HE PULLED HER TOWARD HIM...

Annie was horrified to discover something very female in her was both attracted and repelled by his look and the closeness of his body. But she refused to give him the satisfaction of closing her eyes against the expression of victory on his face.

"You're not the kind of man I want to spend the rest of my life with, Mr. Merrick." Annie Lash spoke slowly and unemotionally. "I want more out of life than a house to tend and food to eat. I want more than to be a vessel to satisfy a man's lust. The man I marry will have to want the same things I want, and that is to build something permanent together." Despite her best efforts, she could not keep the tears from welling in her eyes. "I'll not stand on the fringe of a man's life and hunger for something I know can be real and beautiful. I want to love and be loved. I want my man to be a part of me and I of him. And," she added with finality, "I am determined to hold out for what I want or have nothing at all!"

* * *

"Highest rating, five gold stars! Ms. Garlock has, as usual, caught the flavor of the times in both description and dialect—it's her forte!"

—*Barbra Critiques*

Also by Dorothy Garlock

Wild Sweet Wilderness

Published by
POPULAR LIBRARY

This is for you, Amos.
Recalling the first six years of your life
helped me to develop the character, Amos,
in this story. I love you.

Gran

AUTHOR'S NOTE

All the characters in this novel and Berrywood home-stead are the figments of my imagination, with the exception of Thomas Jefferson, General James Wilkinson and Aaron Burr.

After killing Alexander Hamilton in a duel, Aaron Burr traveled to New Orleans and held several secret conferences with General James Wilkinson, the commander of the army and the Governor of the Louisiana Territory.

The truth is not fully known, but it was believed that Burr meant to intrigue for the possession of Mexico, or that he had designs upon the Louisiana Territory.

President Jefferson ordered an intensive investigation in the affairs of the former vice president. Burr was arrested on the charge of treason and brought to trial in Richmond, Virginia.

After a trial that lasted six months, he was acquitted for lack of evidence on September 1, 1807.

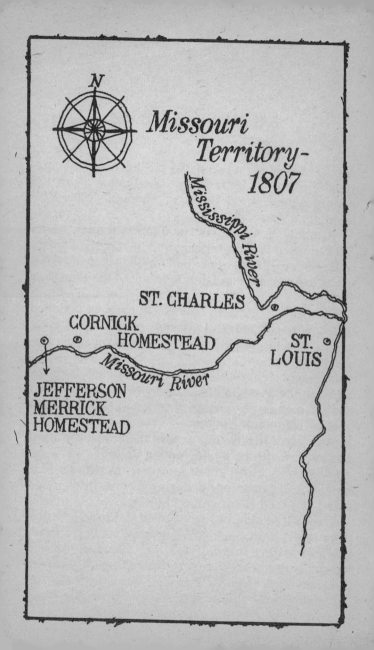

CHAPTER
ONE

Annie Lash Jester walked with an easy stride and almost noiselessly, keeping close to the trees. They grew thickly back about a hundred feet from the riverbank, letting no sunlight through them. For a moment she stepped back into the sun and gazed at them. How great and tall they were. Then she recalled the lesson her pa had taught her and looked searchingly out across the forest. A good woodsman, Pa had said, never fixes his eyes on an object; he shifts them from side to side and far ahead. You get trapped staring at one thing. Her mind reached back, remembering.

Walking beside her pa, during the long journey over the mountains from Virginia, she had been gay and bright, holding out hope that her mother would live to see the broad Mississippi River and the trading post of Saint Louis; but they had buried Mama in Kentucky and, sorrowing, Annie Lash

1

and Charles Jester had continued west. On the worn trail through the woods her pa had spoken of his love of the trees.

"It's odd, the way of trees," he had said. "They know their wants. They grow straight and tall, reaching for sunlight, their roots searching for water. They can survive without man, but man can't survive without them." He pointed out a young elm. "The bark is good for poultices. The oak yonder is as enduring as all time. It's used for sills and framing for cabins. The beechnut trees make good flooring and the honey locust can't be beat for fence posts and railings. Hickory, the best grained of all wood for axe handles, will burn for a long time in the fireplace on a cold winter night."

Annie Lash loitered now among the trees, recalling how her pa had catalogued their uses. He had been solid and enduring like the trees, but like them, he had been struck down by man. How pitiful he had looked during those last months, broken down as if he was of no use. His strength, his proudest possession, had gone swiftly and his pride with it when he could no longer tend to himself and the food that kept life in his withered body had to be lifted to his mouth.

Charles Jester had always been a strong man and a clever one. His strength and his pride had been a shield between himself and life. His huge shoulders could heft a heavy log and his strong legs could track a deer all day without tiring. It had taken a year to wring the life out of him, and in the end he had died old and broken; the dark-skinned *voyageur*, who had thrown the knife, ending the dispute over the furs, would never know the anguish he had caused by the flick of his wrist.

Annie Lash leaned against a tree and looked back at the village of Saint Louis. The ground on which it stood was not much higher than the river bank. On a point of narrow land commanding a view of the river stood a long, low structure enclosed with a stockade fence. On the four corners were little circular towers that bulged out as if to survey what was going on up and down the river. The fort had been occupied by United States soldiers for a short time, but now it was deserted except for the stone towers which were used as a prison. The massive timbers used in the construction of the fort were still standing, and the small dark holes cut into the walls gave the structure a threatening, impregnable aspect.

Below, on the Bank, were many cabins striped with the yellow clay that filled the chinks between the logs. The life and bustle in the vicinity of these dwellings contrasted sharply with the still grandeur of the forest where Annie Lash stood so silently. Farther back from the river, on what was once a flat, grassy plain, were the wagon grounds. Among the canvas covered wagons strung out in deep curls, children played. Several herds of horses grazed on the short grass, and a score of red and white oxen munched at the hay that had been carried to them. One man hammered stakes into the ground from which to hang a kettle and another man swung an axe with a vigorous sweep; the clean, sharp strokes rang on the air when the blade pierced the wood of the log. The smoke of many campfires curled upward, and near the blaze ruddy-faced women hovered over the steaming kettles, scolded children, and greeted neighbors.

Annie Lash looked back toward the river where yet another caravan of settlers had just crossed on the ferry. The lead wagon headed for the wagon grounds, the two span of oxen moving ponderously. On and on they came; wagons, carts, dogs and cows, the children shouting and running alongside while trail-worn men popped the whips tiredly.

This was Saint Louis where, three short years ago in 1804, Captains Merryweather Lewis and William Clarke passed to ascend the Missouri River for twenty-six hundred miles, becoming the first white men to cross the American continent north of Mexico. Here, hundreds of settlers had camped briefly before going on west. They had left farms, blacksmith shops, mercantile stores, and families to pursue their dreams of finding richer, more beautiful country across the wide Mississippi.

"They'll manage," Annie Lash said aloud, and the sound of her voice startled her. Tonight, they'll unhitch and picket the oxen, she thought. The children will stake out the cows; the women will get out pots and spoons, and there will be a cookfire. They'll make a home for the night. Later, each woman will snuggle in her man's arms to whisper the intimate things a man and a woman say to each other in the dark of the night.

Reluctantly, Annie Lash moved along the path again. She wanted to remain to smell the evening. There's no supper smoke like April smoke, she thought. The dry leaves and twigs still have the winter dampness. In no time at all spring will be gone and summer will take its place. She walked swiftly now, not wanting darkness to catch her outside the safety of the sturdy cabin Charles Jester had built when they arrived in this place five years ago. She looked at the western sky. The sun had gone down and she hadn't noticed. Overhead, the clouds were thickening, and to the south, brief flashes of lightning signaled the approach of yet another spring rain storm. Before the night was over the loud clashes of thunder would shake the rain from the clouds, and by morning the streets of Saint Louis would be a sea of mud.

Annie Lash reached the village and slowed her steps.

"Evenin', Miss Annie Lash." The man's voice was respectful, and Annie Lash glanced up, nodded to the man lounging in front of the mercantile store, and hurried past.

She knew good and well that he was wondering, just as nearly everyone in this village of almost a thousand permanent residents was, *What's Annie Lash Jester going to do now that her pa is dead?* She could almost hear the murmur of voices that trailed her. *Foolish old maid tied herself to the old man and let her good years slip past her. She must be all of twenty-two. Never been to a party. Never owned a pretty dress. Never had a man. Almost too old, now, for a man to want her, except one whose woman had gone and left him with a parcel of younguns to take care of.*

Annie Lash was a tall, lithe, strong woman with capable, slender hands which she used with pleasure. She had to be strong to cope with caring for her invalid father and to help Zan Thatcher handle the furs they bought and sold in order to make enough money to put food on the table for the three of them.

She had no fancy opinion of herself or her looks, no vanity about the rich, brown hair with its deep waves nor her delicate white skin that she kept shaded from the sun with a calico sunbonnet so her nose wouldn't peel. Her eyes were what one noticed first. They were large and clear, the kind of blue that was so light it looked faded, yet they shone bright between the layers of dark brown lashes. She had always thought her mouth was too large, so when she smiled she held her lips in such a way that the corners turned up and her teeth only showed partially. This way of smiling put two small holes in her cheeks, but Annie Lash didn't know that because she had never smiled at herself in a mirror.

Her feet hit the walk fronting the shops. She liked the sound her heels made on the board walk. Here, Osage men padded, their moccasined feet soundless; shiny-shoed gamblers strolled; women trod lightly in soft slippers, trailed by barefoot children; heavy-booted workmen clumped along. The moccasined feet of French *voyageurs* walked here, as did the feet of the bragging, fighting boatmen who freighted the furs down the river from the rich country in the north.

Annie Lash turned into a shop at the end of the block and paused until her eyes became accustomed to the dimness before she moved toward the rear of the store. She inhaled the fragrance of the tobacco, the spices, and the kegs of dried fruit, and decided to do something impulsive and foolish. She was going to buy a nickel's worth of sugar, go home, and make it into maple sugar squares to indulge her sweet tooth.

"Evenin', Miss Annie Lash. Ain't this late for you to be afoot?" Old Seth Harthan moved away from the two Osage men he was dickering with and hurried toward her. The Indians and two rivermen were the only customers in the store.

"I suppose so." She placed a coin on the counter. "I'd like this much sugar, Seth." When she spoke there was a taste of the far away South on her lips. "If you'll trust me with the container, I'll see that you get it back."

Seth snorted. "Fiddle! Tomorry? Next week? Makes no matter." He worked fast, scooped the sugar from a barrel into a small tin bucket, and clamped down the lid. "Ain't no nickel's worth here so I'll throw in this dab a raisins if'n ya got a pocket to put 'em in." He reached into a keg and came out with a handful of plump raisins. Annie Lash held open the pocket on her apron and he dropped the fruit inside.

"Thank you, Seth." She knew the raisins were a gift and smiled at the old man so he knew that she knew they were a gift.

Seth followed her to the door of the store. "It's almost dark, Miss Annie Lash. You ain't ought to be awanderin' about this late. You ought to wait and I'll shut up the store and walk you home."

"I'll be all right. In no more than five minutes I'll be inside the cabin." She looked away from him, allowing her eyes to adapt to the gloom up and down the street. "Bye, Seth."

The old man nodded and watched her walk

rapidly across the street and head down the road toward the river. He had seen the two boatmen eyeing her while he was scooping out the sugar. He hurried back inside to engage their interest in case they had a notion to follow her.

Annie Lash knew well the risk of being caught away from her home at night. Once, two rowdy rivermen had captured her and held her pinned to the side of the cabin until Zan and his long gun persuaded them to let her go. She and Zan had backed into the cabin as the drunken men advanced threateningly. They had returned later that night to pound on the door and make insulting offers.

She walked swiftly, her long stride eating up the distance. Zan would be worried about her. She had depended on her father's old friend for so much these last few years. Now it was time to set him free to ride the river he loved. She had to make a decision soon, choose one from among the three men who wanted to marry her. The offers had come in scarcely before her pa was cold. A strong, capable woman, well able to handle a parcel of motherless younguns, tend a garden, wash and cook was what those men wanted. The fact that she was sightly didn't really enter into it at all. A single woman, people said, needed a man to take care of her. It was unheard of for a decent woman to make her way alone. If she was unmarried she lived with a relative and worked for the family, that was, if she didn't want to be a whore and live in one of the bawdy houses farther down the river.

Annie Lash hastened her steps and thought of her choices. Harm Fletcher; short, skinny, almost bald. He had five children, the oldest eight years old, the youngest two. She felt sorry for the children. They were nice, well-behaved little ones. But... oh, she wanted more out of life than tending someone else's younguns. Aside from that, the thought of being in bed with Harm sent cold chills all through her.

There was Mr. Greer, who owned several flatboats and freighted furs down to New Orleans. He didn't make the trips himself. He was too old. He was probably no more than fifty, but he looked older. His shoulders were bent and he suffered from a chronic pain in his joints. Annie Lash knew he was looking ahead to the time when he would be an invalid and need a woman to take care of him. In the meanwhile, he would take what pleasure he could from her young body. She had seen his eyes on her breast, and the thought of those talonlike hands on her naked body brought the saliva to her mouth and caused her stomach to tighten.

The other offer had come from Walt Ransom, a big, brawny, rough-talking man with seven children. He had bragged that he had a youngun for every year he'd had his wife. He drank, brawled, worked as little as possible, and had been on her doorstep before she realized the word was out that her pa was dead.

Annie Lash heard the scuff of boots behind her and quickened her steps. Hoarse laughter followed her and she began to feel panic until she saw Zan coming toward her, the long gun in his hand. She didn't slow down until she reached him.

"What'er ya tryin' to do, gal? Ya know ya ain't got no call to be out when night comes." Zan's voice sounded angry, but she knew it was because he'd been worried.

"I'm sorry. The time passed quickly and darkness came before I knew it." It felt good to slow down and walk beside big, comfortable Zan. This is what my pa would have been like, she thought, if he'd not been involved in the argument with the *voyageur*.

They stopped at the door to the log cabin. Lightning creased the sky and thunder rolled nearer. Annie Lash felt a drop of rain.

"Light the lamp," Zan said. He stood in the open door while she moved into the room, walking with sure steps because she knew every inch of it.

In the soft glow made by the lamp she looked at him. Grizzled and gray, he still stood straight and tall, his buckskins clean, his flat, straight brimmed hat sitting squarely on his head. She knew he loved her like a daughter and that accounted for the impatient scowl on his face.

Darkness had brought a lively wind that whistled in the door. The light flickered and Zan turned to go.

"Bar the door, lass." His voice still held gruffness.

"I will. Zan...thank you."

"I'll be back come mornin'."

"Zan..." She went to him. "I'll make up my

mind soon. Don't worry about me. If you get the chance to take a boat upriver, take it. I'll make out."

"Annie Lash, ya ain't got to take no man ya don't want. Ain't I tol' ya that?" His weathered, roughened face softened. "We'll make out like we done a'fore yore pa died."

"I can't do that, Zan. It's time I made a place for myself and freed you to spend your time on the river. I don't know what Pa and I would have done without you, but now that he's gone I want you to live your dream of following the river up to its beginning and beyond if the notion strikes you." She kept her voice steady by sheer willpower, because... Oh, Lordy, how she hated the thought of his leaving her alone in this place.

"I ain't got no use fer none of 'em what ask ya, Annie Lash. If'n I was a leavin' ya with a good man, one what I knowed ya wanted, I'd go. Till then, I ain't." His voice was determined, as forceful as it was sometimes when he was selling furs.

Annie Lash held his arm and squeezed it—as much demonstration of feelings as Zan would allow. Even that embarrassed him.

"Annie... Annie Lash." The slurred voice came from the rutted path that served as a road. "Are ya waitin' fer me, darlin'?" The brief lightning flash outlined Walt Ransom's brawny frame. "I brung someone ta see ya," he called, and came lumbering toward the door. "What ya a doin' here with my woman?" he demanded belligerently when Zan blocked the doorway.

"Annie Lash ain't receivin' no callers."

"Ain't... receivin' no callers?" Walt repeated

Zan's words in a disbelieving tone, then roared
with anger. "Ya want me ta wring yore head off
that scrawny neck, ya old river rat?" The man with
Walt reeled drunkenly and snickered. "What ya
doing here, anyways? Ya stay way from my intended. Hear?"

"I'm not your intended, Walt Ransom! Get your-
self and your drunken friend off my doorstep."
Annie Lash squeezed into the doorway beside
Zan.

"Ya shut yore mouth up, woman! This here's
twixt me 'n the ol' man."

"You lay a hand on Zan and I'll blow a hole in
you big enough to drive a team of mules through."
Annie Lash drew her pa's musket out from behind
her and pointed it at Walt's bloated stomach.

"Jesuz Christ!" Walt swore. "Ya ain't got no
hankerin' fer this ol' man, has ya?"

"I've got a powerful lot of love for this man, but
you wouldn't understand that." The sneer in her
voice enraged Walt more than her words.

"What ya need is a whip on yore back! An' I
got me a notion ta let ya have it."

"That ain't what her needs, Walt." The man's
voice was so raspy it sounded like it hurt him to
talk.

"She'll get *that*, too!" Walt hitched up his trousers. "I'll be back tomorry with that preacher man,
gal. An' I ain't better hear no back talk outta' ya."

"You come around here tomorrow or any other
time, Walt Ransom, an' I'll fill your hide with
buckshot."

His laughter was loud and full of bravado. "Hear

that, Samuel? I'm goin' ta have me a fightin' squaw, but I kin take the fight outta' her."

"Get!" Annie Lash snapped. "Get on away from here and don't come back!"

"If'n it ain't me, t'will be them river rats. Ya know ya can't live here without no man, 'n I'll treat ya square. I was just a funnin' 'bout the whip. Ya know I'd not mark up a purty thing like ya be." His black, hairy face split in a grin and he moved closer to the door.

Zan had stood quietly, but now he lifted his rifle and the muzzle touched Walt's chest.

"Don't ya come anosin' 'round here no more, ya no good hunk a fish bait. That's all ya be ... fish bait. Ain't no decent man on this here Bank'll stand 'n let Annie Lash take no slack from the likes of ya. Now back off, or ya'll be a long way downriver come mornin'."

Walt stepped back. His pride had suffered a blow. Samuel would spread the news at the tavern that he had been rejected by the gal he'd been bragging about. He shook his fist at Zan.

"Ya ain't got no chance a'gin me, ol' man. I be back tomorry, 'n I'm a havin' that woman! Me little ones needs a ma, and she's gonna be it." His voice dropped to a whine and he turned away. "C'mon, Samuel. That ol' man ain't gonna walk easy fer the rest a his days. Ain't I tol' ya the gal was sightly? An' ya ort to see her with her hair down. I seed her a washin' it in a bucket a rainwater once ... purtiest sight I ever did see. Now, oncet I git 'er, ya fellers what's ..." His booming voice trailed away in the darkness.

Annie Lash and Zan stood for a long moment. When Zan lowered his rifle, Annie Lash lowered hers and stood it just inside the door. She moved back into the room, her shoulders slumped dejectedly.

"Oh, Zan! What am I going to do?"

"Ya can mark that'n off. Ya ain't havin' no truck with him," Zan said firmly.

Annie Lash went to him, wrapped her arms about his waist, and leaned her head on his chest. Zan stiffened and stood still.

"Let me lean on you for just a moment, Zan. I'll be all right. I'll make out, but sometimes it's so hard...to be alone." Her words were muffled against the soft buckskin of his shirt.

"Ya ain't alone, Annie Lash." His rough hand came up and patted her back gently. This was a big concession for Zan, who had never, by look or touch, allowed his affection for her to show. He hid it with his gruffness, but Annie Lash had long known it was there.

"It isn't fair to you, Zan. I know you'd have gone long ago, but you stayed because of me and Pa. I don't want to be a millstone around your neck." She willed herself not to cry.

"Ya ain't, gal. A good man'll come, 'n till then we'll go on as we've done. I got me plenty a time ta see the north country. Ain't no call fer ya to be a frettin'. If'n I don't go this spring, I'll go next."

"Oh, Zan! Thank you." She lifted her head and his soft gray beard brushed her face. "There'll be other offers and I promise I'll take one before it's too late for you to go upriver."

"Ya jist take yore time a choosin', Annie Lash.

I be in no hurry." He carefully examined the rough hinges on the door, and gave the chain that hung beside it a tug. "Ya'll be all right with the chain up. If'n it gives, shoot the bastard."

"I think I would. I think I could do it."

"Ya better, if'n they come, 'cause they ain't a comin' ta talk," he growled.

"Take care of yourself! Walt's a sneak—he might be going to back-stab you."

"Humph!" Zan snorted. "I git on the docks 'n he come a lookin', he'll git a pike in the belly. Ain't nobody on the docks what's got use fer Walt Ransom."

"Be careful, Zan." Annie Lash went to the door and Zan stepped out into the darkness.

"Put up the chain, Annie Lash."

Large drops of rain were falling now, and the lightning flashes were almost constant. Zan was out of sight almost instantly, dodging around a pile of debris in the road. Annie Lash remembered her father telling her that Zan was "slick as an eel, quiet as a cat, the best woodsman I ever knew or even heard about." Annie Lash wondered whatever turned him from the woods and toward the river.

A gust of wind blew raindrops in her face and whipped the loose strands of her hair. She shivered, backed into the cabin, and closed the heavy door. She looped the chain across and hung it on the iron hook Zan had put in a heavy oak log. The windowless room was a safe haven.

Annie Lash stood with her back to the door and surveyed the square that had been her home for the last few years. Different—oh, so different from their farm home in Virginia. Her pa had apologized for it many times before he died. The bunk where he had lain for so long was covered with a faded patchwork quilt. The corner where she bunked had been curtained off by another of her mother's quilts. She had taken it down as there was no need now for privacy, and folded it across her bunk.

The crude log cabin had a slab wood floor, one of the few floors in the entire section of cabins that fronted the river. Her pa and Zan had just finished laying the floor when her pa was stabbed. Charles Jester had laid the cobblestones to make the fireplace and the lumber from the wagon that brought them from Virginia was used to make a table, benches, and a work counter. Her mother's rocking chair, trunk, and gilt-edged mirror that hung over the walnut washstand were the only furnishings in the room. As if she were drawn by it, Annie Lash picked up the lamp and went to the mirror.

The reflection that looked back at her was that of a beautiful young woman, but Annie Lash was unaware of it. In a day when a young woman was considered to be in her prime between fifteen and twenty years old, Annie Lash felt old. In a month she would be twenty-three. Many women had had six children by the time they were her age. Not that Annie Lash wanted six children, but she was sure that she wanted more than one. She had been lonely all her life, longing for a brother or a sister.

On impulse, she began to remove the pins from her hair. It fell to her waist and below in wide, deep waves. If Annie Lash had any vanity at all, it was about her hair. It was rich brown, and thick, kept shining clean with the rainwater she caught in the barrel at the corner of the house.

She picked up the brush and began stroking. It was soothing to brush her hair. She thought of the times she'd seen her father stand behind her mother and run the bristles on the brush from her scalp to the ends of hair that hung to her waist. Annie Lash had been only a child then, yet it seemed to her that Pa got such pleasure out of doing this simple service for her mother. She wondered what it would be like to have a man run the brush lovingly through *her* hair.

The eyes that looked back at her were dreamy. Unconsciously, she puckered her mouth into the shape of a kiss. A loud clap of thunder shook the cabin and jarred her into awareness of what she was doing.

"Fiddle!" she said aloud, and carefully placed the brush in the combcase that hung beside the mirror. She swung her hair back over her shoulders and picked up the lamp. "Fiddle, and be damned for foolish notions," she said under her breath.

As the thunder rolled and the wind-driven rain lashed the house, Annie Lash stirred the melting sugar in the iron pot she had suspended over the flame. A small puddle of water began to form under the door. She laid the wooden stirring paddle aside and placed part of a rag rug against the door to absorb the water.

"Oh, fiddle," she groaned. She had completely forgotten the lamp was still lit. The lamp fuel was almost gone and she had intended to use it sparingly. Holding her loose hair back from the flame, she bent to the fire, lit a candle, and blew out the lamp. Dark smoke rose from the glass chimney. She shook the lamp to judge how much oil was left in the base. It scarcely sloshed at all. Damn!

A stunning crash of thunder seemed to fill the room. It was still echoing when another roared in its wake. Sheets of rain hit the sides of the cabin with such force that small trickles of water began to run between the logs, carrying with it the stain from the yellow clay. Annie Lash removed the picture of her mother from the wall and placed it on her pa's bunk. It was warm in the windowless cabin, and she unbuttoned several buttons on her dress and wiped her perspiring forehead on her sleeve.

Eventually, the storm passed, but a soft, steady downpour of rain followed.

When the heavy rap sounded against the door, Annie Lash almost jumped from the chair. She settled back again and remained perfectly still, her eyes fixed on the door. The rap came again and again, deliberate and loud in the silence of the night, but she made no attempt to open the door.

"Hello, the house. I'm looking for a woman by the name of Jester." The man's voice was crisp, and she was sure she had not heard it before. "The man at the store sent me down. His name was Seth something-or-other."

Annie Lash stood and moved slowly to the door.

"What do you want?" Her voice had a frightened tremor.

"Open the door. I want to talk to you."

"Say what you've got to say from there."

There was silence and she thought she heard him swear.

"I mean you no harm. I want to talk to you, that is, if you're the woman that nurses the sick."

"I only nursed my ma and pa."

"Well? Are you going to open up or not?"

The hollow in her throat was beating and the pulse was jumping in her wrists. He didn't sound like a tavern rough or a Pittsburgh boatman. She picked up a candle and lit it from the one on the table, then slipped a few links of the chain down on the hook so she could open the door a crack, but still have the security of the chain blocking the door. All she could see through the crack was the shadow of a man, a big man. Water dripped from his hat and the slick poncho cloth that covered his upper body.

"I can't say what I've come to say through this door, ma'am. If you're scared, here's my gun. Be careful, it's loaded." He held the butt of the gun to the crack in the door and she reached for it, checked to be sure it was loaded, slipped the chain from the hook, and stepped back.

The wind from the open door blew out the candles. Annie Lash's heart almost jumped out of her breast when the big figure loomed in the doorway. She backed against the table, holding the gun in front of her with one hand and fumbling with the buttons on her dress with the other.

CHAPTER
TWO

He stood in the doorway, the wind that curled past him firing the spattering of coals in the fire-place into sparks. He made no attempt to come farther into the room.

"Do you mind if we have light?"

Annie Lash retreated back into the darkness, but he saw the hand she lifted in a gesture of consent. Leaving the door open, the man went to the table, picked up the candle, and lit it from the small blaze in the fireplace. The wind from the open doorway threatened the flame and he shielded it with his cupped hands.

"We'll have to close the door. At least partway."

Annie Lash felt her hand motion again, but he had already swung the heavy plank door to within a foot of closing and set a piece of wood to hold it. The thought came to her that she had never behaved in such a brainless fashion. It had been stupid to open the door a crack, stupider yet to let him in. He came to the center of the room and stopped.

"I'm not going to pounce on you, if that's what you're thinking. I want to talk to you and I'd like to have some light so I can see you and you can see me." He picked up the lamp and shook it, seemed satisfied with the slush of the oil, and lit it without asking permission. He replaced the chimney and the soft glow of the light reached into every corner of the room. "That's more like it," he said without looking in her direction. He took off his hat and hung it on the peg beside the door, then slipped the oilskin slicker from his shoulders and hung it beside the hat. He turned and stood perfectly still so she could see him.

He was dressed in clean buckskin trousers and shirt such as many of the French trappers wore, but without the fringe and bead decorations. The deerskin moccasins on his feet accounted for the noiselessness of his movements on the plank floor. He was tremendously tall and broad. Handsome in a completely masculine way. Everything about him was big: big shoulders, big hands, feet... bones. In the semi-darkness she was unable to see the color of his eyes, but she could tell they were dark, either brown or black. His hair was light, very light. She had seen women with hair this light, but never a man. At first she thought it was gray, but when he turned she could see he was not old enough for it to be gray. It was cut short, so short she had scarcely noticed it until he took off his hat; but it was incredibly thick and curly and a sharp contrast to his dark face which, although it was unlined, showed him to be a man "who had been over the mountain," as her pa would have said.

His face went with the rest of him; big nose, prominent cheekbones, and a wide mouth. Most surprising were his eyebrows and lashes. They were unusually dark for a person with light hair. His eyes, through the dark lashes, were studying her with the same intensity as she was studying him.

The silence lengthened. She could smell the tallow of the burning candle, the smoke of the burned log, even the scent of the maple candy cooling in the pan. Her thoughts stirred, awakening lazily. Her precious lamp oil was being savaged; she was alone with this big, silent stranger. Apprehension began in her, crept up her spine, throbbed in her temples, but no part of the feeling was fear. No, she thought clearly, she wasn't afraid of him. Then why was she holding the gun?

The wind whined around the corner of the house and rolled a piece of debris against the wall. She'd have to tell Zan about this tomorrow. He'd be sure to scold. While she was thinking this, the man shifted his feet and lifted his hand to his belt and hung it there by his thumb. His hands were large, too; the fingers long with square, clean nails.

She waited, her eyes doing battle with his. She couldn't move, couldn't speak, could scarcely breathe. She was in a waiting pool. She must wait until he said what he had to say and left. He would do it ... now. She was wrong. He said nothing. She was here, he was there, and there were no words between them. His mouth was motionless and stern.

She felt a small outrush of air stir her lips. She heard a voice that was her own, because the words came from her mouth.

"Won't you sit down?" Actually, the only way she was sure she had really said the words was that he answered.

"Thank you." He remained standing, but took his hand from his belt and waved it toward the rocking chair.

She moved around the table, backed into the chair, and sat down, holding the gun in her lap. She couldn't stop staring at him. Her legs were weak and she was grateful to be off them.

In one long stride, he reached the chair at the end of the table and moved it out to the side so the lamp was no longer between them. He sat down, his forearms on his legs, his hands hanging between his knees.

"I'm sorry I frightened you." The words came out slowly and fell into the quiet pool of silence.

She inclined her head and waited.

"My name is Jefferson Merrick."

She inclined her head again and shifted the gun to lie across her knees, its muzzle no longer pointed at him. She wished her knees would stop trembling, she wished she didn't feel as if she were off somewhere, out of her body, watching what was going on. She wanted to think clearly so she could remember every detail of this visit with this man who was like no other she had ever seen or talked with.

"I saw you today on the street and I asked the storekeeper about you. He said your name is Annie Lash Jester."

Again she inclined her head. What was the matter with her, for goodness sake! Couldn't she say anything? He didn't seem to care whether she spoke or not; he went on talking, and she felt immense relief.

"I have a farm up on the Missouri River. My half brother and his family live there. I had been away for a year and returned to find my brother gone and his wife sick. She has two small children and needs help. There are two black men, freed black men, who work the land, but no other woman on the place."

He stopped and Annie Lash met his eyes. Instinctively, she knew he was not used to talking about himself.

"Buy a black woman."

His eyes held hers. "I don't buy human flesh."

Her face burned. She felt suitably rebuked. Her pa didn't hold with slavery, either. Why had she said such a stupid thing? His next words brought an even deeper flush to her face.

"I heard talk of you in the tavern." His voice was set, his eyes on her were unwavering. She turned hers away from them and looked into the dying fire. "The talk is that you're a lone woman, a decent woman." She looked back at him at that. "I looked over the three that had asked for your hand, and I think I can make a better offer."

Her eyes widened and for some reason unknown to her she felt a spurt of anger. Now she was up for barter, like a cow! He saw the sparks light her eyes and what he said next took her completely by surprise.

"I should have your eyes and you should have mine."

She thought about what he said. Her blue eyes, his light hair; his dark eyes, her dark hair. She was still thinking about it when he shrugged his shoulders as if what he had said was of no consequence. The action spurred her to say, "I won't."

His dark eyes searched her face and she felt a stir of something in the marrow of her bones, in her brain, in that secret corner of her heart that she kept locked away and brought out only occasionally as she did tonight when she had looked in the mirror and took down her hair. *Hair!* She had forgotten about her hair hanging down her back! Only a loose woman allowed a strange man to see her with her hair down. She lifted her hands and gathered it into a bunch at the nape of her neck. With it safely behind her back she leaned back against it.

He seemed to know what she was doing, how she felt, but it didn't soften his features.

"I realize I came without notice," he said, as if to put her at ease. "But I don't have time to dally around. I go back upriver tomorrow. Why did you say you won't? Have you accepted one of your suiters?"

She shook her head vigorously. "No. I won't marry one of them and I won't marry you!" It was what she had known all the time. She'd not marry a man who didn't yearn for her as she would yearn for him. He must be a man who had the same hunger for love that she had, she thought. He must have the same longing that the seed from that love would produce children who would be equally loved, nurtured, challenged to grow to adulthood with the same values. Before she would settle for less she would take her chances on the river.

"I'm not asking you to *marry* me!"

For heaven's sake! What in the world was he asking, then? Her face warmed from the pounding of her heart and the embarrassment that fought with her pride. One wanted her to cringe, turn her eyes away, the other demanded she keep her eyes fixed on his. Pride won, and she and the stranger continued to regard each other with deep soberness. Neither spoke. Both were used to waiting.

Finally, she was forced into speech which came from stiff lips. "State your business."

"What do you plan to do if you don't marry?"

"I don't know."

"Zan Thatcher is an old man."

"You know him?"

"Every mountain man between the Alleghenies and the Mississippi knows about Zan Thatcher."

"You're a mountain man?"

"You might say that." He waited for her to speak, and when she didn't, he asked, "Can you be ready to leave come morning?"

"I never said I was going."

"It stuck in my craw to hear the talk about you in the tavern." He spoke as if she hadn't said anything.

Annie Lash gazed at him, the beat of her heart picking up speed. "Why?"

He ignored the question and asked one of his own. "Why haven't you married? You've had offers." The last was a statement, not a question.

"That's none of your business." She thought he was going to smile, but he didn't. "I've not loved a man, except my pa and Zan, and that's not the same." She had decided in an instant to be candid.

He took his eyes away from hers and swung them slowly around the room. Annie Lash thought that perhaps she had shocked him with her frankness, but when his eyes returned to hers they held the same quiet, serious look.

"I have a good, strong house with neighbors no more than five, six miles away. It isn't fancy, but it's snug in the winter and airy in the summer. You would be safer there than here on the Bank. Although, in all honesty, I must tell you we are bothered some by the Osage."

"What would I do when you no longer need me to care for the woman?"

"I'd bring you back here, but you'd be welcome to stay." He continued to regard her with deep soberness.

"Who's taking care of her now?"

"A friend."

"A woman?" She spoke before she thought and her face reddened with embarrassment. To her astonishment, she saw his lips curl and amber flecks appear in his dark eyes. The smile rearranged his features in a fascinating way, and suddenly she smiled at him, felt her own lips move, lengthen; felt her cheeks curve and her eyelids half close. "It's none of my business," she hastened to say before he did.

"I wasn't going to say that," he said as if he had read her mind, but he was still smiling. "A friend, Will Murdock, is minding the younguns. Callie is taking care of herself."

His smile vanished as quickly as it came and she wanted suddenly to bring it back. He leaned back in the chair, an ankle crossed over a knee, studying her.

"Would you like a piece of candy?" The words came off her not-quite-steady lips, but the smile returned and it was worth the effort it took her to say them.

"I can smell it. It brings back memories of maple time when I was a boy."

Annie Lash placed the pistol on the table and got to her feet, forgetting about her loose hair. There was exultation in her; it was rising, pulsing in her throat, making her eyes shine. She glanced at him from the high bench counter where she went to break the cooled slab of candy into bite-size pieces. He was watching her, and a light flush came to her face. She turned her flustered attention back to the candy, the beat of her heart faster now. She opened a drawer and took out a thong, caught her hair back with it, and tied it behind her neck before she carried the plate of candy to the table.

Jefferson had not expected to find a woman such as Annie Lash Jester on the Bank. When he had turned after lighting the lamp, he was almost stunned into believing someone else was in the room, but it was his pistol the woman held in her hand, so he knew she was real. Could this be the same woman who had been talked about at the tavern—the spinster who had to take a man? The talk was that she was sightly, but no one had praised her perfect features: her straight, finely-boned nose, her soft brown brows arching away from eyes that were not quite blue, not quite gray. Her hair was the color of rich chocolate and lay, soft and luxuriant, in careless disarray along her shoulders and down her back. Loose tendrils framed delicate cheekbones flushed with uneasiness. He had seen her from a distance, talking with the storekeeper, and his impression of her was merely that she was a tall, slim young woman. He hadn't been prepared for the face that went with the body.

He continued to study her. Cleanliness. She was shining clean from the top of that glorious hair to the toes of the soft shoes that peeked from the hem of her skirt. It surprised him that a woman living on the Bank could be so faultlessly clean. She had looked him over with the same degree of interest as he had looked at her. The straight-forwardness of her stare was also a surprise. This was no empty-headed beauty, but a strong-willed, determined woman.

"Mr. Merrick." His name rolled off her tongue easily, softly slurred in the accent of the middle South.

He accepted the plate, selected a chunk of the confection, and leaned back to watch her nibble at the sugary lump she held between her thumb and forefinger. The candy was a treat and she didn't mind his knowing she was enjoying it. They sat in the silence looking at each other. When Jeff reached for another piece, she smiled with her

lips together because her mouth was full, and the
dimples appeared in her cheeks. She finished eating and drew a square of cloth from her pocket to
wipe her fingers.

"I can't give you my answer tonight, Mr. Merrick. I'll have to talk it over with Zan."

"Is Zan on the docks? I'll bring him here so
you can speak with him tonight. I want to leave
by first light. We have a five-day journey."

Annie Lash caught the word *we*, but made no
mention of it. There were other matters to be discussed.

"I won't leave my mother's trunk."

"We can take it."

"I would hate leaving the rocking chair," she
said wistfully and rubbed her hand lovingly over
the polished curved arms.

"You won't have to leave it." His voice, though
soft, seemed to fill every corner of the room. "We'll
be taking a flatboat upriver until we get out of the
bottom land, then we'll transfer to wagons for the
rest of the trip. There'll be room for whatever you
want to take."

Her head whirled in a quickening eddy. Was it
possible that her troubles were over? Would this
man take care of her and ask nothing more than
that she care for his sister-in-law and her children? She wouldn't have to take a man. Heavenly
Father! Let all that he says be true, she prayed.
Her sanity argued, this is madness. She couldn't
leave this place with a man she had known less
than an hour. She had to talk to Zan.

She opened her mouth to say so, but the words

never came out. The door crashed open and Walt Ransom sprang into the room. Instantly, Jeff jumped and whirled to face the intruder, a knife in his hand. Annie Lash drew in a frightened breath, too numbed to move.

"Ya bitch!" Walt was drunk, shaking with anger. Two men crowded into the doorway behind him. "Ya ain't goin' to be givin' out no bit a tail when I git ya!" He was either too drunk to see the knife in Jeff's hand or too mad to care. He lowered his head and charged him like a mad bull.

Annie Lash grabbed the pistol from the table and backed out of the way. Her disbelieving eyes focused on the men at the door and she pointed the gun at them. They made a move to come farther into the room.

"No!" The word burst from her mouth and they heard it above the crashing noise made by Walt's body as it was slammed against the floor. They were not so drunk or so foolish as to argue with a woman holding a gun, and they backed to the doorway and stayed there.

Jeff's fist had collided with Walt's nose. It had taken just one blow. Walt lay on the floor, blood running down over his mouth and into his beard. He shook his head and tried to get to his feet. He made it on the second attempt and stood, swaying, his eyes glazed.

"Get him out of here," Jeff said. "I don't want to kill him."

One of the men picked up Walt's hat and the other took his arm. Docile and still reeling, Walt stumbled to the doorway, muttering incoherently.

"Walt ain't goin' ta fergit this," one of the men said over his shoulder. The threat was directed at Annie Lash, but Jeff answered.

"He better forget it if he wants to live," he said quietly.

The man was roughly shoved aside, and Zan's broad body appeared in the doorway.

"Gawddamn!" he roared. "Annie Lash, ya be all right?"

"I'm all right, Zan," she called from the corner where she stood with her back to the wall, the gun still pointed toward the door.

Zan's eyes flicked over Jeff and then away. "Ya tell that thar bastid when he sobers that he pert nigh got his head blowed off," he told the men moving away with the staggering Walt between them. "Now then... put down the firearm, Annie Lash, lessin' yore aimin' to shoot me." Then, quick as a cat, he snatched his hat from his head and struck Jeff on the chest with it. "Jeff Merrick, ya ol' son of a grizzly b'ar!" Zan threw his arms around Jeff and they whirled around the room.

It was crazy! In all the years she had known Zan she had never seen such a wild display. The two huge men pounded on each other, laughed, roared greetings. One time they banged against the table and jarred the precious lamp. It was a miracle it didn't topple over. Jeff's face was split into a wide, wide grin. His teeth were white and even, his face years younger.

"Zan Thatcher! I thought the buzzards had picked your old bones clean, by now."

"Ain't no goldanged buzzard goin' to get a hunk of Zan Thatcher. How ya be, boy? Heared ya was off up the Trace. Wat ya doin' in Saint Louis? What ya a doin' with my little gal, Annie Lash?"

"Your little gal, Zan?"

"Same as," Zan said firmly, still pumping Jeff's hand.

"I heard talk as to how a man would have to reckon with Zan Thatcher if he made a move toward the girl."

"Yup, that's kerrect. Her pa was a man what I owed. Took up fer me agin' a parcel a riffraff 'n took a knife fer his bother. But I'd a seen to the gal anyways, she's gen-u-ine."

The two men were talking about her as if she wasn't there. Neither had given her as much as a second glance. She stood silently watching them, the pistol hanging from the hand at her side.

Jeff reached down and righted a chair that had been upset during the brief struggle. "How long have you been here, Zan?"

"Two, three year, off and on, come pie time." Zan's eyes were brighter, happier than Annie Lash had seen them before. "Do ya recollect that thar widder woman on the Trace what made apple pie?"

"I remember several widows on the Trace that had an eye on you in those days," Jeff teased. "You always managed to find one that could cook a good pie."

"How's thin's on the Trace, boy?" There was a certain amount of wistfulness in Zan's tone.

"Changed, Zan. It's a solid nest of cutthroats and robbers. Not like five years back when all we had to worry about was Indians. Now roving bands of thieves have almost taken it over."

Zan shook his head sadly. "People is worser than varmits. They's crowded in clear to the mighty river, now they's crossin' 'n spreading their ruin."

"It's something that can't be stopped, Zan. The country is growing; people are spreading out. Folks like you and me are going to have to find us a spot, hole up, and make the best of it."

Annie Lash moved toward the door. The wind threatened the light, and the small hoard of oil was finally going to peter out. The men didn't seem to notice the flickering light, or even remember that she was in the room. She placed the pistol on the table when she passed it and grabbed the straw broom. Mud and water littered the floor, and as she swept, her irritation grew. Not an hour ago she had been sitting quietly, waiting for her candy to cool. Then, all of a sudden, her house was full of muddy feet. Not a man had stopped on the step to scrape the mud from his boots. Well ... maybe one man. She hadn't noticed the mud after Jefferson Merrick came in.

She looked out the door into the black night. The rain had stopped and she could see a few stars. The campground would be a sea of mud, and she pitied the women who had to keep the wagons clean. Cleanliness was a mania with Annie Lash. She couldn't abide dirt on her person or in her house.

Behind her the lamplight flickered and died, but the soft glow from a candle Jeff lit from the glowing embers of the fire pushed back the darkness. Annie Lash closed the door before the draft created by the door and the chimney was too much for the small flame. When she turned, both men were looking at her.

"Would you rather discuss my proposition with Zan alone?" Jeff asked, looking full into her eyes.

She hesitated a moment before she answered. "No. You may as well know when you leave here if I'm going with you or not. Your being here won't make any difference in what Zan advises me to do."

"You know him well." He gave her a faint smile and his eyes darted to Zan.

"Yes. Perhaps not as long as you have, but just as well. Shall we sit down?"

Jeff gestured toward the rocking chair and remained standing until she was seated. Annie Lash noticed the courtesy and her curiosity about this man grew.

"Do you want me to put the words to Zan, or would you rather do it?"

Zan hung his hat on the peg and looked at the mud that clung to his moccasins. "I ne'er thout 'bout the mess I was a draggin' in, gal."

"It's all right, Zan. Sit down and listen to what Mr. Merrick has to say, then tell me if I should consider his offer."

"Do you remember my brother, Jason Pickett, Zan?" The old man nodded, and Jeff turned his eyes on Annie Lash. "Jason and I had the same mother, but different fathers."

"If'n I recollect, Jason was short on brains 'n long on temper," Zan said dryly.

"Six years ago I started a place up on the Missouri. I knew the minute I set eyes on that land,

Zan, that that was the place I wanted to be, where I could build something solid and enduring. Will and I came back, cleared the land, and built a cabin. Then we got a message to meet with a representative of Tom Jefferson. How could I refuse, Zan? Will and I have known the President all our lives. Tom was my pa's best friend. I was his namesake. The mission took a year and a half. In the meanwhile, I put Jason and his wife and two black men that I had freed on the place to look after it and clear as much land as they could for planting. Will and I returned to find Jason had been gone for almost a year. Callie has been alone out there with the two blacks. Thank God, they're dependable men and didn't run off and leave her. When I get my hands on Jason, I'll beat him within an inch of his life."

The coldness of his tone made Annie Lash glad his anger was not directed at her.

"It should a been done years back. I allas knowed he was a no-good. His pa gived him too much. When hit was gone he'd a'ready been spoiled rotten. Ain't much ya cin do with a grown man spoiled rotten."

"I reckon you're right, but that still leaves me with the problem of what to do about Callie. She's worked herself almost to death and she's sickly. She's also got two little boys to look after. Her husband deserted her and she had no one but me and Will."

"Wal, what ya awantin' with my Annie Lash? Air ya awantin' to marry up with her and take her upriver?" Zan asked bluntly.

Annie Lash's neck and cheeks grew warm. Jeff

captured her eyes with his, the amber flecks appeared in them again, and the corners of his wide mouth twitched.

"She already turned me down. She said she wouldn't marry me. I want her to go back with me and take care of Callie and the babes. It's not right for Callie to be out there alone. She needs a woman with her."

Zan turned his steady gaze on Annie Lash. "What air ya athinkin' 'bout that? Hit's the best offer yet. You'd not have to bed no man ya didn't want. Hit 'pears to me like ya ort to study on hit."

The warm glow on Annie Lash's cheeks turned to scarlet. To make matters worse, her glance at Jeff told her he knew how mortified she was at the mention of bedding a man. Damn him! she thought. And damn Zan, too. What got into him, talking like that? She'd not be pushed—

"Wal, Annie Lash?" Zan prompted.

"I'm studying on it, Zan, like you told me to do." She spoke with a strong hint of impatience.

Jeff leaned back in the chair, ankle crossed over knee. Zan sat silently on the bench, his hands clasped together, his thumbs twirling around each other. The only sound was the squeak of the chair as Annie Lash rocked. Finally, she spoke to Zan as if they were the only two people in the room.

"Is he trustworthy, Zan?"

"Trusty as any man I ever knowed."

"It's a long way. He says they're bothered some by the Osage."

"There's worser thin's."

"Well, my land, Zan! What's worse than being scalped by the savages?"

"Bein' raped by river rats."

"I've not been out of Saint Louis since I came here with Pa."

"Ya don't like town, no ways—"

"What if I want to come back?"

"There ain't nothin' fer ya to come back to, Annie Lash."

"There's you, Zan. I don't think I could bear it if I thought I'd not see you again."

"Ain't no worry 'bout that, gal. I jist figgered I'd mosey along to see ya get settled in."

"Oh, Zan. You'd go, too?"

"Ain't I said hit? I ain't alettin' my little gal go off with no raskallion what's run the Trace." His eyes twinkled. "He be a rough 'n tumble man, but as fer as I knowed allus on the side of what's square 'n right. But that's as fer as I knowed. He's aged since I seed him last."

Jeff's laughter filled the room. Annie Lash could feel the rush of affection between the two men. It was strange. This was the only man she had ever known Zan to loosen up and tease with. He was almost like a different person. There was a new vibrancy about him and he was more talkative than he'd been in a long while.

"You old scutter! I guess in order to get Annie Lash to come help me out, I'll have to take on a battle-scarred old grizzly b'ar."

"Humph! Jist consider yourself lucky, ya young skutter, that I didn't nail yore hide to the wall when I found ya lallygaggin' 'round here."

Her future was being decided, Annie Lash thought irritably, and they sat there funnin' with each other!

"You'd have had your hands full, old man. I was taught to fight by the best man to cross the Alleghenies and go down the pike."

Zan let out a loud guffaw. "Time ya was asayin' somethin' worth a listen to."

"Zan..." Annie Lash's patience was wearing thin.

"Have ya turned yore mind to what ya'll do, Annie Lash?"

"That's what I want to talk about, Zan. If you can be serious long enough. Do you think I should go upriver with Mr. Merrick?"

"Hit's more'n what I'd hoped fer ya, gal."

She turned to Jeff and studied him before she finally spoke. "I'll go with you, Mr. Merrick—if I can take my things." Her eyes left him and sought the familiar furniture her parents had brought over the mountains from Virginia.

"Take what you want. There'll be plenty of room." He got to his feet. His head almost touched the rafters and Annie Lash was shocked once again by how big he was. "I'll be here an hour before daylight with a wagon."

Zan followed Jeff to the door.

"Are you going, too, Zan?" She had hoped he would stay so he could tell her more about Jefferson Merrick and why he had decided to go along.

"I'm goin', gal. Drop the chain, Annie Lash." He turned as if remembering. "Why'd ya open the door fer 'im?" He jerked his head in Jeff's direction.

Annie Lash raised her shoulders. "I don't know. I just thought... He seemed—"

"Women!" Zan snorted. "C'mon, Jeff. We got us a powerful bunch of catchin' up to do."

Annie Lash shut the door and automatically dropped the chain in place. One short hour ago she had been wondering how she was going to fend off the attentions of Walt Ransom, how she was going to free Zan to go upriver, what direction her life was going to take. Now it was settled. In one short hour a body's whole life can be shifted in a new direction.

It was like a miracle.

CHAPTER
THREE

Shortly after the first glint of dawn appeared in the east behind a bank of low clouds, a freight wagon loaded with barrels, wooden crates, an assortment of tools, coils of rope, and numerous other items pulled to a creaking stop in front of the cabin. Annie Lash had heard the jingle of the harness and the clip-clop of the horse's hooves on the hard-packed clay. She opened the door a crack, and after seeing Zan's fur hat and hearing him swear as he crawled down from the high seat, she swung it wide.

"Air ya ready, gal?"

"I'm ready." She stood in the doorway in her plain woolsey dress. There was nothing fancy about it, no touch of color, no apron on its front. It was a serviceable dress, dyed nut brown and well worn. She had a dark shawl thrown about her shoulders, and a three-cornered cloth, tied

securely beneath her chin, covered the thick braid
she had pinned on the top of her head.

"Mornin'." Jefferson Merrick loomed out of the
darkness and stepped into the cabin.

"Mornin'."

He looked around the room, then placed a box
in the seat of her rocking chair, picked them both
up, and maneuvered them through the narrow
door.

Zan crawled over the wagon seat and onto the
goods already loaded on the wagonbed. He
stacked her chair, the walnut washstand, a round
keg containing some of the things her parents
brought from Virginia, and the feather mattress
from her bed. Jeff threw a rope across and they
tied them securely. Annie Lash carried out a stack
of quilts, a small hand loom, and a few choice fur
pelts Zan had given to her to make a warm cape.

The eaves of the cabin still dripped from the
night's rain, and fog lay like a cover of white snow
over the river. It was a cold, damp morning. She
mentioned it to Zan.

"Hit'll brighten 'fore noon. Hit's a'ready
ablowin' away. When they's heavy fog hit allus
means clearin' weather. Ain't that so, Jeff?"

"Usually," he said and heaved Annie Lash's
trunk up onto the flat top of a crate on the end of
the wagon. "Is this everything you want to take?"
He looked directly at Annie Lash for the first time.

"Yes," she said and a wistful note crept into her
voice. She looked back into the almost empty
room. Someone else would use the workbench
she had kept so meticulously clean and the feet
of some unknown person would muddy the plank

floor. She had made a home in this small cabin, although she had never lost the feeling of temporariness while she lived in it. Now that it was emptied of homey things it looked lonely and forsaken.

"Stop your lallygaggin', Annie Lash, an' climb on up here." Zan's voice seemed loud in the foggy stillness. "Ya ain't agrievin' fer this ol' place, air ya?"

"'Course not, Zan Thatcher!" Her voice was sharp because she was grieving in a small way. She couldn't help feeling some attachment to the place that had sheltered her these past years.

Annie Lash picked up the cloth bundle that held her brush, a washcloth, a bit of scented soap, and a clean dress; things she would need during the journey to the faraway homestead. She blew out the candle, left the smoking stub on the mantle, and went quickly out the door. Zan reached for her bundle, then took her hand and helped her climb up the big wheel and onto the wagon seat.

"I didn't know ya set sich a store by this old place," he said with a hint of impatience in his voice. He moved to the far side of the seat and drew her with him to make room for Jeff on her other side.

"I lived here, Zan. And if I come back it'll not be to this cabin. Someone else will have it by then. I can't help it if I feel I'm leaving a part of my life behind, even if it wasn't a happy part."

Jeff picked up the reins and flicked the backs of the horses, setting them into motion. Crowded between the two men, holding the bundle on her lap, Annie Lash braced her feet against the lurch of the wagon. They made a wide circle and she caught a glimpse of the cabin one last time before they turned the corner. The team strained to pull the heavy load up the hill to the main street, which at this hour was deserted and dark. Behind a building a dog barked and a hoarse voice cursed it. Nearby a rooster crowed. A muskrat, lumbering toward the river, ignored their passing.

With her shoulders tucked behind those of Zan and Jeff, her hips and thighs snug against theirs, Annie Lash looked straight ahead. She was exhilarated, saddened, and frightened, if it was possible to have all those feelings at one time. She had longed to leave the Bank; she despised the stench of the slop and human excrement, the rough Pittsburgh rivermen who were forever drinking and brawling, and the constant fear of being subjected to their pawing and lewd suggestions. Now, at last, she was leaving it to go to a homestead deep in the wilderness with a man she had not yet seen in the light of day.

She glanced at Jeff, but could only see his clean-shaven cheek and the white-blond hair that his hat didn't cover. Somehow she sensed that he had a frown on his face and wondered why. He had been politely aloof while loading her belongings on his wagon. Was he already regretting his offer of employment? Did he doubt now that she would earn her keep?

Jeff seldom, if ever, wondered at the wisdom of a decision once it was made. One part of his mind knew that he was right to get Zan out of Saint Louis. He also knew his old friend wouldn't leave without the girl. The other part of his mind wondered how she would adapt to life at the homestead. She seemed to be a calm, sensible woman. He couldn't imagine Zan taking to a woman who was a flibbertigibbet. But would she and Callie take to each other? If she hated the isolation, would she make life miserable for Callie? He glanced down at the hands clasped tightly around the bundle she held in her lap. She was used to having people around, watching the comings and goings on the river. Would she become dissatisfied and want to come back? He was glad when Zan spoke and interrupted his thoughts.

"Hit's been a right smart spell since I been aridin' a wagon. I'd a heap druther be takin' to my feet or aridin' a horse."

"I agree." Jeff sailed a short whip out over the backs of the horses and urged them to pick up speed. "I'm not partial to riding the river or bouncing on a wagon, either. But it's easier to haul by wagon up to the Missouri than to pole against the current on the big river."

"Hit makes sense."

"A neighbor, Silas Cornick, and one of his boys came down with me. They left late yesterday with another wagonload of supplies. They'll have it unloaded and on the raft by the time we get there. We'll pole up to Saint Charles, then load again onto wagons for the rest of the trip home."

"This ain't yore rig?" Zan asked the question while Annie Lash was trying to sort out the puzzle.

"It belongs to a friend, Fain MacCartney, who lives about five miles north of the mouth of the river. Isaac, Silas Cornick's son, and I will take them back tonight."

"I heard 'bout that MacCartney feller, but I ain't met up with 'im. Gunsmith, ain't he?"

"One of the best I've run across. He made my rifle. I'll put it up against any I've seen. Even that old blunderbuss you carry around," he added and tossed Zan a grin.

"Wal..." Zan leaned out and spit over the side of the wagon. "One a these days we'll have us a little match an' jist see 'bout it."

Annie Lash was glad to sit back and listen to the men talk. She could give her mind over to looking and seeing. The sun was just coming up and the whole sky was flushed with a warm, rosy light. It lay over the land, and beneath it the grass was silver from the rain of the night before. A great owl, patrolling the border between the forest and the river, swooped low over the wagon and she could almost feel the stir of the air from the slow beat of its silent wings.

At first, the trail was flat and wound between the giant oaks and ash that bordered the river, but as they penetrated farther north it became rougher and higher with short sweeps of meadow in between. High above, a pair of hawks circled in amorous pursuit of each other, squirrels scampered in the underbrush and raced for a tree trunk to scold the intruders from their lofty perch. A flock of colorful parakeets dipped and dived before settling in the top of a giant tree. As the wagon lurched along, there were occasional glimpses of the river, tearing through the dense woods on its seaward course.

Sitting there on the high seat of the wagon, Annie Lash began to feel a strong sense of well-being. She was a part of this vitality, this vast land, this movement into the wilderness. She was sure Zan felt it, too. He had an eager, lively look on his face, and the tone of his voice as he talked with Jeff held more enthusiasm than she had heard in a long while.

The day passed quickly. They stopped every few hours to rest the horses and to let them drink. Zan always helped her down from the wagon, although they both knew she was quite capable of getting down on her own. Jefferson Merrick was distantly polite, seldom looking directly at her, but she noticed his eyes were continuously moving, searching, even as he squatted beside a stream to drink. Once he caught her looking at him and it made her feel foolish and awkward, stiff-handed and clumsy, as she accepted the drinking cup. A deep embarrassment spread within her, making it impossible for her to look at him. A feeling of heat crept up her throat and into her face, and she could scarcely make herself mumble, "Thank you."

The size of the raft and the amount of goods on it were a complete surprise to Annie Lash, as were the three men who were waiting to help load the wagon. Silas Cornick and his son, Isaac, were farmers. The father, big, gangly and gray-bearded wore a loose, homespun shirt. His trousers were held up by galluses. His son wore similar garb. He was a lean young man with a quick easy smile, a head of heavy dark hair, and eyebrows that grew together over the bridge of his nose.

Jeff was pleasantly surprised to see the third man. They greeted each other warmly. He was dark and quiet, wore buckskins and knee-high moccasins with fringe down the sides. His hair grew well back from his broad forehead and was held behind his neck with a thong. He was slim and wiry and had about him a solitary air. Although his dark eyes roamed the edge of the forest constantly, as did Jeff's, Annie Lash had not caught them looking directly at her. His high, prominent cheekbones and skin the color of smooth copper proclaimed the blood of his Indian ancestors, but when he spoke it was with a pronounced French accent. Jeff said his name was Lightbody, but he was called Light. He made a small stiff bow when introduced to Annie Lash.

The raft was rectangular in shape with a platform running down the center of it so the waves that broke over the logs could not reach the goods piled on it. Annie Lash's trunk and boxes were placed on the platform and tied down. Her rocking chair and walnut washstand were tied to the top of the canvas-covered kegs and crates that were already loaded when they arrived.

They camped beside the river and after a meal of broiled catfish and fried cornpone, Zan fixed a place on the raft for Annie Lash to bed down for the night. He was happy to be out of Saint Louis. It was evident in the smile that stripped years from his face. He talked freely with the men, joked with Jeff, and lightly teased Annie Lash.

"Git yoreself settled in, gal. We're aleavin' at first light an' we ain't awaitin' fer ya."

Annie Lash was sure she wouldn't sleep a wink. Isaac and Light left before dark to take the borrowed teams and wagons to the MacCartney's. When they returned, the five men sat beside the dying campfire and talked. The murmur of low male voices was comforting. She heard Jeff laugh, and it occurred to her that he didn't laugh often. That disturbed her somehow. Then her mind, now free of the burden it had carried since her pa died, allowed her tired body to relax and she slept a deep and dreamless sleep.

Annie Lash sat on the edge of the platform and watched Light slip off the rope holding the craft to the stake on the bank. All morning she had tried to avoid looking at Jeff, but she could often feel his eyes on her. Once her glance locked with his. In spite of her excitement and that of the others, there was no merriment in his eyes, only quiet watchfulness. He was as disturbing this morning as he had been last night and the night before. She'd had a hard time pushing him out of her mind long enough to pack her belongings, and his voice was the last thing she'd heard before she went to sleep last night. Now, she marveled at how easily he and Light moved about on the bobbing, swaying craft, and how his voice was in tune with the morning quiet as he spoke to the men.

They traveled steadily upriver, and by sunup the bluffs were high along the edge. The trees that topped them merged into a solid wall of dark forest, their tops edging jaggedly against the sky. From her perch atop her trunk on the platform, Annie Lash watched the men toil, sweat, and ma-

neuver the clumsy, heavily loaded craft away from
the swift current in the middle of the river and
edge it along the shoreline.

The wide, muddy Missouri River was famous
for being cussedly wicked. It was devious, treach-
erous; it twisted and turned like a snake, it narrowed, it widened; its eddies could snatch a boat
and send it whirling. The river could rise unex-
pectedly, lifting logs and driftwood off a hundred
sandbars, hurling them with a vicious force downstream where they would lodge on other sandbars, forming concealed traps for the unwary
traveler.

Along the bank of the river, quick-springing
willow roots caught together a mass of branches
and young trees yanked up by a sudden surge of
flood waters. Then, tucked beneath its muddy
waters were what boatmen called sawyers, the
Missouri's most dangerous trick of all. A log floating downstream would anchor its roots or branches
in the muddy bottom on the river, giving it free-
dom of movement to ride up on the current, seldom breaking the surface but lying concealed until
it pierced a boat or ripped off a gunwale. They
were as much a danger as the sucking pockets of
quicksand, hungry and relentless, that rivermen
called the Missouri's secret pockets.

Zan relieved first one man and then the other
at the poles. Jeff was the last to surrender his
position. He dipped a cup in the river and brought
it to Annie Lash.

"I don't have a fondness for river water myself,
but sometimes it has to do."

"Thank you," she murmured. She took the cup,

drained it without breathing, and handed it back to him. "It's better than down by Saint Louis."

"More?"

She shook her head. "I feel useless sitting here. I can take a turn at the poles."

"That's not necessary. Just sit here and enjoy the ride." His dark eyes caught hers and he seemed to not want to look away.

Annie Lash wanted to ask him about the place where they were going and about the woman, Callie, but decided this wasn't the right time. Instead, she said, "I've got two pieces of candy in my pocket. Do you want one?"

He smiled at that, his dark eyes holding her sky blue ones. Annie Lash ignored her jumping heart and dug her hand into her pocket. He popped the small square into his mouth when she handed it to him.

"That's almost better than catfish." His eyes gleamed with a sudden light that was plainly mischievous.

"Catfish? Ugh!"

She knew he was laughing, but no sound came from his strong, bronzed throat. His eyes were so dark, so mirror dark, she could see her own reflection in them. She felt a spurt of intense pleasure. A tingling thrill traveled down her spine, making her almost giddy.

"No taste for catfish, huh?"

"Not much."

"How about turtle? There are snappers in the river as big as washtubs." He continued to look at her—really look—and she felt a flush steal up her throat into her face.

"Jeff," Light called softly.

Jeff looked past Annie Lash and his face instantly lost its merriment. She turned to see what he was looking at. Jagged rocks protruded out from the shoreline, a potential hazard for their small craft. He quickly picked up a pole and helped the men edge the craft into deeper water.

By midday it was so warm she took off her shawl and tucked it under the rope holding the trunk. She was not used to prolonged inactivity and was stiff and tired from sitting for so long. She got up from her seat and stood holding onto the rope. She hadn't, as yet, learned to keep her balance on the bobbing, swaying craft. Her stomach growled noisily and she ate a handful of dried fruit and a biscuit provided by Jeff. By the middle of the afternoon the question foremost in her mind was how she was going to relieve her full bladder. She ached with the pressure of it.

Annie Lash watched the river ahead and wondered what was around the next bend. It was wide and deep at this point, but not swiftly flowing, and it curled in looping bends. They were able to move along faster now. There was a low, grassy bank that separated the river from the thick growth of trees. It was still and quiet. Only the creaking of the boat and the sucking sounds as the river bottom released its hold on the poles that propelled the craft broke the hush.

Suddenly, as if some unseen force had pulled a string, she turned her head toward Jeff. It was as if he had willed her to turn and look at him. He laid a finger against his lips, then looked away from her toward the band of trees. She sensed now the alertness of the other men, although the rhythm of their poling was not broken. Light, from his position on the front, righthand side of the boat, kept his head turned toward the shore as did Jeff and Zan. Silas and his son poled strongly on the outside, taking an occasional quick glance in the direction of the river's edge.

Annie Lash forgot her almost overfilled bladder and her not quite empty stomach as she strained her ears for sound and her eyes for movement along the thick curtain of foilage. The silence pressed down on her. There was not a whisper of a branch or a birdsong to break the stillness on this warm April day.

Jeff caught her glance and motioned for her to climb down from the piled cargo and stand on the river side of the platform. Her skin prickled and her heart knocked, but when she moved her legs they were steady. With her feet planted firmly on the floor of the raft, she looked at Jeff for more instructions. He and Light were communicating by hand signals. Light wanted to move the craft farther out into the stream as they rounded a bend. Jeff agreed, and the four men poled strongly until they were almost on the edge of the faster moving current. Zan, his long gun in his hand, moved up beside Annie Lash and stood looking over the pile of freight, his narrowed eyes searching constantly along the edge of trees.

"What is it, Zan?"

"Dunno. Somethin' fer dadburn sure."

"What can I do?"

"Keep yore eyes peeled 'n stay outta the way."

It was hard work poling against the strong current and progress was slow. They had just rounded the bend when a shot rang out like the crack of a whip, echoed, and was lost down the river. Not a movement was lost as the men strained against the poles. Several more shots were heard before they cleared the point in the river and could see what lay ahead.

A clumsily constructed raft was drifting with the current toward them. One man stood against a crude log hut built in the center of it and fired his gun while another poled the craft away from the shore. A group of Indians mounted on ponies broke from the trees and raced along the bank, yipping and holding their bows high over their heads in a threatening manner. Their near naked bodies hugged the backs of the small, surefooted, ponies as they sped over the rough ground. The panic-stricken settler continued to fire his gun.

"My Gawd!" Zan snorted. "Hit's jist a bunch a younguns a showin' off! They ain't even dry behind the ears yet." He put his hand to his mouth. "Hold yer fire!" he yelled.

The settler continued to fire while the raft, caught in the dangerous, swift current, raced downriver. Annie Lash heard Isaac curse. Then Jeff shouted to Light to pull in toward shore. The settler continued to fire while the Indian boys danced their ponies along the shore well out of rifle range, enjoying the havoc they were creating.

As the raft raced closer to them, Annie Lash could see the women and children huddled beneath the log shelter. The settler, who suddenly seemed to realize the immediate danger was not with the Indians but a collision with another raft, dropped his rifle and grabbed a pole.

"Gawdamned ignoramus!" Zan shouted. "Hold tight, gal, they jist mought ram us!"

Annie Lash gripped the ropes and braced her legs against the platform, more frightened for the people on the other raft than for herself. The Indian boys on the shore were forgotten as she watched the space between the two rafts narrow rapidly. The men pushed with all their strength to avoid the path of the out-of-control craft coming toward them. The raft was so close, Annie Lash could see the terror on the faces of the women as they hugged the children to them. She felt the jar as heavy logs scraped against each other.

"Now!" Jeff shouted. He and Light leaped to the other craft.

Annie Lash watched it move away with four men now straining at the poles to steer it out of the swift current. Her quick feeling of relief that they had not crashed was replaced by a spurt of pride in the way Jeff and Light had jumped to aid the people on the other boat.

Zan shoved his rifle beneath the canvas and grabbed a pole.

"Can I help?"

"Stay where ya is, gal. We ain't got no time to be a fishin' ya outta the river."

The Indian boys raced their ponies along the edge of the water to harrass the craft coming in toward the shore. The boldest among them urged their ponies out into the water, while the others raised their bows over their heads and shook them menacingly as they had done to the panic-stricken settlers on the other boat. Zan cupped his hands and yelled at them in a strange dialect. The yipping ceased and Zan yelled again. They drew away from the water's edge, retreated to the edge of the forest, and sat quietly watching for a moment. Then, with defiant yells, they wheeled their ponies and raced away.

"Thank Gawd fer that!" Silas snorted.

"What'd ya say to 'em?" Isaac looked at Zan with new respect.

"I tol' 'em to git on back to their lodge or I'd kick their butts up atween their ears an' put a feather in 'em."

"Ya didn't!"

"Wal, I'll be a horned toad!" Silas chuckled.

Zan turned his back and spit in the river. Annie Lash could see the grin on his face and felt a rush of affection for the grizzled frontiersman. Zan had never talked much about himself. She wondered now, as she had done dozens of times before, about his life before he came to Saint Louis.

Thoughts of Zan and whatever life he'd had before fled her mind when she saw the other craft coming around the point in the river. It was smaller and lighter than the one they were on, and the four men at the poles moved it along faster.

Their own craft jarred against the shore, and Isaac scrambled up the muddy bank to tie a rope to the stump of a tree. Zan and Silas dug their poles into the river bottom and lashed them to the raft to steady it. Annie Lash stood beside the platform while the second raft was secured and the women and children helped up the three-foot bank. She went to the end of the craft, holding onto the platform to steady her wobbling legs. Jeff was waiting at the top of the bank with his hand extended. Without hesitating, she put hers in it, braced her foot on a root, and he hauled her up onto solid ground.

A pair of deep dark eyes studied her face. She smiled at him without being aware that her lips were pressed together and two deep holes appeared in her cheeks. As his eyes studied her, hers noted that his leather shirt had shrunk from repeated wettings until it fit him like the skin on an animal and that his hair was damp and curled around his ears; its startling, white-blond color drew her eyes to it again and again. His powder horn, knife, and tomahawk were as much a part of him as were his arms or his legs, and the long rifle fit in his hand so naturally that he seemed to be unaware it was there. They stood gazing at each other as they had done earlier. Annie Lash couldn't turn her eyes away.

"Be careful of snakes. They'll be coming out to sun themselves." The tone of his voice was soft, as though he were saying other words, and her lips parted so she could take a trembling breath. She prayed that he wasn't aware of how girlish she felt or how excited she was.

"Snakes?"

"Are you afraid of them?"

She tried to suppress a shudder. He had touched on one of her real fears. She was deathly afraid of snakes and moved uncomfortably.

He grinned down at her and his glance dropped toward her feet. She lifted the hem of her homespun dress, disclosing strong, high shoes. He nodded his approval.

"Carry a stick. Snakes are just as afraid of you as you are of them and will get you out of your way if they can. They won't strike unless startled or cornered."

The shudder shook her shoulders. "I had to kill one a few weeks back and drag it out of the house. It had a flat head and beady eyes. It was clammy and...slithery. Zan said it was a diamondback rattler and very poisonous."

His grin became a smile. "They're not bad eatin'. That is, if you're good and hungry."

Annie Lash felt the saliva flood her mouth and her stomach do a slow roll at the thought. He observed the way her mouth turned down at the corners and laughed. She knew, then, he was teasing.

"Oh, you. I couldn't!"

"You'd be surprised at what you'd eat if you were hungry enough. You might even eat grub worms."

"No! No—" She shook her head vigorously. Her eyes shone and her dimples deepened as she smiled.

She was still smiling as she walked away from him.

CHAPTER
FOUR

The women from the other raft stood together, silently waiting for Annie Lash to approach them. Their faces reflected the kind of resigned patience that was typical of women who had left their homes to build a new life on the frontier. Their clothes were ragged and mud splattered. One held a sleeping baby on her hip, the other clutched the hands of two small children. A young girl stood beside them. Annie Lash smiled. The women returned the smile shyly, apologetically, as if they feared their presence was somehow offensive to her.

The young girl stared at her with a mixture of curiosity and hostility and then looked away toward the line of trees. She was not much bigger than the small boy who stood beside her, but her young breasts pushed against the thin material of a dress that was too small for her. The hem came

a good two inches above her bare ankles. A tangle
of jet black curls that looked as if they had never
known a brush tumbled around a beautiful, fine-
boned face that could not possibly be that of a
young child. There was an elfin, untouchable
quality about the girl, as if she were with them
in body but not in spirit.

"Hello." Annie Lash instinctively knew the
women would not speak first.

"Howdy." The two older women spoke in un-
ison. The girl threw her a quick glance, then ignored her.

"Annie Lash," Zan called. "Hit's a'right if'n y'all
go in the woods a ways. Not deep mind ya, just
outta' sight like."

"Thank you, Zan."

Jeff appeared beside her with a long, slim willow stick. She took it from his hand without looking at him and despised the shyness that caused
the heat to come up from the base of her neck to
flood her face with color.

Annie Lash followed the women, the girl, and
the children into the clearing behind the bushes.
She looked around carefully and then beat the
leaf-covered ground with the willow switch to
make sure there were no crawly things before she
squatted to relieve herself. The girl and the children squatted also, but the two women stood in
the sprattled stance, as was the habit of backwoods women, to attend to their bodily needs.

"Is the one with hair like sheep's wool yore
man?" the girl asked. Her large hazel eyes were
as clear and as innocent as a young child's. The
foilage of thick, dark lashes that surrounded them

contrasted vividly with her translucent complexion.

Annie Lash was so intrigued with the girl's beauty that she almost forgot to answer. "Oh, I'm sorry," she said with an embarrassed little laugh. "You're just so pretty that I forgot..." Her voice trailed off as if she couldn't find the right words to explain.

"Hit's all right, ma'am. Maggie's used to folk astarin' at 'er. I'm her ma, Mrs. Gentry."

"I'm Annie Lash Jester. And, no, he's not my man," she said to the girl. "I'm not married. I'm going upriver to Mr. Merrick's homestead to take care of his sister-in-law and her two small children."

"Ah..." The sound came softly from Maggie and her thick brush of lashes lowered. Her lips tilted in a smile and her arched brows raised slightly. Annie Lash wasn't sure what the sound meant, but she didn't have time to dwell on it. The girl's mother was introducing the other woman.

"This here's another Mrs. Gentry. We wed up with brothers."

"Howdy, ma'am."

Annie Lash nodded. "Where are you from?"

"Kaintuck." Maggie's mother answered with a yearning in her voice. "We left us a snug cabin with a good stand a fruit trees, good huntin', a garden—"

"Our men's been hankerin' to try new land," the other Mrs. Gentry said with a deep sigh. "Hit's certain they got wanderin' feet."

"It wasn't that a'tall." Maggie turned flashing

green eyes on her mother and her aunt. "It was
'cause them loony ol' hill folk thought I was a
witch, and Pa was feared they'd get a notion to
burn me!"

Annie Lash looked from one woman to the other,
expecting one of them to deny what the girl had
said. To her surprise both women nodded their
heads in agreement.

"Folks is funny," Maggie's mother said sadly.
"My girl's a good girl fer all her queer ways. Nobody'd pay her no never mind if'n she didn't have
the face of an angel. Menfolk say she puts a spell
on 'em an' they trail 'er like she were a bitch in
heat. Times is when she takes to the woods to get
away from the pesterin'. The womenfolk back thar
in Kaintuck were talkin' witchcraft, so we up and
moved on."

Annie Lash thought surely Mrs. Gentry was ex-
aggerating. The girl was beautiful, but—Maggie
stood silently watching to see what effect her
mother's words had on Annie Lash. Annie Lash
smiled at her, but the girl's expression was de-
fensive, as if she expected her to dislike her. Suddenly, she whirled and darted into the woods,
disappearing among the trees like a shadow. Mrs.
Gentry gave her attention to the baby that had
awakened and was pawing at the bodice of her
dress.

"Don't you think we should wait?" Annie Lash
asked when the women started to leave the clearing.

"Don't give no worry 'bout Maggie. She'll come
when she's aready."

Mrs. Gentry seemed unconcerned about her

daughter's disappearance. A feeling of uneasiness about the girl settled on Annie Lash. She had seemed taut, like a bird ready for flight, and had moved away from them so swiftly and silently Annie Lash had hardly been aware of it until she was gone. She's like a wild, shy, forest creature, and quite the most beautiful thing I've ever seen, Annie Lash thought. At the riverbank, she looked behind her, but there was no sign of the girl.

Overhead, the rustling wings of migrating, northbound birds caught her attention. Ahead of her the Missouri, so often hostile, repellent, lay shimmering in the late afternoon sunlight. The channel where they had entered and tied the rafts was smooth, sheltered from the main current by a string of little islands. The islands seemed to be floating in the river, idyllic ships of green carpet. The northern riverbank was splendid with the masses of darkly growing redbud set against the snow-white blooms of wild pear and plum.

Annie Lash drew in a long, satisfied breath, consciously permitting herself to enjoy the view. She was in new country and from now on every hour, every bend of the river, would reveal new and interesting views. She went to stand beside Zan. The old mountain man was her family now, and she had the feeling of belonging when she was near him. She felt every bit as close to him as she had to her pa. Zan cut a chew of tobacco, stuffed it in his jaw, and listened closely to what Jeff was saying.

"We'll not make Saint Charles by nightfall, so we might as well make camp," Jeff told him, then turned to Silas. "That all right with you?"

"Hit's the onlyest thin' to do."

"What do you think, Light?"

"Is that not a good place?" The scout pointed toward a narrow strip of land that jutted out from the store. "Waterfowl to rise up if disturbed. A belt of rose thicket on the land side to keep out bear or wolf." The man's dark, alert eyes caught and held Jeff's in unspoken communication.

Jeff nodded. Light jumped off the bank onto the raft and made ready to cast off.

Silas came close and spoke to Jeff in low tones. "These folk ain't got no river know-how a'tall. Hit's a wonder they ain't got them younguns drowned afore now."

"What do you want to do, Silas?"

"I'm a thinkin' we ort to help 'em."

"Are you suggesting we let them come along with us?"

"Hit's our Christian duty," Silas said firmly.

"All right." Jeff waited a long moment before he spoke. "We'll see them as far as Saint Charles, then they're on their own."

The older Gentry brother came hesitantly forward and stood twisting his hat in his hands. "How far air ya agoin' upriver, mister?"

"From Saint Charles? Quite a ways. It'll take us the better part of four days unless we have a mishap."

Annie Lash listened for a hint of impatience in Jeff's voice. She could detect none and was surprised because she had heard Zan's snort of disgust when Silas suggested that they help the ill equipped settlers. Zan didn't suffer fools easily, and it was plain he considered the men fools for bringing their women and children into the wilderness without the know-how to protect them.

"Is they a settlement thar?" Mr. Gentry asked.

"No." Jeff nodded toward Silas and Isaac. "Silas and his family are my nearest neighbors. They have a place five miles this side of mine."

"Is thar decent land what's not took up?"

"Plenty for those who want to work and clear it."

"Hiram . . . could we?" The woman with the baby moved forward hopefully.

The man ignored her. "We needs to git set, git a crop in an' git up a cabin afore winter sets in."

Jeff lifted his shoulders. "There's a Territory man at Saint Charles. He'll point out the parcels available. We'll help you get that far."

"We'd be obliged—ah, beholdin' to ya. We be hill folk an' that river be plumb worrisome," he said with a shake of his head.

"Get ready to shove off. We'll camp on that land that juts out from the shore." Jeff lifted his arm toward the timbered island about a half a mile upstream. "The water's smooth between here and there. You'll make it without any trouble." He jumped down onto the raft.

Annie Lash looked around for Zan, wondering how she was going to get down onto the bobbing craft. Jeff was watching her, his eyes darkly amused. He tossed his hat onto the platform and extended his hands. The sun flinted on his white hair. He was smiling.

"C'mon. I'll catch you."

"You can't. I'm . . . too big."

He laughed. "Not as big as me. C'mon."

"But I'll knock you down."

"I doubt that. Lean forward. I'll not let you fall."

"Don't blame me if we go into the river." She tilted her body toward him. Just before she leaned so far there was no turning back she closed her eyes tightly and let herself fall forward.

Miraculously, his hands found her armpits and hers his shoulders. She was swung down and her feet struck the floor of the raft. Her shyness gone, she giggled softly, her eyes shining up at him. His face was alive with smile lines that fanned out from the corners of his mouth and his eyes. She took her hands from his shoulders and he let his drop to his sides.

"I told you I wouldn't let you fall."

"I didn't...believe you."

Weakened and made clumsy by the exhilarating experience, she stumbled, and his hands shot out again to grip her upper arms. His dark eyes, as they watched the crimson flood her face, glinted with devilish amusement.

"Whoa, now."

"I'd never make a...boatman. I'd better sit d-d...down." Ashamed of the stammer in her voice, she moved toward her seat on the platform. Jeff clasped her elbow to steady her when Isaac leaped from the bank and the craft rocked on the water.

Seated once again on the trunk, Annie Lash watched the girl, Maggie, walk slowly out of the woods, cross the grassy clearing to where her parents waited, and leap lightly down onto the raft. She is so curiously lovely, she's like someone from a fairy tale, Annie Lash thought. Her skin was honey gold, her dark hair a soft swirling cloud about her thin, beautifully constructed face. Her body was boyishly slim except for her small pointed breasts. Her mouth was soft and as red as an apple. She reminded Annie Lash of a picture she had seen of a dark-haired angel floating down out of a misty white cloud with flowers in her hand and a crown on her head.

A pole struck hard against the side of the craft and Annie Lash turned to see Isaac staring at the girl as if he was seeing a vision. His admiration was so open, so frankly intent, that she could not help but think of what Mrs. Gentry had said: "Menfolk say she puts a spell on 'em." Her swift glance took in the other male members of their party. Light was also watching the girl with the same intensity, and his arms were moving the pole automatically. Zan and Jeff were straining to push the raft away from the bank, their attention absorbed with that task. Silas Cornick leaned on his pole and watched the other raft with a puzzled look on his face.

Annie Lash looked back to where the settlers were hurrying to get their craft into position to follow them. She felt a tinge of apprehension and drew the tip of her tongue over dry lips. With her eyes focused on a raucous cloud of gulls working their way upriver she tried to force her mind away from the thought that something truly new and unimaginable was going to happen, something for which she was totally unprepared.

* * *

The campfire of dry cedar knots and splinters burned with a clear, hot flame and what little smoke there was drifted away to be dissipated among the thick, overhanging branches of the cedar grove. They ate fish again. In a quarter of an hour, Light had caught three perch, a bass, two small white catfish, and a giant pike. Annie Lash had watched him wade out beyond the reeds and, using a hand line, cast a hook to which he had tied a bit of feather as a lure. It had barely hit the water when it was struck by the bass with a violent lunge.

Fish was not Annie Lash's favorite thing to eat and she wondered why they were eating it when the island was alive with waterfowl. The birds were restless and noisy, and when disturbed the whole island would erupt in raucous clamor and then gradually quiet as they settled down once more. She mentioned it to Zan.

"Ain't no sense in lettin' every livin' thing know we're here, Annie Lash. A shot'd carry five mile downriver. Hit's jist a mite easier to catch a mess a fish an' be on the safe side." He looked down the shoreline to where the Gentrys were camped. "Damn fools!" he barked loudly. "They ain't got no brains a'tall."

Annie Lash watched him lope down the sandy shore toward the big, blazing fire that lit up the whole area. In a few minutes the bonfire was reduced to a small glowing blaze with a shield of dry brush between it and the river, and Zan came back to where she was waiting.

"Jeff done tol' 'em not to shoot. He ne'er thought

'bout 'em buildin' a fire big nuff ta roast a buffalo,"
he grumbled.

"I've heard about the renegades who attack the
settlers on the river, robbing and killing—"

"Hit ain't only river rats, Annie Lash. Injuns
use the river fer travelin', if they cin do it. Hit
bein' spring, they take to prowlin' considerably.
Hit's plumb queer them Gentrys ain't had a brush
with 'em afore now."

"I'm glad you're with me, Zan." Annie Lash
impulsively hugged his arm.

"Ya ain't got no cause to worry none, gal." Zan
chuckled. "I'm a thinkin' thar ain't much what
goes by Jeff and that Frenchman. I ain't ne'er seen
a man use a knife like that Frenchie. He ain't no
slouch, that's sart'n."

The moon came up over the treetops. Annie
Lash took her soap and washcloth and walked
through the trees to the other side of the small
finger of land to the water's edge. With a quick
nervous glance behind her to be sure she was
alone, she unbuttoned her dress to the waist and
pulled it back over her shoulders. The water was
cold, but she scrubbed herself briskly and splashed
water onto her face. It was wonderfully refreshing
to be clean again, even though she shivered in
the cool night air.

After she pulled her dress up over her bare
shoulders and buttoned the bodice, she moved
back under the trees, sat on a boulder, and took
the pins out of her hair. She freed it from the braid
and let it fall about her shoulders to her hips. It

felt good to have the heavy weight off the top of her head. Her fingertips massaged her scalp and raked through the long strands to remove the snarls before she began the long sweeping strokes of the brush.

Night fog began to rise from the river in wispy patches. She lifted her hair and swung her shawl around her shoulders to hold off a chill. It was peaceful here in the darkness. It had been a long time since she had been alone out under the stars so she lingered, brushing and then braiding her hair.

Annie Lash saw the girl as soon as she came out of the woods. She darted from the tree line to the water's edge, stood poised for a moment, then lifted her dress up over her head. Her naked body was merely a white form in the darkness. Quick as the wink of the eye, she was in the water and disappeared from sight.

Annie Lash thought her heart was going to stop beating and never start again. She got to her feet, keeping her eyes on the place where Maggie had gone into the water. She knew the perils of the river; the pockets of quicksand, the whirling eddies that could grasp a stout log and draw it to the bottom. Just as she was about to shout for help, Maggie sprang up out of the water and leaped up onto the bank. She picked up her dress and slipped it over her head. Annie Lash sank back down on the rock, her heart pounding with anger at the girl for giving her such a scare.

Anger was soon replaced with awe. She stared in openmouthed amazement at the girl on the sandy riverbank. She was singing softly and the beauty of her voice was both surprising and delightful. It was as clear as the song of a lark and Annie Lash thought it no wonder the hill folk thought she was a witch. Maggie began to dance, her bare feet scarcely touching the soft sand, her arms curved gracefully upward, her hair flying as she dipped and swayed and turned and spun in perfect harmony with the tune she was humming. She was completely absorbed, twirling, dancing, singing to herself. And then—almost like the mist—she was gone.

For a fleeting second Annie Lash wondered if she had dreamed she saw a girl dancing and heard the bell-like tone of her singing. She sat for a long while, her hands in her lap, thinking about it. It was almost as if the girl were enclosed in a timeless world.

"What are you doing out here by yourself?" Jeff's sharp words from behind her caused Annie Lash to jump to her feet in alarm. "I thought you had bedded down on the raft until Light told me you were here."

"I came here to wash—"

"Zan thought you were on the raft, too. You should have told him where you were going."

"I'm not a child, Mr. Merrick. I was within calling distance." Annie Lash was astounded at the coldness of his voice and then angered. He certainly was a man of many moods.

"It's foolish and stupid to wander off alone."

"I knew there was no danger."

"No danger? This island is crawling with snakes,

not to mention the hostiles that could beach a canoe and carry you away before you had time to take a deep breath."

"You're just trying to frighten me because you know my fear of snakes!" It had been on the tip of her tongue to tell him Maggie had even been in the river, but she held back, knowing he was in no mood to listen. "I'm sorry for being a bother to you. It won't happen again." She turned and marched stiffly back through the thick stand of trees toward the glowing coals of the campfire, very much aware that Jeff stalked angrily along beside her.

"Here she is, Zan. I'll thank you to keep an eye on her until we get home."

"Where ya been, Annie Lash?" Zan was on his feet. Light and the Cornicks were not in sight. "You ain't ort to be goin' off by yoreself."

"Don't you go jumping on me, too. I just went over there to wash myself and to brush my hair."

"Ya warn't dirty. All ya done all day was sit on that raft. Gawd amighty! Ya coulda brushed yore hair here," he insisted impatiently.

"Well, I never—" she sputtered. "If you gentlemen will excuse me I'll go to bed and you can rest your minds about me for the rest of the night." She tossed her head defiantly and was grateful for the darkness that hid her flaming face and the tears that sprang to her eyes on hearing Zan's rebuke. She strode briskly toward the raft, her head high, litheness and grace in every line of her body.

Zan chuckled. "She c'n get her back up quicker'n scat. She ain't no namby-pamby, my gal ain't."

"She's ... headstrong," Jeff snapped, and kicked dirt onto the coals with his moccasined foot.

Zan looked at him sharply. "Ya got a burr under yore tail 'bout somethin'?"

"Godammit, Zan! Why'd you say that? It was foolhardy for her to go off like that and you know it as well as I do."

"Yup, 'twas. But hit didn't call fer no lashin' out like ya done. Air ya gettin' stuck on my little gal?"

"You ragged ol' son of a grizzly b'ar! If you wasn't so damned old I'd knock that chaw of tobacco down your throat. Don't go reading any meaning in my words. Women! They're just a mess of trouble anyway you look at it."

Zan doubled over laughing. "I don' know as I ever seed a man bit so hard."

Jeff stared at him in cold silence, then turned on his heel and walked away.

CHAPTER
FIVE

Darkness lay upon the river. It had been a relief
when, in the middle of the afternoon, they had
glimpsed the low roofed cottages of the little
French settlement of Saint Charles, the first and
last white habitation of any consequence on the
river. They beached the raft a half-mile upriver
from the town, and the men unloaded it, stacking
the goods back from the shoreline. Silas and Isaac
left immediately to bring the teams and wagons
for the trip to the homesteads.

Dusk came and they built a fire. Almost before
the fire had a good start they heard shots, six in
all, and Light loped into camp. He knelt beside
the water with six plump mallards, their heads
neatly shot off. He disemboweled the birds with
one stroke of his knife, washed them, and then
plastered the carcasses with river mud. Jeff

scooped a hole in the sand beside the fire and pushed a part of the burning embers into the bottom of the hole. He dropped the clay covered birds in, scooped in more embers, and filled the hole with sand.

Jeff came to hunker down on his haunches beside a second fire Zan had built well back from the river. He was glad to have his feet on solid ground. The river to him was a means of getting from one place to another and nothing else. He had no romantic illusions about the river that knew no recognized banks. Yet destructive as it was, it was permeated by fertility. It teemed with life. In the tributary creeks were trout, in the pools, bass and pike. And in the muddy depths of the main stream, there were great catfish weighing up to a hundred pounds. Geese, ducks, brant, tern, and snipe swarmed in incredible numbers above the river and fleets of goslings and ducklings cruised in each backwater.

Jeff was anxious to get home to Berrywood. He had never uttered the name he had given his holding aloud, but in his thoughts home was Berrywood, where sycamores, walnuts, cottonwood, and willows attained an enormous size. The tallest were crowned by the foliage of huge grapevines that shot upward from stems the thickness of a man's arm, and beneath the spreading branches were strawberry plants, blackberry and raspberry bushes, as well as grapevines and pawpaw. There was also an abundance of hickory nuts, pecans, and acorns providing food for the forest population of deer, bear, racoon, turkey, and squirrel.

A place to call home had taken on a new meaning during the last few months. Jeff wanted some permanence in his life, a strong, calm woman to bear his children. He studied the oval face of the woman sitting across from him. She was lovely. He judged her age to be at least five years less than his twenty-eight. He admired her wide hips, generous bust and her tiny waist. He liked her voice; it was low and soothing. In fact, he liked everything about her from the dark lashes that fringed her remarkable light eyes to the way she tried to suppress laughter by smiling with her mouth closed. He wondered what her laughter would sound like: deep, satisfying gulps or light, high trills. He turned his eyes away from her. Light and Zan were bound to notice how often he looked at her.

It had been distinctly typical of Jeff to take exception to the rough talk he had overheard in the tavern about the girl. He'd already been irritated by the sour-faced man with the snaky look who was not quite drunk, but nearing it. His talk about the woman he planned to wed and the fact he planned to share her once Zan Thatcher took a boat upriver had brought him up short. Jeff had come out from Virginia with Zan when he was no more than a stripling, and Zan had taught him how to survive on the Trace.

Jeff's inquiries led him to the mercantile store and he saw the slender young woman walk away. The reluctant storekeeper had told him where she lived, and while he was on his way there, it occurred to him to offer to take her to Callie. At first his interest in her was merely a means of locating Zan and upsetting the plans of the bully in the tavern, but when he turned and saw her in the soft glow of the lamplight, he had held his breath until his chest hurt, then breathed deeply to ease it, still watching her. A tightness had crept into his throat and he had thought, how foolish. He was a grown man, not a callow youth to spin fancies around a pretty woman. Still, three evenings later, he was sitting across the campfire from her trying to ponder up an excuse to talk to her.

Jeff's stomach rumbled with hunger. He got to his feet and went to lean against a young sapling growing near the river. The glow from the campfire the settlers had built downriver caught his eye. He watched it with disinterest. A poignant loneliness possessed him. He was filled with a quiet unrest. He suddenly felt the desire to hold a soft woman in his arms, not any woman, *that* woman, and have her respond to his lovemaking. The thought was so real, that before he could comprehend what was happening, his own body was responding to his thoughts and he turned toward the line of trees fronting the river and moved among them.

Annie Lash watched Jeff walk away with regret. "How long have you known Jeff, Zan?"

He was whittling on a stick with a long, slim blade, his mouth puckered and twisted to the side.

"Fer a right smart spell." He rubbed his foot over the shavings on the ground. "Met up with 'im acomin' over the mountains. Jist a wet eared kid astrikin' out, he was. He done good. Warn't no time a'tall till he was full learned in the ways of the trail."

Annie Lash waited for more. She knew the futility of trying to hurry Zan into speech. When it was apparent to her he wasn't going to say more, she was forced to ask another question.

"Did he leave a family behind?"

"If'n ya want to know so goldarned much, what'cha askin' me fer? Ask 'im." He chuckled when he saw her bristle.

"Sometimes, Zan Thatcher, you make me so... so darned mad!"

"Hold yore tater, gal. I was just a funnin' ya."

"I get tired of having to pull every word out of you, Zan. I'm just curious about this place where I'm going and what kind of man is taking me there. What's so wrong about that?" she asked waspishly.

Zan chuckled again. "Nothin'."

Annie Lash clamped her lips together and the foot of her crossed leg began to move back and forth in a rhythmic movement that reflected her frustration.

"Ain't much I kin tell ya, gal. He be a good man, best I ever knowed. He come from moneyed folk. His pa died and his ma wed up with Harrison Pickett of Caroliney. He got a brother named Jason. He ain't nothin' like Jeff. Dandy, is what he is. Hit's 'bout all I knowed. Never figured hit was my business where he came from. Wed up with 'im, gal. He'll make ya a good man."

"Don't talk like that!" she snapped. "That's what makes me so damn mad about being a woman! There's no place for me unless I take a man. Why can't I have a business, homestead a tract of land, make my own way? It's not fair, Zan!" She ended her torrent of words and glared at his set face.

"Hit's foolishness yore atalkin', Annie Lash.

You'd a wed up with one of them no-goods back in Saint Louis."

"I'd of done it to free you, Zan. Not because I wanted to do it." She regretted the words instantly and placed her hand on his arm.

"I knowed that, gal. I warn't 'bout to let ya wed up to one of 'em what asked ya."

She rested her forehead against his arm. "Thank you for looking after Pa and me. Just don't push me to marry someone who doesn't love me. I want more than to be a man's possession. I want to be his partner, the other part of himself. I want the closeness that my mother had with my father."

Zan threw the stick on the ground. "Humph! Ya don't know nothin' bout your ma and pa."

"What do you mean by that?"

"Ya was jist a snot-nosed kid."

"I was not. I know my father loved her. It almost killed him when she died." Her voice was little more than a hissing whisper.

Zan half turned so that he could look directly at her. Her face glimmered in the firelight, floating with disembodied paleness in the dark aura of her cloudy dark hair.

"Yeah, hit did," he admitted softly. His gnarled hand came out and swept the hair back from her face.

Annie Lash was so surprised and touched by the gentle gesture that tears sprang to her eyes. "I loved him. I love you, too, Zan." Zan let out a snort. She knew his affection for her ran deep, but he was unable to voice it. "But don't think that gives you the right to boss me, Zan Thatcher," she said saucily.

Zan took an unnecessarily long time picking up the stick he'd tossed to the ground. He began to carefully shape the ends with his thin-bladed knife.

"What ya needs is knittin' needles, gal. A woman ort to keep her hands busy 'n her mouth won't flap all the time. Hit's been awhile since I had me a pair of stockin's."

"You didn't wear the last pair I knit for you. All you wear are those moccasins."

"Don't argue. I weared 'em in the moccasins."

Annie Lash laughed, heartier than any she'd enjoyed in a long time. It was melodious. A happy, friendly laugh that floated on the night air to Light and Jeff, who were bent over the pit where they had buried the ducks. Jeff glanced up to see Light watching him with a perceptive look on his usually solemn face.

"What's the matter with you?" he growled.

"Not me, *mon ami*." He shook his head. "Ho, but your eyes stray often to the woman. Is mating on your mind?" He winked and shrugged his shoulders. "My own eyes have enjoyed her beauty."

Jeff gave no indication he had heard. He dug something out of the ground that resembled a melon. This was one of the mud-plastered ducks, the encircling clay now baked brittle and hard. He rolled it onto a piece of bark and moved away from the pit as Silas and Isaac, hungry after the day of toil on the river, came forward to get their supper.

Outlined against the glow of the fire, he knelt in front of Annie Lash and began cracking the shell with his tomahawk. The clay broke off readily, the feathers adhering to each piece, so that the smooth brown body of the roasted duck was exposed.

"Wal, now. Thanky, Jeff." Zan tucked his knife in his belt. "Hit's right friendly of ya to wait on a ol' man."

"This is for the lady."

"Annie Lash ain't used to be a waited on," Zan said stubbornly. He stood. "Wal, if'n I got no invite—"

"You don't." Jeff said it sharply, abruptly, as if he was angry.

Zan began to whistle and moved out into the darkness. Annie Lash wished a crack would appear in the ground and swallow her up. What in the world had gotten into Zan that he would act this way? She was grateful for the darkness that hid her burning cheeks.

Jeff broke off a portion of the duck and handed it to her. She stood and leaned over while she ate it so the abundant juices would not soil her dress. It was delicious. They ate without speaking until their hunger was satisfied.

"Will the people from the other raft be traveling with us tomorrow?" Annie Lash asked just to have something to say.

"No. If they plan to settle here they must see the Territory man and select a tract. We'll leave before sunup. We'll load the wagons at first light." He threw the duck carcass into the fire and it blazed briefly. "You'll bed down on the raft. I'll take you there."

He was standing close to her and they were

both aware of a sudden tension. She started to speak, but would not trust her voice. She had the feeling that there was nothing anywhere that could frighten or disturb this man. He was a man who knew himself, knew what he wanted. He had measured himself against the mountains, against the river, against the land and its wilderness. He knew his strength.

The wind stirred the leaves and moaned softly in the treetops. Downriver an owl hooted. It was a lonely sound, a sound that always frightened her because it brought to mind her aloneness. She turned swiftly, fighting down an overwhelming urge to run, to escape from this man. There was something big and hard and sure about him, something in the way he moved. It was impossible, ridiculous, but she had the feeling he had made a decision about her. She hugged her shawl about her shoulders, feeling suddenly chilled and unsure of herself.

Jeff put his hand beneath her elbow and guided her down to where the raft was beached.

"I've fixed a spot under the canvas and left the pelts for you to use for cover."

"Thank you. But I could have slept on shore." She couldn't make out his features in the dark, but his light hair was visible.

"It may rain."

"Oh? It doesn't look like rain."

"Light left the pelts on the raft so you might as well use them."

"He looks ... part Indian."

"He is part Indian. The other part's French."

"Does he work for you?"

Jeff smiled. "Only when he wants to. Light is a very complicated man. He pleases only himself."

Annie Lash laughed. "It would be a nice way to live."

"Don't envy him. He's had much sadness in his life. He's the son of an Osage woman and a French trapper. He's seen his mother, his brother and sisters killed by white men and his father killed by Indians. His young wife was raped and murdered by French rivermen."

"Oh, the poor man!" She was shocked by the story, and equally shocked by the dispassionate way he told it. "He must find it hard not to hate all mankind."

"When I first met him his depression was deep, and at times I was sure he had lost his mind. For days he wouldn't eat and at night he couldn't sleep. Whenever his grief became unbearable he would go into the woods and raise his head to the sky and howl like a wounded animal."

Annie Lash shuddered and turned away from him, although it was too dark for him to see the sparkle of tears in her eyes. It had been unfair of her to think he didn't care. It was there in the tremor of his voice.

"How long ago?" She voiced the question huskily.

"Five years come summer. It isn't a very pretty story."

She was silent for a long time. Then, in a strange tone of voice, she said, "Life is so short. Sometimes you don't have time to make it beautiful."

With his hand beneath her elbow he guided

her to the edge of the platform and they sat down. She was increasingly aware he was in a different mood.

"Beautiful?" He shrugged. "The important thing is for a man to leave something behind to show he has passed through this life. If he doesn't, he's just put in his time."

What a strange thing for him to say. She stared at him, her eyes straining in the darkness. "Is that what you want to do?"

"Yes."

She fought to still her trembling. "What is your home like?"

"It's the best I could build in this place. It's not elegant by Virginia standards, but it's sturdy and will do for now. I call it Berrywood."

Annie Lash felt a strange tenseness come over her and fought it with a sudden desperation. She was uneasy, and to cover it she rushed into speech.

"Berrywood? It sounds like a Virginia mansion."

He was silent and a queer little shock of something almost like panic went through her. Had he thought her frivolous? What if he did? What could it possibly matter? The thought disturbed her. Today she had looked at his face and wondered what was behind it. Zan respected him. The men trusted him. What sort of woman would he want? She looked at him keenly and knew he was watching her. A woman could strengthen a weak man, but this man didn't need to be strengthened. A woman wouldn't make a whit of an impression on him. She would have to conform to what he wanted, be what he wanted. Resentment edged its way into her thoughts. On the shore she could see Zan moving about the campfire. She wanted to call out to him, but she didn't because Jeff had placed his hand on her shoulder to get her attention.

"I want to talk to you about something and I think now is the best time to do it."

Slowly, she shifted her gaze to him. "About what?"

"I've decided to marry you. There's a man here in Saint Charles who can do it and it'll be legal. We'll go see him in the morning."

Annie Lash wasn't sure she had heard the words correctly. Had he really made that shocking statement? *I've decided to marry you*. That's what he said! She drew a quivering breath into her lungs and stiffened as the hand on her shoulder slid down her back and he began to pull her toward him.

"*You* have decided?" Her throat was so dry and lumpy she almost choked on the words.

"Yes, I've decided."

"If this was what you had in mind, why didn't you say so last night, or the night before?" Anger burned in her independent heart.

"I didn't have it in mind last night or the night before. I thought about it today ... tonight. I need a woman if I'm going to leave something to show I've passed through this life." He repeated the words he had said earlier, but somehow she knew the meaning was different.

"You've decided you want a woman and I'm the only one available." Resentment stiffened her. She put her hands on his chest to push him away. It was like pushing against a mountain.

"Why are you angry? You need a man to look after you. There are other women here in Saint Charles. A widow, the fur trader's daughter, and the girl with the settlers." He jerked his head toward where she'd seen the glow of the settler's campfire.

So he'd noticed the beautiful, elfin girl after all. The knowledge only increased her anger. "You may think I should be grateful to be *chosen*, but I'm not. I refuse your generous offer!"

"You haven't had a better one," he reasoned calmly. "Ransom was going to pass you around, Fletcher was sickly, and Geer was old. I'm young and strong. I'll provide for you and no other man will touch you."

Her humiliation was almost complete. "Well, thank you! That's most kind of you!" The words burst from her with bitter sarcasm. He seemed not to notice, and suddenly she was crushed against him. His arms wrapped around her like a steel trap.

"You'll get used to the idea. I won't rush to bed you. But, Lord, girl! You tempt me!"

Her temper ran out of control. "You ... pompous ass! I wouldn't take you if you were the last man on earth. Get your hands off me. I'll scream," she threatened, her voice husky and trembling. "I'll scream for Zan and he'll kill you!"

His face, only a breath away from hers, was like carved stone. He watched her mouth spilling out the angry words. One hand gripped the nape of her neck, the other was flat against the small of her back. When she opened her mouth to make her threat a reality, he clamped his mouth to hers.

His mouth savaged hers relentlessly, prying her lips apart, grinding his teeth against her inner lips. She tried to drag her head back, but his hand held her in position and she couldn't wrench it from his grasp. His teeth were biting into her lips, his fingers wound into her hair; she moaned in pain and struggled as violently as she could. He was taking her breath. When she thought her lungs would burst, he moved his mouth to the side of her face and she took in great gulps of air through her open mouth.

His hand had moved around to cup her breast. The shock of feeling his hard fingers kneeding her flesh made her giddy. She tried to speak, to protest, but her voice seemed to have dried up. Her heart was racing beneath the breast he was holding and she felt a sudden revulsion in the pit of her stomach. He looked down into her face, his breath quick and warm on her wet mouth. Trembling, she tried to shake her head in silent protest.

"I told you I needed a woman. I guess I didn't realize how much," he said in a strange, thickened voice. "I won't always be this rough."

Helpless tears gathered in her eyes. "You... animal! Find yourself another woman to maul. I don't want you!"

Her words made him angry. "What do you think you'd have got from Walt Ransom?"

"There's not a speck of difference between you!"

"You think not? He'd not have stopped at kissing you."

"You call that a kiss? You jackass! Force and take is all you know!"

"What else is there? You wouldn't have let me kiss you, and I'm not the type to beg for what I want." He drew in a harsh breath and put his mouth to hers again.

She silently shrieked a bitter protest and resisted with all her strength. She had never felt a man's lips on hers and her disappointment was so complete she went cold and stiff, but he didn't seem to notice. He was using her for some satisfaction of his own. She felt like an object and she hated him. When he lifted his head she was crying. He tasted the tears on her lips.

"What's the matter with you? You're a grown woman. You act like a mare whose seen her first stallion."

Her lips felt swollen. "You'd never understand," she whispered on a ragged breath.

"I mean to have you for my wife," he bit out close to her ear.

"No!"

"Goddammit! I'll talk to Zan."

"Zan won't make me." She said the words quickly because she believed them.

"Then go back to Saint Louis and let the dogs fight over you," he said harshly.

The words made her tremble. She tried to move away from him, but his hands on her shoulders gripped them tightly. He looked down at her, his eyes savage. She looked back at him, her own eyes stricken, dazed by what had taken place.

"All right. I'll ... go back." They were the only words she could manage.

His hands shook her. "You're the stubbornest woman I ever met!"

"You think I'm stubborn because I want to have a say in the direction my life will take? You think that just because I'm a woman I should take a man I don't want so I'll have a roof over my head and food to eat? I'll not take one male *animal* to keep the other *animals* at bay!"

He looked at her as if she had lost her mind. She felt her skin grow icy, her head throb with agony. Yes, she thought, that's what he thinks. He's shocked that I want more. He doesn't even know what I'm talking about!

"I want to talk to Zan." Her words were strong, not at all a reflection of what she was feeling. She felt the probe of his stare and was ashamed of the weak tears on her face.

"He won't take you back to that...muck!"

"Then I'll go alone. There'll be someone in Saint Charles who will help me. I wouldn't have come if I'd known what you had in mind. I thought I would have work, care for your brother's wife, *earn* my way, keep my self-respect."

"You still can."

"No. Things are different now."

"Because I offered for you?"

"Because you hold me in such low esteem."

"You're insulted by my proposal?" The tone of his voice was incredulous.

"Is that what it was?" she sneered, enjoying knowing she had angered him.

His fingers bit into her shoulders and he stood, bringing her up with him. As he towered over her, she felt his rage and frustration.

"Woman! I could—" He bit back the words he intended to say, so she said them.

"Beat me? Oh, yes, I can well imagine that would be the way you would control a rebellious wife." Her voice more than her words made her contempt for him known.

"Careful," he cautioned through teeth clenched tight with suppressed anger.

"I'm aware of your brute strength, Mr. Merrick," she said in a cool, steady voice and indicated the hands that clenched her arms so tightly it rounded her shoulders. "I'm sure I'll have evidence of it on my arms tomorrow."

A full moon had come up over the edge of the treetops and shone on her resentful face. Her light eyes did battle with his dark ones. He was breathing deeply, erratically. So the stone man can be jarred after all, she thought. Slowly, he let his hands slide from her arms and she saw a smile twitch at the corners of his wide mouth.

"Don't bait the bear, *Annielove*. The beast just might go for more honey."

Her throat choked with bitterness. The emphasis he put on the name he called her was like rubbing salt into a wound. She stuck out her chin, and at the same time realized the futility of the gesture.

"I want to talk to Zan."

"Go to bed. We'll be loading the wagons before dawn." He reached out a hand and touched her cheek lightly with his fingertips. "I might point out that Zan is on my side in this matter." He tapped her cheek and laughed softly. "He'd like nothing better than to see you wed to me. He told me so."

Annie Lash felt her heart sink to the pit of her stomach and lie there, thumping in a strange and disturbing way that alarmed her. She edged away from him until the back of her knees struck the platform.

"It's not saying much for your manly charms that you have to use threats and the help of an old man to get a wife," she said quietly, rashly uncaring that she would arouse his anger again.

His eyes rested on her face for a long time without movement, without any discernible emotion, then he grinned. His face was tilted down toward hers and she could see the amusement that narrowed his eyes.

"I never liked a mountain that was too easy to climb, or a smooth, calm river, Annielove. You and I will hitch well together."

"Stop calling me that ridiculous name!" His grin almost shattered her control. Her heart was pumping madly and her insides were quivering from the effort it took to keep from slapping his face.

His laugh rang out. It was a hearty, happy laugh, and she hated him for it. Laughter spilled into the words he spoke.

"Get under the canvas and go to bed, or ... I'll come in there with you."

She swallowed dryly, feeling the frantic clamor of her throbbing pulses even as some devil prodded her to say recklessly, "As I said before, you're no better than Walt Ransom!"

His hand shot to her throat and choked off the

words. For a long moment he looked down into her beautifully structured face surrounded with dark hair that had come loose from its pins. She stood quietly, refusing to humiliate herself by struggling.

"Don't think for a moment that your opinion of me matters in the least," he said, knowing full well that he was lying and wondering why he was doing so. "At this moment, all I'm concerned with is what I want."

She felt a surge of panic as his arms went around her again and tightened their hold until she was crushed against him so tightly she could feel every tense muscle in his body throbbing with life. His mouth was hard and angry and she made only a small sound before his lips cut off both breath and sound.

Moon and sky were blotted out by his dark, angry face. His kiss was possessive, demanding, and she suffered it numbly, too shocked to protest. He kissed her deeply, again and again, as if he had long been thirsty and was drinking at a cool well. Violently and ruthlessly, he plundered her mouth until she was unable to stand and sagged against him.

She didn't know when his mouth softened and his tongue forced its way between her compressed lips. The feel of it was strange, soft and caressing. She thought she would swoon; a strange feverish pounding in her temples spread to her stomach and lower into her genitals. His hand slipped down to her buttocks, holding her there, his hard muscular thighs forcing intimate pressure upon her. The feeling of something rock hard pressing against her lower stomach jerked her to awareness. With a sob in her throat she began to struggle.

He raised his head. He was trembling. She could feel the tremor in the body pressed to hers.

"Please—" she whispered shakily.

"When the time comes, you'll sleep with me," he growled softly. "You'll sleep with me and you'll like what I do to you."

At his words her body went cold inside. She strove to pull back, but his grip was too strong. She glared at him with eyes that looked like bits of blue glass.

Something about the way she looked at him made him hesitate. He could see the heaving of her breasts, even though the shirt she wore was loose, and the thought of them, the sweet softness he felt when he held her, caused his heart to lurch suddenly. His eyes searched her face and found her eyes, and he marveled at their beauty.

Annie Lash seemed to lose herself in his eyes. He was less frightening somehow, but his words pounded in her head. She was trembling, and when she drew away from him he let her go. She was drained of thought and will and just managed to find the opening in the canvas and crawl into the nest of soft pelts, tears of humiliation coursing down her cheeks.

Jeff watched her go, a peculiar feeling moving through him. He scowled to himself, wondering what she thought now. Why should he care? For a moment, he speculated on how it would be if she had responded to him out of love, and not in response to his passion, as other women had done. How would it feel to have a woman whisper true words of love in his ear, to see a softening look come to her eyes when they sought and found him? He felt the twinge of desire to know love, but seconds later he discarded the idea. That wasn't what he wanted. He would not be bound!

Why had her rejection aroused such a devil in him? He certainly had had no intention of man-handling her like that. But once he started he just couldn't seem to stop. Damn her! She'd think he was no better than Walt Ransom. In fact, she'd said that. Well, what the hell to do now? By the Lord Henry, he swore to himself, he'd sure made a mess of things!

He turned restlessly, hating the strange, twisting feeling that churned about inside of him. He leaped to the sandy bank and walked quickly to where Light was adding a few sticks to the small blaze beneath a blackened coffee pot.

"*Mon ami,* you flee like a rejected lover."

"Mind your own business, damn you!"

Light laughed softly and settled down beside the fire. He lifted a harmonica to his lips and began to play a French love song. Usually the music he played came from his own feelings, but tonight he was playing to soothe the feelings of his friend. He finished the song and glanced at Jeff, who was hunkered down on his haunches staring into the fire. That in itself was atypical of the wary woodsman. A man who looks into a fire cannot see for several seconds when he looks away, and those few seconds could cost him his life.

"It is painful, no?"

Jeff scowled, but didn't answer.

Light got to his feet and walked away, pondering the obvious cause of his friend's irritable mood.

CHAPTER
SIX

Yawning, Annie Lash took her place at the end of the small caravan. Today was like that first morning, except that now she knew what to expect. This morning she couldn't see her surroundings, could only follow the dark shape of the wagon, or swing herself up to ride on the tailgate. She did that now, because the grass was wet with dew and the forest beyond loomed thicker and darker in this hour before the dawn streaked the eastern sky. They kept to the outside edge of the timber, making good progress.

In travel, they followed the pattern established the morning they left Saint Charles, that of keeping to the open, avoiding swampy places, making camp at dusk. Always, they moved with caution. Jeff said there were thirty thousand Indians along the Missouri including Osage, Sioux, Pawnee, Ponca, and Delaware. Light, mounted on a spotted Indian pony, and Jeff, on a frisky black, watched endlessly for signs of them. At night the men took turns standing watch. They rarely talked, for if they were not eating a hasty meal they were resting.

The goods from the raft filled two wagons; one pulled by a team of oxen and led by Isaac, the other by a team of mules driven by Silas. Zan walked beside her, his long gun within easy reach, or, if the ground was rough and the going hard, he would sit beside her on the tailgate.

The first day she had walked most of the way and had grown increasingly tired; but gradually her stubborn pride had given way, and now she rode for a short time each morning and each afternoon. She had toughened until she could walk for hours over the rough ground without suffering extreme fatigue. She had always had an awed affection for the forest. Here on the banks of the mighty Missouri, she marveled at the beauty of the towering cottonwoods and the great walnut trees, which were sometimes as much as six feet around and up to forty feet to the first branches. She learned to identify the various sounds of the forest and knew that when they were suddenly still, something foreign moved. Each minute of each day was filled with looking everywhere at once, ahead, to each side, and to the rear. The moment at hand filled her and her spirits lifted. She would make out, she still had Zan to rely on.

An early morning mist rose from the river. Annie Lash sat on the back of the wagon, her shawl wrapped about her. Every so often she had to lift her feet as the wagon passed through the tall grasses, heavy with dew. Jeff, on the black horse, was trailing the wagon. The darkness prevented her from seeing him, but she could hear the soft plops of the horse's hoofs on the sod. She hadn't said a private word to him since the night on the raft. She had been distantly civil and that was all. If Zan noticed, he didn't mention it.

After her confrontation with Jeff she had cried herself to sleep for the first time since she was a child. When morning came she promised herself she would wait a few days before she talked to Zan. Perhaps today the opportunity would present itself. She had to pick a time when they were walking well back from the wagon because Isaac and Silas picked up every sound.

The mules and oxen plodded along patiently. The trail was rough and rugged with tree stumps pressing close on either side. The river road curled as the river curled. It was only occasionally, when the road cut across country, that they lost sight of the muddy, turbulent Missouri.

The morning grew increasingly hot and sticky. By afternoon a suffocating sultry calm had settled over the river road. The birds fell silent. Not a leaf stirred. A fringe of dark clouds appeared above the forest ridge. The fringe became a bulge that swiftly boiled upward until it spread across the sky. From the distance came the muttering of thunder.

Jeff rode up beside Annie Lash. "Hop on the wagon," he said tensely. "We're going to try and get out of the lowland before the rain hits."

As soon as she was settled on the wagon, Silas whipped the mules and the wagon picked up speed. Zan had been beside her when the day started, but since mid-morning she had been alone at the end of the caravan. Zan had veered off through the forest and would be waiting ahead. He had done this several times since the journey had begun at Saint Charles.

Annie Lash bounced viciously on the end of the wagon, groaned, and muttered an unladylike word. She knew many such words from the years on the Bank, but it was only on extreme provocation that she used them. This was one of the occasions. She was hot, tired, and irritable because she hadn't been able to corner Zan long enough for a private conversation. She was rehearsing in her mind what she would tell him when she heard the shot. The sound came from up ahead and her throat was suddenly choked with fear. Zan?

Almost before she could gather her scattered thoughts, Jeff was wheeling his horse around the end of the wagon.

"Get under the canvas," he ordered. "Stay out of sight."

"Zan—"

"Do as I say!" he snapped.

Annie Lash slid back under the canvas that covered the barrels of flour and sugar, her heart galloping madly in her breast. She could still hear the steady plops of the horse's hoofs, so she knew Jeff was riding beside the wagon. She adjusted the canvas to make a crack to peek through, and minutes later, she saw a horseman ride out of the woods leading a pack mule.

Tall and thin, the horseman had a dark, narrow

face with a beard as black and kinky as his hair. He was wearing buckskins similar to those Jeff and Zan wore, but they were ragged and dirty. He had a leather, round-brimmed hat pulled low over his eyes, and he sat loosely in the saddle with his shoulders slumped.

Jeff had slowed his horse and was directly behind the wagon. The face that had looked so sober for the last two days now looked deadly sober. His mouth was tight, his eyes hard and fierce, his body tense. He held his rifle across his knees, the muzzle pointed toward the approaching horseman. Fear gripped Annie Lash and sweat dripped from her face unnoticed.

The man had come out of the trees at an angle. He turned his horse and was beside Jeff before he spoke.

"Howdy," he said lazily. "Where y'all headed?"

"Upriver. You?"

"Saint Charles. Was a goin' to do me a bit of scoutin' fer a place to settle till I run into a pack of murderin' redskins." He hesitated and scratched the side of his head. After a moment he spoke in a guarded voice. "Murdered a family up north. Reckon ya heared 'bout it."

"You ran into them?" Jeff asked quietly.

"I saw 'em. I heared 'em and hid myself. They was all smeared up with paint, a whoopin' and a hollerin'. They was wearin' feathers and a dancin' round a fire. They had some poor devil lashed to a stake. There warn't nothin' I could do fer 'im, so I got the hell out."

"You traveling alone?"

The man hesitated and then laughed. "You don't see nobody else, do ya?"

Jeff nodded toward the pack mule. "You've got a lot of tucker."

"Yup. Was a goin' ta stay out fer a good spell. Say...ya got any whiskey?"

Annie Lash watched the man through the split in the canvas. His eyes shifted from left to right. They were never still. Was she imagining it, or had Jeff deliberately let his horse slow until it was a step behind the stranger's, and had his hand always been resting on the rifle so his thumb could jerk the trigger?

"We've got none for sale."

To Annie Lash, Jeff looked like a coiled spring. Did he think the man was going to do something? The heat and the tension under the canvas was almost unbearable.

"Warn't lookin' to buy it. Thought we could do us some swappin'. Got a dandy pair of black boots." The man was slouching even farther in the saddle. The mule he was leading was loaded with what looked like a large bundle. A canvas was carelessly thrown over it.

"What else have you got?"

The man grinned. "You ask a powerful lot a questions."

Jeff lifted his shoulders in what was now to Annie Lash a familiar gesture. The stranger laughed. She thought he was being too friendly and wondered if Jeff noticed. He remained silent.

"Hit's all right. A man cain't find out nothin' if'n he don't ask," the stranger drawled. "Wal now,

let's see, I got me one a them lookin' things what'll
let ya see for a long way off. I ain't got no use fer
the thing. It cain't see through trees. Got it off'n
a dead Injun. Then I got me a right pert gold
watch."

Annie Lash was about to suffocate. She shifted
her position and her knees came down on her pa's
rifle. Zan had cleaned and oiled it only the night
before. *A gun ain't no more than a club if'n it
ain't primed 'n ready when ya need it.* His words
came to Annie Lash with a rush of fear. She would
need it. Somehow, she knew she had to get it and
be ready. Slowly, carefully, so as to not move the
canvas or scrape the barrel against the floor of the
wagon, she picked it up.

"You homesteadin' out here?" The man's voice
was a lazy drawl, slurred, but with a curious twang.
There was a rough, raspy quality to it, as though
it was seldom used. If that were the case, why
was he as determined to talk as Jeff was to listen?

"Why do you ask?"

"Just sort a thought ya might know most folks
'round these parts."

"Who're you looking for?"

"Ain't said I was a lookin' fer anybody."

Annie Lash suddenly realized the man was listening. There was a peculiar look on his face. He
seemed to be contemplating something, weighing
the pros and cons while keeping Jeff occupied
with conversation. Uneasiness was like a tangible
thing in her breast. She let her eyes wander from
him to the mule he was leading. She looked away
and then back again. Was she loosing her mind,
or had the pack on the mule's back shifted? She

fastened her eyes to the load the animal was carrying. The wagon rolled over a deep rut and she was jolted. Her eyes left the opening for a second. When she looked again the canvas covering the pack seemed to hang longer on the outside. She held her breath while she watched the canvas move. Slowly, the load on the mule's back changed shape, and as she watched in horrified fascination, she saw the canvas part ever so slightly. Her head throbbed viciously with the realization of what was about to happen.

"Jeff! The mule!" She screamed the words even as she threw back her covering.

There was a thundering blast, a streak of flame, and a man's scream. Jeff's rifle was smoking. The frightened mule broke his lead rope and began to plunge. A man lay on the ground, his face strangely missing.

Eyes wide with shock, Annie Lash saw the stranger and the handgun aimed at Jeff. Her action was instantaneous with what she saw. She lifted her pa's rifle, pointed it, and fired. The blast not only deafened her, the gun's recoil knocked her back against the barrels, momentarily stunning her.

When she came to her senses, someone was pulling her up from between the barrels. Her vision cleared and Jeff's face swam before her eyes.

"Are you all right?"

"I think so." She reached to pull down the skirt bunched about her thighs. Silas and Isaac stood at the end of the wagon. "There was a man on the mule ... under—"

"I know. Thanks for the warning."

"The other man—"

"Don't look. He would have killed me if not for you."

Despite his warning, Annie Lash glanced down at the body sprawled on the ground; arms and legs flung wide, his head and shoulders were a mass of bloody pulp.

"Oh!" It was an agonized wail. "Oh... what have I done? He was going to kill you! He had the gun raised! I couldn't let him—"

"Ya done a plucky thin', little gal." Silas reached up his arms and lifted her out of the wagon as Isaac ran to catch the horse and the mule. "That varmit was out to kill Jeff, shore as my name's Silas Cornick."

"Where's Zan?" Annie Lash was trembling like a leaf in the wind. "I heard a shot before—"

"We'll be catching up with him and Light," Jeff said quickly. "Walk with Silas. We've got to load the bodies on the back end of the wagon. We have to get away from here. The shots will be heard for miles."

The patient oxen were waiting. Silas rapped them smartly on the rump and they began to move. Annie Lash moved automatically on trembling legs. Reaction to what she had done was just setting in and she held the side of the wagon and let it help her along. It seemed an eternity before Jeff rode up beside her.

"Are you all right?" he asked for the second time.

"I'm worried about Zan."

"He'll be up ahead. Do you want to get up on the wagon?"

"No. I'm all right." She turned frightened eyes up to him. "I...just shot. I was scared, so scared I forgot I had the rifle in my hands. I couldn't call out, I just...swung it around and fired."

"It's a good thing for me you did. I fired the rifle and let it drop so I could jerk the pistol out of my belt. Time ran out. I'd of been a goner if you hadn't fired when you did."

"Who were they? Why did they want to kill you?"

He shrugged his shoulders. "Probably for the goods on the wagons." He wheeled the big horse around and Annie Lash could hear him talking to Isaac, who was keeping the heads of the mules as close to the end of the lead wagon as possible.

Overhead, the sky was dark with thunder clouds. "We don't need no more goddamn rain," Silas said, and urged the oxen to walk faster.

Storms had always excited Annie Lash. She thought there was something grand and spectacular about the lightning slicing across the sky. She plodded alongside the wagon and didn't raise her eyes to the skies where the winds were whipping the clouds into a roiling mass. She scarcely looked up when Jeff went by. They had topped a rise and the ground was hard and rocky. The wagon jolted over the rocks until they started downhill.

"Goddamn bastids!"

When Annie Lash heard Silas curse, she left the side of the wagon so she could see ahead. At the bottom of the hill was a densely wooded area. Hundreds of tall, gigantic trees reared like leafy giants among a scattering of underbrush. She saw Light's spotted pony first, then Jeff's black horse.

The next thing to register in her mind was Jeff's white head bending over something on the ground. A knot of fear tied itself in her stomach and she began to run.

"Please...No! Oh, please..." She ran, stumbled, fell, picked herself up and ran again. "Please, not Zan—" Her cheeks were wet with tears and she wasn't aware that she was crying. It seemed a million miles down the hill. Her hair had come loose and was sticking to her wet face. She lifted her skirt with both hands to free her legs as she sped over the short grass. "Zan!" she screamed. "Zan!"

Jeff got to his feet and took her arm. She jerked away from him and fell on her knees beside the old man. Zan lay with his head on his hat, his face deathly pale, his breathing labored. His buckskin shirt had been slit and a pack of moss was pressed to his side.

"Oh, Zan..." Annie Lash took his hand and held it in both of hers.

He opened his eyes and grinned weakly. "Ol' Zan got a mite careless."

"Are you hurt bad?" Her sight was blurred by her tears. She sniffed and wiped her face on her sleeve.

"Hit could be a sight worse. I could be dead."

"Don't say that, Zan Thatcher! You make me so mad when you joke about things like...this." She raised her eyes to Light, who was staring off into the woods. Angered, she jerked on his trousers that were tucked into his knee-high moccasins. He looked down, then knelt beside her. "What happened to him?" she demanded.

"Knife."

"Who did it?"

"Feller what got his head blowed off," Zan said weakly. "Gal, quit yore frettin'. What's done's done." He rolled his head so he could see Jeff. "Heared rifle fire. Thar was two more."

"We got them, Zan. One was on a mule under a tarp. Annie Lash spotted him and yelled a warning. We got both of them." He looked at Annie Lash. She avoided his gaze.

Zan closed his eyes wearily. "I tol' ya my little gal ain't no rattlehead."

"You were right." Jeff reached out and clasped his shoulder. "We'll make a place for you in the wagon. If the rain holds off we can be home by morning."

"It'll be a heap a trouble fer ya, Jeff, but I'd be obliged. I want ta see where my Annie will be." His voice was strong, determined. "Ain't had me so much 'tention in all my born days. I even got me a purty little gal a blubberin' over me."

"I ought to hit you, Zan, is what I ought to do. You scared the daylights out of me."

Zan let out a half snort of disgust and winced. "Hush yore prattle, gal, and wrap a rag 'round me."

Annie Lash smiled through her tears. "I'm not tearing up a good petticoat to wrap you, Zan Thatcher," she teased to hide her fear. "A piece of old tablecloth will do."

His eyes flew open. "Not the one Lettie put the fancy stitches on!"

For a moment Annie Lash was so surprised he had mentioned her mother's name and remembered the cloth that she couldn't answer. When she did it was with an excessive tone of exasperation in her voice.

"I should say not! It'll be the cloth you put your knife through when you picked out walnut meats last Thanksgiving."

The once sharp old eyes held hers before they closed. Oh, Lordy, she thought. He looks so old! She hadn't thought about him being old. He must be older than her pa was, she thought suddenly. She glanced up to catch Jeff exchanging a look with Light and her heart plunged. Zan couldn't die! Dear Lord in Heaven, she prayed, don't let Zan die. She clutched his hand and peered into his face. *She wouldn't let him die, damnit! She wouldn't!*

Oxen can pull a heavier load than mules, so some of the barrels were transferred to that wagon to make room for Zan. While Light and Jeff cut pine boughs to cushion the bed, Silas and Isaac dug a shallow grave for the men who had attacked them.

Annie Lash was too busy with Zan to question why the three men had made and tried to execute such a complicated plan to kill Jeff. She had overheard Light telling Jeff that Zan had found where they had camped and the horses hidden in the brush. He knew two of the men had ridden away on a horse and a mule and the other lay in wait down the trail. He was scouting to locate the waylayer's position when he was discovered. They fought and the man got his knife into Zan before he could get his gun into position to fire. Light found him shortly afterward and stopped the flow of blood with moss or he would have bled to death.

Annie Lash watched the sky anxiously. A breeze had come out of the southeast and seemed to be pushing the rain clouds around them. Jeff had assured her that Zan would be kept dry. If necessary, they would use the canvas from the pack mule. Annie Lash looked at the blood-splattered cloth and shuddered.

The would-be assailants' personal possessions, guns, and provisions had been rolled in the canvas and thrust beneath the wagon seat. In the wilderness nothing was discarded that could be used. The only thing the men took with them to their graves were the clothes they were wearing. Light rode ahead, leading a horse and the mule. The other two horses were tied to the back of the wagon pulled by the oxen.

Evening came. They didn't stop for a meal. Just before dark they reached a clear stream that flowed out of the hills toward the river. Jeff stopped the wagons to allow the stock to drink. He dug into his pack for a pewter cup, filled it with cool, fresh water, and carried it to Annie Lash. She drank it gratefully. When the wagons started up again she had a flask of water beside her. Zan lay quiet and uncomplaining on the bed of pine boughs. In their haste to make as good time as possible, the wagon wheels would occasionally strike a rock and jolt the wagon. At first Zan would wince or a faint groan would escape his lips, but after the first hour he seemed to be sleeping and Annie Lash was grateful that he was no longer suffering.

The night was agonizingly long. The only good thing about it was that the sky cleared and the

stars came out. The moon, obscured occasionally
by a thin drifting cloud, hung like a giant orb over
the treetops. When Annie Lash could no longer
endure the cramped position beside Zan, she got
out and walked, her hand holding to the end of
the wagon, her eyes and ears alert for any sound
or movement from the old man. At times Jeff led
the way and Light rode behind. At other times it
was reversed. In her anxiety about Zan, Annie
Lash forgot her anger at Jeff and her desire to go
back to Saint Louis.

"We should reach the Cornick farm in about an
hour. It'll be daylight by then." Jeff was walking
beside her, leading his horse.

"Will we stop there?" Fatigue had almost
numbed her and she spoke tiredly.

"I wanted to talk with you about that. I think
that, as long as we're moving, we should go on.
Zan wanted to see my place."

It took a while for the import of his words to
reach her stupefied senses. When they did, she
looked up, trying to see his face, but only his light
hair was visible in the moonlight.

"You think he'll die." It was a whispered statement.

"We must face the possibility, Annie Lash," he
said gently.

A sob rose in her throat. "We've got to do...
something!"

"Light has already done all that we can do. His
quick thinking has kept him alive this long. It's a
bad wound and Zan's not a young man."

"You're wrong! He won't die." Oh, Lordy, she
hurt all over; her head, her feet, but mostly her

heart. She was unable to stop the tears that spilled down her cheeks. In her grief she turned angrily to the person who had brought them to this wilderness. "I wish I hadn't come with you! If I'd said no Zan and I would be back in Saint Louis and he wouldn't be about to ... die!"

"Zan wanted to come. He was itching to get back in the woods and get you out of Saint Louis. If you had stayed he'd have been killed trying to keep the rivermen away from you."

"He'll die anyway, and it's your fault!" She lashed out unreasonably and she knew it, but couldn't stop herself. She wanted him to be angry, to defend himself.

"I'm aware of that and I'll regret it all my life. Zan saved my hide more than once. Without Zan I'd never have made it over the mountain." His sincere words took some of the anger from her.

She bit back more harsh words, and instead she asked, "How far to your place from Silas's?"

"A little over an hour."

They walked in silence. The sky was getting lighter in the east. Birds were beginning to wake with pleasant chirps and rustlings. Distant colonies of ducks quacked companionably as the new day arrived.

First she heard a dog yap, then the squealing of pigs. A rooster announced his superiority over the clucking, quarreling hens. The wagon creaked to a stop beside a split rail fence and a woman came out of the low, log-hewed house and stood wiping her hands on her apron. A tall lad came from a brush-covered shed with a bucket in his hand. His shout of, "Pa's home," brought two more boys out, and all three came on the run toward the wagons.

Silas greeted his wife with hugs and kisses and then embraced each of his sons. Annie Lash stood at the end of the wagon beside Jeff. Silas spoke with his wife, then urged her forward with his arm about her waist.

She was the plainest woman Annie Lash had ever seen, young or old. She was a thin shadow with sharp features and thin lips. She wore a butternut-dyed dress and a black apron. Her hair was pulled back into a tight, round knob that sat on the back of her head, and her eyes, which were bright blue, homed in on Annie Lash and played up and down and over her like a blue flame. Her taut face relaxed, and when she spoke her voice was like music.

"Landsakes, child! You look all tuckered out! Why, I do declare, a good meal is what you need ...but Silas says you got to push on to Jeff's. Let me run and get you a hoe cake while them boys are changing the mules. Ain't that right, Jeff? This child needs somethin' in her stomach. Well, Lordy me, you men thinks us women ain't got no quit a'tall!" Her light, lilting voice seemed to drone on and on, around and over Annie Lash.

"Thank you, Mrs. Cornick, I—"

"Call me, Biedy. Lester," she called, "wrap some hoe cakes in a towel and bring a jar of that fresh milk. Hurry, now." Her bright eyes fastened on Jeff. "Things is fine at yore place. Me and the boys been over to chew the fat with Callie. My land, that girl's thin."

"This is Annie Lash Jester, Biedy. She's come out to stay with Callie."

Again the birdlike eyes searched her face. "Ain't she pretty? Not silly pretty, like some, but pretty." Biedy sighed. "I always did want me a girl. I love my boys, but they won't let me fuss on 'em." Instantly, she turned to Jeff. "Is there nothin' I can do for the hurt man?"

"He's sleepin', Biedy."

"No, I . . . ain't." Zan's voice rasped weakly.

"Zan! Oh, Zan! I thought you were asleep."

"I need a swaller of water, gal."

Annie Lash lifted his head and held the flask to his lips. The water slushed into his mouth and down on his beard. He drank thirstily, then she lowered his head gently. He closed his eyes wearily and sucked air in through his open mouth.

"Oh! My goodness sakes alive!" Biedy chirped. "I know you got to be gettin' on. Annie, you 'n me will have us a talkin' get-together some other time. I'll build a fire under them boys o'mine so they'll stop diddlin'." She turned, threw her hands in the air, and issued orders like a drill sergeant. Her boys didn't seem to mind in the least. "Get to changin' that team, now. Move those mules on in here, Martin. You'n Walter, get to humpin'. Help him, Walter! What'er you standin' there for? Landsakes! You boys is slow as a ol' woman at times."

While the Cornick boys moved out the tired team of mules and hitched a fresh span, Jeff took the canvas with the dead men's belongings from under the wagon seat and gave them to Silas.

"You take their plunder, the mule and one of

the horses, Silas. They had some good guns, powder, and shot."

"If'n that's what ya want, Jeff. Me'n Biedy will be acomin' along. If'n there's anythin' we can do, anythin' a'tall—"

"I'll come arunnin' if'n ya need me, Annie," Biedy said. "Tell a hello to Callie."

"I'll tell her. Good-bye."

The wagon moved with Jeff at the reins and Light leading the spare horses. Annie Lash sat beside Zan and waved to the bright, perky woman who stood beside her husband and tall sons. Under different circumstances she would have enjoyed visiting with Mrs. Cornick, but now... Her eyes mirrored her distress.

"Somethin' I'd like to say fer what'er hit's worth," Zan said clearly.

Annie Lash peered sharply at him. "Yes, Zan?" she asked quietly.

"Ya got'a goodly supply of pride, gal. Hit could be Jeff's stuck on ya. Don't get stiff-necked and prideful. Give yoreself time to..." His voice deserted him, but his lips still moved. Then he closed his eyes.

Annie Lash held his hand and watched his labored breathing. The agony within her clawed fiercely.

CHAPTER
SEVEN

Emptiness, heavy as a stone, pressed against Annie Lash's heart. The speech she had rehearsed
to urge Zan to take her back to Saint Louis now
seemed foolishly childish. She tried to close her
mind to the agony that Zan was going to die and
leave her alone in the sparsely settled wilderness
with a man she had known less than a week. She
had never allowed herself the luxury of self-pity,
but now, as she held Zan's gnarled, work roughened hand, she cried silently for herself and for
Zan. *Don't die and leave me, Zan. Please don't
die!* She had never felt so utterly helpless nor had
tears that came so easily.

From far away she heard a wild turkey gobble.
There came an answering gobble, then another
and another. Everything has something, or someone, she thought. She had her ma and pa, then
her pa and Zan. Now only Zan. A poignant wave

of homesickness came over her and she longed with all her heart to be a little girl again back home in Virginia with her mother and father.

Zan stirred restlessly and she dampened a cloth with the water from the canteen and wiped his face. His brown, leathery skin was cold to her touch. She folded the cloth and let it rest on his forehead. Then she noticed his eyes were not fully closed. It was too late to wipe the tears from her face.

"So you caught me bawling, Zan Thatcher. Shame on you for watching me when I thought you were asleep." Her nose was stuffy and she sniffed as she strove to control her quivering voice.

"I ain't n'er seed ya bawl, gal. Not e'en when yore pa died."

"He was in such pain and wanted to be released from it. But I did bawl. I just didn't let you see me with my eyes all red and my nose running."

"Ya'll be a'right, Annie Lash. Jeff'll take keer a ya. It's a heap more'n I'd hoped fer."

His eyes looked extra bright. Oh, Lordy! He'd got the fever on him. She controlled her panic with forceful words.

"Don't be making any matches for me, Zan Thatcher," she said scathingly and was rewarded with a twitch of a grin on his lips. "And don't think for a minute I don't know what you're up to. I can work and look after myself. I hired on to work for my keep and that's what I'll do. Cooking and washing and taking care of younguns is better than marrying Walt Ransom!" She forced a laugh that didn't come out quite as convincingly as she hoped.

"I'd a kilt him first."

"Why, Zan! What a thing to say!"

"I warn't lettin' them no-goods have ya, gal."

"Oh! You're going to make me bawl again, and I don't want to." She wiped her eyes with one hand and held his with the other. There was surprising strength in the hand that gripped hers.

"Air we 'bout thar?"

"I don't know. Do you want me to ask Jeff? He's driving the wagon."

"I know hit, gal. No. Just keep a lookout and tell me what ya see." He closed his eyes and let his head roll to the side. "Hit's a purty day, ain't it?"

"Yes. It's a pretty day. It's pretty country, too."

"Ain't nothin' smells good as the woods. Ya like being in the woods, gal?"

"Yes, I do. I got awfully tired of the river. We're well back from it now and on higher ground. The soil is black and rich. I wish you could have seen Mr. Cornick's farm. The garden patch was spaded and planted. Mrs. Cornick had brought some buttercups and wild ferns out of the woods and planted them in a rotted out stump. She seemed so birdlike, the way she moved and talked, but her men jumped when she hollered just like they thought she was grand." She stopped talking. His eyelids flickered and she continued. "The land around the house was cleared and fenced with split rails. It looked like Mr. Cornick and his boys had been busy burning off brush."

"I could tell he warn't no slouch...Keep talkin', gal."

"I...saw a few cowslips trying to get through

the grass along the trail." Annie Lash hastily wiped
her nose on the hem of her dress. "We're near the
river again and the bank is a solid mass of scarlet.
The redbud is in bloom, Zan. And all along the
trail I can see berry bushes and wild plum. Ma
loved berry bushes and plum and cherry trees.
She used to make plum jelly."

"She made plum butter," Zan said without
opening his eyes. "Said she didn't like throwin'
out the pulp."

Annie Lash felt a tightness in her throat. "I
didn't know you knew my mother."

"Hit was a mighty long time ago. She were jist
a slip of a lass, all eyes 'n chestnut hair. Talk, gal.
What're ya seein' now?"

"I can see Jeff's house. The name Berrywood
is fitting."

Annie Lash sat there with a cloud of hair tum-
bling about her face in the warm morning breeze
and stared at Zan's whiskered face for an endless,
empty moment, knowing these were the last minutes she would spend with the man who was the
link with her past. When he was gone she would
be cut loose from everything she had ever known
and loved. Suddenly, she could not go on and had
to wait until she could master her voice again.
She saw Zan's eyelids flutter. Her head came up
then, her eyes enormous in her drawn face.

"The house is backed up to a wooded slope.
Someone's been busy splitting rails. There's a big
pile at the edge of the timber." She drew a ragged
breath and forced herself to go on. "Everything
is laid out in patches and fenced, Zan. There's a
garden, an orchard, and a fenced pastureland with

a creek running through it. It looks like Osage-plum planted along the fence. Pa always said they grew fast and were so wiry and thick they were better than a fence once they got going. Inside one of the patches the black soil is plowed open. There's a barn and a railed barnlot, a smokehouse, and a chicken house. The lower part of the buildings are stone and the upper part split logs. The house is made like that, too, and it sits in the center of its own grassy yard." She blinked her eyes rapidly so she could see through the tears. "It's really a double cabin, Zan. One roof covers two separate buildings, with a dogtrot connecting them. The roof slopes down and covers a run across the front of the house that's paved with flat slabs of stone. There's a big rock chimney at the outer end of each of the cabins." Annie Lash's heart trembled. It was a lovely homestead.

"Air we thar yet?" The voice didn't sound like Zan's voice.

"Almost, Zan." She spoke with trembling lips, but with gladness in her voice despite the constriction in her throat.

"Do ya like what ya see, Lettie?"

Lettie? Her mother's name. Oh, Zan!

"Yes. It's—" Her voice broke. "It's beautiful and peaceful here, Zan."

The old man let out a long shuddering sigh. Tears rolled from Annie Lash's eyes and fell on the wrinkled, brown hand she held to her cheek.

Light had gone ahead and now stood holding open the rail gate so they could pass through. Weariness enveloped Annie Lash like a dark cloud. She put nervous hands to her hair and pushed it back from her face, not knowing or caring that it was coming loose from the pins or that her dress was dirty and she had grime on her face and hands. Her insides quivered when she looked at Zan's face. To her he looked a hundred years older than he had yesterday at this time, and he was a million times dearer.

The hoarse barking of a dog and a hallooing came from the distance. The team picked up speed, sensing the end of the journey. The wagon made a half turn and Annie Lash saw a woman with a small child astraddle her hip come out of the dogtrot. The wind was blowing her skirts against the backs of her legs and lifting the blond hair on top of her head. A small boy with cotton-white hair ran across the barnlot, crawled through the fence, and raced for the house on short, stubby legs. A man in buckskins stepped from behind the house and scooped him up with one arm. The child let out a squeal of laughter and hung limply from the middle like a sack of grain.

Annie Lash watched the scene with tired, dull eyes, painfully aware that nothing would ever be the same again. The wagon slowed and rolled to a stop. She sat there holding tightly to Zan's hand, her stomach knotted with tension and her heart heavy with pain, but reconciled to the inevitable.

Zan's eyes opened. They were as vacant as a blind man's eyes. He blinked at her and she felt a surge of guilt and...love.

"Yore a good lass. Ya got Lettie's eyes an' her hair, an' ya got 'er ways. Get Jeff, gal. I got a thin' to say to him." He was lucid and spoke clearly, but his face had turned a blueish gray.

He was going to die! There was nothing she could do for him. A cold, gray dread was pressing down on her, crushing the last of the energy that had held her upright and gotten her through the night. Horrified awareness that she was losing her dearest friend was reflected in her eyes. Zan saw the expression on her face and snorted in the old familiar way.

"Don't lollygag, Annie Lash. Hit ain't fit an' proper fer ya to be bawlin' an' carryin' on. Ain't nothin' ya can do fer me, nothin' a'tall. Get Jeff."

"I'm here, Zan." Jeff leaned over the end of the wagon, his eyes on a level with Annie Lash's tear-blurred ones.

"We've got to do something! Help me get him in the house. We can get herbs and bind the wound—" In an agony of despair she groped for words.

"No, lass," Zan was gasping for breath, now. "I ain't a leavin' this here wagon. If'n I warn't so goldurned stubborn I'd a been dead back yonder a ways."

"Don't talk nonsense, Zan." She tried to hide her pain behind a scolding voice.

"Hit's a good place ya got here, Jeff. Hits a good place fer me to leave my little gal. I ain't ne'er ask no man fer nothin' till now. I'm a askin' ya to be seein' after Annie Lash. See she don't end up with a no-good, the likes of what's back in Saint Louis. I thought she'd take to ya 'n want ya fer her man, but my gal's got 'er own mind 'bout such as that. I'd..." His weak voice trailed away.

"I'll do it, Zan. I'll take care of her. She'll not go back to the Bank. You have my solemn word on that." Jeff bent over and spoke low and firm.

"I knowed I could count on ya. Hit's purty here—the woods 'n ... all." His eyes closed and his chest heaved with a deep sigh. A trickle of blood came from his nose and Annie Lash wiped it away.

The morning sun beat down on her bowed head. She was weeping silently. She heard nothing, saw nothing but the still gray face of the man who had been like a father to her during the trying years her own pa had been sick. Afterward, he had stood between her and the toughs of Saint Louis. His breathing was so faint, the hand she held in hers so limp, that she never knew when the breath finally left him. Jeff stood at the end of the wagon, his broad shoulders and her own body making a private place for Zan to die. After a while Jeff reached over to take Zan's hand from hers and place it on his chest.

"It's over, Annie Lash."

She sat still for a long moment, her head bowed. When she stirred and tried to stand, her numbed legs wouldn't hold her and she grasped the side of the wagon for support. Jeff placed his hands beneath her armpits and swung her to the ground, holding her against him until her lifeless legs found the strength to hold her.

"Are you all right?" It seemed to her that he was always asking that. She nodded and stood away from him. "Callie," he called over his shoulder. A woman came from the shadows beside the house. She was young, her oval face a pale apricot and her thick, honey-blond hair braided and twisted around on the top of her head, making her appear taller than she was. "This is Annie Lash Jester. She needs a cup of tea."

Annie Lash glanced at the woman and then back to Zan's still face. Her eyes found the sunbonnet she had discarded the day before crammed down in the crack between her trunk and the side of the wagon. She reached for it, spread the brim, and covered Zan's face.

The silent woman was waiting, and Annie Lash walked with her toward the house. Under the shelter of the sloping roof, on the flagstone run, were several benches. She made for one of them, her legs suddenly so weak she was staggering.

"Do you mind if I sit down here?"

"No, ma'am. If that's what you want."

Annie Lash leaned her head back against the stone wall of the house and closed her eyes. She felt as if there were a wide chasm between her and everyone else in the world. Her thoughts finally became orderly. Was this the woman she had come to take care of, the one that was so sick she couldn't care for her babies? She didn't look sick, but if she were, she shouldn't be waiting on her. Pushing herself away from the wall, she got to her feet as the woman came from the dogtrot with a steaming mug in her hand.

"You don't need to wait on me."

The woman looked at her with dark-circled green eyes. They were large and clear and unsmiling. She was shorter than Annie Lash, slightly built and small-boned. Her breasts were full and gently rounded under her brown linsey dress.

She held the mug out and Annie Lash took it.

"I'm sorry about your pa." She spoke slowly with a soft slur to her words.

"He wasn't my pa. He was a very dear friend who was like a father to me." *Was*. She closed her mind to the agony the word brought her. Her lips pressed together to trap a sob that longed to escape.

"Are you homesteadin' 'round here?"

Annie Lash sat back down. The calm question had just barely penetrated her mind when Jeff rounded the corner and stood looking down at her.

"I've picked out a burying spot in the woods. Would you like to see it before we start digging?"

She shook her head. "Any place in the woods would be all right with Zan."

"The burying won't be until the middle of the afternoon. Will's making a box. He knew Zan the same as I did."

"It's good of him."

Light brought her rocking chair from the wagon and set it in the shade of the porch. Callie's eyes shifted from the chair to Annie Lash with an unmistakable question in their depths that Annie Lash sensed immediately to be one of displeasure.

"I'll not be staying long," she said numbly and took a deep, dry, hurting breath. Everything was a blur of fatigue.

"It's not *my* house," Callie said wearily, and walked away.

Jeff stood looking down at the top of Annie Lash's bent brown head. She kept it bowed over the cup in her two hands, and after a while she saw his moccasined feet moving in the direction Callie had taken.

Oh, Lordy! She wasn't wanted or needed here, that was plain enough. Her eyes flooded with new tears of despair. She'd have to study on what she was going to do, but... not now. She was so tired. It felt like a hundred years since they left Saint Louis. Zan... was so happy... Her brain seemed to be aimlessly whirling, spinning fragments of thought into space as fast as they formed. In this terrifying state of tiredness and confusion, Annie Lash knew only that she could not face the woman again without breaking down. She set her empty mug on the floor under the bench and lay down. She covered herself with her shawl and fell into a sound sleep.

Feeling strange, almost like an intruder, Callie went back into the house. The kitchen door was standing open and the sunny breeze played across her, moving the hair at her brow, fluttering it against her cheeks, stirring up the clean smells of soap, wood, and mush bubbling in the iron pot at the fireplace. Absently, she moved to the crane, swung the pot away from the heat, and filled two small wooden porringers with mush to cool for Amos and the baby. She looked around the big, cozy room, at the clean, stone floor and the massive fireplace with its baking chamber on the side. She took stock of the work shelves, the washstand that was attached to the wall near the back door, the water bucket and the wooden washbasin waiting there. The long trestle table and benches that would be replaced with chairs when Will got around to making them occupied one end of the room. This had been hers for almost two years. She had come to believe it would be hers forever. How foolish of her to dream...

Will. How she had enjoyed being here with him during Jeff's absence. It wasn't decent for a married woman to be yearning for another man, she scolded herself as she had done more than once before. But she didn't feel married to Jason, she argued silently with her conscious. It seemed as if she'd lived a lifetime since he ran off and left her and Amos with Henry and Jute.

Will had been with Jeff when he brought them to this place. It had always been Jeff and Will. Almost inseparable since childhood, she had known Will for as long as she'd known Jeff, but he had always been politely reserved until lately. The last few weeks had been the happiest of her life. Now that time was over. Jefferson had not only come back, he'd brought a woman with him. What would she do now?

The tall, beautiful woman had come to stay. She was sure of that despite what she'd just said. She'd brought her rocking chair and in the evening, when the work was done, she'd sit in it beside this fireplace. This would be her house, the food-stuffs in the cellar would be her doing. She would decide if they would eat the smoked turkey or a cut from the side of venison that hung in the smokehouse. Would she rearrange the pots on the shelves and take down the bundles of dried onions and peppers Callie had tied to the rafters?

"Callie?"

Jarred from her thoughts, she turned quickly, guiltily; her glance taking in the serious look on Jefferson's face. She went to the bearskin rug, loosened the harness that kept the baby from crawling toward the fireplace, and lifted him to her hip. Somehow the warm, little body of a child was a comfort when something unpleasant was about to happen.

"Callie?" Jeff said again. "Are you feeling better?"

"It was just a cold in my chest, Jefferson. It wasn't nothin' a dab of coal oil and goose grease couldn't cure." With one hand she laced the baby's mush with molasses from a crock. "I've been a feedin' Abe in the middle of the mornin' and he'll sleep through the noonin'. Amos will be in, if he can bring himself to let Will be. I'll swan, Jefferson, that child thinks Will is as grand as a shiny new dollar." Words came out in a nervous little rush without her even thinking about them.

Jeff smiled, so she smiled at him, picked up the spoon, and managed to get the first bite into Abe's mouth without spilling it down the front of him. Jeff filled a mug with tea and sat down across from her. *Now he'd tell her that he wanted his home for the woman, that he'd send her and the boys to Jason. He'd tell her that he found him in Saint Louis or Natchez. He'd say that they were Jason's responsibility, not his.* The thoughts raced through Callie's mind as she steeled herself for what she was sure he was going to say.

"I was hoping that you and Annie Lash would take to each other, Callie. It would make it more pleasant for you, and for her if you did."

"Are you going to marry her, Jefferson?" Callie kept spooning the mush into her son's little mouth, grateful for the chore so she didn't have to look at him.

"I asked her, but she turned me down."

She looked at him with astonishment on her face. He wasn't smiling. He wasn't making a funny joke.

"Why, Jefferson? Landsakes! Why in the world would she turn you down?"

He lifted his shoulders in a shrug. "She's proud. Real proud. She won't wed in order to have a roof over her head. She'll work to pay for her keep or she won't stay. I gave my solemn promise that I'd look after her. I'd have done it anyway, Callie. She was like a daughter to that old man and I owed him my life. You can ask Will. He'll tell you that Zan Thatcher saved our hides more than once."

"You want her to stay here and...take care of the house?"

"You're working yourself down to skin and bones. I thought she'd be a help to you."

"Then...you don't want me to...go?" She was about to cry.

"Want you to go? Whatever gave you that idea? Of course I don't want you to go," he ground out. "You and the boys are my family."

"Well...I thought that maybe you'd found Jason and—"

"I've no intention of looking for Jason unless you want me to find him, Callie. Do you want him to come back?"

"No, Jefferson," she said smoothly. "Jason don't

want me and the boys. You know that. I'd just as soon never set eyes on him again, even if he is my boys' pa. But I've got pride, too. I've got to feel that I'm some help to you. I've got to pay back just a mite for all you've done—"

"You've more than earned your keep. You've held this place together, Callie. When I came back and found Jason gone, I thought he'd met with an accident and was killed. I refused to believe he would leave his pregnant wife and child out here alone with no one to take care of her but two black men. He's in Natchez, Callie. I could have gone downriver and found him, made him come back to you, but I figured you and the boys were better off without him."

"I hope he never comes back. He didn't want to marry me. Pa and the boys made him. I hadn't been ... with him, but they thought I had." Her eyes filled. "We were so poor, and Jason was from landed gentry. They thought they were doing good by me."

"I know." Jeff said, then after a pause, "Annie Lash was living on the Bank in Saint Louis among the riverman, the trappers and toughs. When her pa died all the loose men from miles around were after her like dogs after a bone. The only man she had to protect her was old Zan Thatcher. He wouldn't have been able to hold out a week longer against the toughs from the taverns and the docks. He told me so. He would have ended up floating downriver with a pike in his back." For a moment Jeff was silent. "Instead, we'll bury him in the woods. My God, Callie. I'll hate it until my dying day that he died the way he did!" He spoke in a tone of deepest regret, looked away from her and out the open doorway toward the western sky. "The woman's got spunk. She shot a man to save my life. That's another reason I must do everything I can for her."

He stood and went to the mantle, rummaged, found a pipe and filled it. From the woodbox he took a splinter of wood and held it to the flames, then to the tobacco and sucked on the pipe.

"Annie Lash is a name I've not heard before," Callie said when he sat down again.

"When Will and I first met up with Zan on the Trace, some of his trail mates called him Lash because he was tall and whiplash thin. It was a name he said was tacked onto him when he was a boy in Virginia. I'd not heard it since, until I met Annie Lash. I was going to ask Zan about it, but it never came right. Now it's too late."

"Mama! The woman's sleepin' on the bench. I looked at 'er." A small, barefoot boy ran in from the door leading to the dogtrot. He came directly to the table and grabbed the arm Callie was using to feed the baby.

"Oh, flitter, Amos! You've made me spill the mush! And don't talk so loud, I'm not deaf. Not yet, anyways."

"Uncle Jeff, Will's 'bout done with the box, 'n Henry 'n Jute's gone to dig a big hole. I wanted to go, but Will said I'd fall in, but I wouldn't a! I ain't gonna fall in no buryin' hole!"

The boy's small face was beautiful. The hair that curled loosely about his head was cotton-white. He could have been a miniature of his uncle except for the large green eyes that now

sparkled with excitement. The sadness of death
had no meaning for him. He was excited by the
unusual and interesting things that had happened. A strange woman was asleep on the bench
on the porch, Will was building a box for the dead
man in the wagon under the lean-to, and Henry
and his boy, Jute, had gone to the wood, singing
a moaning song. To Amos, this day was like fair
day to a town child and he could scarcely contain
his excitement. Now, he spied the second bowl
of mush cooling on the workbench.

"You can have it, but bring it here to me and
I'll syrup it," Callie said. She looked up to see
the fondness on Jefferson's face when he looked
at her son. Both he and Will were patient and
understanding with Amos, far more so than his
own father had been. Jason had thought of his
children as an added burden to tie him down.

Amos half-sat, half-stood, and spooned the mush
into his mouth as rapidly as he could bring the
spoon from the bowl to his face. He had things to
do. He was determined not to miss out on a single
happening on this momentous day.

Jeff watched him with an amused smile. He
hoped and prayed the boy would be as different
from his father in actions as he was in looks. He
looked at the child's square, blunt little hands and
thought of Jason's long slender fingers manipu-
lating a deck of cards.

"What's 'er name, Uncle Jeff? Do ya think she'd
care if I'd rock in her chair?"

"Her name is Annie Lash, and I don't think
she'd mind at all if you sat in her chair." Jeff
reached out a hand and rumpled the child's hair,

looked up at the man coming in the door and grinned. "It seems like our hired hand had to pause and fill his stomach, Will."

"Ya know, he don't believe me a'tall when I tell him Dan'l Boone eats one time a day, an' sparingly at that." Will hung his hat on the peg and went to the washstand. He was not as tall nor as big as Jeff, but he was lean-hipped, with a deep-muscled chest and brawny forearms. His light brown hair hung straight and clean to his shoulders and matched the mustache that sprang from his upper lip. His eyes sought Callie when he turned, and Jeff caught the look.

"Godamighty, Jeff. I'd a shore liked to a visited with old Zan." Will helped himself to tea and sat down on the bench across from Jeff. "He'd changed a mite since I seen him last. He looked pert near ninety years old."

"He was right spry until he got the blade in his side," Jeff said. "He held off dying until he got here and it aged him. That girl out there meant the world to him and he was determined to stay alive until he found out what kind of place she was coming to. I heard her telling him about it as we came up the lane."

The dog began to bark and Amos raced for the door. In a second he was back. "It's the Cornicks," he shouted and was gone again.

"Silas said he and Biedy would be over for the burying," Jeff explained. "Both Silas and Isaac took a liking to Zan." He stood, leaving his empty tea mug on the table, and knocked the ashes from his pipe into the fireplace.

"Give me that youngun." Will reached over and

took the baby from Callie's arms. "You go on out and meet the company. This one's 'bout asleep anyhow." He lifted the baby to his shoulder, careful to balance the sleepy head until it rested in the curve of his neck.

Callie's face was flushed with color. She stood behind Will and rearranged some of the pins in her hair. Oh, flitter! she scolded herself. Why did she act like a skittish pony everytime Will Murdock came near? He was just being nice, same as he'd been all the time Jefferson was gone to Saint Louis. It wasn't his fault she'd been so stupidly happy doing for him, and in the smallest part of her heart pretending that they were all a family living on their own homestead. She hurried out into the dogtrot and to the front of the house just as the wagon pulled up and stopped.

Amos's shouting had awakened Annie Lash. She sat huddled on the bench, her shawl around her shoulders. Her dull eyes were circled with dark rings of fatigue and her face felt stiff, as if it would crack if she moved her mouth. She smoothed her dress and poked the hair on her neck back into place. Callie went past her to meet Biedy Cornick, to give her a little more time to arrange herself.

Biedy got down from the wagon talking non-stop. "My, my, my! What a bright, fine day it is! Is he dead yet?" she whispered to Callie. Callie nodded and Biedy threw her hands up. "Whar's that poor girl at?" She made small clicking sounds with her tongue. "I'll swan to goodness if she didn't look like she'd been dragged inside out through a knothole! Now, ya ain't to be afrettin' 'bout feedin' us, Callie. I brought fried pie and a hunk a deer meat. I tol' you, didn't I, 'bout Lester shootin' them wild hogs? Meat's stringy less'n you put it in a pit. I tried to roast some, but, my land, it was tougher than boot leather. Boys drew straws again. Walter got the short end and had to stay behind. He's all up in the air, madder than a flitter he was ... said he'd made Amos a reed whistle, said Lester cheated. Silas had to put a hush on 'em. Silas brought his hymn book. He'll say a piece over that poor soul, that's if it's what Jefferson wants."

Annie Lash waited beside the bench. She was groggy from her short, deep sleep. Biedy swooped down on her as if she had known her forever, folded her in her arms, and hugged her to her thin frame. The expression of sympathy from this bird-like woman was almost her undoing. The well of tears she thought had dried up threatened to overflow, but she held them back and returned the hug.

"You poor thing!" Biedy crooned. "I know yore jist wore out. Hit ain't easy what you done. Isaac tol' me how spunky you be and all. Now, Callie and me'll look after you. You'll be jist back on yore feet in no time a'tall."

"Thank you." Annie Lash looked over the woman's shoulder at Callie. Was that a warmer look she saw in her eyes?

"Light brought your trunk in while you were sleeping," Callie said shyly. "If you want to clean up a bit, I'll bring you a washbasin."

"I'd like that." Annie Lash looked down at her soiled, wrinkled dress with distaste. "It seems like I've worn this dress forever." She turned to see

Jeff looking at her. His dark eyes met hers, and his head moved almost imperceptibly in greeting. It was she who looked away first.

The group that walked behind the wagon taking Zan to his final resting place was larger than it would have been if he had been buried in Saint Louis where he had spent the last few years. Eleven adults and two children; a sizable crowd, Annie Lash thought as she watched Jeff and Will with the help of the two black men lower the box into the grave. Her face was tired looking and white, and her lips were tightly crimped. She held her grief inside of her, not wishing the comfort of tears, but hurting with a kind of knotted sadness that wouldn't come loose. She had looked at Zan before Will closed the box and smoothed his sparce hair the best she could. A spasm of pain crossed her face; the only thing that betrayed her feelings.

The women walked away after the grave was filled. Annie Lash looked back once and saw the men carrying heavy rocks to pile on the soft, black earth. She knew it was so that wolves or some other wild animal wouldn't get curious and dig.

She felt a small hand work its way into hers and looked down to see an impish face grinning up at her. This was life. Zan was gone. Her ma and pa were gone. But life still went on.

CHAPTER
EIGHT

"We'd be pleased to have you come," Silas said. He was waiting to help Biedy into the wagon.

"She knows we'd be plum tickled, Silas. Come visit, Annie Lash, come 'n stay a spell, that's if'n Callie'll let go of ya. My, my, my, yore mouths will go like a couple of bluejays once ya get the newness wore off. Callie 'n me've jawed fer hours. I reckon that girl's heard ever' tale I ever knowed a dozen times over! I got me somebody new to listen, Callie!" Biedy laughed, and the sound was so utterly pleasant it seemed impossible to Annie Lash that it came from the mouth of this plain woman.

"You'll come now, hear? Hit's a pity it takes a buryin' fer us to bunch up, eat, 'n have us a good palaver. What air ya a waitin' fer, Silas? Landa-livin'! I thought ya said we had to be a scutterin' on home. Hit's goin' to be near dark if'n ya don't get a move on."

"Thank you, Biedy, for all you've done to... make the day easier." Annie Lash held her hand out, and Biedy grasped it and gave her a brief hug.

"Why I didn't do nothin' a'tall, girl. Nothin' any neighbor wouldn't a done. You make them men hitch up the wagon, Callie, 'n haul ya over fer the day. Ya got the garden in, ain't ya?"

"It's mostly in. I'm waiting for the dark of the moon so I can plant potatoes."

"Hit's the way to do it. Plant 'em when the moon is full 'n all ya get is runts. I did it oncet a thinkin' the moon didn't know what I was a doin' down here, 'n we was eatin' them blasted turnips all winter! Watch what yore a doin', Silas. You'll dirty up my good dress."

Silas climbed up to sit beside his wife and slapped the reins. The mules moved. "Giddap, thar. We can't be a waitin' fer Biedy to stop talkin', or we'd be standin' here this time tomorry. Bye, folks."

"Why, Silas Cornick! What a thing to say! Bye, Annie Lash. Bye, Callie. Amos, did I tell ya that Walter's got a whistle fer ya? Bye, Abe. Oh, I ne'er did get to hold that little dumplin'. We'll be back—" Her voice was lost in the jingle of harnesses and the rumble of the wagon wheels.

Annie Lash watched the wagon leave with regret. Biedy Cornick had a way of filling a void, of taking over so that all a person had to do was respond once in a while. Now Annie would have to get her thoughts together and figure out what she was going to do.

Callie had been a surprise. Although she had been shy, she'd been friendly and helpful, too. The resentment that Annie Lash had felt in the air when she first arrived seemed to have disappeared. However, she wasn't needed here as Jeff Merrick had led her to believe. She had to make her thoughts known to him. She couldn't stay here on sufferance when Callie seemed to be perfectly able to cope. Had he intended Annie Lash to be a servant? If so, why hadn't he said so?

Not being one to dawdle once her mind was made up, she turned and headed straight to where Jeff stood beside Will and Light. His eyes caught hers as she approached and she looked at him squarely before shifting her eyes first to Light and then to Will. She spoke to him.

"Thank you for what you did for Zan," she said, her words not stressed by any emotion. "Zan would have liked it, if he knew that it was you who did it for him."

"No thanky needed, ma'am. Zan was one of the first real men I knowed. Guess Jeff told ya 'bout us meetin' up with him on the Trace?" Will took his hat off when he spoke to her.

"Yes. Zan would have enjoyed visiting with you about old times." She smiled wanly before addressing the other man. "Mr. Light, ah...Mr. Lightbody—"

"Call me Light, *mademoiselle*. I have become used to the name."

She held out her hand and he gripped it strongly.

"Thank you Light. Zan was happy these last few days—happier than I had ever known him to be."

"He was a man I could have learned much from. I was glad to call him friend."

"And he you." She tilted her head and looked up at Jeff. "I would like a private word with you."

If he was surprised by her request he didn't show it. He was watching her, amazed at how well she was holding together despite all she'd been through. Zan was right, he thought. His little gal was no rattlehead. He reached out and cupped her elbow with his hand and they moved away from the other men.

"I was expecting it."

The sun, a crimson, glowing orb, had disappeared long ago behind the towering trees in the west and the air had turned cooler. After going a short distance, Jeff released her elbow and Annie Lash wrapped her shawl closely about her shoulders. He didn't stop walking until they were among the trees, out of sight of the house. He leaned against a large oak, crossed his arms over his chest, and surveyed her with his eyes. He started at the top of her head and took in every feature of her face before moving down her body and then up to her throat and breast. His eyes lingered there long moments before moving to her face again.

She shifted, uncomfortable under his intense gaze. "Why did you lie to me?" she demanded. "You said Callie was sick and couldn't care for her children. You brought me here under false pretense!"

"Yes, I did," he admitted. "I wanted to get you out of Saint Louis before some rejected suitor put a knife in Zan."

"Oh..." She looked at him long and hard. She knew he regretted the term he'd used and she didn't want to taunt him with the obvious. "If that was the case, why didn't you say so?"

He lifted his shoulders in a gesture she had come to recognize as characteristic of him when he considered another's opinion unworthy of words. It angered her.

"You brought me out here to help a woman who doesn't want or need my help and I lost Zan in the process. I'll not stay here as extra baggage. I'll not be thrust upon your household because there's nowhere else for me to go!" She spaced each of the words to give emphasis to her statement.

"Extra baggage? Anyone who can do a day's work on a homestead is not extra baggage. You saw how thin and run down Callie is. Her lot hasn't been easy. She was here alone when the baby came. Henry sent Jute to fetch Biedy or she'd have died with only Henry and little Amos to hold her hand. I thought I saw a way to make things easier for her and to pay Zan for past favors."

She turned her face toward him and looked at him quietly. The silence stretched between them like a taut thread. She drew in a ragged breath. "If what you say is true, I can understand why you did it," she admitted reluctantly. "But Zan is gone and Callie has had the running of the house for so long it would be difficult for her to let go even a part of it to a hired girl."

"Did she say that?"

"No. But I know how I'd feel in her place."

He waited for her to continue. When she did not, he asked, "How would you feel?"

"I'd probably resent it. I wouldn't want another woman in my house." She dipped her head and plucked at her skirt. "If Zan had lived I was going to ask him to take out a homestead with me." She looked up and her clear eyes met his.

"He'd have done it, even if he didn't want to. You meant the world to him."

"Can a woman take out a claim for herself?" The question was out. What now? she wondered in agonizing silence.

He shook his head, but he didn't laugh as she expected him to do. "I've never heard of it. I don't know if the law would stand. It's hardly a thing a woman would do, or *could* do alone. You've got to raise a crop and build some kind of a place on the land, and you've got to live on it."

"I could do it," Annie Lash said simply.

He shook his head. Now, he laughed. "I don't know but what you could, if you set your mind to it. But there's no need even if the law would allow it. You've got me to take care of you. You can help me improve on this place. I've only started to do all I've planned to do."

"I have some money—almost a hundred dollars. And Zan...would want me to have whatever he left. It's enough for a start," she said stubbornly.

"Get it out of your mind, Annie Lash," he said firmly. "If necessary I'll build another cabin if you don't like being in the house with Callie." His hands snaked out and grasped her shoulders.

"I don't want you to build me anything! I want my own place!" she snapped. Her eyes became two bright, angry stars.

"I wouldn't be building it for *you!* I'd build it for Callie and the boys. My *wife* stays in *my* house." His words wiped out her thoughts completely.

"You're ... out of your mind!" she snapped, appalled at the nerve of the man. "I'm not marrying you!"

"Are you going to live with me in sin?" His rugged, intense face was close to hers and she could see his lips twitch. *He was laughing at her!*

She gasped, her pulse racing, then chills caused her legs to shake. He had not said one word about love, about wanting or needing only her.

"What I said on the raft still holds," she said cuttingly. "I'll not marry in order to have a roof over my head. That's my final word on it!"

"Things have changed since then. What choices do you have? Oh, I don't doubt that Biedy would take you in. She'd like nothing more than to match you up with Isaac. He's old enough to make babies and Biedy would delight in having grandchildren."

"You're disgusting!" she declared staunchly. Her hands went instinctively to his chest to push him away from her. "I can go back to Saint Louis and take a boat down to New Orleans and get a job as seamstress or caring for children."

"There's plenty of darkies for those jobs. And don't count on Will or Light to help you. They already know my plans for you."

His cool taunts struck sparks against the temper

she was so certain she could control. The very
fact that he could ignite it so easily was added
fuel to the blaze.

"You are lower than I thought!"

"Why are you so stubborn?" His brows drew
together as he studied her mutinous face. "Do you
dislike me so much? I could swear you didn't
dislike me when I lifted you down on the raft
from the bank. What have I done to change your
opinion of me?"

Through the fog of her anger she realized the
look in his dark eyes reflected a new and perhaps
more dangerous element. A very male hunger
stirred there now, and she was horrified to discover something very female in her was both attracted and repelled by that look and the closeness
of his body as he pulled her toward him. Word-
lessly, she stared up at him. With a cool air of
possessiveness that defied her to protest, he slid
his hands from her arms down to encircle her
waist. She sucked in her breath, refusing to give
him the satisfaction of closing her eyes against
the expression of victory on his face. She must
not let him have full control of the situation, she
realized dimly. She must maintain her dignity,
keep her pride intact.

"You're not the kind of man I want to spend the
rest of my life with, Mr. Merrick." She spoke slowly
and unemotionally. "Is that so hard for you to
understand? I want more out of life than a house
to tend and food to eat. I want more than being
a vessel to satisfy a man's lust. I want more than
what Callie got when she married your brother.
The man I marry will have to want the same things

that I want, and that is to build something permanent together. When I meet him, I'll know him, and I'll put all my thoughts, my toil, my smiles, my pain, and ... my love into my family." In spite of all she did, she couldn't keep the tears from welling in her eyes. "I'll not stand on the fringe of a man's life and hunger for something I know can be real and beautiful. I want to love and be loved. I want my man to be the other part of myself. I want us to be truly one in every sense of the word. I'm sure this is too complicated for a man of your sensibilities to grasp. I'm also determined to hold out for what I want or have nothing at all."

She was completely wrung out by the time she finished and would have liked nothing better than to lay her head on his chest and cry. She held back the sobs, but there was nothing she could do about the tears that rolled down her cheeks.

She felt the deep breath that shook his body. His hands at her waist tightened and he drew her to him. A gentle hand on her head brought it to his shoulder and the dam that had surrounded her emotions broke. She cried long, low, agonizing sobs that rose from the center of all the pain that had come from the loss of her pa and the cabin on the Bank, the killing of the man on the trail, and Zan. Gentle arms held her while the grinding sobs wrenched her slight body. Gentle hands smoothed the tangled hair from her white face as she clung to him. Finally, the racking shudders ceased and she leaned against him, utterly exhausted.

Jeff held her, wondering about the depth of this

startling, lovely creature that had come to him like a gift from heaven. He felt a stirring of excitement and hope that he might possess what she sought. His chest warmed from the quickening of his heart, and he questioned himself silently. Could he live up to her expectations? Would she ever voluntarily choose him to be her life's partner? He'd been wrong. He'd been brash, too sure of himself, too uncaring of her feelings. Good God! He'd been dumb, stupid and blind! How could he make her understand?

"Annie Lash, I don't know much about women or what they want. I've been too busy trying to stay alive and carve out a place for myself here in this wilderness. Callie and the wives of a couple of friends of mine who have places up on the big river are all the decent women I've had much to do with. I'd like for you to meet them sometime. Rachel is married to my friend, Fain MacCartney." He smiled suddenly. "You remind me of Berry Witcher. She's the spunkiest woman I ever knew until I met you. She and Simon live up on the river, north of where the Missouri flows into the Mississippi. When I saw you, I knew you were a decent woman, like Rachel and Berry, and I guess I wanted to get you out of Saint Louis as much for your sake as for Zan's. I'm sorry for what I did and said that night on the raft. I don't know what came over me."

Rough fingers wiped the tears from her cheeks. "I'll not bother you about marrying me. Stay and help Callie with the work. You'll more than pay your way. After awhile, if you're still of a mind to, I'll find a way to get you to New Orleans and help you find a means of staying there. I'll not be doing it for Zan, but for you."

His mouth was close to the top of her head and she could feel his breath stir her hair. Slow, hesitant fingers lifted her chin and his dark eyes looked down into hers soberly and intently, hers were shimmering with the moistness of her tears.

"I'm a rough, hard man, Annie Lash. The softness was crushed out of me a long time ago."

Annie Lash felt as if she were adrift on a cloud. The tears had released the tight knot of pain in her heart and euphoria spread throughout her taut body. She felt a wonderous warmth and a rightness to the feel of his arms and his fingers that wiped the tears from her cheeks. She felt no awkwardness about the arms she had wrapped about his hard body, no guilt about the comfort she received from leaning on his strength. His blond head and huge shoulders seem to block out the world. There was a tiredness to his face she hadn't noticed before. Was that tender regard that she saw in the depth of his eyes? It was almost enough to make her weep again. Her breath bubbled through her parted lips.

Suddenly, she was aquiver with the desire to comfort him, to soothe away the tight lines at the sides of his mouth, to make them twitch into a smile. A long quiet had slipped by while they gazed at each other.

"No man before me has kissed you?" It was a softly voiced question.

"No."

"You didn't like it?"

"I was disappointed."

He drew in a trembling breath and looked away from her for an instant, then back, as if his eyes couldn't stay away from her face.

"Why didn't you like it? I did."

Her heart stopped, then raced wildly. She took her time answering, trying to find words that wouldn't destroy his gentle mood.

"I always imagined a kiss to be gentle...and sweet. I thought it would be an expression of... loving. That it would be shared, not hurtful and humiliating." Her words trembled from unsteady lips.

"I was too rough," he groaned. "I scratched your soft skin with my whiskers." There was regret on his face, and his voice echoed with it.

Her lips spread in a slight smile while her eyes locked with his. "It wasn't the whiskers—"

"Then what was it?" he insisted.

"It wasn't what it was, it was what it wasn't!" She was beginning to panic. "Did the other women you've kissed like it?"

"I never asked them." He hesitated, then added, "I guess I really didn't care if they liked it or not."

"Jefferson..." She meant a gentle rebuke, but his name was more of a caress when it came from her lips.

"I want to kiss you again." The look in his eyes made her melt inside. "I'm asking this time."

Thoughts of future heartache drifted through her mind and she rejected every one of them even as she raised her slightly parted lips to receive his.

His mouth was firm yet gentle as it sat upon hers. His lips touched hers softly at first, then eagerly tasted them as she yielded to the delicate pressure. There was controlled power in the way he moved his lips over her mouth with a sensual deliberation, taking care not to crush the feeling from hers, but to coax them to respond and vibrate to his warm tender movement. Her lips followed his, seeking, caressing. The feeling became so intense that her entire body shivered with sheer delight. Never in her life had her senses known such excitement.

There was not a whimper of protest from her when he drew her so close that he hurt her against his hardness. Her mouth opened to the gentle persuasion of his and she melted into a mindless dream as his tongue stroked the softness of her inner lips. Her arms tightened about him and she clung, unaware of his restraint, unaware of the tremor in his arms. She allowed him access to her unexplored mouth. Locked in his embrace, glowing waves of pleasure spread like wildfire throughout her body.

Somewhere along the way she lost her identity and became part of him, and untamed intensity swept her on. They were two beings blended together in a whirling tide. His mouth moved a fraction from hers and a sound, half groan, half sigh, exploded on a breath that came from him. She moved her face to find his lips again. His tongue moved lightly over her lips, not daring to go inside again, holding back. His hoarse, ragged breathing accompanied the pounding thunder of his heartbeat.

Slowly, haltingly, he raised his head so he could look directly into her eyes. His eyes devoured her. Relief and surprise at what he saw there made his voice husky and relaxed his taut features. "Annielove..."

They stared at each other for a moment that was so quiet it seemed the world had stopped. She was fully aware that they were breathing the same air, and that the taste of his mouth was flavored with tobacco. The rough plains of his cheeks were warm and caressing against her face. And when his large hand moved beneath her arm to find her full breast, there was a pleasant, natural feeling to it.

"I didn't mean it to go on for so long!" His breath was warm on her lips. He studied her face, the sparkle of tears on her lashes and her quivering mouth.

She returned his searching look. The pale light of evening slanted onto his light hair, his thick lashes, and the hollows of his cheeks. She raised her hand and trailed her fingertips across his chin and moved up to where the slashes appeared in his cheeks when he smiled. She wished he would smile now, so she could feel them.

"Didn't you like it this time?" She could feel life pounding in her throat, her temples.

"Of course I did!" he said almost savagely. "But I..." His voice trailed away and he seemed to be drowning in her eyes. Her tongue came out and moistened her lower lip while she waited. "But I—I wanted you to like it, too. Was I too rough?"

"No. You weren't too rough, but..." A rosy flush came up from her neck to flood her face.

"Were you disappointed this time?" The question came hesitantly.

"No," she said again. "I was surprised. I thought you held your lips like this when you kissed." She formed her lips in a tight pucker.

He laughed and she could feel the vibrations against her breast. She found herself beaming with pleasure.

"Shall we try it?" He puckered his mouth and touched hers lightly. "Did you like that any better?"

"Did you?"

"The only thing I liked about it was that I had to be close to you to do it."

Strange, tempestuous feelings swirled inside her again, and she struggled desperately to keep her head. Her senses commanded her to move back out of his embrace, but her body ignored the order, remained pliable, and molded itself against him. She could feel the hard muscles and bones of his chest and arms, and the steady thumping of his heart. The problems that had clouded her life since the death of her pa seemed to leave her, and she was engulfed in a peaceful void.

"You're about worn out." His voice was soothing against her ear. "You've been through a lot and you've held up. But now you need a good sleep." His hands moved up and down her back and for a moment she allowed herself the luxury of being held and comforted.

It wasn't until she moved out of his embrace that she realized it was dark. There was a smoky smell to the cool air that caused her nostrils to twitch. They walked out from among the trees and into the grassy clearing around the house. The grass was already wet with dew and the forest beyond loomed thick and dark. They walked silently along the rail fence, Jeff's hand firmly attached to her elbow. When they reached the dogtrot he pulled her to a stop.

"Annie Lash." He said her name softly.

The hair on the back of her neck lifted, her breath shortened, her cheeks warmed, and her lips parted tremblingly when she looked up into the dark face that loomed over hers.

"Have we come to an understanding?"

She nodded. "Jefferson." She'd liked the sound of his full name ever since she heard Callie using it. "I'll work hard and be a help to Callie, but—"

"You and Callie will find a meeting ground," he said confidently.

She was quiet for a moment, listening to the far-off hoot of an owl. "It seems so peaceful here, yet you said you were bothered some by the Osage."

"Not for some time now, but you can never completely let your guard down. They're on the warpath with the Delawares now, and as long as they are having trouble among themselves it makes it easier on us. There are a few Osage that hunt these grounds. They've always been friendly. Henry and Jute, his boy, move among them, so we're reasonably safe here."

"I didn't get a chance to thank Henry and Jute. I'll do it tomorrow." She put her hand to her mouth to suppress a yawn.

"Come on." Jeff chuckled. He took her arm and turned her toward the door. "Let's get you bedded down before you fall asleep on your feet."

CHAPTER
NINE

Annie Lash woke to the sound of a scolding blue-jay sitting on a branch outside the window. She identified it, lazily opened her eyes, and lay resting in the nest her body had made in the feather bed. She turned on her back, stretching luxuriously, pleasantly aware of the clean sheets and the soft comforter that covered her. Last night she had been too tired to do more than murmur a good night to Callie when she brought her to this room. Earlier, before the burying, she had washed and put on a clean dress in Callie's room beyond the kitchen. On this side of the dogtrot there were two more rooms and Annie Lash was sure that she was in the larger of the two.

It was a cozy room with white birchbark walls and a stone fireplace with a generous mantle that held an oil lamp. The wide double bunk she lay on was fastened to the wall, its foot extending to the small, high-set window. To the left of the entrance was a washstand equipped with a wooden bowl. There was a cupboard, expertly made from walnut and put together with stout pegs, the wood oiled and rubbed until it glowed softly in the early morning light. A dark braided rag carpet covered a section of the stone floor between the fireplace and the bed. Annie Lash had not slept in a room as fine as this since she and her parents left their Virginia home.

The clatter of a bucket and voices in the dogtrot brought her out of her dreamlike state and her feet hit the floor. She whipped her nightdress over her head and shivered, pausing only long enough to rub her arms and feel the bumps the cold air raised on them before scrambling into her clothes. After pinning up her braids, she slipped her feet into a pair of fur-lined moccasins Zan had made for her and went through the dogtrot to the other room.

Callie was at the fireplace. She swung a crane so that the iron teakettle hanging from it was clear of the intense heat of the fire.

"Good morning," Annie Lash said.

"Mornin'."

"Mercy! I slept like a log. I didn't mean to sleep so long."

"I've not been up long myself."

Annie Lash went to the washstand and splashed water from the bowl on her face, then washed her hands with a small cake of soap that lay in a dish beside the bowl. The towel she used to dry her face and hands was damp from previous use, so she hung it over the end of the washstand to dry.

"You'll have to tell me what to do, Callie."

"I'm going to set another batch of tea to steep. Will and Jefferson have gone through one batch already this morning. I swear, I don't know when those two sleep. They set up half the night chewing the fat and were up hours ago." She wrapped a rag around the handle of the teakettle and poured boiling water into a large crockery pitcher. "Jefferson likes mush after he's been on the trail. You'll find meal in that keg on the floor under the work shelf. I keep the lid on tight so the mice can't get to it. Will likes his mush fried. I'll slice yesterday's for him as soon as he brings me some bacon from the smokehouse."

"How much mush should I make?"

"I usually fill this kettle about half full of water. That'll make enough so there's some left over to fry."

The kitchen and the pots she worked with were spotlessly clean, the tableware and food containers placed handily on the shelves, the cookpots arranged on the proper fireplace cranes, and the set of trivets, skillets, and other implements were neatly lined up along the hearth. Annie Lash's liking for Callie increased.

A lusty cry came from the other room and Callie clamped the lid down on the tea can.

"That's Abe. He don't do anything halfway. When he wakes up he bawls for his breakfast so loud he could wake the dead. I'll have to get him before he wakes Amos." She hurried into her room and Annie Lash could hear her trying to quiet him. Abruptly, the cries ceased. Callie came back holding the blanket-wrapped child in her arms.

"I'll nurse him in here until the men come in. It's cold in there unless I get under the covers."

"Mornings and evenings are cold even if it is almost the first of May. Sit here, Callie." Annie Lash pulled her rocking chair from the corner and placed it close to the fireplace. "Sit here and feed that hungry baby and tell me what to do."

Callie sat down and rested her arm holding the baby's head on the smooth curved arm of the chair and adjusted the blanket to cover Abe's face and the breast he was pulling at so greedily. She rocked gently and her eyes smiled into Annie Lash's.

"It's been years since I sat in a rocker. I thought Amos was going to wear it out last night. Jefferson said he didn't think you'd mind if he sat in it."

"Of course I don't mind. My mother rocked me in it when I was a baby and I couldn't part with it. Jefferson...said I could bring it. Callie, I've got to tell you. He said you were sick, needed help with the babies—"

"I know. He told me. I was sick when he left to go to Saint Louis. I had a terrible cold and it went down in my chest. Will helped me with the younguns. I stayed in bed for almost a whole week. Imagine! He cooked, and took over—kind of. I just never had someone doin' for me like that..." Her voice trailed away with the wonder of what she was telling.

"My pa was the only man I ever knew who would do woman's work without complaining." Annie Lash bent over the kettle of boiling water and sprinkled the ground meal, stirring all the while to keep the batter smooth and free of lumps. "My ma was sick for a long while and Pa did for her. Even after I was older and could have done it all he bathed her and combed her hair."

Callie made little clicking noises with her tongue. "Imagine that! I never knew my ma. I was raised up by my pa and my brothers," she said regretfully. "I never had no sister, either, or a woman friend, so I hardly know how..."

"Me, either," Annie Lash said and her eyes caught Callie's. The faint, shy smile she received from the other woman lifted her spirits and she returned the smile.

Abe began to fuss. His small fist pounded on his mother's breast.

"Mercy me! You're a glutton, Abe Pickett. You've drained it already!" She shifted the child to her other breast. "You're going to get weaned just as soon as you can learn to drink out of a cup, young man." She placed a kiss on the child's head and hugged him to her breast as if to soften the threat. "It don't seem right for me to be sitting here and you doing all the work."

"It looks to me like you're doing plenty, filling that youngun's stomach," Annie Lash replied, and swung the crane holding the bubbling mush clear of the heat.

"Ah, Abe!" Callie grimmaced and got to her feet. "It goes in one end and out the other. I can't get enough paddin' on his behind to hold all the water he lets out. I'll change him and myself while I'm at it. He ought to sleep a good long while."

Annie Lash had no time to prepare herself for meeting Jeff, who came through the back door while she was setting the table.

"Mornin'." He carried a bucket of water to the

work counter. "Will's coming with the milk pail.
How Callie ever got to him to do that chore is
beyond me."

A rosy flush had come up to flood Annie Lash's
face, and her tongue stuck to the roof of her mouth.
Callie's return to the room covered her confusion.

"I never asked him to do it, Jefferson. He said
he had milked back home in Virginia and he didn't
mind a'tall."

Jeff gave her a puzzled look, but Callie had
turned away.

"We're going to burn the brush off that patch
Henry and Jute cleared last fall," he said as he
hooked the bench out with his foot and sat down.
"That is, if the wind stays out of the south to blow
the flames toward the river."

"Will Light be around for a while?"

"Long enough to help Will put up some buildings on the land to the west of here."

Callie turned in stunned surprise. "I didn't
know Will had filed on any land."

"I took out the papers for him on my way to
Saint Louis. Will figures, same as me, that it's time
to squat on a piece of land and hold on to it."

Annie Lash saw the radiant look on Callie's
face. Her flushed cheeks made her blue eyes seem
all the brigher and clearer as they traveled from
her to Jeff before she turned back to the cook-fire
and the big iron spider she had set on the grate.

Jeff's sharp eyes caught the blush on Callie's
cheeks and his dark, somber eyes caught and held
Annie Lash's. Her mind groped like a bat in bright
daylight for something to say. She didn't under-

stand Callie's sudden elation or Jeff's look of concern.

The voice from the doorway saved her from trying to erase the sudden silence.

"I got a pailful, Callie. I set it in the cellar and brought up yesterday's milkin'. Looks like a good dab of cream on top. Ya'll be able to make butter, after all."

"Did you put the cloth over it, Will?"

"No. I left it so spiders 'n bugs could fall in."

"Will!" Callie stood with hands on her hips trying to look cross.

He set the bucket on the workbench and went to the washstand. He grinned over his shoulder at Jeff, who sat resting his elbows on the table.

"I don't know why she gets all up in the air over a few bugs in the milk. They got to eat, same as us."

"If you want to eat, Will Murdock, you'd better get yourself out to the smokehouse and get the meat or you'll get nothin' but fried mush."

"Hold yore taters, Callie gal. Light's fetchin' the meat." Will splashed water on his face and wiped it with the towel.

Three men and two women sat down to breakfast. As the men talked about the work they planned for the day, Annie Lash was painfully aware that Jeff looked at her often, but didn't address one word to her. She was relieved and grateful that she didn't have to talk. What had happened between them the night before was too new for her to exchange casual remarks with him in the company of these people.

"There are four hundred acres on the other side of Will's, Light. Why don't you go file on it?" Jeff dipped his spoon into the edge of his mush, tested it for hotness, then put it into his mouth and swallowed. "Tastes good," he said in the general direction of the women sitting at the end of the table.

"Not me, *mon ami*. I've not the patience to wait and see corn sprout up from the ground. There's wild new country upriver waiting for me." His face creased with a smile. "It's a good way to live. I'll not swap it."

"I've been over the mountain 'n down the Trace," Will said soberly. "I've had my fill of solitary winterin' around a campfire."

Light laughed and Annie Lash suddenly realized he was much younger than she had at first thought he was. He was probably no older than she was, she mused. He would have been a boy in his teens when his wife and family were killed. Her gaze was caught by Jeff's. His face was expressionless, giving her no clue as to what he was thinking. When his eyes left hers they went to Callie, and a vague uneasiness began to stir within her, an intuitive sense told her he was bothered by something connected with his sister-in-law.

"How big a cabin do you plan to build, Will?" When he spoke his voice held nothing but calm interest, and Annie Lash wondered if she was wrong in thinking there was an undercurrent of tension.

"I figure 'bout eight axe handles long 'n five wide, for a start."

"For a start? Ho, *mon ami* plans to add more room for the *enfant* to come!" Light's eyes sparkled mischievously and his teeth flashed briefly in his dark face.

Watching them, Annie Lash realized how deep the friendship between them must be to allow them to talk this way to each other.

"And for my friends who come crawlin' in the dead of winter with their tails a'tween their legs lookin' for somethin' to fill their bellies and a fire to warm their backsides," Will retorted grinning.

"Ah...ha!" The Frenchman put a world of meaning in the words. "If you wish the use of my axe, *mon ami*, we should not linger here." He got to his feet, bowed his head respectfully toward the women, and backed away from the table. Will and Jeff followed. The bench made a scraping sound on the stone floor as they pushed it from the table.

"Don't look for us till night, Callie. Fire the gun if you need us. It's loaded. I checked it last night." Jeff's eyes rested for a moment on Annie Lash's face. "This will give you women a day to get to know each other without us men underfoot."

Annie Lash felt oddly exhilarated by his look and was only able to nod her head before he turned and followed Will and Light from the room.

When Amos woke and came to breakfast, he was upset because the men had left the house without him.

"Oh! Poot!" he said, and stood glaring at his mother as if it was her fault.

"Amos Pickett! I won't stand for such talk!"

"Will says more'n that."

"Will's a man. You're a little boy." Callie was carefully skimming the cream from the milk Will brought from the cellar.

"But he said—"

"I don't want to hear what he said. Sit down and eat your breakfast before you wake Abe. Annie Lash, put just a dab of syrup on his mush. If he does it, there'll be just a dab of mush with his syrup," she said in a soft, exasperated tone. "The men are going to burn off the patch near the river today," she said to her son. "They don't need your help, but I do. You can work the dasher on the churn."

"But, ma, that's women's work! Will said—"

"No buts, Amos."

"Oh, poo—"

"Don't you dare say that word again. What will Annie Lash think of you?"

Annie Lash couldn't keep a smile from her lips, but she turned her face away so Amos couldn't see it.

Working in a leisurely manner, the two women tidied the kitchen, all the while keeping up a steady stream of chatter. Callie told Annie Lash about the garden, the foodstuffs in the cellar and the smokehouse, and about the pigs to be butchered in the fall. She never mentioned her husband or her ordeal while living here alone after he left her. It was only later than Annie Lash realized that.

Annie Lash told Callie about her life on the Bank in Saint Louis and about Zan, the people they met on the raft and about how frightened she had been when she realized there was a man under the canvas on the mule.

"Jefferson said you've got spunk. He said you saved his life."

"I didn't even stop to think about it. I just did it."

"Thank God you did," Callie murmured.

"It sits hard on me. I never thought I'd take a life, especially without giving it any thought."

"By doin' it, you saved Jefferson. He's a good man. Him and Will are the best I've ever known," she said wistfully.

Annie Lash waited, hoping Callie would tell her more about Jeff and Will, but she changed the subject to canning and preserving.

Callie, with the baby on her hip, and Amos followed Annie Lash to the room across the dogtrot. Amos had finished the churning and carried the pail of buttermilk to the cellar after Callie removed the butter. He had decided it was rather nice to sit quietly and listen to the women talk. Even the things his mother said took on a new meaning when she told them to the pretty woman.

Callie spread a blanket on the floor for Abe and put a beanbag in his hands.

"Who's room was this?" Annie Lash moved her trunk out from the wall so she could open it.

"Jefferson uses it when he's here. He built this side for ... us. But it's handier for me to have the other room, so when I was here by myself I moved me and Amos into it and shut up this side." She picked up the picture Annie Lash laid on the bed. "Is this your mother?"

"Yes. Pa said it was painted by a traveling artist when she was sixteen."

Callie looked from the picture to Annie Lash and back again. "You favor her, but you're prettier. I guess you're about the prettiest woman I ever saw."

"Why, thank you. But I feel so big and ... gawky beside you!"

Callie's laugh rang out. "Ain't we somethin'? Standin' here braggin' about each other!"

"You don't mind me being here?"

"Well, at first. But not after I talked to Jefferson. Now I'm glad." Her smile disappeared. "It's been so lonesome."

"I know what it's like to be lonesome. I was. You don't have to be by yourself to be lonesome."

Callie looked around the room. "Where are you going to hang the picture?"

"Oh, I'm not going to hang it."

"Why not?"

"I'll only be here for a while. I can't put my things out. It would seem like I'm taking over this room, permanent like."

"Jefferson wants you to stay."

"I want you to stay, too." Amos spoke from beside the trunk where his busy eyes were taking in all the treasures inside.

"Thank you, Amos. Would you like to look at my picture book?"

"Oh, my goodness!" Callie exclaimed. "Are you sure you want him to hold it?"

"Of course, I am. I can tell by looking at him that he's a very careful boy."

"You can?" The boy's green eyes became round

with wonderment and a broad smile spread across his freckled face. He sat down on the floor and Annie Lash placed the book in his lap.

"My mother put together this book of pictures. They were sketched by the artist who painted her portrait. He spent the winter with the family, and this was his way of paying for his keep. If you take the top corner of each page between your thumb and forefinger, like this," she turned the page to show him how it was done, "you won't tear the pages. Now, you try it." She watched the boy's stubby fingers carefully turn the page. "I knew you could to it. I'll not worry one bit about my book as long as you're in charge of it."

Callie stood watching, holding the portrait hugged to her breast. Her eyes lingered tenderly on her son, then moved to Annie Lash with admiration and gratitude in their depths.

Annie Lash hung her dresses on the pegs beside her shawl and sunbonnet, then laid out her brush, comb, and small mirror. She placed her soap on the washstand and looped a towel over the bar alongside it, then closed the trunk and pushed it against the wall.

"There. That's done." She glanced around to make sure she hadn't taken more liberties than a guest should take in making the room her own.

"You don't plan to stay?" Callie asked quietly and placed the portrait on the bed.

"I don't know. I need time to figure out what's best for me. Zan...asked Jefferson to look after me, and he feels obligated to do it because Zan befriended him a long time ago, but—"

"Jefferson wouldn't do it if he didn't want to,"

Callie said. "He and Will are like that."

"Has he known Will for a long time?"

"Since they were boys. They're like what brothers ought to be like, what I hope my boys will be." She turned her face away, but not before Annie Lash saw the shadow of something like fear on her face.

"Jefferson said he had been gone for a long time. Was Will with him?" Annie Lash was sorry she asked the question. It wasn't her way to pry into someone else's affairs.

"Some men came here and asked Jefferson and Will to do somethin'. Jefferson wanted to stay here and work on the land, but whatever they had to do was awful important, so they left Henry and Jute here and went away. They came back about a month ago." She picked Abe up off the floor and sat him astride her hip. "Jason left a few months after Jefferson and Will. We were alone here for most of a year, except for the two black men."

"You must have been terribly afraid."

"Of Henry and Jute? Oh, my, no! We would've died but for them. They saw to it that we had food, and fuel to keep us warm. When Abe was coming, Jute went for Biedy in a raging blizzard and Henry stayed right beside me until she got here. I feel closer to those two black men than I ever did to my pa and brothers." She went to the door. "I'd better get the turnips ready to go in with the meat we're boilin'. Oh, but I'll be glad to have new potatoes and cabbage and turnip greens."

Annie Lash stood for a long moment looking

down on the top of Amos's head. Callie and she were not so different, she thought. They were both dependent upon the charity of Jefferson Merrick.

CHAPTER
TEN

Will stood with a rake and a gunnysack in his hand to beat back the flames should they jump across the break they had made at the edge of the field. The wind was gently pushing the fire toward the river where it would burn itself out. He wiped his grimy face with the sleeve of his shirt and leaned on the handle of the rake, his eyes sweeping the long grassy patch, alert for a sudden burst of flames that would need his attention.

He didn't know exactly when he had decided he wanted to homestead a piece of land for himself. Certainly not when Jeff filed on this place, or during the backbreaking labor of putting up the double cabin. It was while they were on the mission for Tom Jefferson, when each day that they lived to see sunset was a miracle, that he first started to think about a place of his own.

Jeff came toward him from the direction of the river. He had washed the soot from his face and it was a dull red from the heat of the fire. Will watched him approach. More than once his life had depended on this man, and he had great respect and affection for him.

"The fire's 'bout to peter out. It's been a good day for burnin'." Will made the comment just as Jeff reached him.

"This patch'll be ready to plow with a little raking."

"It's a sightly piece of ground. It'll make a good field for corn or oats."

"How much of your land do you plan to clear?"

"Enough to meet the requirements." Will grinned. "I figure on puttin' me a tradin' post on that high ground by the river and gettin' rich asellin' supplies to boat people."

Jeff didn't laugh as Will thought he would. Instead, he nodded thoughtfully. "It could happen."

Will moved down the line of the fire, beating at it with the gunnysack; Jeff followed.

"Light found out in Saint Louis that Jason spent the winter in New Orleans." Jeff squatted down on his heels and pulled at a blade of grass. "He's in Natchez. It appears to me he's headed this way."

"Light told me." There was a tense, angry tone in Will's voice.

"Light wouldn't think twice about slipping a knife in Jason's back if he thought you wanted his woman," Jeff said flatly, and got to his feet. He stood with legs braced, looking out over his land.

"I know that." There was an edge of irritation in Will's voice. "I'll not give him a reason."

"Callie might. She lights up like a full moon when she looks at you."

Will looked at him then, his mouth drawn tight. "She's obliged to me for helpin' her out, is all."

Jeff shrugged. "She's had a hell of a time with Jason. I don't want any more hurt piled on her."

"If ya think I'd hurt Callie—"

"You know I don't think that. I'm worried about what will happen if Jason comes back. She's his wife, man. Those are his boys."

"I'll not let 'im take her if she don't want to go. Hell! You and I know he'd leave 'er and the kids once he got 'em away from here." He rubbed the back of the rake with an angry motion over the flames that were eating the dry grass. "The gawddamn bastard married her to keep her ol' man from blowin' his head off. Brother to ya or not, Jeff, he'll not hurt 'er again." The eyes that looked into Jeff's were blue and hard and raging.

"Christ, Will! Are you in love with her?"

"Why in hell do ya say that?" he demanded, and looked away. "Callie and them boys ain't goin' to be sittin' in a shack on a river bank ever again awaitin' for that bastard to remember where he left 'em!"

Jeff stared into eyes filled with the unfamiliar gleam of hate. "Have you talked to Callie about it?"

"Naw."

"I have. She doesn't want Jason back. She told me so."

"What kind of woman'd take a man back after what he done? Goin' off and leavin' her like that in the middle of the winter, and her expectin'!

Shit, Jeff! Ya know he ain't worth the powder it'd take to blow him to hell!"

"Callie might figure he has a right to his boys."

"Shitfire! They don't even know 'im!"

"He's got a legal claim, despite what he did. It would be best all around if we raised your cabin, Will. It'll give Callie time to sort out her feelings before Jason gets here."

Will spread his legs and leaned on the rake. He looked defiantly into the face of his friend. "If he lays a hand on her, I'll kill 'im. Henry tol' me how he used her after we was gone. He said Jute come within a inch a doin' it on account a what he done to Amos. Jute would a killed him an' gone to live with the Osage, cause he couldn't a faced ya."

"I couldn't stand by and let you murder a man, Will. And not just because he's my brother. But I promise you this: he'll not abuse Callie or the boys while she's in my house."

"And if she leaves?"

"She's a grown woman. It's up to her. If she chooses to go I'll not stop her."

Will looked away from the sympathy in his friend's eyes. He knows, he thought, and hated himself for revealing his innermost feelings about Callie. All the beauty in life that he had ever dreamed of was summed up in her. His love for her, so long imprisoned, was escaping. It seemed to be thrusting outward and upward, demanding release. He had never so much as held her hand, yet he could feel it clasped in his own, could see the soft gleam of her hair in the firelight, the shadow of her lashes on her cheeks. He had resisted the temptation to step over the bounds of friendship, although he was almost sure his advances would have been welcomed. She had been lonely and it may have been that loneliness that made him seem desirable to her. He didn't want that! Gawd! What a trap he had fallen into!

"You know that they'll do everything they can to kill us before we can testify at Burr's trial." Jeff's voice brought him back to the present. "They know where we are, Will. I'm surprised they didn't ride in here, take care of you, and wait for me. That attempt to kill me on the trail is the third try since we delivered the evidence to Tom Jefferson. Without us, Aaron Burr will be acquitted of the treason charge."

"He's an ambitious bastard, and vicious," Will said coldly. "His murder of Hamilton proved that. He's out to set himself up a little empire in the South and Wilkinson will go along with it."

"Could be all that's standing in his way is you and me and Tom Jefferson."

"James Wilkinson is bein' used. You'd think the governor of the territory'd know better."

"It'll all come out in the trial this fall."

"If we live to get to Richmond," Will said dryly.

"That brings up another question. What about the women?"

"What about 'em? They're better off here than anywhere. They'll have Light, Henry, and Jute to look out for 'em. I'm glad ya brought the woman out to be with Callie." Will grinned and his eyes narrowed as he watched Jeff's face. "That's why ya brung her, wasn't it?"

"I guess at the start I was doin' it for Zan, then things changed. I got to thinking that I want a woman of my own, a son to carry on the Merrick name."

The grin left Will's face. "Ya think ol' Aaron'll be able to waylay us?"

"There's a good possibility he might. He's got some of the best in the business working on it. It would have happened back there on the way from Saint Charles if not for Annie Lash."

The brushfire was almost out. Only a few scattered patches smoldered, sending up wafts of smoke. The men reached the river and Will tossed his hat onto a wild plum bush and knelt beside the water to wash his face.

"Ya always shied away from gettin' hitched with a woman," he said when he stood back from the river's edge and ran his hands over his face to rid it of the water.

"They had their uses." Jeff's eyes searched the landscape, a habit of almost a lifetime.

"And this 'un? She 'pears to be a special kind a woman."

"She is. I guess I never thought I'd meet a woman like her. I don't know how to treat her, to make her feel comfortable with me."

Neither man spoke while they studied each other. Will's light brown hair had grown down to his shoulders and the mustache that curled down from his upper lip added a certain fierceness to his expression. Jeff, taller by half a head, clean shaven, with hair that clung to his head like the wool on a sheep, seldom showed to anyone other than this man the softer side of his nature.

Will nodded, as if in answer to something, and plucked his hat from the bush.

"I'm goin' to raise my cabin on that bare hill yonder, overlookin' the bend in the river."

"It's a good place near that stand of oaks, but a hell of a long way to drag the logs unless you're planning on using them."

Will laughed, slapped his hat against his thigh to rid it of ashes, and pulled it down onto his head. "It won't be like haulin' all that rock up from the river when we raised yores."

Jeff grinned. "I worked the hell outta you, didn't I?"

"Ya shore as hell did! We made a dandy cabin even if'n it did 'bout break my back."

"We can do the same to yours."

"Naw. A stout log cabin with a slab floor will do fine." He shifted his shoulders and loosened the strap which held the long rifle that had been riding on his back. The gun fit into his hand as naturally as a cane might fit the hand of another man. "Think Light will show up tonight?"

"Can't say. He was going to scout downriver. Did you notice he let the women think he was cutting trees?"

"It's good of him not to worry the women. I was hoping that when this was over he'd settle someplace, find himself a woman and some peace."

"His bitterness runs deep and he covers it well. We're fortunate that we, and not Burr, have his allegiance."

"He stops now and then at Simon's. He likes Fain, too, but he takes a special interest in that little 'un a Berry and Simon's. He fetched his Indian aunt to help in the birthin'."

"Nowatha is quite a woman," Jeff said with a

broad grin. "I think the first English words she learned were 'damn you.' I wonder what would happen if she'n Biedy got together."

"It might end in a hair pullin'." Will laughed. "I can't see either of 'em steppin' back fer the other'n."

They walked up out of a gully and the house was in sight. Jeff's eyes settled on it. It nestled cozily in the stand of oak and cedar trees. Thin, white smoke drifted from the kitchen chimney and lost itself among the towering branches. While he watched, Annie Lash stepped into the yard, Amos tugging on her hand. The boy spied them, broke loose, and raced toward them. She stood there, not moving, her gaze fixed on them.

"Will! Will! Guess what?" Amos reached them and danced alongside. "Annie Lash let me hold her picture book! She's got another one 'bout a man left on a island by some mean fellers. She's goin' to read the words. Her 'n ma is gonna make grape raisins 'n go berryin'! They'll put maple sugar in bars if'n Uncle Jeff'll slash a sugar tree. She said the Injuns call bees white man's flies, 'cause there warn't none till the whites come. All of 'em was tame; now they're wild and all over. Annie Lash said maybe we could find us a honey tree. She said—"

"Whoa, muley! Ya had better a day'n if ya come a burnin'. Tomorry ya go work with Uncle Jeff 'n I'll stay home 'n talk to Annie Lash."

"They're washin' tomorry." Amos screwed his face up in disgust. "I'll have to watch ol' nasty britches!"

Will laughed and clasped the small hand that

crept into his. Abe's growin' fast. This time next year he'll be a runnin' ya down."

"He won't! And he stinks!"

"So did you at that age."

"I never!"

"Shore ya did. Even yore Uncle Jeff did."

"Uncle Jeff did *it* in his pants, too?" He gazed up at his uncle, who was looking straight ahead at the woman standing in the yard.

"He didn't wear any pants. He lived in the woods with the grizzly b'ars."

"Ah, Will..."

Jeff didn't really hear the chatter going on beside him. All his senses were focused on the woman standing in his yard. This was something he'd always remember, he thought. Someday, when he was really old, when the living part of his life was done, he'd remember the way she looked at him that first day when he came home from burning the field to find her waiting with her quiet face turned toward him, the evening sun shining on her glorious hair, the gentle breeze pressing the skirt of her blue dress to hug her slender legs. Jeff was troubled by the thoughts that spiraled through his mind.

What is she thinking, he wondered, when she looks at me with eyes the color of a robin's egg? Does she hate me for what happened on the raft? Suddenly, he felt sick. Not physically, but in another way, worse than sick. Scared. This woman could take his heart, and more of his soul than a man could spare. She could be his only joy, his love, the all-consuming factor in his life. Everything had gone wrong. His plan was to take a woman, get a son from her, and that was all. All his dealings had been with women who knew their trade, loved nothing, wanted nothing but the coins he'd placed in their hands. His thoughts were an unwieldy jumble as he approached her. The urge to protect this woman was stronger than the urge to take what he was sure he could have by gentling her as he would a skittish mare. It was an odd feeling and it made him uneasy.

Annie Lash's first thought was to escape back to the house and the safety of Callie's presence when she saw Will and Jeff following the creek to the house. It took only a few seconds for her to reconsider and realize the absurdity of that first impulsive reaction. Now she waited with her hands clasped in front of her, holding fast to each other so they wouldn't fly up and smooth the hair that floated about her face. Her thoughts were so absorbed with the approaching men that she failed to notice the two that came from around the barn until Will raised his rifle over his head and hailed them.

"Henry! Jute!" Amos shrieked, running to throw himself at the young black giant of a man who caught him and tossed him in the air before settling him on his shoulders.

They were both huge men and it was hard to tell which was the father and which the son. Their skins were as black as any Annie Lash had ever seen; so black that her only impression was of white eyeballs and flashing white teeth. They wore homespun shirts and leather britches similar to Jeff's, and low moccasins on their feet.

"How's it goin', Henry?"

"Hit's a doin' good, Mista Jeff. Dat mule don' know he's a pullin' dat new plow." The man's huge black hands twisted the hat he'd removed when he saw Annie Lash. "Lawsy me, we's goin' to be done wid plantin' afore ya knows it."

"This is Miss Jester, Henry," Jeff said, then looked at Annie Lash. "Henry and Jute live down along the creek beyond the cottonwoods, yonder." He lifted his hand and gestured.

Annie Lash had never been introduced to a black before. She didn't know what to do, so she smiled and nodded her head.

The man's smile widened. "Missy," he said, and bobbed his head up and down a few times.

Callie came out of the house. "Jute," she yelled crossly, "I'm goin' to take a stick to you, if you don't stop spoilin' that youngun!"

Henry laughed. "Ya do dat, Miz Callie. Ya take a board to dat boy if'n ya wants. Ya ketch 'im. I helps ya hol' 'im down."

Jute started galloping around the yard with Amos shrieking and holding onto his short, woolly hair. Will shoved his rifle into Jeff's hands and lifted Abe from Callie's arms.

"Come to Will, boy. If yore ma's goin' to be takin' a stick to a body, it's best ya get outta the way."

Callie lifted her skirts and chased after Jute. Annie Lash stood in wide-eyed astonishment. Gales of laughter came from Will and Henry, who stomped his foot and shouted, "Get 'im, Miz Callie. Git dat boy 'n whack 'im!"

The realization suddenly came to Annie Lash

that this was a game that had been played many
times before. She laughed herself as she watched
Callie, a switch in her hand, try to catch up with
the young black man whose immense body
dwarfed hers. She couldn't have prevented the
laughter to save her life. It welled up in such an
overwhelming wave, she could hardly breathe. It
spilled from her lips while her eyes sparkled like
twin stars.

Jeff was frozen for a moment. The sound coming from Annie Lash seemed so strange. Then he
was laughing with her. He'd not heard her laugh
before, not this full voicing of amusement. He
watched her face and couldn't remember ever
hearing such a beautiful sound, or seeing such
utter delight on a woman's face.

The game ended without Callie having caught
the "culprit," and she came back to them panting
and smiling happily.

"I'm sending home a pot of turnips and fat back,
Henry. Don't let Jute have one drop!" Her teasing
eyes looked back over her shoulder at the grinning young giant. "Well ... maybe a cup."

"Dat all he gonna' git, Miz Callie. Dat all!"
Henry promised.

Now Annie Lash looked closely at the black
man. There was a kindness to his features, from
his wide, thick-lipped mouth and large flat nose
to his wide-set dark eyes. A few sprinklings of
gray edged his temples, but his expression and
physique gave proof that he was far from old.

She had watched the play with shock, then fascination, but also with the feeling of having taken

part. She no longer felt shy, and reached to take the baby from Will's arms before following Callie into the house.

Jeff's eyes followed her until she was out of sight. He stood quietly, his rifle butt and Will's resting on the ground.

"Mista Light comed to where I's plantin'," Jute said. "He tol' me to say dem folks yaw'll met up with on the river is squattin' ter other side of Mista Silas. He say dem is downin' trees, fixin' to build."

"Did he say if he was coming back tonight?"

"He say he a takin' off down de river. Dere's nothin' 'twixt here'n yonder, he say."

Jeff nodded gravely. "I had to tell Silas, after the attack on the trail, that the assassins were killers sent out by Burr to keep us from going back for the trial. He suspected that there was more to it than a killing for the goods on the wagons. He'll watch out for strangers roaming around and will send one of the boys over if he thinks there's reason."

"Dere ain't nothin' comin' on dis place less'n ol' dog know hit." Henry jerked his head toward a big, shaggy, dark-haired dog laying beside the shed, his large head rested on his crossed paws.

"That may be," Jeff said dryly. "But that dog is as wild as a wolf. I've not been able to get close to him."

"Ain't nobody c'n but Jute," Henry said. "Dat dog, he don' need nobody." The dog lifted and seated himself as if he knew he was being discussed. "He c'n smell Injin fer a mile, c'n heer a bird fly."

Amos darted from behind Henry and headed for the shed.

"Amos!" Jeff barked. "Stay away from that dog!"

Amos's short, stubby legs didn't stop until he reached the dog, whose head was level with his own. He put his arms around the furry neck and leaned on him.

Jeff started toward them, but was stopped by Henry's hand.

"Dat dog jump ya, Mista Jeff. Dat boy 'n Jute, dem is de ones. One time I seed de boy a layin' by de dog. I comed wid de gun 'n de hair rared up 'n he growled. Dat child, he git up 'n hug up to dat wild beasty. 'Hush yore mouth,' he say, 'n dat dog, he quiet down 'n switch his tail. I ne'er seed such."

"He won't hurt me, Uncle Jeff." Amos's small arms circled the dog's neck and his stubby legs straddled his back. "See? He likes me."

The dog stood perfectly still, but his black eyes were alert for any movement from the men.

"Maybe he does, but I'd feel better if you came away from him," Jeff said sternly. He glanced over at Will, who stood relaxed, his rifle cradled in his arms.

"Scared me crazy when I first saw it. Ain't it the damnest thing ya ever saw?"

Callie came out carrying a black iron kettle, a rag wrapped around the handle. She set it on the ground beside Henry.

"The bail is hot. Don't burn yourself."

"Hit smells larrupin', Miz Callie."

"Keep your eye on that blackberry patch, Henry.

Let me know as soon as the berries are ready and
I'll make you a cobbler."

"Dat I do, Miz Callie. I sure do dat."

"There's a crock of buttermilk in the cellar. Take
it when you go."

"What about us? Don't we got a cobbler?" Will
demanded.

"Find the berries, same as Henry, and I'll cook
you one." Her sparkling eyes met his in quick
exchange and her face reddened under his devilish gaze. She turned and made for the house.

The first day of May came and went. Everyone at
Berrywood worked from dawn to dark; Annie Lash
and Callie were busy with cooking, washing,
cleaning, and gardening; Will, Jeff, Henry, and
Jute labored in the fields, planting the new orchard or felling trees for Will's cabin.

Jeff made no attempt to speak with Annie Lash
alone, but more than once she found his eyes on
her before he turned abruptly away, and her heart
would throb painfully.

Coaxed by Amos, Annie Lash inaugurated her
bedtime custom of reading aloud from *Robinson
Crusoe*. Jeff sat in his armchair, legs outstretched,
and smoked. His eyes, dark and intent, seldom
left her face. Callie rocked the baby and Will
stayed in the shadows. When she finished a chap-
ter, Annie Lash would close the book, stand, say
good night, and go to the room across the dogtrot.

The days flew by.

May was warm and scented with blooms from
the wild honeysuckle growing in thick profusion

along the bank of the creek that passed through the pasture. Jeff had made sure, when he laid out the farm, that none of the runoff from the barnlots would reach the creek until after it passed the house. The spring-fed stream was swift, clear running, and cold every day of the year, according to Callie. Annie Lash found a spot where she could bathe and wash her hair. She longed to remove her clothes and plunge into the water, but she had to content herself with washing the lower part of her body under her skirts and the upper part while her bodice hung open. On these rare occasions, when her breasts were free from the confinements of her clothing, she would lift her arms above her head, stretch, and feel wonderfully free.

Jeff and Will announced one evening that the preliminary work on Will's cabin was completed and in two days' time they would be ready to raise the walls. It had taken the two men, with the help of Henry, almost a week to build a sled and haul the rocks up from the river to lay the foundation. Another week went into cutting and notching the trees; oak for the sills and walnut for the walls. Light, on one of his frequent visits, had been told to pass the word to the Cornicks.

The day before the cabin raising, Will brought in a giant turkey for the women to clean and bake, and Annie Lash made huckleberry pies for the feast in the middle of the day.

The Cornicks arrived just after daybreak. The wagon paused only long enough to let Silas lift Biedy down and set out a number of cloth-covered baskets. Annie Lash went out to help her carry in the food and to wave to the men who guided the team down the path toward the building site.

Biedy talked nonstop as usual. "Landsakes! Hit's a grand day for a raisin'. Isaac got the short straw'n had to stay back. He said he might amble over to Gentrys'. That's them folks that took up land the side a us. Hit's brothers what married up with sisters. You know, you met 'em on the river. They put cabins side by side, but each is on hits own ground. They're slouchy builders, so Silas says," she said in an almost whisper, as if someone would hear her criticism. "That's bread and fresh churned butter," she jerked her head toward the basket Annie Lash was carrying. "This'ns dandelion greens, all washed and ready for the pot. Got mincemeat cake, too. I had to leave a sliver for Isaac. Silas'll send one of the boys with the wagon afore nooning. I do love a cabin raisin'. We'd a helped them other folk, but they is still standoffish like. Where's that baby? Where's that little darlin' that's almost mine?"

"He's still asleep, thank goodness." Callie took the baskets from her hands, and Annie Lash took her shawl and bonnet and hung them beside the door.

"Stand right thar and let me look at you. She's just as purty as I thought, Callie. And you, girl, you look fitter than a flitter. Hit's the best I seen you look for a good spell. Hit was a cryin' shame how you wore yourself out! Now, which one of them is courtin' you, Annie Lash? Is it Jeff or Will? I swan to goodness, if'n there's anything I like better'n a cabin raisin', it's a birthin' or a weddin'. Last good'n we was at was when Berry married Simon Witcher. Oh, my! What a doin's. Isaac fiddled and we sang and clogged till it was a shame. We'll throw us a real doin's when you get married up, Annie Lash."

Amos came out of the bedroom rubbing the sleep out of his eyes with one hand and holding his wet gown away from his body with the other.

"Ma...I didn't mean to."

Callie went to him. "I know that. Let's get you out of this." She pushed him ahead of her through the door.

"You won't tell Will?"

"Of course I won't tell Will. Next time we'll make sure you go outside just before you go to bed."

"One of my boys wet the bed until he was waist high on his pa," Biedy said. "It ain't nothin' they can help." She lowered her voice to a whisper. "Callie ain't said nothin' 'bout the boy's pa comin' back? Why, that polecat! Hangin's too good fer the likes of him. I'd a filled his tail with buckshot, is what I'd a done. I tell you, Jeff was fit to be tied when he come home and found that skunk had run off, a leavin' her without no cut firewood or nothin'. I ain't never had me no use fer niggas, but them two, that Henry and his boy, they took over the doin' for Callie. They're a better lot than some white folks I know."

Callie came back with a subdued Amos, and Biedy burst into small talk. Annie Lash joined in. Callie cut the fresh bread for Amos and smeared it generously with blackberry jam. As he ate his spirits rose. By the time he finished his breakfast he was almost bursting with excited anticipation of the day's events.

Martin came with the wagon an hour before the sun was straight overhead. The women loaded the wagon with the prepared food, blankets, baskets of plates, mugs, and eating utensils. Biedy, Callie, and the baby got up in the wagon and Annie Lash and Amos walked ahead to open the gates.

The walls were already partway up when they reached the house site. It was a wonder to see how the eight men paired off, teamed up, and worked together so fast. Four men lifted a log, and two men at each end notched it, making the chips fly. It looked easy the way they did it, but Annie Lash knew the weight of those logs and how they had to be cut just right so they would lie straight and level.

The water for tea was put to boil over a make-shift fire. Biedy fussed and clucked over Abe while Callie and Annie Lash, being careful to keep out of the way, looked over Will's new home. He was inside the structure marking with a stick where the fireplace would go.

"Callie."

She turned in the door and looked over her shoulder. Annie Lash had started back toward the wagon. Callie paused. This was the first time she had been alone with Will since Jeff had come home. She stood just inside the partially framed doorway, her throat tight, her eyes locked with his.

"Do ya like it?" he asked, as if her answer was the most important thing in the world to him.

She nodded. "Is that where the fireplace will go?"

"Along this wall. I wanted to put a window on

the back, but thought it best to keep the back side solid."

She nodded again. "It'll be warmer without a window on the north. Safer, too."

"I left this side free so I can build on later." He walked through the chips and the shavings to the other side of the room. "I thought to build a dog-trot like Jeff's. What do ya think?"

"It's a good place for one. This will be a good, snug cabin." She spoke slowly, thickly, her voice trailing.

They heard the men shout as one of the Cornick boys, riding the mule, pulled another log up to be placed on the growing walls.

"Callie...it's yores anytime ya want it." Will's hand grabbed hers for an instant before he went out the door.

Callie stood with her face to the wall after he had gone. She had heard the quiver in Will's voice and felt the trembling of his hand as it touched hers. It was there. All the love and comfort she had ever dreamed of having was there. She had seen it in his face and felt it in his hand. Her eyes smarted with tears. *My love, my love.*

Annie Lash and Callie helped Biedy lay out the dinner. Biedy, in her sweet, melodious voice, ordered, commanded, and advised, and everyone obeyed. She kept the men laughing with her remarks. But when Henry and Jute hung back while the others came forward to fill their plates, it was Callie who ordered.

"Get yourselves on over here, Henry. I don't want to be messing around with you and Jute when I got the younguns to feed. Come on, now.

I'm not waiting all day for you to diddle around," she scolded. "Get some of that turkey and ham, Jute, and some greens. I know you like fresh bread and berry jam, so get some. Annie Lash made huckleberry pie outta the ones you brought up, Henry. I know you'll want some of that."

"Yas'm, Miz Callie. Yas'm." The two black men came shyly forward and filled their plates, then moved away to squat on the grass to eat.

Annie Lash had never seen black men eating with whites before, and she glanced at the Cornicks to see how they were taking it, but they seemed to be paying no more attention than if it was an everyday occurrence, and she breathed a sigh of relief.

Jeff came back to get another helping of huckleberry pie. His shirt was wet with sweat or from the dipper of water he had poured over his head before he came to eat. Annie Lash's heart began to surge; she couldn't speak, but smiled up at him. He was so handsome, with his unruly, bright hair and his dark face. Her eyes found his, and they were soft with amber lights. He smiled back at her, his face younger and free of the sober expression it had worn for days.

"Good pie," he murmured for her ears alone.

"Anything is good when you're hungry," she answered lightly, and was happy she could do so.

"I *was* hungry. The other stuff took the edge off my appetite. I'm going to crowd this in because it's good."

"It might make you sick."

"It would be worth it," he said with rockline certainty.

What was the matter with her? Annie Lash thought angrily after he had turned back to join the men. She was as giddy as a schoolgirl because he came and spoke a few private words to her. She worked swiftly, packing away the dishes and leftover food for the trip back to the house. But in a little corner of her mind she couldn't help wishing she had been clever enough to prolong the conversation.

CHAPTER
ELEVEN

June arrived and the weather grew warm, the air
sweet with the thousands of blooming bushes and
trees along the river. Sunny days were inter-
spersed with days of gentle rain. The weather was
of no particular concern to Annie Lash. She was
wrapped in her own brand of warm contentment.
Never in her life had she known companionship
and sharing as she knew it now, though fleeting
memories of Saint Louis and her life on the Bank
with Zan and her father still brought back the chill
of loneliness. The constant work of tending the
garden, harvesting the berries that grew so abun-
dantly in the woods, cleaning, cooking, and helping Callie by watching over the children kept her
whirling through the days with a song in her heart
and laughter on her lips.

Jeff and Will worked from dawn to dusk. The
evening meal was eaten by candlelight. The story

of *Robinson Crusoe* was finished, and if Annie Lash read aloud, it was from *Poor Richard's Almanac*. Jeff's eyes were on her frequently, softly dark and intent. He never withdrew his gaze when she looked full into them, but rather studied her openly as he had done on that night when he had come to the cabin on the Bank. Once she smiled deliberately and shyly when their eyes were holding and he returned the smile. It set her heart glowing. She dared not let herself wonder at his intentions regarding her. Often, when he romped with Amos, she would find herself gazing with longing at his broad shoulders, at the width of his chest, and remember the hardness of his arms and the tender way he'd held her on the day they buried Zan. It was strange, but she never thought about the other time he had held her, the time on the raft when she was sure she hated him.

The last of the shingles had been put on the roof of Will's cabin and soon he would be spending his evenings there. Annie Lash had noticed, during the first few days she was at Berrywood, how his eyes strayed to Callie. He was in love with her and she with him. It surrounded them in an aura that was unmistakable. She had watched the light flare in Callie's eyes when Will was near and noticed how he managed to keep his conversation light and teasing, although his eyes held a world of yearning in their depths.

Annie Lash was too sensitive to have missed the fact that Callie clung to her company as a shield between herself and Will. It had been particularly noticeable since the day they went to the cabin raising. All was changed between them.

Callie never directed any of her conversation to him, and there was a marked changed in the timbre of his voice when he spoke to her and in her response.

Annie Lash had no way of knowing if Jeff was aware of the emotional strain between his sister-in-law and his friend. Every night for the past week he had left the kitchen immediately after supper. And after the dishes were put away Callie would take Abe to the bedroom to nurse him and put him to bed. This night, while Will wrestled with Amos on the floor, Annie Lash slipped out into the near darkness of the dogtrot, deciding to give them some time alone.

She smelled tobacco smoke almost at the same instant she saw Jeff sitting on the bench where she had sat the first day she arrived. His long legs were stretched out before him and his white head rested against the dark logs of the house. She paused momentarily, embarrassed that he might think she was seeking his company. Then he spoke, and what he said surprised her so much that she walked directly to him.

"I was hoping you would come out." He was on his feet, holding his pipe in his hand.

"I don't like the end of the day. I like it to be daylight or dark." She didn't know why she told him that. What she wanted to say was that this was the most lonesome part of the day for one who was alone.

"Night will begin in a little while."

"Something ends, and something begins." She went to the end of the house and looked at the fading light in the west.

"The moon will be coming up soon. Last night I watched it come up over that clump of bushes next to the pines."

She tried to follow his gesture, then shook her head. "There are so many bushes, so many pines."

He moved behind her, and with his hands on her shoulders turned her slightly and pointed.

"Oh, those bushes. Why didn't you say the blackberry bushes? I know them well. I left some of my skin on them." There was laughter in her voice because she suddenly felt happy, young, and breathless.

"Would you like to watch the moon come up over the river?"

"Is it safe to be so far from the house at night?"

"I think so, although you can never be absolutely sure of anything." He knocked the ashes out of his pipe and left it on the bench. "It won't be long until we'll not be able to get near the river this time of evening because of the mosquitos. They swarm in almost as thick as hairs on a dog's back."

They followed the rail fence to the creek and then turned toward the river. When Annie Lash stumbled on the uneven ground and her hand went instinctively to his arm for support, he captured it with his and held it there, then eased it into the crook of his arm. She didn't deter him. For now she gloried in his touch and pushed away any thought that she would regret this impulsive behavior later.

"The flowers you planted beside Zan's grave are doing well."

"I didn't know you knew about that."

"Were you keeping it a secret?"

"No..." She drew the word out and peered up at him to see if he was teasing. She felt as well as heard the chuckle that came from him.

"I don't miss much that goes on around here. I even know you have a favorite place to bathe."

Annie Lash felt her heart jump out of rhythm, felt her blood pound and drain away. Her feet ceased to move and she tried to pull her hand from the crook of his arm, but he held it tightly to his side. He let out a snort of laughter and she thought she would die of embarrassment.

"I haven't been spying on you. Callie told me to stay away from that part of the creek one day when you were gone from the house."

"Well, my goodness! Why didn't you say that in the first place?" she said testily to cover her feeling of relief.

"Because I knew you'd get your hackles up. I haven't seen you mad for a while."

They continued walking. She thought he must have eyes like an owl. He held back branches so she could pass and one time he jumped down a bank, then reached for her and eased her down beside him. When they resumed walking he took her hand. His was large, rough and warm, and almost swallowed hers. They came out of the woods into a grassy clearing. The river was below them. They heard the plop of a large fish as it cavorted in the water. Behind them something scuttled in a thicket. To the right an owl glided between the branches searching for a meal. The night was alive with sounds and Annie Lash unconsciously drew nearer to Jeff.

"Catfish," he said, and led her to the edge of the bank. "We'll come down here sometime and throw out a line."

They were standing a good six feet above the river and Annie Lash drew back sharply when she realized they were so close to the crumbling bank. Jeff laughed softly and refused to release her hand.

"I didn't know we were nearly at the edge. I don't see as well in the dark as some. Zan said I had night blindness."

"I can see well enough for both of us. I could even see a snake crawling across the grass."

"Snake?"

Jeff could hear her sudden intake of breath and was instantly sorry he had conjured up her fear. She tried to suppress a shudder.

"I'm sorry! God, I'm sorry Annielove. There aren't any snakes here. They'd be out on the rocks, not here in the damp grass." His arm across her shoulder pulled her closer until she stood in his embrace.

The tender touch of his hands and the warmth of him verified all the concern his voice implied. It filtered through her fear slowly at first, and then burst upon her consciousness. He was giving her more comfort than anyone had ever given her, and he had called her "Annielove." How different it sounded from the first time he had used the nickname.

"Are you all right, now?" He bent his head until his lips were close to her ear. She could feel her hair drag on his chin when she nodded her head. "Turn around and look. You're going to miss seeing the moon rise."

Annie Lash could scarcely move. She was mesmerized by his gentle voice, drugged by the warm pressure of his hands. Her pulses were throbbing. She felt as if he were touching her everywhere. He turned her in his arms until she faced the river, then drew her back against him and folded his arms about her. Her hand rested on his folded arms and one of his moved to cover it. She stood there, hardly knowing where she was or what it was he wanted her to see, but fully aware that she wanted this closeness more than she had ever wanted anything before. She wanted to see his smile, hear the sound of his voice and his laughter. She wanted to know what he was thinking and what he dreamed about. She wanted to know why he was so hard on the outside when there was so much tenderness just beneath the surface.

Jeff felt her trembling, felt the pounding of her heart against his arm beneath her breast. He wanted to soothe her, calm her with gentle words, tell her not to be afraid, that he wouldn't rush her. But he remained silent and let his lips caress her hair. This feeling was new to him, too. He had thought about it for days, weeks; agonized over the decision of whether or not to speak to her about his feelings or just ask her again to marry him, bed her, and hope that before his life was ended he would have a son. Now he wanted more than to spawn an offspring so that his bloodline would be carried into another generation. Now, all the treasure he wanted, he held in his arms.

Other thoughts flashed through his mind as the red orb that was the full moon rose slowly above the river. Life on the frontier was perilous, his own doubly so due to Aaron Burr's determination to end it. Could he allow her to share the uncertainty of his future? He thought of the days ahead without her, and he damned himself for not wanting to face them without telling her the depth of his love for her, no matter what would come in the weeks ahead.

He shifted his body slightly to form a more comfortable cradle for her and she leaned her head back against his shoulder. The full moon shone on her face and he could see that she stood with eyes closed, her lips slightly parted, trying desperately to control her breathing. He was certain now that he held some part of her heart, and his own swelled with the need to comfort her. He turned her around to face him.

"Annielove," he drew the word out into a long, soft caress, "I've thought often of that kiss we shared the day I brought you home to Berrywood." She was trembling violently. Her teeth were clamped against chattering, but she couldn't seem to stop shivering. "What is it, sweetheart? Are you cold? Are you afraid of me?"

"It's nerves, I expect," she managed shakily, and drew in a deep breath.

He snuggled her against his chest and stroked her back leisurely. His need to soothe and protect her was far greater than his need to gratify his physical desire to plunder her mouth with his. Her arms crept around his waist, timidly at first, then stronger. Her trembling ceased and now unfamiliar sensations were prickling her body. She hoarsely whispered his name, her lips against his neck.

She didn't know she had moved her head until his mouth closed over hers and moved with supplicant precision until, unknowingly, her lips parted, yielded, accepted the wanderings of his, then became urgent in their own seeking. It was what he wanted, she could feel it in his response, in his muscles that flexed beneath her palms on his back.

Her mouth was warm, sweet beyond imagination, but he was wise enough not to spoil the mood by demanding more than the instant of sharing. He raised his head and looked down at her, his lips just inches from her lips, his breath on her mouth.

"I forgot to pucker my lips." There was no trace of teasing in his voice.

"So did I." Had she mouthed the words? She hadn't heard them, but she must have because he smiled, his arms tightened, and he held her in a protective, sheltering way. She could feel his heart beating against her breast that was pressed so tightly against his chest. He smelled of woodsmoke and she liked it. His mouth tasted of tobacco and she liked that, too.

They separated to look into each other's eyes. She found his face different from the way she remembered it. It was younger, happier. Gone was the stern, arrogant expression it had worn the night on the raft. His dark eyes ranged over her upraised face. She wanted his lips again; desperately wanted the sweet ecstasy of their possession. And when their lips met in joint seeking and need this time, she answered his demand by rising on her toes to press her mouth hungrily to his. Nothing had ever stirred her so. She wanted to give every inch of herself to comfort him, to satisfy his hunger. His hands roamed over her, caressing every inch of her back and sides. The long fingers of one hand cupped her round breast while his other hand shaped itself over her lean buttocks and held her to him. His hands, lips, and body were consuming her.

"Annielove, Annielove..."

His mouth moved and she felt the gentle stroking of his tongue over kiss-swollen lips that remained still and parted. The wet sweetness continued to lick, and caress, to feel along the sharpness of her teeth, to explore her inner lips, to withdraw only to enter her mouth again. She thought only of the sweetness, of the gentle, healing touch. He drew back a second time and his hand came up to the back of her head and cradled it.

"What's happened to us?" she whispered between quick breaths. Tears glistened in the corners of her eyes.

"Don't you know?" He kissed the soft skin of her temples, then moved to her eye and tasted the salty tear that hung there. "I've known for some time that there was something rare and wonderful between us."

"We're in love." They breathed the words together. Hers a question, his a statement.

She drew a deep, quivering breath and began to smile. Looking down into her wide, clear eyes, he laughed, intimately, joyously, lifted her off her feet, and swung her around.

With his face buried in the softness of her hair, his words tumbled over each other. "I love you, love you so much. You're so beautiful! I've not been able to think of anything but you. Do you really love me? Do you? You like my home? You like Berrywood? You'll stay and be my love!" His mind was empty of everything except her. "And I love you, love you, love you..." The words trailed off as his mouth traced the pattern of his love.

"Jefferson." His name came shivering and sweet from her throat.

Their lips caught and clung, released and smiled, caught again. Their kisses spoke not of passion, but of newly discovered love. His lips covered her face, stopping at each closed eye to feel the flutter of it, moved down her smooth cheeks to lips that waited, warm and eager.

"Say it, sweetheart. Say it."

"Jefferson...I love you." Her whispered words came haltingly.

He laughed and laughed and hugged her tighter. "Was it so hard to say?"

She squirmed and rubbed her ear against his shoulder. To her surprise a giggle bubbled out of her. "It's so new!"

"For me, too," he confessed huskily.

"When did you know?"

"The night you came here and told me you wanted to love and be loved, and that you wanted your man to be the other part of you...after we shared a real kiss." He took a strand of her hair between his fingers, one that had come loose from his nuzzling, and held it to his face.

The moon was well on its way across the sky and they had scarcely noticed it. An owl hooted nearby. Long habits of vigilance are hard to break, and Jeff lifted his head to listen. The call came again, and he relaxed.

Arms entwined, they moved back toward the house. When they came to the bank, Jeff jumped up to the higher ground, then reached down to pull her laughingly up and into his arms. They exchanged quick, sweet kisses before moving on. They reached the split rail fence and paused again. They stopped at the lilac bush and Jeff picked a blossom and tickled her nose with it. Never was a night so beautiful, nor air so sweet, nor a future so full of promise.

They sat down on the bench at the front of the house. Jeff wrapped his arm around her and fitted her shoulder into his armpit. Her thigh nestled against his thigh, her head fitted into just the right place on his shoulder.

"There's so much I want to say," she murmured.

"And I just want to look at you and hold you," he whispered and turned her to tuck her more closely against his chest, facing him so he could still see her expression.

"Thank you for bringing me here. I was so scared on the Bank in Saint Louis and on the raft at Saint Charles."

"I know." He feathered kisses on her forehead. "I'm sorry I was so rough. I know now I was fighting my feelings for you."

"I love it here. I love everything about Berry-wood. I want to stay here forever," she whispered, planting a kiss in one of the creases beside his mouth.

"And you shall—with me. Silas can marry us, or there's a magistrate in Saint Charles." There was so much tenderness in the look he gave her and in the timbre of his voice that she blinked back the tears and smiled at him.

"I...think I'd rather it be Silas."

"We'll wait for a while. Light will be back in a day or two and we'll have him spread the word. We'll ask the MacCartneys and the Witchers and the folks we met on the raft. They're building on the other side of the Cornicks." He pushed the hair back from her temples. "Take it down," he whispered.

"Now?"

He laughed. "Shall I do it? The first time I saw you it lay along your shoulders and down your back. I thought you were the prettiest woman I'd ever seen." His hands were carefully searching for the pins. "And there you stood, holding my gun on me!" His words teased her, his eyes loved her.

"Jefferson! Be serious. Tell me about Light. He comes and he goes. I asked Callie about him and she said he scouts to be sure there are no hostiles about. Does he have a home? Someone to care about him?"

"For the last few years his home has been wherever Will and I are. Light is a wild, free man. He lives the way he chooses to live."

"It must be a lonely life." She lifted her hand to his cheek. "You shaved tonight."

"I shaved every night, hoping you'd come out." He turned his lips into her palm. "Now I think I'll grow a beard. I won't have time for all that shaving." He loosened her hair from its braid and carefully combed his fingertips through it.

She became braver and trailed her fingertips up and around his ear, then through his hair. It was thick and clung to her fingers. She laughed with pure joy and wonderment. He remained still, his eyes devouring her.

"Oh, Jefferson ... I didn't know it would be like this," she breathed.

"Like what?" His face nuzzled her hair, her neck, behind her ears. "Talk to me sweetheart. I want to know your thoughts, your hopes, your dreams. I want to be the other part of you."

"You are. Oh, you are! I just feel so light and feathery. Just as if I could flit about like a butterfly, as if I could sing like a bird, but as if I could move mountains, too, or hold back a river. Do you think that sounds silly?"

"Silly?" He took her hand and slipped it inside his shirt and placed it over his heart. "Feel my heart pounding. I've crossed mountains, ridden the rapids, and fought Indian wars, but none of it made my heart jump with fright so much as the thought that you might not like it here, that you might not like me. I thought of a hundred different ways to keep you here. I knew that Light or Will would take you back if you really wanted to go."

The rhythmic thump of his beating heart

pounded against her palm. Her fingers were flattened against the hardness of his chest and now they curled, gently, into the soft golden down that covered it and found a small hard nipple to examine curiously. He took a quick breath and settled his mouth on hers. He kissed her with hunger, taking care not to bruise her lips as he had done on the raft. His ragged breath was trapped in her mouth by his plundering kiss. Her fingers continued to move over his chest, and had she been able to think clearly, she would have wondered at the trembling of his body. He moved his mouth from hers and took great gulps of air.

"Annielove, Annielove...I'm afraid I'll not be able to wait for the gathering of our friends before I take you in all the ways a man takes the woman he loves. You're so sweet, so soft, and I love you so much."

She moved the hand inside his shirt up to his throat and rested it there. "I don't know much about men except what I've heard women talk about," she said softly, calmly, and was astonished she could speak to him about such things. "I heard only one woman, my mother, say that what happens between a man and a woman in love is beautiful."

"What did the others say?" he asked in a hoarse whisper.

"They said it was a woman's duty to accept a man inside her and it was best to do it and get it over with. But my mother said I was conceived out of love, not duty. She told me this a long time ago when she realized she'd not live to see me a grown woman."

"Ah...I was such a fool that night on the raft. It's no wonder you wouldn't look at me or speak to me for days. It took all the courage I had to ask you to marry me, and when you refused so bluntly, my pride was hurt. I knew then I wanted you more than I had ever wanted anything. And later, after you faced the renegade and I realized he could have just as easily turned his gun on you, I almost died of fright."

She closed her eyes against the intense look on his face and he bent to kiss her eyelids, then her cheeks, forehead, and lips.

The moon passed over the pines, arced overhead, and still Annie Lash and Jeff sat on the bench. He wrapped her in his arms to shield her from the cool night air and they whispered to each other their innermost thoughts, hopes, and fears— all except the one Jeff held back, the one that he'd not tell her until the very last.

"Jefferson," she whispered after numerous tender kisses, "what about Callie? I think she's in love with Will. Not that she's ever said anything. But I can tell by the way she stays with me when he's around. She's afraid to be alone with him."

"I know, sweetheart. Will loves her, too. It's a mess they'll have to straighten out. Now that I have you, I know what hell Will is going through. Callie deserves better than my half brother; but she's married to him, and he may come back to claim her and the boys most any day now."

"Will she go with him?"

"I don't know. But if she wants to stay, I'll see to it that she stays."

"I wish she could be as happy as I am."

"Are you happy, Annielove?"

"Oh, yes!"

"I can make you happier," he promised huskily.

"Hummm..." She didn't sound totally convinced.

CHAPTER
TWELVE

Callie stood hesitantly in the doorway of her room. "Where's Annie Lash?" Her voice trembled as she asked the question.

"She went out a minute ago." Will lifted Amos off his chest and got to his feet. He could hardly bear to see the look of panic on her face.

"It's bedtime for you, Amos." She spoke to the child more sharply than she intended.

"Ah, Ma..."

"Don't give me any back talk. It's your bed-time."

"Will was goin' to show me how to fight. I don't want to go to bed!"

"You're goin'. You almost fell asleep over your supper."

"That was afore Will—"

"That's enough!"

"But I gotta pee first."

"Amos!" Callie was sure she was going to cry.

"Now what'd I do?" The boy's chin quivered, but he lifted it stubbornly.

"You know what you did, and you know what you'll get for it!"

Big tears filled the green eyes staring defiantly up at her. "You're mean! You said not to say *poot*, you didn't say not to say *pee!*"

Callie groaned inwardly and tried to ignore her son's pleading eyes and quivering lips. Color came slowly up her neck and turned her cheeks crimson. Her eyes went to Will as if drawn there. The candlelight showed his face clearly. His mouth, so grim of late, was slightly parted and tilted at the corners, his eyes were warm and bright and watching her intently.

"I'll take him out." Will's big hand rested on the top of the cotton-white head.

"I ain't got to poot, Will. Just pee. Ma lets me do it by the house at night. If'n I got to poot, I got to go—"

"Amos!" Callie felt the hot blood pounding in her face and was sure that she was going to melt and run all over the floor.

"C'mon, cottontop. We'd better get outta here afore yore ma takes a stick a wood to us." With his hand on the child's back, Will urged him toward the door.

"Will my hair be brown like yours when I get big, Will? I'm gonna have me a mustache like yours. Ma said if I eat lots I'd grow up to be big like you, but she said I'd better not swear like you or I'd get a hidin'. She said..."

Will looked back over his shoulder at Callie.

She was staring straight ahead, her cheeks red, her hands buried in her apron pockets. He carried the image of her anguished expression with him out into the darkness.

Callie sank down on the bench beside the table. She sat there, feeling an aching torment, suddenly tired and bewildered, depleted of all her strength. She had been so nervous and strung out she could hardly think since the day, in his half-finished cabin, Will had grasped her hand and whispered to her. All she had ever yearned for was there in that gentle man. She felt a tiny thrill at the thought of that cabin being her cabin, that man being her man, but it faded quickly in the face of logic. She had a man, sorry as he was. He was the father of her boys, and for that reason alone she couldn't wish him dead, even if that was the only way she would ever be free to go to another man.

The image of Will's sun-bronzed face with its neatly trimmed mustache, high cheekbones, well-formed nose, and sharp but kind blue eyes floated before her. He wanted a woman, a home, and a family. Could she bear it if he took another woman to that cabin?

"Will said for me to say I'm sorry." The sound of the child's voice startled her. "He said mas have 'nuff to do without havin' to make men outta boys like me. He said it was a man's job. I asked him to do it, 'cause I ain't got no pa."

Callie looked up into the face of the man standing beside her son, and his eyes looked down into hers as if he could see straight through her and read her innermost thoughts.

"You have a pa, Amos. He's just not here."

"I don't want *him* for my pa! I don't like him. He's a old...pissant! I don't want him ever to come back. If he does, I'll go stay with Jute and Henry. I wish Will was my pa. He'd show me how to be a man!"

"Amos, please—" The words choked in Callie's throat.

"Get goin', young scutter." Will gave the boy a gentle push toward the bedroom. "Get yourself ready for bed. The first step to bein' a man is to not depend on yore ma to do everythin' for ya."

"You'll wait so I cin say good night?"

"If'n it's a'right with yore ma."

"I'll hurry, Will. I'll hurry!" The last words came from the bedroom.

"Don't wake Abe." Callie didn't know if she said the words or thought them. All she really knew was that Will was standing there looking down on her head.

"Do ya want me to stay away from the boy, Callie?"

"No!" The cry of protest came straight from her heart. She was on the verge of tears. Her mouth trembled and she blinked rapidly to keep the tears from disgracing her. "It... would break his heart."

"I don't want to cause ya worry," he said softly.

"I know." She sat stone still, willing the tears back until she was alone.

"I'm ready, Will."

Callie was afraid to look at her son, afraid he would see that she was about to cry. They had spent some agonizing times together before and after Jason left them, and he had become sensitive to her moods. He went straight to Will and was lifted up into his arms. Callie glanced up and an emotion rose up in her as acute as pain when she saw the loving look on her child's face as he looked at the man who held him.

"Tell yore ma a good night."

"Night, Ma."

"Good night, son."

"C'n I go to your house tomorry, Will? I'll pick up chips. C'n I hold your knife? I'll be careful."

"Shhhh...ya'll wake up Abe."

Callie sat in troubled silence while Will took Amos to bed. She hadn't counted on her life being disrupted in this way. All she'd ever wished for in life after Jason left her was to live here with her boys and work to pay for their keep. She wiped the tears from her cheeks with her fingers, knowing only vaguely that she wept. Why was she so dissatisfied? Why did she ache for this man she couldn't have, and why didn't her common sense come forward and take hold as it had always done in the past when she was in a bind and didn't know which way to turn? Will was the finest man she had ever known, him and...Jefferson. They had taken her and Amos out of a shack down on the river and had brought them here to this grand place. What if Jason came back and forced her to go away with him? It was a thought that filled her heart with terror.

"Why're ya cryin'?" Will was there, kneeling beside her.

"I'm not."

He lifted a finger and gently wiped a tear from her face. "Is it 'cause yore 'fraid Amos is gettin' too attached to me?"

"No. He's been happy since you came." She swallowed hard, fighting back the tears.

"Then is it 'cause of what I said that day? Ya've been like a drop a water on a hot griddle since then. Ya don't even look at me no more." He studied her face, the sparkle of tears on her lashes, her trembling mouth. "I jist wanted ya to know that ya and the boys'll always have a place. Ya don't need to be worryin' 'bout goin' back to that other way a livin', if'n ya don't want to."

She looked at him then, her eyes wet, her vision blurred. "You'll want a wife and boys of your own ... someday."

"Yes, I want that, but not just any wife," he said softly.

She refused to acknowledge anything personal in his words and rushed into speech.

"Jefferson will be wanting his home for Annie Lash." She regretted the words instantly, and longed to recall them. He'd think she was hinting for something. Her hands played nervously with the fabric of her apron.

"Does that bother ya, Callie?" Will was still squatting on his haunches beside her.

"Jefferson would never ask me to go, and Annie Lash wouldn't hear of it, either!" He was relieved to see she showed some spirit. "Annie Lash is just right for Jefferson. I want him to be happy. I owe you and him so much."

"I want you to be happy. I don't want ya to worry about Jason comin' back 'n takin' ya away from here."

"I don't think there's much danger of that. He

don't want us," she said scornfully. "We don't want
him, either!"

They stared at each other for a moment that
was so still that it seemed time had stopped moving. Then slowly, haltingly, Will got to his feet
and stood towering over her. He held out his hand
and hers went into it. He pulled her to her feet.
She looked at him searchingly. The pale light from
the candle flickered over his dark face. His thick
lashes made fans over his eyes, but she knew they
were focused on her face.

"Come live with me in my cabin, Callie. Let
me be a pa to yore boys."

She wasn't sure she'd heard him correctly. Then
the full import of the shocking words reached her
dulled brain. She looked at him and a trembling
set in. "Oh, Will!"

"I'll take care of ya and the boys for as long as
I live. Even after, ya'll be took care of."

"Will, I couldn't!"

"Ya don't care 'bout me?" he asked in a hoarse
whisper.

Her hands went to his chest of their own accord.
"It isn't that!" She was crying on the inside. "Oh,
Will! You know it isn't *that*."

"I built that cabin for ya, Callie." His hands
were on her arms. "If ya don't want to live in it
with me, it's a'right. It's still yores."

"Don't feel sorry for me!" Her words came out
on a strangled sob.

"Feel sorry for ya? Gawddamnit! I love ya, ya
crazy woman. I've loved ya e'er since I saw ya
sittin' in that hovel, so clean 'n proud, holding

yore boy in yore arms. I wanted to kill Jason Pickett, would've if he'd not been brother to Jeff." A
sound, half groan, half sigh, exploded from him
and he snatched her into his arms. "I want ya,
girl, 'n I don't care what I got to do to get ya."

Callie's breath left her in a sudden rush. Her
hands, trapped between them, could feel the
thunderous pounding of his heart. The moment
quivered with tension. Sometime during those
tense seconds she lost all caution and a fierce
desire to comfort him swamped her. She struggled
to free her hands and slid them around him, pulling him to her.

"Sweetheart... Darlin' Callie! I don't want ya
to be hurt ever again," he said against her hair.
He tilted her face so he could look directly into
her eyes. "Ya care for me. Ya do!" Relief made his
voice husky.

The first gentle touch of his lips awakened a
poignant longing in her to satisfy the hunger in
this man who had been all things to her except
lover. Although his lips were gentle, they en-
trapped hers with a fiery heat that flamed her
cheeks and spread down her throat. The soft brush
of his mustache against her cheek, the tobacco
taste of his mouth, and the hard strength of his
embrace made her head swim. She was dreamily
aware when his hand traveled down her back to
her hips to press the full length of her to him.

His kiss was long and deep. His lips seemed
unable to leave hers. When they did it was to trail
up over her cheek to her eyes. He was trembling
violently when he lifted his head and looked into
her shining eyes.

"I've waited...a long time to do...that." His voice quivered with the power of the emotion he was feeling. "Sweet, sweet Callie," he whispered and leaned his head forward to kiss her reverently on the forehead.

"Oh, Will! We shouldn't!" Her voice was grief-stricken.

"Why shouldn't we? I love ya!"

"Someone will see, will know."

He held her away from him. "I don't care if the whole gawddamn world knows!" he said urgently. "I want everyone to know that yo're mine. Come live with me in my house. Be my wife, Callie."

"You know I can't do that! What would people say? What if Jason came back?"

"I'd kill 'im." He spoke with cold finality.

"No! I'll not let you dirty your hands on him! I could never come to you if you killed him so I'd be free." She buried her face against him. "What can we do? Oh, Will, I know I shouldn't tell you, but I love you so much. I'd give my life if I knew my boys would pass into your hands to raise. Amos loves you. He was only four years old when Jason was here, but...he saw enough, was punished enough, so that even now he wakes up in the night screaming. I won't let that happen to him again, Will. He was so afraid—"

"My sweet, sweet woman..." He cradled her to him and rocked her gently. "It won't happen. I promise ya it won't happen agin. Come sit with me. Let me hold ya, just for tonight." As they went past the table he pinched the flame from the candle. The narrow bunk attached to the kitchen wall was straight ahead. When they reached it, Will sat and pulled her down across his lap.

She went to him like a small child and nestled against him, her wet face pressed in the curve of his neck. He wrapped her in his arms with tender strength, murmured love words in her ear, and nuzzled his face in her hair. The warm safety of his arms was heaven!

Callie didn't want to talk. She only wanted to be close to him, savor the delight and enjoy the wonder of being held by him. She wanted to forget everything that had happened before this night, and refused to think about what would happen tomorrow. She felt fatigued and weakened by the emotional ordeal of the last few weeks. Minutes passed without words. Will kissed every part of her face. The sweetness of his touch caused tears to gather in her eyes. He tasted them on his lips.

"It's goin' to be a'right, darlin' girl," he crooned as if to a child. "What happens from here on out will be ahappenin' to both of us. We'll weather it. Ya'll see." He leaned his back against the wall and moved her closer into his arms. He tucked her skirt down over her legs and her hair back behind her ears.

Callie couldn't remember ever being held so lovingly or comforted so tenderly. This strong, hard man was holding her as gently as he would a baby, and her heart swelled with love for him. She kissed his neck, his chin, his rough cheek. His head bent and he carefully sought her lips. The kiss lasted for a long time and was full of sweetness. She sighed his name.

"I was hungry for that. I'm hungry for the feel

of ya. Gawd! It's been a lifetime since I touched yore hand. I won't be able to stay away from ya, now. Don't ask me to. I've got to hold ya, love ya, kiss ya." His humbled voice vibrated with emotion.

Her arms moved up and about his neck and she raised her lips. He took them gently, lovingly, explored them with his tongue, parted them, nibbled. He began to tremble and the pressure of his mouth increased. His hand moved up and he threaded his fingers through her hair. She could feel that his body was demanding more now than the gentle touch of her lips, but still he held back.

"Callie, darlin', I promised myself I'd just hold ya," he whispered hoarsely and rained fervent kisses on her face. "But, Gawd help me, I want more!"

She cuddled up against him, her head in the curve of his shoulder, her arm about his neck. His skin was cool, his hair soft and silky, his breath ragged and uneven. She reveled in a happiness that was beyond anything she'd ever dreamed about; feeling loved, secure. She wanted with all her heart to take away the hunger that tormented him. It would give her a deep satisfaction to give him so much pleasure.

His lips moved over her face and neck, his mouth soft and warm and almost unbearably pleasurable. His hand moved beneath her loose shirt and cupped a firm, full breast. The pressure of his long fingers started the milk to flow. She felt a moment of panic, and then a low, soft moan came from his throat.

"I envied the babe the havin' of these. Darlin'

girl, I was awishin' it was me. Sweet girl...let me..."

With trembling fingers, she opened her bodice and pressed his lips to the soft skin of her breast. His lips kissed the smooth flesh while she brushed the hair back from his face. The soft tug of his firm lips and tongue, rough and wet, on her nipple was the most pleasurable feeling she ever experienced. Never had she imagined a man being so gentle, never in her life had she been stirred like this! She could feel the milk leave her body and fill his mouth, could feel the moan in his throat as she hugged him to her breast. Then, as if the sweet ecstasy of her breast could no longer satisfy him, he raised his head and moved his open, demanding mouth to hers. He clutched her so tightly to him that she felt the milk from her naked breast wet his shirt.

His mouth was sweet and wet. He kissed her deeply, but lovingly, always holding back, trying not to devour her. He cradled her, rocked her, longed to be inside her and satisfy the urge that had tormented him for so long. His mind told him to leave her and end the torture, but he couldn't bring himself to draw away from her.

Callie stirred in his arms, seeking desperately for words to tell him that she knew of the struggle going on inside him, and that she wished with all her heart she could open herself to him and ease the pain that throbbed in his loins.

"Will...I want to, but I can't! Darling, Will, please understand." She grabbed his hand and guided it to the bulky cloth, looped and pinned over the string that encircled her waist. Oh, please know and understand, she pleaded silently. Know that I want you, too, but for this night and the next few nights, this is all we can have.

At first the feeling was disappointment, then an awareness of what she was trying to say without words dawned upon him, and he remembered seeing the stained cloths drying on the bushes well away from the house. Sexual desire left him as a flood of compassion for this precious girl swamped him.

"It's a'right, darlin'. It's enough to know that ya want me. Our time will come, 'cause I'm not a leavin' ya, ever." He pulled her face close to his neck and moved his chin across her cheek. The sweetness of it brought tears to her eyes.

Will sat there, holding her gently, rubbing her back, and his life, meaningless and empty up to now, danced crazily into his thoughts. He was the bastard son of a wealthy, influential man, a man greatly loved and respected. How did he know that fact for sure? He had his mother's word on it, and the sum of money paid into his accounts by the man who sired him. He'd never really belonged anywhere, been loved by anyone except his mother. He had been a friend to Jeff and Light, adventure and danger his only pleasure. Now he had this woman and her children. By God, nothing would take them from him; not Jason Pickett, not Aaron Burr's henchmen, and not Thomas Jefferson! He was going to live here on this land with this woman, be a father to her boys, and sire some of his own.

Will's ears, attuned to the night sounds, picked up the murmur of voices. He listened, then smiled with lips against Callie's face.

"Darlin'," he whispered. "We're not the only ones courtin' tonight. Jeff an' Annie Lash are on the porch."

It was nearer to dawn than to midnight when Will opened the door and stepped into the dogtrot. When one lives in the wilderness one acquires a quality of stillness and learns to listen. He stood with his back to the building, absorbing the sounds. He had cultivated the art of listening. There is never complete silence, and one learns to distinguish between the sounds such as birds rustling after food among the leaves and squirrels scrambling in the branches. He heard both of these sounds and yet another. It was the sound of light, running footsteps.

Will sidled to the end of the dogtrot, blending into the shadows. Now he heard faint, panting breaths. The runner had stopped. The moon was shining brightly and he didn't dare move from the shadow of the house. He stood waiting, his hand on his knife, carefully scrutinizing every shadow, every clump of brush between the house and the woods.

A slim shadow at the edge of the woods caught his eye. It jumped lightly from one shadow to the other, staying close under the trees. He watched, fascinated as the human figure flitted across an open space, coming even closer to where he stood beside the house. Not even Light could move so lightly and so swiftly in the darkness. Will had no time to think of what or who it was. He scarcely breathed as he waited to see what the creature would do.

He knew the instant his presence was known. The creature froze, hunkered down, and waited. It was no more than two dozen paces away. The stillness was almost complete. Will decided to wait a moment longer. He heard a sharp intake of breath and then a small hiss. The hissing sound came again, urgently, and still he waited.

"Mister."

Gawdamighty! It was the voice of a woman or a child. Even realizing this did not lessen his caution. He remained perfectly still, his eyes glued on the small figure squatting beside the bush.

"Are you Will or Jeff?" The slim shadow stood, poised for flight.

"Who are ya?" Will whispered.

"I got a message from Light."

"But who are ya?"

"Maggie."

"I'm Will. C'mon out where I c'n see ya."

Maggie hesitated for a second and then raced for the shadow of the house. She was as tiny as a child, but her long, flowing hair and rounded breasts beneath a tight cloth shirt said she was more woman than child. She wore britches tucked into knee-high moccasins.

"I'm Maggie," she said in a voice that was barely a whisper.

"Where're ya from?"

"Over yonder, t'other side a the Cornicks." She waved her hand toward the woods. "Light told me ta come and tell ya he's watching men on the trail from Saint Charles, and two more're comin' upriver by canoe."

"Does he think they're comin' here?"

"They travel by night. They be comin' here."

"He sent ya through the woods to tell us this?"

"He knows I c'n find my way. Light's very much a man. We meet at night. I'm a goin' ta be his woman," she said proudly.

"Ya've been here before?"

"The dog didn't bark." She laughed softly, musically. "He don't bark if I come at night, but he barks when Light comes. I laugh at Light fer this. I got to go now."

"Wait. Who're the men Light is watching?"

"Light don't tell me. He says they're bad men. He may kill them." She jerked her head toward the river. "Light says they're a comin' to kill you."

"Tell Light that we'll be waitin' for the men in the canoe."

Will knew it was useless to ask her to stay. Somehow he knew she was as wild and as free a creature as Light. He watched her speed across the clearing and disappear into the woods. It was like watching a wood nymph from a story he had heard long ago.

After she had gone, he circled the house and tapped on Jeff's window, then stood beside the door and waited for him to open it.

CHAPTER
THIRTEEN

Jeff caught the horses and the mules and put them in the fenced area next to the barn while Will went to get Henry and Jute. Both men knew Light well enough to know he wouldn't have sent the girl through the woods to warn them if the danger wasn't real. Jeff had told Will about meeting the settlers on the raft, but he had failed to tell him that, even then, he thought there was something curiously different about the girl. It didn't surprise either man that Light hadn't mentioned the girl on any of his frequent trips to Berrywood.

Henry and Jute appeared, suddenly and quietly.

"Will and I have got to go downriver, Henry. Keep an eye out and don't let anyone near unless you know them."

"We do dat, Mista Jeff," Henry said. "Jute, tak

dat ol' dog 'n sit yo'self down by de smokehouse. Me, I hide me out on de utta side."

"I think the women were goin' to wash today. Tell 'em not to start till we get back," Will said.

"I do dat."

The hour before dawn is the quietest time of night in the wilderness. Jeff and Will took off in a trot toward the river, their running steps scarcely breaking the silence. No words were needed between these two men who had faced death together more times than they had fingers and toes. Each knew he could count on the other in any situation. Will was leading the way and veered off into the woods before they reached the river. Several times they stopped and listened. Their ears were trained to tune out the usual noises, ignoring them. It was the strange sounds they listened for, or the lack of the normal sounds. Each time they stopped they would wait patiently to see if the insects would begin their singing again, or if something other than themselves was near, something not known or understood by them.

The ground began to slope down gradually and they followed a gulley, leaping over rotting logs. When they left it, they came up the other side and took a well-worn game trail. They trotted eastward and came out on a bluff overlooking the river. When they stopped, Jeff touched Will on the shoulder. Both men had heard the rhythmic splash as a paddle hit the water. Silently, as shadows, they moved down through the thick stand of oak and ash trees toward the river. Instinctively, Jeff knew where the men would beach the canoe.

They had passed bluffs all along the river's edge, and in the faint light they would see only bluffs ahead of them.

Waiting was something Jeff and Will were used to doing. Standing shoulder to shoulder, they watched the river patiently. The shadow that was the canoe turned toward shore as they expected it to do. It never entered Jeff's mind that the men were on any mission other then to kill him and Will. Burr must be getting desperate, he thought, to send such unskilled hunters to do what two groups of assassins had failed to do. The men were rivermen. That was evident from the way they handled the canoe, their cloth clothing, and the knit caps on their heads.

The canoe was pulled up out of the water, turned over, and the oars stored underneath.

"I ain't a budgin' from here till daylight. I ain't traipsin' off through them woods not a knowin' where I'm goin'."

"All ya've done is bellyache! I wisht I'd a ast Farnan to come 'stead a you."

"I wisht ya had. I ain't a likin' none of this here."

"Ya'll be likin' yore part of the purse," the smaller man sneered.

"Ain't no purse gonna do me no good wid my gullet slashed," the other grumbled. "'Sides, ya ain't set eyes on 'em. How're ya gonna know 'em?"

"I ain't got me no worry 'bout that. I heared the man say bring the scalp of the white-haired bastid, and the upper lip of the other'n and he'd pay."

"Wal... soon's it gets daylight we kin walk in a sayin' we's lost. Seems like hit's jist too easy."

They sat down on the overturned canoe. Both men took guns from their belts and checked the load.

Jeff motioned to Will and they moved back among the trees. Will was grinning. He reached up and stroked his mustache.

"I didn't know this hair on my lip was so valuable."

Ordinarily, Jeff would have laughed with him, but his life had suddenly become so precious to him that he couldn't laugh off the threat to it even if it was from the two fools beside the river.

"We'll face them before they get in the woods."

"Why face 'em? Call out 'n shoot the bastards," Will said coldly.

"We'll give them a chance to back off."

"Back off? Christ! They'll back off 'n come at us again. That ain't all, they'll spread it up 'n down the river there's a purse for my lip 'n your scalp! We'd have every cutthroat from here to New Orleans a lookin' for us."

"I know you're right, but I don't like killing if I don't have to. I'd like to find out who the agent is that's paying the purse."

"One of 'em said he *heard* the man say to bring the scalp. That means he overheard the agent hirin' someone else to do the job. These two bastards are a tryin' to jump the gun on 'em and get the reward." Will took his gun from his belt and moved his knife around into position.

"So we've got some others back up the trail," Jeff said wearily. "God! It'll never end!"

"That's the one thing we can be sure of," Will said with a twitch of a smile. "It'll end. We got to be sure it ends the way we want it to."

They returned to the river, separated, and hunkered down out of sight to wait for daylight. Light from the eastern sky soon dispelled the gloom of dawn and the rivermen got up to pull the canoe into the bushes. One was still grumbling.

"I don't like bein' in the woods. I don't like nothin' 'bout hit. I could be havin' myself a time in Natchez. I could'a got me a woman—"

"Ah, shut up! Ain't ya got nothin' on yore mind 'cept shovin' it in a woman? The purse'll buy ya a dozen whores."

"Whooeee! All a playin' on me at once!"

"Yo're a stud. A gawddamn stud. Get your mind off that stick ya carry atween yore legs and help me with this fuckin' canoe."

Will lifted his hand and motioned. Jeff nodded and stepped out into the open, gun in hand. He was no more than a dozen paces from the men when they saw him.

The taller man, still grumbling, turned and saw the man dressed in buckskins, his head covered with white, close-cropped hair. A look of recognition came over his face. The look was quickly replaced by one of fear when he saw the man's eyes; dark and cold and angry. There was no mistaking who he was and what he intended to do. The man made his decision in an instant and jerked at his gun. He never raised it. Will's knife caught him between the shoulder blades. His mouth opened, closed, and he fell on his face.

The other man, confused and scared, tried to

take aim, and Jeff shot him. The charge struck
him in the chest. He backed up a few steps and
fell, hitting the ground hard.

"Damn!" Jeff said. "We didn't find out anything."

"We found out they was goin' to kill us," Will
said dryly, pulling his knife from the back of the
man who lay face down and wiping it on his bloody
shirt.

"The fools!"

"Dead fools," Will added.

Jeff took the feet of the man he had shot and
dragged him to the river. He waded out and
pushed at the body with an oar from the canoe
until the swift current caught it and the dead man
began a journey downriver. Will removed the
powder horn and shot bag from the other man and
Jeff also let the powerful river take him.

Tired, weary of the killing that had become
necessary for them to stay alive, the two men stood
for a long moment beside the river, then turned
into the woods and started home.

It was past sunup when they came out of the
woods and into the house yard. Smoke was coming from the kitchen fire and Callie was carrying
the milk pail from the dogtrot. Henry waited beside the shed and Will went to detain Callie so
Jeff could talk to him.

"Mornin'," he called out before he reached her.

"Mornin'." She looked tired, but equally calm
and happy.

He ignored the question in her eyes. "I'm hungry as a b'ar."

"Then go eat some berries," she teased.

"I ain't hungry for berries." He grinned suggestively. "Need anything from the smokehouse?"

"Jute brought it in."

"I figured he had, but 'twas the only place I could think of to get ya out of sight for a minute." His eyes twinkled at the red flush that covered her face.

"Now stop that! You're goin' to have me blushin' all the time."

"And a purty blush it is, Miss Callie." He swept his hat from his head and bowed from the waist.

"Oh, what'll I do with you, Will Murdock? I swan to goodness. I don't think you've been to bed a'tall. You look wore out."

"I am tired," he said seriously. "Tired and hungry." He took the milk bucket from her hand. "I'll milk so ya can cook."

"Wash your hands first."

"What's a little dirt in a pail a milk? A'right, I'll do it. Now scoot, woman, 'n cook me some vittles that'll stick to my bones."

Smiling to herself, Callie turned back to the house.

When Annie Lash saw Jeff and Will come out of the woods a vague uneasiness came over her. Why was Jeff wet? Had he been in the river or the creek? She watched him through the small window as he went to the shed. Henry came out to meet him and they talked. What had happened to take him away from the house in the early morning hours?

It had been well past midnight when Jeff had brought her to her bedroom door and it had been hours, it seemed to her, before she fell asleep. Her heart had felt so quivery and the fluttering in the pit of her stomach had refused to go away. This morning she was filled with boundless happiness, and it reflected in her face, her bright eyes, and in her bouncy step.

"Is Will going to milk?" she asked Callie when she came in.

"He offered. He and Jefferson have been up to something. Jefferson is wet from the waist down and Will came to head me off so he could talk to Henry. My land! They must think we don't have any brains a'tall. I knew the minute I got up that there was a reason why Jute was sitting by the smokehouse." She moved the big spider over the grate in the fireplace and began slicing thick strips of smoked meat to go into it.

Uneasiness shot through Annie Lash again. The picture of the robber trying to get his gun into position to shoot Jeff flashed across her mind. She trembled so violently that the plates she was carrying made a clattering sound as she sat them on the table.

The two women worked in silence, each occupied with her own thoughts. Each knew she would confide in the other before the day was out about the happiness that had come to her.

Breakfast was almost ready when Jeff came to the house and went into the room beside the kitchen. Annie Lash longed for, yet dreaded, the moment when he would come in the door. She didn't know how she should act, didn't know what he expected her to do. She smoothed her best apron down over her skirt and moved the hair from her forehead with the back of her hand.

Will came in with the milk. "Here ya are, Miss Callie, ma'am."

Annie Lash didn't hear Callie's reply. Jeff stood in the doorway. He had changed into dry clothes and his hair was already rebelling against the brush that he had used trying to smooth it. He looked tired, but relaxed and happy, too. She met his eyes and her pulses leaped in excitement. Her slightly flushed cheeks made her light blue eyes seem all the brighter, clearer. Her mind groped for something to say, but all thought left her.

"Mornin'."

"Mornin'." She stood as if mesmerized.

He came to her, put his arms around her, and kissed her on the lips. "Mornin'," he whispered just to her this time.

"Mornin'," she whispered back and her heart took wings. He kissed her again, his big body shielding her from the others in the room.

"What's Uncle Jeff bitin' Annie Lash for?" Amos came from the bedroom, holding his nightshirt up so he could walk.

Jeff lifted his head and laughed. Callie hurried toward her son, but he slipped past her and ran to Will, who scooped him up in his arms.

"He wasn't bitin' her. He was kissin' her," Will explained laughingly.

"Why'd he do that for?"

"'Cause I wanted to," Jeff answered. With an arm across her shoulders, he hugged Annie Lash to him. "I like kissing her."

Annie Lash looked up. Will was watching with a wide smile and twinkling eyes. Jeff's eyes on her face brought even more color to her cheeks. The smile he gave her spread a warm light into his eyes and she found herself beaming with pleasure.

"Will don't kiss," Amos announced proudly.

"Now, just hold on there, cottontop," Will said sternly. "There's a lot to be said for kissin'." He planted a loud smack on the boy's cheek.

Amos shrieked. "It tickles!"

"'Course, it does. Shall we see if it'll tickle yore ma?"

"Yeah!" Amos yelled. "Tickle 'er, Will."

"Will! Behave yourself!" Callie scolded and scooted around to the other side of the table, her cheeks a rosy pink.

Will sat down at the table and sat Amos on the bench beside him. "We'll let her get away this time, if'n she feeds us." He put his arm around the giggling child.

Jeff reluctantly let Annie Lash leave his side. He pulled out the bench and sat down opposite Will.

"When's the marryin' gonna be?" Will asked with a wide grin, his eyes going from Jeff to Annie Lash.

"Soon. It'll take a while to let folks know," Jeff said, his dark eyes glowing with heady brightness.

"Did ya tell 'er ya snore like a razorback hog, an' did ya tell 'er 'bout that time we was holed up in a river shack and that gal what weighed a good three hundred pounds took a shine to ya? Did ya tell er—"

"Will! Stop teasin', now," Callie scolded.

"Ah, Callie."

Annie Lash listened to the joshing. She wasn't concerned about anything that had happened in Jeff's life up to now. It was enough that he loved her and she loved him, and that he really was a tender, caring man and not the arrogant, demanding person she had thought he was. This smiling, gentle, wooly-haired giant who watched her with such tenderness in his eyes was her man, and she was going to spend the rest of her life with him right here on this homestead. A wonderful, warm feeling of permanency, of really belonging, wrapped its arms around her as happiness filled her heart and shone in her eyes.

Her shyness gone, she went to where Callie was turning the meat in the spider skillet and put her arm around her.

"I've always wanted a sister, Callie. Now, I'll have one. Don't go away from here, ever," she whispered with a world of feeling in her voice.

Callie didn't say anything, but Annie Lash could see her lips tremble and a tear appear at the corner of her downcast eyes.

From the other side of the room, Jeff saw the gesture with a gigantic surge of pride. There was depth to Annie Lash and a quickness of mind that he liked and it surprised him constantly. She was like no other woman he'd ever known. He wondered again about Zan's connection to her family. The pack containing all the old man's worldly belongings was still hanging in the shed. Annie Lash hadn't asked for it, and he had waited until she had become comfortable being here without

Zan before mentioning it to her.

They sat longer than usual at the breakfast table. Their laughter mingled and the atmosphere
was charged with excitement; everything was new
and wonderful. Not only was there a special
understanding between Jeff and Annie Lash,
which they proclaimed with clasped hands and
clinging eyes, the tension of the last few weeks
between Will and Callie had eased and in its place
there was something special and unspoken. Will
teased, Callie scolded, one's eyes continually
seeking the other's.

It was mid-morning.

Annie Lash and Callie set up the washtubs on
a bench under a shade tree near the creek. They
were getting a late start with the washing, but it
was a good drying day. The sky was sunny, the
breeze warm. Callie spread a quilt on the grass
and put Abe in the middle of it. Amos, provoked
because Jeff and Will had left on some business
of their own and had refused to take him, played
along the graveled edge of the creek. Callie cautioned him to stay away from the iron wash pot
that bubbled over a small blaze and not to throw
stones at the wet clothes hanging on the bushes.

"He needs something to keep him busy," Annie
Lash said, smiling at the tow-headed child who
stomped down to the creek to throw pebbles in
the water. "This winter we can spend a couple of
hours every day on lessons. I'll teach him to read
and to cipher and to write his name."

"Oh, Annie Lash," Callie's mouth curved in in-
voluntary delight at the suggestion, "I'd hoped

that somehow my boys'd learn. Would it be all right if I tried my hand, too? I always wished I could read. Do you think I'm too old?"

"Of course you're not too old! We'll set aside regular hours this winter and I'll ask Jefferson if we can send word to Saint Louis for a slate and a book or two."

An hour slipped by while they worked and talked about the reading and writing lessons.

"I hope there's enough soap to last the summer." Callie poked at the clothes in the boiling pot, selected a shirt, and wrapped the stick around it so she could transfer it to the rinse tub. "There won't be any more grease until we butcher the hogs."

"When do you do that?" Annie Lash spread a sheet on the rail fence to dry.

"Not until after Thanksgiving. The weather's got to be good and cold or the meat'll spoil."

"Ma! Abe's eatin' rolly pollies."

"Lordy mercy, Amos! Take 'em away from 'im!" Callie ran to the quilt, wiping her hands on her apron.

"He likes 'em."

"Landsakes!" She poked her finger in the baby's mouth and pulled out several small bugs that had rolled themselves into a tight ball. "Ah, Abe!" She continued to poke into the small slobbering mouth until she was sure it was empty. The baby smiled up at her with spittle running down his chin. "I swan to goodness, you'd eat anything," she scolded. "How did he get them, Amos?"

"I was showin' him how they roll up in a ball an' he ate 'em."

"Well, for cryin' out loud! I never! You know better than to give him something he'll put in his mouth."

"I don't like 'im anyhow. He stinks!" Amos walked away, his mouth set stubbornly and his back straight.

"You're due for a switchin', young man," Callie called after him. She laid Abe down on the quilt, took a sugar tit out of her pocket, and put it in his mouth. "Now go to sleep so I can get on with the washin'."

"Callie, we've got a caller," Annie Lash said softly and nodded toward the yard. At first she had thought it was a young boy, and then she saw the black hair cascading down and recognized the girl from the raft.

"Who is it?"

"It's the girl I was telling you about. The one called Maggie."

"I never saw a woman in breeches before. And where's she going?" Maggie was walking across the yard toward the shed, completely ignoring their presence.

"Don't go near the dog," Callie called.

The girl looked over her shoulder at the two women and went directly to the dog, patted its head and let it lick her hand, then poked her head inside the shed door, leisurely looking around as if she were at home.

"Don't that beat all? What's got into that ol' dog? He's usually as touchy as a cow with her tit caught in the fence." The astonished Callie stood with her hands on her hips and gawked. "The only time I was ever near him he acted like he wanted to chew my leg off."

On her way to the house, Maggie merely glanced at the women beside the washtubs. She disappeared into the dogtrot.

"Well, I never!" Annie Lash exclaimed and started toward the house. "She doesn't have any manners at all," she said over her shoulder to Callie, who had gone to pick up Abe so she could follow.

Maggie stood just inside the kitchen door. Her eyes were taking in everything from one end of the room to the other.

"Are you looking for something?" Annie Lash tried to keep the irritation out of her voice.

"No." The girl moved past Annie Lash and went out into the dogtrot. "What's o'er here?" She pushed open the door to where Annie Lash slept. "This be where Will and Jeff sleep?"

"No. It's where I sleep." Slow anger at the girl's rudeness burned in Annie Lash.

"Where do they sleep?" Maggie's large hazel eyes turned to Annie Lash. They were as unpretentious as a child's. The girl was so utterly lovely that Annie Lash was awed into silence for a moment as she stared at the perfectly formed features and milk-white skin framed with dark, shiny curls. Her almond-shaped green eyes were large and her lashes were so long they almost reached the curved brows above her eyes. Her soft red mouth was slightly parted and she tilted her head to one side as she stared back.

"Jefferson sleeps in there," Annie Lash gestured toward the other door. "Will stays at his own place ... some of the time."

"Who's that?" Maggie looked beyond her to Callie, who had come into the dogtrot with Abe in her arms and Amos behind her.

"Callie Pickett and her sons, Abe and Amos. Callie, this is Maggie. Her folks are homesteading on the other side of the Cornicks."

Callie nodded. Maggie studied her, letting her eyes go from the baby to Amos.

"Why'd yore man go off 'n leave ya here?"

Callie was so startled by the question she couldn't reply. Maggie waited for an answer and when one didn't come she shrugged her shoulders.

"I'd a killed 'im," she said simply. Then, dismissing the subject, she said, "I been here at night. I wanted a see it in the daytime."

Callie came forward. "What do you mean?"

"I come at night and look."

"I don't believe you," Callie gasped.

"Ask the wolf-dog. He knows me. Ask Will." She frowned, as if provoked because she wasn't believed.

"Why do you come? How do you get here?" Annie Lash asked. "Why didn't you let us know you were here?"

Again the girl's thin shoulders lifted. "Sometimes I come with Light. Last night I come ta see Will."

Callie's face went white. "You're lying!"

The girl's features seemed to freeze. "I don't lie. How did Will and Jeff know the men was comin' upriver to kill them? I come to tell 'em."

She gave Callie a scathing look and stalked past her into the yard.

"What men are you talking about?" Callie called anxiously.

Maggie didn't answer. She tilted her head hautily, her face mutinous. Annie Lash went to her.

"We're not questioning your honesty, Maggie. Callie and I find it hard to believe that you came through the woods alone." Still Maggie didn't answer. "Would you like a cup of cold buttermilk?"

Annie Lash turned anxious eyes from the silent girl to Callie, who was looking toward the river. Jeff and Light were coming toward the house.

"I don't like buttermilk," Maggie said absently, her eyes on the men.

Amos sped down the path. "Uncle Jeff! We got a caller. Her name's Maggie and she's purty." He stopped suddenly and began to hop along on one foot. "Oh, shitfire! Oh, poot! I got a burr!"

Jeff reached down and scooped him up with one arm and sat him astraddle his hip, never even breaking stride.

"Your ma said you'd get a hiding if she heard you say those words again."

"Don't tell 'er, Uncle Jeff."

"I'll tell you what I'll do. If she didn't hear it, I won't tell this time. How's that?"

Annie Lash couldn't take her eyes off the big man and the small boy riding so easily on his hip. His long stride ate up the distance between them and she suddenly remembered her apron, wet from leaning over the washtub, her damp forehead, and her windblown hair. She longed to escape to her room and tidy herself, but remained

where she was beside Callie and called out a
greeting to the scout that walked beside him.

"Hello, Light. We haven't seen you for a spell."

"Ah, *mademoiselles,* it's good to see the both
of you." He smiled at them, his dark eyes shining.
"You've met my fairy of the woods, no?" His smile
deepened when he looked at Maggie. She moved
to his side and took his hand.

"Fairy? Is that good?"

"It is not bad, *cherie,*" he said and laughed.

"We've been visiting with Maggie." Annie Lash
hardly knew what she was saying. Jeff had come
up beside her.

"This youngun's got a burr in his foot, sweetheart. Can you get it out so I can set him down?"

Annie Lash bent her head over the small dirty
foot and took out the sharp spine with her fin-
gernails. Happiness sang in her heart like a bird.
Sweetheart. Would she ever get used to hearing
him say it?

"I want us ta go from here, Light." Maggie
looked smaller than ever standing beside Jeff. Her
head scarcely came to his armpit.

"Stay and noon with us," Callie invited.

"No." Maggie shook her head vigorously and
pulled on Light's hand. "I want ta go from here,
Light."

"*Oui,* little one. We will go." Light's voice was
full of amusement. He winked at Jeff. "How can
one resist one so beautiful, no?"

"Is there anything you need?" Jeff asked.

"There is nothing, *mon ami.*" His dark, ex-
pressive eyes looked into Jeff's for an instant be-

fore he let Maggie pull him away. "*À demain,*" he called over his shoulder.

They were like two children as they leaped over the rail fence and sped into the woods. Inside the dark, quiet forest, Maggie's laughter rang out, a trilling, happy sound. Light tugged on her hand and they stopped beneath a huge cottonwood tree, its trunk entwined with the stems of grapevines, its branches filled with their foliage.

Maggie looked up at him, her green eyes sparkling. She looked beyond him as if she saw something. Light knew this was a ploy and she was poised for flight. He smiled and reached for her, then let her slip out of his hands. Instantly, she darted behind the tree, leaving peals of laughter behind her. Light waited a moment, then wheeled around and sped through the shadowed forest. She was where he thought she would be, and he moved up behind her and clasped her in his arms.

"I got you, *cherie,*" he whispered menacingly. "You did not hide well. You wanted me to find you, no?"

"Yes." Maggie turned in his arms and clasped hers about his neck. "I'm yore woman, Light."

"Woman?" He ran his hands down her slight form. "You're hardly more than a child, *ma cherie,*" he teased.

"I kiss like a woman." She held up her slightly parted lips and Light took them against his own. The kiss was gentle and sweet at the beginning, then her lips worked on his, her tongue darted into his mouth, and he unconsciously increased

the pressure of his arms and his lips. He drank
from her mouth greedily for a long moment before
he lifted his head and looked down into her face.
He was stunned by the depth of his emotion.
Something that he had thought long dead had
come alive in him.

"See? I tol' ya I'm a woman. I c'n make ya
tremble!" The eyes that looked into his were like
sparkling pools of clear, cool water.

"Vixen! Don't try that on another man," he
warned in a stern, quiet voice. "Another man might
not stop with a kiss."

"I don't want ya ta stop," she whispered and
wiggled against him.

"Behave yourself, *cherie*."

"Yore are my man. I kiss only you," Maggie said
tartly. "They grab and their mouths're all wet and
slobbery—ugh!" She hid her face against his shirt.
"I like fer you ta touch me, Light. I feel all swoony,
and my heart goes like I've been a running for a
long way. Now when we kiss I get a hurty feelin'
and all wet between my legs. Why do I do that,
Light?"

"Oh, *cherie*, I think perhaps you are a woman!"
He held her to him and rocked her gently in his
arms. A fierce desire to protect her came over him.
This little wood nymph was as innocent and as
rare as snow in the summer.

"Am I yore woman, Light?"

His woman? He felt a queer pant of fear. He
didn't want to love a woman, he didn't want to
expose his heart to the pain of loving and losing.
Yet the lonely years stretched ahead and this precious child—

"Light?"

"We'll see, little one. Come. We go downriver by canoe." He started off in a slow trot. Maggie's hand worked its way into his and she kept pace easily. He looked down at her and smiled. A new peace of mind had come to him.

Toward evening, while Annie Lash was taking the clean, dry clothes from the rail fence, Jeff went into the kitchen to talk with Callie.

"Where's Amos?"

"He saw Jute coming in from the field and went racing off to meet him. I swan, Jefferson. That boy gets wilder every day."

"Not any wilder than any other boy, I expect. Callie..."

The way he said her name brought a chill of fear to Callie. He had bad news to tell her. Will? Oh, dear God! Had something happened to Will? Did the men that Maggie spoke of—

"Jason is on his way here."

At first his words were a relief. Will was all right! Then the full impact of what he had said struck her. She felt her face freeze and then a trembling set in.

"Oh, no," she whispered fearfully.

"He's with another man. Light has been watching them. He said they'd be here tomorrow."

"What'll I do, Jefferson?" It was a pathetic plea for help.

"What do you want to do, Callie?" he asked gently.

"I don't want to see him ever again!" She trembled violently. Please, please, her inner voice cried. How could she tell Amos? She had to get a hold of herself, she thought wildly. She didn't dare let Amos know how scared she was. *Will*. He would know what to do about Amos. How would her son act when he saw the man who had abused him so terribly? She didn't know.

"You'll have to see him, but you don't have to ... have him in your bed if you don't want to. He gave up that right when he left you and Amos here alone."

"Does Will know he's on his way here?" Callie asked. Her time with him seemed like a dream now that she was plunged back into the nightmare.

"Yes, and he'd ride out to kill him if Jason wasn't my half brother. I'll handle Jason. I don't want any trouble between him and Will."

"Sometimes it's hard for me to remember that you and Jason had the same mother. You're so different," she said tiredly. "Jason has been like a millstone around your neck for years, and now, me and the boys are an added burden."

"You and the boys are a pleasurable burden, Callie. You'll always have a home here with me and Annie Lash."

"Thank you, Jefferson." Calm and dry-eyed, she turned back to preparing the evening meal. "Jefferson ... did Light say who was with him?"

"He said a dressed-up dandy with his own body servant was with him. You know the type Jason usually hooks up with; a fop, a gambler—that sort."

"What would a man like that be doing out here?"

Jeff shrugged. "Light heard rumors that he has

big plans for hauling settlers upriver. Claims to have a line of keelboats in New Orleans."

"Something big. That would interest Jason."

"Jason dreams of rebuilding his pa's fortune. I keep telling myself that Jason can't be all bad. He's got some of our mother's blood in him."

"It worries me, Jefferson. Amos and Abe have the same blood," she said dejectedly.

"But they won't be spoiled rotten as Jason was. Will and I will see to it."

Callie worked automatically, filling the teakettle, stirring up the corn pone. Her mind clung to Jeff's words, *Will and I will see to it.*

CHAPTER
FOURTEEN

There was none of the gaiety at the evening meal
that had been so evident at the breakfast table
that morning. Callie sat quietly with Abe on her
lap and spooned small bits of food into his mouth.
She seldom lifted her fork to her own lips. Will
scowled down at his plate and grunted an occasional reply to Amos. Jeff's dark eyes missed nothing as they traveled from his sister-in-law to his
friend. He had come out to the fence where Annie
Lash was taking in the dry clothes and told her
the news Light had brought. Later, she had heard
him talking to Will while they sat on the porch
waiting for supper; his voice calm and even, Will's
angry and laced with curses.

The meal would have been eaten in total silence if not for Amos's continual line of chatter.
He was enjoying himself immensely. The grown-

ups seldom interrupted him. His mother had said "hush up" only one time and that was when he was telling about Abe eating the rolly pollies.

When Will finished eating he reached over and took Abe from Callie's arms and went to sit in the rocking chair. He held the sleepy child to his shoulder and gently patted his back. Abe yawned and stretched contentedly, snuggled his face into Will's shoulder, and was soon asleep.

Annie Lash helped with clearing away the table, feeling an urgency to hurry, not only so she could be alone with Jeff, but to give Callie some time with Will. She dried the last of the plates and placed them on the shelf.

"Amos, how would you like me to start another story tonight?"

"I'd like it! You tell good'ns, Annie Lash. Tell one 'bout ships." He fairly danced with excitement.

"All right. I know a good one about ships and I'll tell it to you in my room. But first, I think we'd better wash some of that dirt off your face and hands and put your feet in the washpan. You know I don't like dirty feet on my bed. Besides, if you're ready for bed we won't have to end the story so soon."

"Can't you tell it in here?" Nothing dampened Amos's spirits as fast as the thought of a wet washcloth.

"Not tonight. We'd wake Abe," she whispered.

"Ol' stinky ruins ever'thin'," he muttered.

"Run and get your nightshirt so we can get started."

Annie Lash's eyes sought Jeff's nervously, hoping he would understand her reason for postponing their time alone together.

"Can I listen to the story, too?" He smiled, a consuming tenderness in his dark eyes.

She smiled back, the ache of love on her tremulous lips.

Callie was weary, but calm now. She had managed to stumble through the horrible meal and had not broken down and cried. The shock had worn away to some extent, and she had regained some use of her mind. What she had feared would happen, had happened. But now she was not alone. Thank God for Will, Annie Lash, and Jeff. The heavy lump of dread in the pit of her stomach had lain there since Jeff had told her Jason was on his way back. It had sapped her strength, controlled her thoughts. Now she was alone with Will. Will, her love. She turned to see him sitting with her child on his shoulder, the big hand that could grip an ax handle and split a log with one stroke gently cupped the sleeping head of her child— her child by another man. What made some men so full of goodness and others so mean and rotten?

"Abe's sleepin'." His voice broke the silence.

He held the child as if it was the most natural thing in the world for him to do, and the sight of it made her heart slip out of rhythm. Her voice stuck and it was an effort to bring it out of her tight throat. "I'll put him to bed."

"I'll do it."

She followed him to the bedroom and smoothed the blanket over the straw tick in the box Henry had made just after Abe was born, then moved

aside to make room for Will. He laid the baby
down, gently rolled him over onto his stomach,
and drew the cover up over him. Tears started in
Callie's eyes and she left the room quickly to stand
at the small kitchen window that looked toward
the woods.

Almost immediately, Will was behind her, his
arms pulling her back against him, his lips kissing
the side of her face. All the agony of the past few
hours gushed from her like a storm. She turned
and flung her arms about him, blindly seeking
comfort. Strong arms drew her against his solid
chest. Her face found refuge in the hollow beneath his chin and the floodgates broke. She cried
as she had not done in a long, long time.

Will cradled her to him, rocking her, stroking
her hair, whispering to her, "Sweet, sweet Callie.
Let it all out, my darlin' girl. I'm here. Yore Will'll
not let nothin' hurt ya."

When it seemed to her she had cried herself
dry she found herself cuddled on his lap. He sat
on the short bunk and smoothed her golden hair
back from her wet face. His shirt and throat were
wet with her tears. She felt as weak as a baby, but
so safe, and so at peace.

"Do ya feel better?" Will's lips were against
her ear.

She bent her head so she could lift the hem of
her skirt and wipe her eyes and nose. She was
almost giddy, as if her tears had washed away her
strength.

"I'm sorry. I don't know what got into me."

He pressed her head down on his shoulder.
"Don't be ashamed of cryin', darlin' girl. Ya've had

to bear more'n any woman ought to bear. But I'm here, now. Ya don't have to face anythin' by yore self again."

The words were muffled in her hair. His hand traveled down her back. He could feel the warmth of her body through her thin dress and the steady beating of her heart against his. He wanted to kill Jason Pickett, provoke him into doing something that would justify killing him. Yet he knew he couldn't do it, no matter how badly Jason needed killing. How could he face the boys and tell them he'd killed their pa so he could have them and their ma? And there was Jeff, who, for the sake of his mother, would do everything he could to prevent trouble between him and Jason. There had to be another way, and the one that had kept his thoughts occupied while he rocked Callie in his arms was the most logical one.

"Ah, Will. You're so comforting." A strange, relaxing warmth was spreading through Callie. "It's like being in the cellar during a storm. All the trouble in the world can't touch me as long as I'm here."

Will felt indescribably moved by her words. Her hand stroked his cheek with a little comforting gesture. He was acutely aware of her soft body, of the warm flush of her skin, the soft sweetness of her mouth. This woman and her children were home. He would never leave them; not for Tom Jefferson, not if a hundred Aaron Burrs were found innocent of treason. Somehow he'd find the words to make Jeff understand that he had given a year and a half of his life to Tom Jefferson, and that was all the bastard was going to get!

His eyes wondered over the upturned face of the woman in his arms, then found and held hers. They were full of concern for him now. His arms tightened and he slowly lowered his mouth to hers.

Callie lifted trembling lips to meet his kiss. They slackened and parted as his mouth possessed hers with insistent pressure. He kissed her mouth, her face, her ears, her throat, before returning to her mouth and making it his own. Callie closed her eyes as his mouth, hungry for her, swept her every nerve with intense pleasure. She heard his harsh breathing in her ear, the hoarsely whispered words of love.

"Callie...Callie, my sweet Callie. I'll kill 'im if'n he touches ya!" Muttered words tumbled from his lips as he pressed fevered kisses along the soft skin of her throat and the beginning swell of her breast.

"He won't touch me. I promise he won't. I couldn't bear it."

Tenderly, he pushed the damp hair from her face and his heart swelled. He had never dared to hope, to dream of finding a woman like this.

"Yore not to worry, sweet Callie. He won't be astayin' long, 'n when he leaves he won't be acomin' back."

"Oh, Will! No! You can't—" She looked up at him with eyes wide and fearful.

"Shhh...I'll not kill 'im," he assured her. "What does Jason love more'n anythin'?"

"The only thing that Jason loves beside himself is money," Callie said bitterly.

"Exactly." He hugged her to him. "Forget

ever'thin', but me, sweet girl, 'n let me kiss ya
some more, 'n tell ya how much I love ya."

"I think he's finally gone to sleep," Annie Lash
whispered and pulled a cover over Amos.

"Stubborn little scutter!" Jeff said teasingly. "I
thought he was going to stay awake all night."

"He's not a scutter. He's a darling little boy."

"Maybe. But come here to me. He's had your
attention long enough." He pulled her down onto
his lap as soon as she reached him. "I never
thought I'd be jealous of a little kid," he growled,
and kissed her soundly.

"Shhh. You'll wake him and I want to talk to
you."

"What I want to do to you won't make any noise
at all," he murmured against her cheek.

"Jefferson..." When he bent to kiss her again,
she forestalled him, pressing her hand over his
mouth, and slipped from his lap.

"Henpecked already," he said with exaggerated
weariness as he picked up the candle.

Arm in arm, they went through the dogtrot. At
the door of his room, he stopped, looked at her
for a moment, then entered and placed the candle
on the mantle.

Long habits of proprieties are hard to break,
and Annie Lash stood hesitantly in the doorway.
The room was small and neat. It had two single
bunks attached to the walls, a washstand, a large
trunk, and a wooden chest. She had been in the
room before to hang Jeff's clothes on the pegs
fastened to the inner wall, but that was different.
This was more...intimate.

There was a long moment of silence, dominated by the pounding of her heart. Jeff came to her; the flickering light from the candle played over the hard angles and planes of his face and added to the dark hue of his eyes. Annie Lash was conscious of the steadiness of his look. He took her hands. She backed away a little and stared up at him.

"You look so tired. Didn't you get any sleep at all last night?" she questioned in a sensually soft voice.

Jeff let his fingers trace her hairline along her temple. He followed it to her cheekbone and rubbed his knuckles across her jaw.

"It's been a long time since I've had anyone to worry about me," he said softly.

"You've got someone now, Jefferson." She felt the vibrations of her throat when she spoke. His hand was stroking the sensitive underside of her chin and jaw. "It was something Maggie said today that worried me. She said she came last night to warn Will about the men coming up the river to . . . kill you and him. Is it true?"

"Is that what's taken the shine from your eyes?" She gazed into his bronzed face, stamped with strength and the proud arrogance of self-assurance. A thin thread of panic ran through her. Oh, God, how could she bear it if something happened to him?

He read the haunting fear on her face and pulled her into his arms. She clung to him, her lips parting under the probing insistence of his. It didn't matter that he was drawing away her strength, because he had enough for both of them. A tiny moan trembled from her throat. She couldn't give herself up to his kisses just yet.

"Jefferson?" she whispered his name against his lips.

"Light sent the girl to tell us some men were coming upriver," he told her.

"But don't people come upriver all the time? Settlers come looking for land."

"These men were in a canoe, traveling at night, and Light thought they were up to no good," he explained patiently. "Will and I went down to head them off. They didn't come up as far as the creek before they headed back downriver." This was as much as he could tell her, he thought. Someday soon, he'd be able to tell her all.

"But, Maggie said they were going to—"

He stopped her words with small kisses. "Something she added to make her trip seem more important."

"She's a strange girl. Imagine coming through the woods at night like that. And, Jefferson, that old wolf-dog let her walk right up to him as if he knew her."

He led her to the bunk and pulled her down beside him. "Long ago I gave up trying to understand people and accepted them the way they are. Light is different, too. He has a moral code all his own, one that he believes is right. He wouldn't hesitate to kill if he thought a man was offensive and the world would be better without him. He wants no ties to hold him, gives loyalty but not love. I suspect the girl, Maggie, is a free-spirited creature, too."

These precious new confidences were as heady

to Annie Lash as his kisses. They talked together for an hour in the sweet surety of domestic intimacy.

"What do you think will happen when your brother gets here?" She lay across his lap and he rested his back against the wall. "Callie has never talked about him. It's almost as if he didn't exist."

"I don't know what will happen, sweetheart. A lot will depend on Jason's attitude. Will is in love with Callie. I've never known him to be so angry and so full of hate. I can understand the way he feels, but there's nothing I can do to help him." His arms tightened and his lips moved across her cheek to her mouth. "The thought of another man having any right to you would drive all logic from my mind."

The kiss took away her breath and her desire for any more conversation. She curved a hand around his neck, letting her fingers slide into the thickness of his hair. They strained together, hearts beating wildly, and kissed as lovers long separated. His hands roamed restlessly from her shoulders to her hips and up to the delicate white glimmer of her throat and cheek. He began to shake and his kiss became deeper, deeper, and she moved against him, seeking closer contact. He laid her down on the bunk and stretched his long length beside her.

His mouth broke free of hers, and as she gasped for air his lips descended to the hollow of her throat. She closed her eyes with pleasure as his lips trailed down to the neckline of her dress. When his fingers, trembling with uncertainty, moved to work on the buttons of her bodice, she covered his hand with hers, gently moved it aside, and her slender, experienced fingers took over. In a moment there was no barrier between her soft breasts and the large hand that cupped and caressed them.

His mouth moved to her breast and sensation after sensation washed over her. Her fingers stroked his hair and alongside his face. He seemed to take great pleasure in her caresses while his mouth intimately investigated the perfection of her nipple. A stifled moan of searing delight escaped her lips as he rolled his tongue around it and gently nibbled with his lips.

"You taste so clean and fresh." His mouth formed the words against her flesh. The nuzzling bite of his teeth teased her skin, sending quivers along her spine.

"We...shouldn't..."

"You're so beautiful," he breathed against her breast, his voice thick and full of wonder. "Why shouldn't we, sweetheart? I've been waiting for you forever. You'll never be more mine than you are at this moment," he murmured, his voice cracking. "Stay with me and let me show you how it is between a man and a woman."

A sigh trembled through her. She framed his face with her hands. Thank you, God, she prayed silently, for giving me this happiness. "You'll... have to show me how," she whispered.

"Woman of mine."

She wound her arms around his neck, inviting possession. He held her lovingly and pressed gentle kisses on her mouth. His breath quickened, like hers, as his kiss became suddenly fierce.

Annie Lash's reaction stimulated him and sent her own senses spinning. His urgent need communicated itself to her and there was an answering ache within her, exciting and overwhelming.

Abruptly, he left her. She opened her eyes to see him moving across the room toward the candle. Almost before she had time to sit up and swing her feet to the floor, he was there beside her in the darkness.

"Someday soon I'm going to see you, love you in the light of day, but now..." He knelt at her feet and lifted her foot in his hand, unlaced her shoe and removed it, then did the same with the other. Large, strong hands found her armpits and lifted her to her feet. He turned her until he was behind her, his mouth kissing the soft nape of her neck, his hands sliding the dress from her shoulders, pushing it down over her hips until it fell to the floor at her feet. She stayed his hands when he went to remove her shift.

"No," she said shakily.

"What it is, sweetheart? Are you shy with me? Don't be. I want to touch you, love you." Ever so carefully, he pulled the pins from her hair. It fell to her waist in deep, soft waves. He ran his hands through it and spread it out along her back, then turned her around to face him, kissing her eyelids, the curve of her cheek, her mouth.

It was all right! This was *her* man, the other part of herself. Her hands were suddenly urgent on the lacings of his shirt, wanting to be closer to his flesh, wanting him. He moved away from her and pulled his shirt over his head. When his embrace enfolded her again, bringing her back against his warm flesh, only the thin fabric of her shift was between them. Her heart hammered loudly in her chest. A thread of fear ran through her. Would she find pain or pleasure in his arms? Nervous now, she turned her face away from him and buried it in his bare shoulder.

"You're trembling." Jeff's face brushed against her silken hair, stirring from it the clean, tangy smell of vinegar water. He knew he must be gentle or her fear would destroy the moment, but it took an extreme amount of self-control to keep his arms from crushing her to him and his lips from savaging hers. He'd never had a woman who had not had another man and his heart swelled with love for this woman who would be his alone.

"Annielove," he rasped, "I'm the man who loves you. This kind of love is not for taking, but for giving and sharing. We'll not do anything until you're ready."

The tension and resistence went out of her body on hearing the whispered words, and her arms encircled his smooth and muscled waist. She felt the hard, manly, private part of his body against her when his hand cupped the cheek of her hips and drew her tightly against him. The whisper of a gasp escaped her as she leaned her head back upon his shoulder, spilling her hair over his arm. Trembling lips slackened and parted as his mouth possessed hers. A warm tide of tingling excitement flooded her. His hand caressed her, leisurely arousing her, stroking her breast, moving up and down her back and over her hips. Then he was lifting her up, cradling her in his arms, her hips pressed against the flat muscles of his bare stom-

ach. The rounded curve of her breast rubbed
against his sinewy chest. He carried her the few
steps to the bunk, laid her atop the covers, and
followed her down, a bare leg hooked over hers.
His mouth opened on her lips in a hungry kiss,
tongues met impatiently, passion raged vora-
ciously within him, yet he held back, carefully
easing the shift from her body until her breast,
indeed, all of her glorious body lay naked and
beautiful against him.

Annie Lash's mind whirled giddily. Her hands
slid around to the corded muscles of his back,
trying to press him closer. She was shattered by
the sheer pleasure of lying naked beside him, yet
the pleasure had only begun, as she discovered
under his roaming, caressing hands. Free from her
fumbling uncertainty, her only wish now was to
please, to satisfy, to give.

She reached out to explore his warm, hard flesh
with trembling intensity, letting her fingertips find
the masculine nipples and follow the line of fine
golden hair down to his taut, flat stomach and
beyond. She felt the tremor that shook him with
each new caress, each new place on his body she
explored. He reacted to it as if her hand was a
torch being added to his already flaming desire.
Her hand boldly found and caressed the rock hard
part of him that pressed against her thigh. His sex
was large, firm, and throbbing. She didn't feel
threatened by it. He groaned softly and his mouth
broke free of hers.

"You were made to be loved and cherished."
His voice was husky, and rawly disturbed, like his
deep, quivering breaths. He grasped her hand in

his and moved it to his chest. "Sweet...I'll not
be able to wait much longer."

"You don't have to wait, darling. Oh, Jefferson..."

He gently nudged her thighs apart and stroked
the inner part of them. Driven almost mindless
by the hard tension gnawing within her, she moved
her face over his skin, scented of clean lye soap
and so solid to her touch. Annie Lash thought she
was going to die of want when his hand moved
up until it could go no farther and he knew without a doubt she was ready to receive him. The
pleasure mounted so intently, she wondered
wildly if she could stand it.

"So warm, so...wet, my Annielove. Do you want
me, sweetheart? Do you want my loving inside
you?" He held himself rigidly over her. His fingers moved in a stroking motion and she flinched.
They moved again and she gasped, arching herself against him.

"Yes, yes...Oh, yes!" She rolled her head from
side to side. She had never felt like this before.
She had never known this heat radiating from the
pulsing center where his fingers moved so skill-
fully. She whimpered aloud, and he was above
her. Her body opened to him, needing him above
all other things, welcoming the solid length of his
maleness as if it were a part of her own flesh
returned to her. He thrust harder, deeper, faster.
There was a small hesitation, an instant of pain,
and Annie Lash gasped for air. Then she felt him
move inside her and there was no pain in this,
only pain without. A new, higher level of need
raced rampant through her. She felt as if she was

being tossed to the highest treetops by a forceful wind and she clung to the man above her who was the source of the violent storm that was shaking her.

Annie Lash was made to know all the need and power of this large woodsman whom she had come to love so passionately. His large hands closed over her buttocks and held them while his body pressed into hers as if he were trying to draw her into himself. She felt the thunderous beating of his heart against her naked breast and heard his hoarse, murmured cries in her ear.

It was magic! A stunning, beautiful bloom of glorious rapture that made her respond with a fierce ardor matching his. When the explosion came it was so consuming that it was frightening. A bursting, shattering, uncontrollable release and they went sailing out over the world together.

The hands that had so expertly guided her hips now moved to either side of her and relieved her limp body of part of his crushing weight. His mouth moved tenderly over her throbbing lips and she gave quick answer, returning warm, fleeting kisses. He eased himself from between her legs and shifted to lie beside her. Annie Lash rolled onto her side to face him and he smoothed her rumpled hair and traced his mouth along the curve of her cheek, tasting the clean fragrance that seemed so much a part of her. There was a silent claim of possession in the way her hand moved to his hip and remained there.

"What was it, love?" she whispered against his chin.

"Did you like it?"

"It was beautiful. How could I not have liked it? But I still don't know what happened to me."

"The Indians say it's a gift from the gods, and that each time it happens, you give up a part of yourself." Jeff's lips parted and played on hers as he replied.

"It was just that way with me. I gave a part of myself to you. It was so wonderful—I could feel you all through me; in my hands, my feet, my stomach. The tip of you touched my very soul," she whispered.

"Ah...sweetheart."

They lay silently for long moments, simply holding each other, awed by what had happened to them.

When Jeff spoke he placed the tip of his nose to hers. "How does it feel to belong so completely to a...jackass?" he asked with a rich chuckle."

She remembered, vividly, calling him that the night he told her he had decided to marry her.

"You deserved that!" She laughed softly, lightly, nibbling at his chin, touching it with her tongue. "Why did you let me think you were such a cold, unfeeling man?"

"It was my defense against you, you vixen. I was thinking about you too much, my eyes could scarcely move away from you. I resented it."

"And now?" Her fingers moved across his belly where the skin was smooth and taut. He held his breath as she traced the thin line of downy hair down from the light furring on his chest, and again the coals of passion were fanned and flamed.

"Now...you're mine!" His open mouth sought her lips, parted them, twisting, devouring, as if he couldn't get enough of her dewy sweetness. Their breaths merged and became one. His hand moved downward, capturing the soft fullness of a breast before his mouth followed. Annie Lash caught her breath as the wild, sweet pleasure consumed her again. She lost her last touch on reality when his hands slipped beneath her hips, lifting her to him, and again they tasted the full joy of passion.

Much later she lay on his chest, her cheek resting against his shoulder. They were silent and awed by the bliss they had found together. She lay nestled in his arms. Jeff's fingers brushed the soft tangled curls around her ears and his kisses ventured along the smooth whiteness of her face.

A long sigh escaped her. "I suppose I should go back to my room."

"Not yet," he breathed against her ear. "Stay till dawn. Let me hold you while I sleep."

She tilted her face so her lips might meet his, and their mouths played with tender warmth.

"Will you be able to sleep if I'm here? This bunk wasn't built for two."

"I'll sleep." His mouth became insistent.

"I'll stay." Her voice was muffled beneath his kisses.

CHAPTER
FIFTEEN

Climbing up from the depth of sleep, Jeff came awake instantly. He raised his head and listened, identified the sounds of Henry and Jute doing the morning chores, and relaxed upon the pillow. For a brief haunting moment when he woke, he had feared that he had dreamed it all. But then he felt her soft, warm body entwined with his and the memory of her passionate responses fanned the flame of love in his heart. Her effect on him was total and complete. She had brought something into his life that he hadn't realized existed, an all-consuming love that went beyond the gratification of his physical needs. She had filled his heart since the day they buried Zan when she had stood proudly, defiantly, and declared she wanted to love and be loved, that she wanted to put all her thoughts, toil, smiles, pain, and love into her future family.

The fragrance of her filled his brain. Her lovely, curving form nestled close against him; a warm, soft thigh snug between his, an arm flung out across his chest. Gently, he kissed her, urging her to wake as he spoke her name. She moaned sleepily, her arm moving up from his chest to encircle his neck. His mouth lightly caressed her softly parted lips.

"Wake up, Annielove. I've got to get up," he murmured. "God knows I don't want to leave you."

Annie Lash opened her eyes and then closed them, bathing in the peace of her contentment. A long sigh escaped her.

"Do you feel different this morning?" she whispered drowsily.

"I feel like someone just handed me the world by the tail."

"Me, too. I feel like I've just been born."

He chucked softly. "I guess you know that I'll never let you go to bed without me again."

She drew him to her as his kisses came upon her mouth, warm, devouring, fierce with love and passion, then traveled lower to spread their heat over her quivering breasts.

"I thought you had to get up," she teased.

"You make it impossible, love."

Passion spread in the heat of their touch. His caresses were searching, and Annie Lash opened her legs to his questing hand. His wandering fingers brought soft, breathless whimpers of trembling joy from her. She felt the tip of his rigid sex seeking the opening between her legs, and then the flame was within her, consuming, searing, setting fire to every nerve, filling her with unbearable pleasure. His heart beat wildly against her naked breast, and beneath her hands the hard muscles of his back tensed and flexed as the warm, sweet wetness of her surrounded him. She heard harsh breathing in her ear, and hoarse, whispered words of love as they rode the high, swelling tide of rapture to fulfillment.

They lay resting in the aftermath of their sweet storm; peacefully content, legs entwined, fingers gently interlaced in a knot of love. Jeff's lips nibbled at the soft flesh of her shoulder, paused to take her earlobe in his mouth.

The corners of her mouth curved softly. "I don't feel one bit guilty about what we've done, and I thought I would without the parson saying the words."

He smoothed her tumbled hair and nuzzled his face into its fragrant mass, breathing in the sweet scent of her. "I want to take you inside me so I can take you with me wherever I go. This feeling of peace you give me is strange. What is this gift you carry around with you?"

"I'm not sure what you mean."

"Peace and contentment. I find it when I'm with you."

"I'm glad," she whispered. "I'm so glad."

"I love you," Jeff whispered. "I just wish old Zan knew how much I love you and that you'll always be with me."

"I think he knows." Her hand caressed his lean ribs before moving to his muscled waist. "I think the minute he saw you in my house on the Bank, he decided you were the man for me."

"And?" he urged.

"And he was right." The words came on a soft, trembling breath, and she nestled closer.

Will, frustrated and angry, opened the gate to allow the three horsemen to pass through. The stormy session had began at sunup. Will argued against Jeff riding out alone to meet his brother. Finally, Jeff had agreed to take Henry and Jute with him, knowing it was one way to keep Will from going to meet Jason. He would not leave the women unprotected at the homestead.

The three men rode out down the lane toward the Cornicks as the sun rose above the treetops. Jeff looked back and saw Annie Lash standing in the yard waving to him. His face gentled. Annie Lash—calm and beautiful in her faded dress. His life had changed so drastically since she came into it. She could not guess the depth of his feeling for her. It surprised even him.

Jute moved out ahead, the old wolf-dog slinking through the underbrush by his side. When the trail widened, Henry moved up beside Jeff.

"Mista Jason ain't gon' ta be likin' ta see me'n Jute, Mista Jeff. He gon' ta be 'memberin' how hit was 'fore he went."

"And how was that, Henry?"

"Miz Callie, she comed to da shack wid Mista Amos. Mista Jason had don whopped dat child wid da strap, 'n Miz Callie, too. He comed ta git 'er, 'n I hol' 'em off wid da gun. Miz Callie, she stay two day 'til Jute follow Mista Jason 'n know he ain't comin' back. He gon be powerful mad when he see me'n Jute." A worried frown etched the black man's visage.

"Don't worry about it. You and Jute are free men. I bought your papers from Jason and had them recorded. He has no claim on you, and if he has any brains at all he'll not mention that his wife and child had to seek your protection." His words were sharp and angry.

"Yas'suh. Jute would'a don kilt Mista Jason when he seed dat child, if'n not fer you, Mista Jeff."

"I'll handle Jason. He won't whip Callie or Amos again. I promise you that." His tone and his angry face marked the end of the conversation.

They passed the Cornick homestead with only a wave to Biedy. An hour later, Jute rode back to say that Jason and his party had passed the cabins of the new homesteaders. Jeff decided to wait and let the party approach him. He chose a place near the river, dismounted, and turned the horse over to Henry to water. He told Henry and Jute to stay out of sight and sat down on a log to wait.

He heard the party approaching long before he saw them, and marveled at their stupidity. High, almost feminine, foppish laughter carried on the slight breeze to where Jeff sat waiting. It was not his brother's laugh, but the deeper tones that accompanied it were, and Jeff tried to curb his anger, tried to remember this spoiled, selfish man was also the son of his mother.

They saw him immediately and Jeff had to give the fop credit for quickly drawing his firearm, but after a few murmured words from Jason, he tucked it back into his belt. Jeff had plenty of time to study them. Jason looked just the same in his fine coat and silk shirt with the broad ascot looped under his chin. A three-cornered feathered hat sat on his blond head at a jaunty angle. The man with him was dressed equally as fine. Both men wore polished, black boots and rode good horses. Trailing behind them was a black man, dressed in servant livery, leading one mule and riding another. If Jeff hadn't been so angry, he would have laughed at the sight of the ridiculous procession here in the wilderness.

Jason Pickett was a much handsomer man than his brother. His features were not so rugged and his frame not so large. His hair was more the color of ripe wheat than pure blond, and he wore it fashionably long and clubbed. He was witty, charming, and preferred to talk rather than to fight. He spurred his horse ahead, and when he reached Jeff, he swung down and came toward him, a huge smile on his face, his hand extended.

"Jefferson! How are you, brother?"

Jeff stood and stretched himself up to his full height before his fist lashed out and caught Jason on his smiling mouth, dropping him to the ground. He glanced up to see the fop jerk his gun from his belt, but before he could react, Jute sprang into view, his musket in his hand and the old wolf-dog, hunkered down and snarling, at his side. Jeff turned his attention back to Jason, who was picking himself up off the ground, retrieving his hat, and dabbing at his mouth with a cloth.

"Now, why'd you do tha—"

Jeff hit him again, and he staggered back several paces before he fell heavily. This time Jeff followed him and fastened his hand in the front of his coat and hauled him to his feet. He shook

him viciously before he gave him a powerful shove
that sent him rolling in the dirt again.

"You worthless scum!" he shouted angrily. "I
should beat you to death for what you did to Callie
and that boy! Consider yourself lucky we have
the same mother or I'd kill you here and now."

Jason stumbled to his feet, his lip cut and bleeding, his eyes blazing with hatred. He picked up
his hat and jammed it down on his head; his face
was crimson with embarrassment and anger.

"Is she still hanging around?" he sneered.

"Where did you think she'd be when you left
her here alone? Did you hope she and the boy
wouldn't make it through the winter and you'd
be free of your responsibilities?" Jeff's narrowed
eyes watched his brother, saw the glance exchanged between him and the man still mounted
on the horse, saw the effort he was making to
control his temper.

"I'm sorry about that," he said after a while.
"She left me to go stay with the blacks and I
thought she wasn't coming back. You know I was
forced by her pa and her brothers to marry her,
Jefferson."

"I know that, and I also know why you were
forced into marrying her, but that's no reason for
you to treat her the way you have. You took your
pleasure of her quick enough."

"I want to see my boy," Jason said, and looked
his brother directly in the eye. "I've a right to see
my boy."

"You lost any right to that boy when you
whipped him so hard it left marks all over him!"

"Ah, come on, Jefferson. What's that backwoods

slut been telling you? All kids need a taste of the strap. You ought to know, the old man gave it to you often enough."

"I haven't forgotten. I don't want you here, Jason. I don't think I can stand looking at you every day, even for the sake of our mother."

"I want to see the boy," Jason said stubbornly. "I want to see Callie, too. Hartley and I will stay out of your way. We're working up a deal to bring a fleet of keelboats up from New Orleans. Right now we're looking at likely locations for landing stations."

The other man dismounted, left his horse in the care of the servant, and came forward with his hat beneath his arm. He was almost too pretty to be a man, with his pink cheeks, merry blue eyes, and light brown hair that curled to his shoulders. He stood hesitantly, a slight smile on his face.

"Hartley Van Buren, Mr. Merrick. I always think it wise to stay out of family squabbles," he said with a chuckle.

"Smart of you," Jeff said dryly, and took the hand he offered.

"We would appreciate your hospitality for a short while. The magistrate at Saint Charles was good enough to provide us with a map of likely locations for our landing sites, which should expedite matters greatly."

Jeff's eyes went to his brother. "I'll stand for no abuse of Callie or the boys."

"Boys?" Jason's face wore a puzzled look.

"Yes, *boys*. Callie was pregnant when you left her. She had your son with only Henry to help her while Jute went through a blizzard to get the

Cornicks." Anger surfaced again and Jeff's voice
was thick with it.

"I swear I didn't know, Jefferson."

"Would it have mattered if you had?"

"I honestly don't know," Jason said slowly.

The brothers looked into each other's eyes for
a long while, and when Jeff spoke his voice was
low and menacing. "You leave Callie alone."

"What do you mean leave her alone? She's my
wife." Jason attempted a cocky grin, but it faded
in the face of the thundercloud look that spread
across Jeff's face.

"You know what I mean. Stay out of her bed."

Jason threw back his head and laughed. "So
that's the way the wind blows. You've been did-
dling with—"

"Don't say it!" Jeff's hand snaked out and
grabbed the front of his brother's coat. "You say
one rotten thing about that woman and I'll beat
you to a bloody pulp! She's worth ten of you!"

"All right, all right." Jason was trying to
straighten his ascot and bring order to his clothing. He looked beyond Jeff and a smile came on
his handsome face. "Well, look who we have here.
Hello...again."

Jeff turned to see Maggie coming toward them.
He looked back at his brother and found his eyes
riveted hungrily on the small figure with the
hauntingly beautiful face.

Maggie went straight to Jeff and took hold of
his hand. She looked like a tiny, perfectly formed
doll. She was wearing leather breeches and moccasins. Her loose shirt was tied around her small
waist and did nothing to disguise her soft breast.

Soft, tumbled, black curls framed her face and cascaded down her back.

Jason was looking at her in awed silence, a smile playing at the corners of his mouth.

Maggie looked up at Jeff. "Is he your brother? He don't act like you."

"We had the same mother, but a different upbringing. I suppose that accounts for the difference."

She nodded, agreeing to what he said, and went to the wolf-dog, patted his head, then walked around the black servant, looking him over. Jason and Hartley didn't take their eyes off the girl. It was as if they couldn't believe what they were seeing.

"Who is she?" Jason asked. "We've had several glimpses of her since we left Saint Charles. But when we tried to get near her she disappeared like a mist."

"Her name is Maggie and she belongs to the homesteaders you just passed," Jeff said with a frown. He didn't like the lustful look on either man's face.

Maggie came back to him. "C'n I ride with you, Jeff?"

"Of course. Are you going to my place or to the Cornicks'?"

"To Biedy. She makes me pie."

"Won't you introduce me, brother?" Jason said with bright, interested eyes on Maggie.

"And me," Hartley added.

"No, I won't," Jeff said bluntly. "Maggie isn't for the likes of either of you." He mounted his horse and reached for her hand to pull her up

behind him. He motioned for Jute to lead out and
he turned the horse toward the end of the caravan;
Henry followed.

Jason accepted the help of the servant when he
mounted his horse. His steady gaze was focused
on Henry, clearly intending to intimidate.

"You've done all right for yourself, Henry. That's
a fine horse you're riding. Can you shoot that musket?"

"Yassa," Henry said evenly.

Jason edged his horse in between Jeff's and
Henry's. "That's good. You never know when
you'll have to use it."

"Yassa. Dat what Mista Jeff say." He looked
squarely at his former master without a trace of
submissiveness on his black face.

"I was in New Orleans when I heard you were
headed back to your farm, Jefferson. Did old Tom
cut the strings and let you go?" Jason's eyes strayed
continually to the girl riding behind his brother.

Jeff gave him a sharp look. "What made you
think I had any ties with Tom Jefferson?"

Jason laughed. "Don't be stupid, Jefferson. Why
else would Mother name you after him? Papa was
sure you were old Tom's bastard. That's why he
hated you so much."

Jeff's face turned a dull red. His anger was almost choking him. Jason knew how to place his
barbs.

"Your mouth will get you killed, Jason."

Jason laughed again. "Maybe. But not by you,
brother Jeff. You're too righteous to kill your own
brother. It's common knowledge that old Tom fa-

thered bastards all over Virginia. Our ma—"

"Shut up!" Jeff pulled up on the reins and his horse stopped. His brother's horse moved on ahead and Jeff fell in behind, cursing himself for a fool for allowing his brother to antagonize him to the point where he lost his patience.

At the path leading to the Cornicks', Jeff stopped and Maggie slipped off the horse. Without a word or a backward glance, she took off, running lightly toward the house, her dark hair streaming behind her.

Jason stopped his horse to watch her. "That's some little bit of tail," he said when Jeff moved up beside him. "She'd set New Orleans spinning on its ear!"

"Don't get any foolish notions about Maggie," Jeff said sharply. "You just might find a knife in your belly."

"Like that, is it?"

"Jason, you're a fool—a hopeless, stupid fool!"

"Maybe. But I'm not buried in the backwoods like you are, brother."

It was noon when the party reached Berrywood. Jute was waiting beside the railed gate and closed it when they passed through. The black servant slid from the mule and hurried to help Hartley, holding the mount by the bridle while the man dismounted. Jute took the reins of Jeff's horse, but made no attempt to assist Jason. The black servant ignored the two freedmen as if he were their superior, and Henry and Jute went about the chore of unsaddling their own mounts and Jeff's as if the other three were not there.

There was no one in the yard waiting to welcome the visitors. Jeff silently led the group toward the house.

"This is a lovely setting for a home, Merrick," Hartley said, his shorter legs working hard to keep pace with Jeff's long stride. "I can see this place in a few years; sweeping lawns, circular drives, a large carriage house set over there." He waved his arm as he talked.

Jeff scarcely heard him. He had registered the fact that Will was nowhere in sight. Now Annie Lash stepped out from the dogtrot and stood waiting. She had never looked more beautiful, or more sedately composed, and Jeff's chest tightened with love for her. She wore one of her better everyday dresses and had a light blue apron tied about her waist. Her hair, shining in the sunlight, was coiled atop her head. It was the calm, confident look on her face that caused Jeff to feel a surge of pride. He went to her, and with his large body shielding her from the eyes of the other men, dropped a light kiss on her forehead. When he turned he had his arm around her.

"This is my fiancée, Miss Jester." His face wore that terribly sober look Annie Lash had seen on the trail coming from Saint Charles. "Hartley Van Buren and my half brother, Jason Pickett."

Annie Lash nodded to each man. Jason swept his hat from his head and smoothed his thick, blond hair. His face was a wreath of smiles.

"You're full of surprises, brother. What a beauty!"

Hartley bowed after he realized she was not offering her hand. "May I congratulate you, Merrick? You have a lovely lady." His friendly eyes rested on Annie Lash. "We'll try to be of little bother, Miss Jester. I have my manservant who will assist you. He'll be at your disposal at all times."

"That's kind of you, but unnecessary. We're used to doing for ourselves here at Berrywood."

Jason Pickett was not at all what Annie Lash expected a brother of Jeff's to be. He was a very handsome, well-dressed, polished gentlemen of the upper classes. There was nothing in his attitude that even suggested he felt any hesitation about returning here, or any remorse that he had left his wife and child to face possible death in the winter wilderness. He smiled charmingly, his twinkling eyes going from her to his brother.

"You sly fox, you! Why didn't you tell me I was going to meet my future sister? You always had all the luck, Jefferson. Where did you find this beautiful lady?"

"He found me on the Bank in Saint Louis, Mr. Pickett. Your brother has an addiction for taking care of those weaker than himself." Annie Lash carefully kept the sarcasm from her voice.

If Jason felt the barb he didn't let on by as much as a flicker of an eyelash. He laughed easily.

"And what a pleasant task he has, ma'am." His eyes moved beyond her, searching. "Is my wife inside?" He went to go around Annie Lash, but she moved abruptly and blocked the way so he had to follow as she led the way to the kitchen.

To Callie, sitting in the rocking chair with Abe in her lap and Amos standing beside her, it seemed as if the world had stopped and she was waiting to fall off it. She had tried to prepare Amos for meeting his father. The child had listened, round-eyed and solemn, while she tried to convince him he had nothing to fear from this man ever again. They had Jefferson and Will, she explained, who would take care of them. Amos had been unusually quiet and Callie's heart went out to him, wondering how much a small child can remember and understand. Thank God, Will had been persuaded to go to his own homestead and she didn't have to worry about him confronting Jason at this time.

She focused her eyes on Annie Lash when she came through the door. She had been like a rock to cling to. Her calm steadiness and her unshakable conviction that Jefferson could handle his wayward brother had helped her prepare herself for this meeting she had dreaded for so long.

When she looked at the man behind Annie Lash she was surprised to find his bold, amber eyes locked on her with smiling intensity. It was like being caught naked in a public place. Her face must have reflected the revulsion she felt because the smile left his face as he came toward her.

Until now, Amos had stood quietly, holding to the arm of the rocking chair. Now he moved around behind it.

"Hello, Callie. Jefferson tells me I have another son." A smile flashed rakishly across his handsome face.

Callie didn't answer and once more she found him scrutinizing her with a thoroughness that made her again feel undressed. His gaze moved unabashedly over her softly rounded breasts and then along the length of her. She knew he was doing it deliberately to unnerve her and she decided to refuse to let him.

"Me and *my* children are no longer your affair, Jason. We want nothing to do with you and want nothing from you." She was pleased that her voice was so steady, even though she felt as if she were about to crumble into a million pieces.

Jason's face flushed and he kept it turned away from the silent audience that stood just inside the kitchen door.

"We'll discuss that later. Now I want to see my boy." He moved around to the side of the chair, and Amos scooted to the other side.

"Leave him be!" Callie said sharply. She held Abe to her with one arm and circled Amos with the other. "Keep your hands off him!"

Jason's face flushed hotly, but he persisted. He squatted down on his heels. Amos cowered against the chair, his small face set rebelliously.

"Don't you remember your papa, boy? I've brought you a whistle all the way from New Orleans. Wouldn't you like to see it?" He held out his hand and smiled with his mouth, but not his eyes.

Amos refused to look at him. His green eyes found his uncle's face and stayed there. When he felt the hand take his arm and try to pull him forward, all the hate his little heart held for this man exploded, and he flew at him, striking him in the face with his fist before racing past him to the safety of the bedroom door, where he stood and let all his feelings flow out of him.

"I hate you, you mean old puke! You hurt me a—and ma! I wish you'd died an' put in a hole!

Go away! You're a poot! Will's gonna show me how to be a man! Ol' poot...ol' turd...ol' piss ant, and ol'...shit!" With tears streaming down his freckled face, the child stood defiantly and shouted all the forbidden words he could think of to express his hatred.

Callie jumped to her feet. The look of anguish on her son's face was almost more than she could bear. She went to him, not to reprimand him, but to comfort. Jason brushed past her, anger making his face livid.

"That's enough!" he shouted.

Amos darted into the bedroom and slammed the door. Callie heard the stout bar Will had put there only this morning fall into place, and felt a measure of relief.

Jason pounded on the door. "What you need is a good strapping! You're growing up to be a backwoods dolt like your ma's folks. I won't have it! Do you hear? You're a Pickett, by God, and you'll act like one!"

Callie turned on him like a spitting cat. "Leave him alone, Jason Pickett! What's so proud about being a Pickett? The only one I know, besides my boys, is nothin' but a low-down, lazy, shit-eatin' buzzard that never did a day's work in his life! I ain't proud my boys have got to carry the name! It's a shame they'll have to live with it, but they don't have to put up with your meanness! Get out!"

Jason's face swelled with anger. The veins stood out on his forehead and his fists clenched and lifted as if he were going to strike Callie. Jeff moved quickly to her side and shoved him away from her.

Abe began to cry. This was a new sound coming from his mother and it frightened him. Annie Lash came and took him from Callie's arms, walked to the far end of the room, held him against her shoulder, and crooned to him. Her quiet voice reassured him. He stopped crying and lay against her, sucking his thumb.

"What did you expect, Jason?" Jeff stood beside Callie, his hand on her shoulder.

"I didn't expect her to turn my son against me," he replied angrily.

"You always put the blame on someone else," Jeff said dryly. "Leave the boy alone or you'll answer to me."

"Are you threatening me? Amos is my son, not yours. He's a Pickett. I know *he's* a Pickett. I'm not so sure about the other one," he said with a sneer.

Jeff crossed his arms and rocked back on his heels, trying to hold onto his temper. "You're making it impossible for me to allow you to stay here, Jason. You and Mr. Van Buren can ask the Cornicks to put you up for a few days. I doubt if they will, but you can ask."

Hartley Van Buren, who had been lounging beside the door, moved suddenly.

"Jason's been excited about seeing his son again, Merrick. I'm sure you can understand his disappointment. As soon as he's had time to think about it, he'll appreciate the boy's feelings." Hartley put a hand on Jason's shoulder. "My sympathy is with him. It's hard for a man to lose a son." The friendly eyes that looked so saddened when they looked at Jason now looked determined and sincere when they met Jeff's. "We'll not be any trouble to you, Merrick. We'd appreciate your hospitality for a few days."

Jeff was silent for a moment, then said, "You can use the room across the dogtrot for a few days, then I want you gone from here." His eyes locked with those of Annie Lash as he led the way to the door.

"We'll be nooning shortly, Jefferson," she said quietly, then followed them to the door and watched as they entered Jeff's room. She had already prepared the room and, at Jeff's request, moved his personal effects to her room. It had been a pleasurable task. She had hung his clothes beside hers and lined his boots and moccasins up alongside the wall, caring not a whit for propriety, feeling she was his wife every bit as much as if the preacher or the magistrate had said the words.

Callie stood beside the closed bedroom door, tears streaming down her face. Annie Lash went to her quickly. One arm held the baby; she put the other about Callie and hugged her.

"Wasn't it awful? Oh, my poor baby! He hasn't forgotten a thing, Annie Lash. Did you see his eyes? If he'd a been a man he'd have killed him!"

"Yes, it was awful, but somehow we'll make Amos understand that we love him, and we'll keep him safe. Now, go wash your face so he won't see you've been crying. I'll take care of things in here and you keep the boys in the bedroom. We've got several pieces of sugar candy put away. I think this is the time for Amos to have them. Oh, I'm glad Will insisted on putting that bar across the door. Not that I think Jason will do anything," she hastened to say, "but it must be a comfort to Amos to know he can lock himself in."

Callie reached up and kissed Annie Lash on the cheek. "I don't know what I'd do without you. I'm so glad you came here." She sniffed and wiped her eyes on her apron.

"I'm glad, too. I found a wonderful man and a whole new family to care for. Now see if you can get Amos to open the door."

CHAPTER
SIXTEEN

Jason sulked at the table during the noon meal. He left it up to Hartley to carry on the conversation, which he did with enthusiasm.

"I figure that in another year there'll be ten thousand families crossing the Mississippi each year to take up homesteads along the Missouri. I plan for my boats to be the means of getting those people upriver, and in order to do that I must have supply stations." Hartley's eyes darted now and then to Jason, but he sat with his eyes downcast. "I'd appreciate your help, Merrick. I'd not only appreciate it, but will be glad to pay for it. I'm told you and Will Murdock know this part of the country better than anyone."

"We know the country, but we've got our summer work laid out for us. We'll not be able to help you."

"I'm sorry to hear that, but I understand. Jason and I will do some scouting tomorrow. Perhaps you'll take a look at our map and point out the most likely locations."

The meal passed slowly, but it passed, and Annie Lash drew a sigh of relief when Jason and Hartley left the kitchen. Jeff lingered to ask about Callie.

"She'll be all right. Have you seen Will?"

"His horse is gone. I expect he's going to stay over at his place. I'll send Jute or Henry over to tell him things are all right here."

Annie Lash laid her head on his shoulder. "I feel so sorry for them. Callie loves Will. He loves her and the boys. I wish there was something we could do for them."

Jeff kissed her softly on the lips. "Things have a way of working out. Jason may decide he wants another woman and divorce Callie. It's happened before."

"She's afraid he'll come to her room. Will put a bar on the door, but she's still afraid. It must be terrible for her. I wasn't even that afraid when I was on the Bank."

"Tell her not to worry about Jason forcing himself on her. I'll be close by. I'll not leave the homestead while they're here."

"I love you," she whispered against his neck.

"And I love you." He kissed her gently on the lips and went out the door.

When she finished the cleanup, Annie Lash took the wet towels and went out through the dogtrot to hang them on the line. Hartley's black servant sat on his heels, leaning against the back of the house. Annie Lash was startled when she saw him.

"What are you doing here?" she asked sharply.

The man got to his feet and bobbed his head several times. "Ah waitin' fer mastah."

"What's your name?"

"Antone. Mastah doan like Ebitt, so me Antone now."

"You mean he changed your name from Ebitt to Antone? How could he do that?"

"I slave, missy. Mastah say name is Antone."

Annie Lash caught a glimpse of something in the man's eyes that she didn't understand. Was it resentment? He still wore the silly smile on his face as if he was a dog waiting to be petted. She didn't like the thought of it and turned to go back in the house, then paused and turned back.

"Have you eaten anything?"

"No, missy. Not dis day."

"For goodness sake! That's ridiculous," she said and went back through the door to the kitchen.

She returned minutes later with several large pieces of cornbread, slices of meat, and a cup.

"Here." She held out the food and set the cup on the step. "You can get water from the creek yonder."

"Yas'm, missy, yas'm." He bobbed his head up and down. "Ah stay here. Mastah say Antone stay here. Mastah—"

She gave him a puzzled look then, "Well, I never. I need a bucket of water," she said sharply. "Take the bucket. I'll tell him I sent you for water." She went to the kitchen. If that's not the limit!

she fumed. The man can't even leave to get a drink of water!

She carried the half full bucket of water to the yard, dipped the cup into it, and handed it to Antone. She threw the rest of the water on the fern she had planted along the north side of the house.

"Antone," she said loudly, "go to the creek and fetch me a bucket of water."

"Yas'm, missy." A broad smile split the man's face in half, and in spite of her irritation at Hartley Van Buren, she smiled back.

Five minutes later, she heard Hartley call Antone. She waited to see if the black man answered, and when he didn't, hurried to the door. The scowl on Hartley's face quickly turned to a smile when he saw her.

"I'm looking for Antone. I told him to wait outside the door."

"I sent him to fetch a bucket of water. I hope you don't mind."

"Not at all, ma'am. You're welcome to use his services in any way you see fit. In fact, Antone is an excellent cook. My friends say his fish chowder is the best in New Orleans."

Annie Lash inclined her head. Hartley was smiling at her in open admiration. He was younger than Jeff, but something about him made her think he was older than Jason. Although he was extremely nice to look at, almost pretty, he had a hardness about him that she didn't like.

"That's kind of you," she murmured. "But we'll not need his help in the kitchen."

"Well, keep it in mind. I'd like to treat you to his chowder while we're here." Antone came around the corner. He paused and his eyes sought Hartley's face. "Take the water inside for Miss Jester, Antone, then come to my room. Step lively, I can't wait to get these boots off."

Later, Annie Lash was to think the slave had a frightened look on his face, as if he expected some sort of punishment for not being available when Hartley called to him.

Jason sat on a rock overlooking the river. After breakfast he and Antone had ridden out with Hartley to look over the locations Jefferson had pointed out on the map. He tried to work up some enthusiasm for this business venture that Hartley was so sure would restore both their fortunes, but it was hard to do when he was hot and tired. He couldn't understand why Hartley didn't hire someone to do this so they could have stayed in Natchez or New Orleans and overseen the restoration of the boats they were going to buy.

Hartley had somehow got the idea they could get help from Jefferson. He, himself, had thought it possible, but after he saw the look on his brother's face when he met him on the trail, he had known he had gone a mite far in pulling out and leaving Callie. But, goddamnit, he couldn't have stood the boredom of that primitive place or the nagging of that backwoods slut or the bawling of that kid a day longer! What the hell! He knew she'd be all right. Unsinkable, like a river tug, she was. Her kind always got by. Besides, the money he'd gotten from selling Henry and Jute to Jefferson was burning a hole in his pocket. He'd had a high old time in New Orleans for a while. He smiled, remembering. He'd spent his evenings gambling, visiting the brothels, or attending gay masquerade balls until his money had petered out.

Jason looked off down the river. Hartley had gone down beyond the point. He never made a move without that black bastard with him. Jason had to grin. Hartley didn't like women as much as he did. He'd take them if they were offered, but he didn't go out of his way to pursue them. His passion was money, comfort, and clothes, in that order. He kept a servant with him at all times to wait on him hand and foot and he knew how to keep him in line, too. He seldom laid a hand on the man, but when he did, he punished him severely.

Jason refused to think of yesterday's embarrassment. He had thought Callie would be over her sulks by now. And that damn kid acting the way he did! He wouldn't have cared a bit if Hartley hadn't been witness to the whole thing. Oh, hell! The sooner we get this business over with, the sooner we'll be gone from here, and the better it'll be.

He stood, flexed his shoulders, and looked back toward the woods. At first he didn't see her. She stood beside a large tree, her slim, small body blending with the background of thick brush. Her white face was framed with that gorgeous hair, and even from this distance he could see her red mouth. This was undoubtedly the most beautiful woman he'd ever seen! There was a tantalizing aloofness about her that fired his blood to the boiling point. Godamighty! With her on his arm every rich young swain in New Orleans would be clamoring for his company. If he had had any luck at all with the cards he'd not have to tramp through this godforsaken wilderness to help Hartley set up his stupid keelboat business.

Jason stood perfectly still. He knew that if he made one sudden move she would be away like a frightened doe. So he smiled and said casually, "Hello, Maggie."

He waited almost breathlessly, holding the smile on his face. She stood for several minutes, her hand on the tree trunk, her beautiful, clear green eyes on him. Finally, she moved and came toward him.

"Why'd the other man leave ya here?"

Jason had to force himself to look away from her. "He went downriver to look for possible landing sites. I'm waiting for him to come back."

She walked around him, looking at him from every angle. He wondered if she could hear the pounding of his heart. She touched the material of his shirt, holding it between her thumb and forefinger.

"This is purty. Why don't ya wear buckskins like Jeff 'n Will?"

"Gentlemen from New Orleans don't dress in buckskins. They wear fine silk shirts. The ladies wear silk, too. Their dresses are made from silk much finer than this."

"What do they wear under 'em?"

Jason's eyes devoured her, drinking in her beauty, but he kept his voice impersonal and his hands at his side.

"They wear silk underneath, too. Sit down and I'll tell you about it, and about the beautiful silk undergarments I've seen in the shops that come all the way from China and the South Seas."

"They wear China underdrawers?" She had such a puzzled look on her beautiful face that Jason had to bite his lips to keep from bursting out with laughter.

"Silk underdrawers from a country called China." Oh, God! Excitement made his heart knock against his rib cage. She'd be worth a king's ransom in New Orleans.

She moved away from him and leaned against a boulder.

"Why'd ya go off'n leave yore woman?"

Goddamnit! She was difficult to talk too. Did everyone in the country know he'd run out on his wife? He kept his irritation from showing in his face and even managed to look a little sad. "My father was dying and I had to go to New Orleans to be with him. Then I came down with the fever myself and couldn't get back until now."

"Ya don't look poorly."

"I'm not now, but I was." He took the scarf from around his neck and held it out to her. "Would you like to have this? It would serve to tie back your hair."

She took it from his hand and held it to her cheek. "It's soft."

"Would you like me to put it on your hair?"

"No," she said and twisted the scarf around her hand.

She was as small as a China doll and perfect in

every way. Jason could visualize her in a beautiful
blue gown with a voluptuous skirt that empha-
sized her tiny waist. He would bring her hair up
to the top of her head and tie it with a ribbon.
With her innocence and ethereal beauty she'd be
worth anything he had to do to get her. He would
take her to New Orleans and make a fortune.

"I like talking to you," he said in a desperate
attempt to keep a conversation going so she
wouldn't suddenly vanish.

"Why?"

"Well...you're nice to talk to. You seem to be
at home in the woods."

"I like the woods."

"Do you always walk?"

She shook her head. "I run. I like t' run."

"Do you have a horse?"

"No."

"Would you ride a horse if you had one?"

"No." She tilted her head, but kept her eyes on
him.

She was listening. Goddamnit! Was Hartley
coming back? "Will you come talk to me again?"
Jason desperately tried to think of a reason to keep
her from fleeing.

She lifted her shoulders in a careless shrug,
then with a movement so quick he scarcely registered it, she was around the boulder and gone.
He darted after her, but she had disappeared into
the woods like a wisp of smoke. His eyes caught
the flutter of something white, and he cursed viciously. She had left the scarf he'd given her
draped over a berry bush. He hastened to retrieve
it before Hartley arrived.

• • •

It was evening.

Jason had been unable to get the beautiful wood nymph out of his mind. Hartley and the black had come back and the three of them returned to the house. The slave picked up clean garments for them and they went to the creek to bathe. Jason knew there was a big tin tub in the shed that was used for bathing during the winter, but Jefferson hadn't offered it. A creek bath was better than nothing, and besides, Hartley didn't seem to mind.

Callie and Amos took their places at the supper table. Jason ignored them. There was no pressure on him to make conversation when Hartley was around. He was charming to the women and discussed with Jefferson the possibility of all the territory included in the Louisiana Purchase breaking up into individual states.

Jason left the kitchen after the meal and almost stumbled over Antone squatted outside the door. The black had a mark across his face. Jason chuckled. Hartley must have lost his temper and taken a willow switch to his slave.

He walked out toward the outbuildings. When he left here before, he was in a hurry and traveling light. He had left some things that had belonged to his pa behind. More than likely Jefferson had put the bag in the shed, and rats would have chewed it up by now, he thought resentfully. But if he could find it, there might be a few things he could salvage. He entered the semidarkened building and waited until his eyes became accustomed to the gloom, then moved toward the back and a shelf built close to the roof.

He was reaching for the flat leather pack when an arm locked about his neck, digging into his windpipe and choking off his breath. His hands clawed at the arm. He was acutely aware of the knife point in his back. The arm tightened viciously and he felt himself begin to black out. He never thought he'd die like this, he thought just as the arm loosened. He took great gulps of air into his lungs, feeling the bite of the knife even more distinctly now.

"I promised Jeff I'd not kill ya, but, Gawd, how I'd like to shove this here knife into yore gizzard 'n twist the life outta ya!"

"W—ill? Will Murdock?"

"Will Murdock, ya gawddamn hunk a useless horseshit!" Will spun him around, letting the knife rake across his back, and shoved him against the wall. "I never said I'd not beat yore face in." He hit him with such force that Jason stood for an instant, then slid down the wall to the floor. "Shitfire! Don't ya black out on me, ya fuckin' bastard! I want ya to feel ever'thin' I'm goin' to do to ya." Will grabbed a bucket and dipped it into the water barrel. The full force of the water hit Jason in the face and he shook his head groggily. The next bucketful brought him to full awareness.

"Ahh...What?" He rolled onto his knees and got shakily to his feet. He stood swaying and dabbing the sleeve of his shirt to his face.

"Are ya in the mood to talk or do ya want more?" Will stood on spread legs, arms crossed over his chest, the knife still clutched in his hands.

"What the hell's eatin' you? I never did anything to you."

"It's fer what ya done to Callie 'n the boy, ya shithead! Not for leavin' her. That was the only decent thin' ya done for her. But I'm goin' to beat the shit outta ya for the beatin's ya give her 'n the marks on the boy."

"What's that bitch been tellin' you? I whipped him, is all. All kids need a taste of the strap once in a while."

"Ya gawdammed sonofabitch! Ya whipped him till he bled an' ya held his hand over the fire with his ma afightin' and beggin' ya to leave him be!" Will's voice was thick with suppressed rage and the veins stood out at his temples. "Ya tied a string 'round his little dinger 'cause he wet the bed! Yo're a gutless excuse fer a man! Not even Jeff knows what ya done to Callie and that boy!"

"The kid wouldn't mind me," Jason said defiantly.

"If'n ya ever touch her or *her* boys a'gin, I'll kill ya! I'll hunt ya down if'n it takes the rest of my life. I'll kill ya, an' it'll take ya a long time to die." Will placed the tip of the knife beneath Jason's chin. "Be gone by tomorry an' in a week get yoreself on a boat a headin' downriver, else you'll be floatin' down with a knife in yore belly."

"I can't do that! I don't have any money and the only way I'll get some is by sticking to Hartley and his plan to run the keelboats." Jason tilted his head as far back as he could to keep the knife point from piercing his skin.

"I'll give ya money."

"You'll what?" Jason wasn't sure he'd heard correctly.

Will removed the knife and stepped back. "Ya

heard me, ya rotten piece of scum! Ya'll head downriver with money in yore pocket and a draft from my bank in Virginia. Yo're to go to Governor Wilkinson and petition for a divorce from Callie. Ya'll pay the sonofabitch off, and send me the papers. I'll see to it ya have a thousand in gold."

Jason began to laugh. "So that's—"

Will grabbed him by the throat. "Don't laugh at me. I'd get the same results if'n I kill ya and throw ya in the river. Jeff's friendship is all that's keepin' ya alive."

"Where'd you get that much money?" Jason said when he could catch his breath.

"That's none of yore gawdamned business!"

"What are you doing here in this hellhole if you could be someplace else?"

"I'm here because I want to be, but you'd not understand that. Hit's none of yore gawddammed business no how."

Jason was beginning to feel a little more sure of himself. Will wasn't going to kill him. He had something Will wanted: Callie. He couldn't resist taunting him a little.

"So you're hot for my little backwoods woman. She must have showed you something she didn't—"

Will's fist slammed into his face and Jason's head slammed into the wall. He didn't lose consciousness, but his jaw wished he had. He leaned against the wall, holding his sleeve to his face.

"Ya rotten sonofabitch!" Will's knife lashed out and ripped Jason's pants from the waist to the crotch. Jason's yell was one high-pitched screech of terror as the knife nicked the soft skin of his stomach. Will reached out and grabbed his soft male sex in a big, hard hand and posed the knife over it. "One slice from this knife is all it'd take to geld ya. It'd give me a heap a pleasure to do it, too." His voice was deadly quiet.

"No! No," he croaked. "No...pl—please..." He was sure he was going to faint.

With a vicious twist, Will pushed him from him. Jason let out another cry of pain and doubled over. It took several minutes and all the effort he could muster to straighten up, but he managed to do it.

"I'll go," he gasped. "I'll try to get Hartley to go."

"I don't give a gawddamn about Hartley."

"I'll talk to him tonight. I can't run out on him and leave here by myself."

"A'right," Will said reluctantly. "When yo're ridin' outta here, I'll meet ya in the woods with the money."

"I don't want Hartley to know."

"He won't. But if ya doublecross me, Jason, I'll find ya, 'n brother to Jeff or not, I'll kill ya. I want the papers in my hand six months from now. Is that understood?"

"I understand. You'll have them."

"If not, I know where to find ya—suck-assin' up to another shit like Van Buren." Will backed to the door and was gone.

A few minutes later, Jason came out of the shed. It was dark and he headed for the creek to bathe his face. The only thing that had happened that angered him was the beating and the verbal abuse. The rest of it was almost too good to be true.

• • •

Antone was in the room when Jason reached it an hour later. The black man was bending over Hartley's bunk, smoothing the covers. When he straightened up, he saw Jason's cut face, the blood on his shirt, and the split britches he was holding together with one hand.

"What are you looking at?"

"Nothin', suh."

"Get the hell outta here!" Jason's hand flew out and slapped the black man across the face. It was almost as if he was compelled to show his superiority over someone after the beating he had taken.

"Yas'sah." Antone walked stiffly from the room, his dignity taking away some of the satisfaction Jason had received by slapping him.

When Hartley came to the room later, Jason began his argument for leaving.

"I want to leave here in the morning, Hartley," he said casually. "I think it was a mistake to come traipsing through the woods when we could have come upriver by boat."

Hartley sat down on the bunk and held out a booted foot. Antone straddled his leg, and Hartley put his other foot on the man's posterior and pushed.

"We're making headway. I've already found a couple of sites that will be suitable. Everything worthwhile takes some work."

"If we go back to Saint Louis we can hire a boat to bring us upriver, and we can find our locations from the water. It makes more sense to me."

"We don't have that kind of money, Jason," Hartley explained patiently. "I told you when we started this trip that we had to be careful with what money we have. It will be quite some time before we'll realize a profit."

"I think I can get money from Jefferson, in fact I'm sure I can." Jason laughed and hoped it didn't sound too forced. "I suppose you've noticed there's not much love between me and my prude of a brother."

"Then why would he give you money?" Hartley asked quietly.

"To get rid of me. I'm sort of a thorn in his flesh. Jefferson can't tolerate anyone unless they think as he thinks, act as he acts, live as he lives. He's a sanctimonious bastard who is sure his way is always the right way."

"Is that why he busted your face?"

Jason gritted his teeth and winced as pain shot through his jaw. He'd thought Hartley was too much a gentlemen to ask about that. "You might say so," he answered stiffly.

"Have you told him you want to cut our visit short?"

"Not yet. I wanted to talk to you first."

"I suggest we stay over one more day. I want to treat Miss Jester to some of Antone's fish chowder and repay in some small way for their hospitality. Do you think you'd have any trouble catching us a nice, big catfish, Antone?"

"Naw'sah."

"Good. It's settled, then. We'll leave at dawn the day after tomorrow. God, but I'm tired and sore. Rub my back, Antone. Not there, you black bastard! Lower."

Jason congratulated himself. It had been easier

to get Hartley to agree to leave than he'd antici-
pated. Now he'd give Jefferson the news. He was
sure to pass it along to Will. One more day, he
thought, and I'll leave this place with money in
my pocket. It was far more than he'd hoped for.

Annie Lash and Jeff sat on the bench beneath
the sloping porch roof enjoying the evening cool-
ness. It had been a warm, muggy, trying day. Nervous tension had sapped their strength.

"This is good growing weather," Jeff explained.
"The corn is already ankle high, and it's only the
end of June."

"When will it be ready to harvest?"

"About the first of November, if we have a dry
fall."

"We'll have a harvest party and ask the Cornicks
and the two Gentry families. Or maybe we should
wait until Thanksgiving and have a feast like the
pilgrims did." Her voice had a lilting, happy
sound.

Jeff hugged her to him. He couldn't bring himself to tell her that he wouldn't be here in the fall,
that he'd be in Virginia testifying at the trial of
Aaron Burr. God almighty, it was going to be hard
to leave her! She had been beautiful before, but
now, basking in her newfound happiness, she radiated a beauty that caused his hungry eyes to
devour her and aroused him so strongly that his
breath stopped in his throat.

"Sweetheart." His voice was all tenderness and
pride.

"I love you," she said simply, but they were the
most important words in the world to him. She

reached to caress his smooth face with her fingertips. The joy of being in love had smoothed the stern lines from his face and he looked years younger despite his worry over Jason.

"I'm sorry to interrupt, brother." Jason's voice came out of the darkness. "I thought you'd be pleased to know that Hartley and I plan to leave the day after tomorrow."

Jeff kept his arm tightly around Annie Lash. "You've found the locations for your landing sites?"

"You might say that." Jason laughed nastily. "I'm sure you'll be glad to see the backside of me."

"Yes, I will," Jeff said honestly. "I've finally realized there's no more I can do for you. Now it's up to you to do what you will with your life."

"Yes, it is up to me, isn't it?" There was a sneer in his voice, but Jeff ignored it when he spoke.

"The decent thing for you to do now is to divorce Callie. Set her free to make a new life for herself and her children. You don't want them, Jason. They don't fit into your scheme of things."

"No, they don't, but a divorce takes money."

"You could manage it. You always manage to get the other things you want."

"Can I expect any help from you? It takes money to pay off the officials."

"Afterwards. Not before."

"How do I know you'd come through with the money?"

"That's a chance you'll have to take. I've been taking chances on you all your life, now it's your turn. Set Callie free and I'll give you a sum in gold."

"How much?"

"It will depend on how much trouble you cause while you're here."

"You love to have the whip hand, don't you, dear brother? I'll think about it. Do you plan to marry...her?" There was no mistaking the intended slur by not using Annie Lash's name.

Annie Lash felt the muscles jerk in Jeff's arm. She was tense as she waited to see what he would do. He didn't say anything and a long, quiet moment passed.

When he did speak, his voice was flat and wicked, taut with restrained anger. "I'm proud to say that Annie Lash and I will be married as soon as I can arrange it."

Jason's unmistakably contemptuous laugh came out of the darkness. "Congratulations," he said dryly, and went back into the house.

Annie Lash stroked Jeff's arm with a touch intended to comfort. "Shh...He was trying to make you angry. Don't let him succeed."

Sometimes she couldn't believe all that had happened to her. It was so wonderful to be in love, to share his happy moments as well as his trying ones. He filled every corner of her heart without her being able to do anything about it. Her love for him had given the world a whole new brightness.

"Shall we go to bed, darling?" she whispered against his cheek. Happiness flowed in her blood and a little smile of pure delight danced on her mouth.

"My Annielove! I'll never get used to having you with me and knowing you want me." His voice was husky, tender. His lips found her ear. "You smell like roses."

"Of course. Callie and I picked some rose petals, dried them, and tied them in a little bag. I rub them on my cheeks so I'll smell good for you."

The feel of her against him and the scent of her filled his head. He swallowed hard, because he wanted her so much. His hand moved up and down her back, and over her rounded hips in gentle possession.

"This has been a very long day," he whispered passionately against her lips. "Let's go to bed."

"Hummm...I was ready an hour ago."

They went to her room and Jeff struck a flint to the candle on the table beside the bed. "I'll look around while you're getting ready, sweetheart. I always take a turn about the place at night."

Annie Lash removed her dress and hung it on a peg next to Jeff's shirt. It brought a soft smile to her face to see her clothes hanging beside his. Humming a happy little tune, she sat down on the edge of the bed, unlaced her shoes, and walked barefoot across the rag carpet to set them beside Jeff's high moccasins leaning against the wall. Her foot bumped them as she passed and one fell over. She reached down to set it right and drew back, her mind rapidly filling with terror.

A snake slithered out of the boot, its small head just a little way off the floor, its beady eyes on her and its forked tongue sliding in and out of its mouth rapidly. The small body formed an "S" shape, then swiftly coiled. At first Annie Lash was too terrified to move, then she dived for the bed, her horrified eyes riveted to the writhing creature on the floor.

"Oh! Oh! Jeff...erson! Jeff...er...son!" she screamed.

It seemed to her she waited a lifetime before the door burst open and Jeff was there.

"What's the matter? What—"

"Snake! On the floor!" She was trembling so violently she could hardly point her shaking finger.

"Stay where you are. It can't get to you."

Annie Lash saw Jason and Hartley crowd into the doorway. She watched Jeff move around the snake, go to the fireplace and grab the long, iron fire prodder that hung there. She closed her eyes as he smashed the flat head and then looped the snake's body, still in its death throes, over the poker and carried it from the room.

"What is it?" Hartley asked and backed out of the way.

"Water moccasin."

"Ugh! I hate snakes."

Annie Lash sat in the middle of the bed and let the tears run down her cheeks. She hated her weakness. When Jeff returned he closed the door, came to the bed, and took her trembling body in his arms.

"I'm sorry I'm such a coward," she sobbed.

"Where did the thing come from, sweetheart? We've never found a water snake in the house before."

"I knocked your boot over with my foot and the ...thing crawled out." She sniffed back the tears and wiped her nose on the end of her shift.

"Are you sure it came from my boot? I can't believe—" he asked, and just barely bit back the rest of the words he was going to say.

"Yes, I'm sure. I saw it come out."

"It's gone and you've nothing to be afraid of, now. It's rare that a water snake comes in the house and it'll probably never happen again. Come on, get to bed, sweetheart. I've waited all day for this."

Later, with Annie Lash snuggled in his arms, Jeff pondered every detail of the incident. His busy mind worked far into the night, and before morning he slipped from the room to find Will.

CHAPTER
SEVENTEEN

Annie Lash was disappointed to find herself alone in the bed. She yawned, stretched, and let her mind move back to the night before. She should feel disgracefully wanton; instead, she felt a glorious fulfillment and an extraordinary sense of well-being. She bounded out of bed, dressed in the early morning light, and went across to the kitchen.

Callie heard her stirring around, opened the bedroom door, and peeked out. When she saw that Annie Lash was alone, she came through the door and closed it behind her.

"Mornin', Callie. Is your room awfully hot with the door closed?"

"It hasn't been so far. I swear I don't know what I'm going to do, Annie Lash. Amos wet the bed twice last night. He wet his bunk and I put him in bed with me and he did it again. He hates it

306

so! Poor little fellow cried half the night. He begged me not to hang the sheets outside to dry. He's afraid everyone will know."

"No one is going to know!" Annie Lash said fiercely. "I'll take the sheets off my bed and off Abe's and we'll wash them all. It'll be a washday in the middle of the week."

"You always seem to come up with something," Callie said with a relieved sigh. "Annie Lash, that child is a nervous wreck. I don't know what he'd do if Jason makes another attempt to take hold of him."

"Jason told Jefferson last night that they'll be leaving tomorrow. We only have to get through this day. We'll make sure Amos is with us and Jason doesn't get a chance to take hold of him."

"Oh, thank goodness. It can't be too soon to suit me."

"I haven't seen hide nor hair of Will." Annie Lash filled the teakettle and swung it over the flame. "I thought he might take Amos over to his place."

"He thinks it's best that he stay away while Jason's here." Callie moved quickly to slice the slab of bacon Jeff had left on the work counter. "Is Jeff milking?"

"The milk pail is gone, he must be. Callie... I love him." Annie Lash's clear eyes shone. "I'd not have shared his bed if I didn't love him and know that we'll be married."

"I know that!" Callie reached over and squeezed her arm. "I'm happy for you and Jefferson. He's a good man and he deserves someone like you."

"He might not think so this morning. I made a

fool out of myself last night screaming the house down. I just can't abide crawling things. Even worms give me the chills, and... snakes! There's no other way to put it, I have a horror of them. They scare me to death!"

"That's the first snake we've found in the house. I've seen a few little garter snakes in the garden, but they're harmless. Who'd a thought one of them awful things would've come up from the river?"

"I know one thing: I'm going to be mighty careful when I put my foot in a shoe from now on." She shuddered. "When I think about what could've happened to Jefferson I get the cold chills."

Jeff came in with the milk and the three of them had a quiet breakfast. Annie Lash fervently wished the day would be over so that they would have the homestead to themselves once again.

"We're going to wash today, Jefferson," Callie said with a nervous glance toward the door.

"It looks like a fine day for it. I'll set up the boiling pot and bring out the tubs."

It seemed to Annie Lash that Jeff was extra quiet and withdrawn this morning. She was sure it would be a relief to him, as it would be to all of them, when Jason and his friend departed.

Callie fed the children and Annie Lash gathered up the wash. The reason for their haste wasn't voiced, but both women wanted to leave the kitchen before Hartley and Jason came in for breakfast.

When Annie Lash went out through the dogtrot she saw Antone sitting on his heels beside the house. Had he spent the night there? She called to him.

"Antone. Come on in and eat something." He followed her into the kitchen and she filled a porringer with mush and laced it with syrup. The black man hung back until she shoved the bowl in his hands. "Hurry and eat before they come in," she urged. "Mercy sakes! Doesn't that man think you've got to eat and have a place to sleep just like everyone else?"

"Yas'm...." Antone bobbed his head, but his eyes flicked nervously to the doorway.

He moved over to a corner beside the stove, squatted on his heels, and began to eat the mush as though he were starved. Annie Lash filled a mug with hot tea and put in a generous amount of milk. The look on his face when she gave it to him caused her to look at him sharply. There was more intelligence behind those dark eyes than he allowed to show.

"You can fix their breakfast, Antone. Fry grits, or give them mush and milk. The tea is here." She set the tin on the counter. "We're going to the creek to wash."

"Yas'm." He kept bobbing his head up and down and she wished he wouldn't do it. "Missy?"

"Yes?" She looked at him over her armload of clothes.

"I git big rivva fish. Mastah want chowdah."

"Well, all right," she said reluctantly. "Go ahead and fix it. If there's anything you need that you can't find, we'll be down at the creek."

"Yas'm."

Annie Lash looked down at him and shook her head. "If you belonged to me, Antone, the first thing I'd tell you to do would be to stop using that word!" It was impossible for Annie Lash to hold back the giggle that insisted on coming out.

The black man looked at her blankly, then he began to smile. "Yas'm."

"Oh, you're impossible!" she said laughingly. "I put beans on to simmer. If we won't be needing them for nooning, set them aside."

His dark head bobbed again and he watched her go out the door.

It took no more than an hour to do the washing. When the sheets were on the line and the wash water emptied, Callie sat on the quilt with Abe. Annie Lash took Amos by the hand and they went to the barnlot where they puttered with unnecessary chores to fill the time. They scattered grain for the hens, carried water to the already filled troughs, searched for eggs, and found none.

It almost broke Annie Lash's heart to see the subdued little boy trudging along beside her, holding tightly to her hand. The only time he smiled was when he saw the old wolf-dog slinking along behind Jute, who had come to the barn with a broken harness. He ran to the dog and threw his arms about the shaggy neck. She had seen this many times, and each time her heart came up in her throat. It was strange, she mused, that that old dog loved and trusted the child about as much as he hated and distrusted everyone else except Jute and Maggie.

She waited and watched. The rough, red tongue came out and licked the boy's face. Soft mewing sounds came from his throat. Jute came out of the shed with the harness thrown over his shoulder. He stood with his head down, grinning shyly. He was too bashful to speak to Annie Lash.

"Yaw'll stay wid Masta Amos, dawg," he ordered.

"What's his name, Jute?"

Jute tilted his head and looked at the dog as if he had never thought about giving the dog a name. "Dawg, missy. He jist named Dawg."

When she could think of nothing else to do in the barn, Annie Lash sent Amos back to where Callie sat with Abe in her arms and went into the house. She walked into the kitchen feeling like an intruder. Jason and Hartley sat at the table and Antone moved quietly between the work counter and hearth. Hartley got to his feet when she entered. Jason looked up, but remained seated. It was a deliberate snub, and Annie Lash wanted to smile at his sulky, childish behavior.

"Mornin', ma'am. We're enjoying an extra cup of tea. Will you join us?" Hartley was all smiles. His face was clean shaven, his hair ratted into a pompadour high over his forehead with the top hair smoothed over it. He wore a blue silk shirt that matched the blue of his eyes, tight cord pants, and boots that were so shiny black she could almost see reflections in them.

"No, thank you. I came to get my work basket."

Annie Lash deliberately let her eyes linger on Jason's face. There was no doubt in her mind that he'd been handled roughly. But by whom? His mouth was cut and swollen. The side of his face was skinned and bruised. He frowned and flushed when he caught her looking at him, but she refused to turn her eyes away.

"Have you had an accident, Mr. Pickett?" she asked innocently with raised brows. She had to press her lips together to hold back a smile.

"It's none of—"

"Now, Jason," Hartley laughingly interrupted. "We're leaving tomorrow and you shouldn't be rude to your future sister-in-law."

"It was rude of me for asking the obvious, Mr. Van Buren. Excuse me," she said pleasantly, feeling apprehensive and not at all pleasant. "Have you found everything you need, Antone?"

"Yas'm."

"Antone tells me you're allowing him to prepare the noon meal, ma'am. That's generous of you. I haven't had fish chowder since I left New Orleans and probably won't get any more until I return. You're in for a real treat, I assure you."

"I'm sure we are. Antone, there's another crock of milk in the cellar if you need it."

"Yas'm."

Annie Lash made her escape. Her mind was flooded with questions. Who in the world gave Jason the beating? she thought as she left the house. Was it Jefferson? Or Will? Had Will come in the night and called Jason out? Jefferson would have known if he had, but he hadn't said anything about it. She decided not to say anything to Callie. There was a chance Jason wouldn't show up for the noon meal, and there was no need for Callie to worry about it until she had to. Not that she'd care a whit about the beating. She didn't want any trouble between Jason and Will. Personally, Annie

Lash was rather pleased. It gave her spirits a small boost just knowing that Jason had gotten his comeuppance.

The morning dragged for the women sitting by the creek. It seemed to them such a waste of time to be sitting idly when there was so much to be done. Annie Lash watched Jeff's white head move about the barnlots, making chores for himself. It was hard for him to be idle, too. She told Amos stories while she wove her needle in and out of a small hole in one of Jefferson's stockings, pulled the thread through, and wove again. The sheets dried and Amos helped her fold them.

Finally noon came, and there was nothing else to do but go back to the house. Annie Lash was relieved to see Jeff come from the shed. He came down the path to meet them, took the basket of clothes from her hand, and walked into the house ahead of them.

Antone was alone in the kitchen. He looked up, bobbed his head, and looked away.

"I hope he washed his hands," Annie Lash murmured to Callie.

Jeff took the clothes basket to Callie's room, then went out into the dogtrot without a word.

"Jefferson's edgy," Callie said.

"He's anxious for the day to be over just like the rest of us. Isn't it a shame? Jason is his only blood relative with the exception of Abe and Amos. I know he feels badly about the way he behaves."

"Jason hasn't even looked at Abe," Callie said sadly. "Poor little boy. It's just like he don't amount to anything."

"Oh, fiddle! I don't feel sorry for Abe. He'll be

better off if he never knows his father. He's got you and Will. He's got me and Jefferson and Amos to love him. He'll do just fine without Jason Pickett!"

"I swan to goodness, Annie Lash. I can feel so down in the dumps, and you come along and say something that makes so much sense. I just got to keep tellin' myself how good I got it now to what it was. It was just a lucky day for me when Jefferson found you in Saint Louis."

Jason came in followed by Hartley and Jefferson. He stood stiffly beside the door, ignoring everyone in the room. Hartley moved past him and placed some sprigs of honeysuckle on the tressle table.

"Is everything ready, Antone?" He peered into the kettle simmering on the hearth.

"Yas'sah."

"Cut the cornbread in nice square pieces this time," he said pleasantly and looked over the table with a critical eye, rearranging a spoon, moving a bowl. "I'd sure like to persuade you to open a supply station here on the property, Merrick. That piece of land to the west would make an ideal place for a landing. You could be a very rich man in a few years."

"It's something to think about," Jeff said from where he stood beside the door. 'I've not given much thought to business. Farming has been on my mind for a long while."

"Are you ready to serve, Antone?"

"Yas'sah."

Jeff moved to the head of the table and motioned for everyone to take their places.

"May I sit beside you, young man?" Hartley said to Amos, and moved onto the bench beside him after the women were seated.

Jeff remained standing even after they were all seated. Annie Lash watched his face and was swept by a premonition of trouble. She glanced at Callie sitting on the other side of Amos with Abe on her lap. Her hand was behind Amos, touching his back to reassure him. She had looked once at her husband and then away. Jason sat slouched on the bench opposite them, his swollen mouth drawn down at the corners.

Antone moved quietly. He placed a plate of perfectly cut squares of cornbread on the table beside a crock of butter.

"It's a pity we're not going to be here longer, ma'am. I'd have Antone teach one of your blacks to cook. Cooking is one of the few things they—"

"They're not used to quality living, Hartley, so save your breath," Jason said belligerently. "The niggers are free. My brother doesn't *hold* with slavery."

"It's your brother's right to believe what he wants to believe, Jason." Hartley flashed him an odd little smile. "We can't all be right, and we can't all be wrong."

"My brother won't agree with you, Hartley. He's always right! Ask him anything. He'll give you the *right* answer."

"Don't ruin what could be a pleasant meal with your sarcasm, Jason." Hartley's words had a bite in them, but he had an indulgent smile on his face.

Annie Lash sat motionless, her eyes moving around the table. She was unable to say a word. Her thoughts were going wild with speculation as to why Jefferson was still standing and why he had that tense, watchful look on his face.

Antone went to Jeff's end of the table with the kettle and a small dipper. He ladled the thick soup into his bowl, then moved clockwise and served Hartley. He started to fill the bowl in front of Amos, and Jeff reached across and turned the bowl upside down.

"That's enough. Put the pot down." He said the words quietly, but they fell like stones in the quiet room. There was no mistaking the tone of command in his voice.

Visibly shaken, Antone looked from him to Hartley and back again before he carried the pot back to the hearth and hung it on the crane.

Hartley had picked up his spoon. Now he carefully placed it beside his bowl and looked at Jeff, a smiling question on his face.

"What seems to be wrong, Merrick? I think the chowder smells delicious."

"Then eat it," Jeff grated. His jaws were clenched and his dark eyes were hard as agates.

Hartley's smile dropped away and his face turned a dull, angry red. Every head at the table was turned in his direction.

"What? What's wrong with you, Merrick? I... don't understand what—"

"I think you do. Eat your soup."

"I can't... eat, until the ladies are served." He gave his bowl a shove as if to move it away from him. The push sent the bowl over, spilling its contents along the table. "Oh, how clumsy of me! I'm sorry, ma'am," he said to Annie Lash.

She got to her feet to get a cloth to mop up the spill.

"Leave it," Jeff said sharply. She sat down again, dumbfounded. He set his own bowl in front of Hartley. "Eat," he said again.

Jason jumped to his feet and slammed his hand down on the table with such force it bounced the empty bowls. "What the hell is the matter with you, Jefferson? I'll not have you treating my friend—"

"Shut up and sit down!" Jeff roared. He didn't even look at his brother when he spoke. His eyes remained on Hartley.

Caught by Jeff's tone, Jason looked from his brother to Hartley and back again. "What the hell is going on?" he demanded.

"I'll tell you what's going on after your friend eats the chowder his servant prepared for us."

All eyes were on Hartley. Even Amos sat in openmouthed fascination, forgetting for the moment his fear of his father.

"I don't know what your brother is thinking, Jason. If he didn't like the chowder all he had to do was say so. I've been insulted and I shall demand satisfaction." Hartley's knuckles were white where he gripped the edge of the table.

Annie Lash drew in a dry, hurting breath. She had seen Hartley's face change from one of friendly boyishness to the cold face of a hard man burning with anger. The air was heavy with explosive tension.

"Eat your soup and I'll apologize," Jeff said.

He never moved his merciless dark stare from Hartley's face.

"I'll not give you the satisfaction of dragging this insulting situation any further," Hartley snarled and got to his feet.

"What did you give your black to put in the soup?" Jeff demanded.

"What are you talking about?" Hartley's lips were quivering with anger, his nostrils flaring. He looked cornered, desperate.

"It was poison!"

"You crazy fool! I gave him some...flavoring! Ask him."

"Hartley, for God's sake!" Jason's confusion was giving way to doubt. "Drink the soup and prove him wrong."

Hartley placed his hands on the edge of the table, bowed his head and shook it sadly. "You, too?" he said wearily. "My friend—" Then he moved.

Hartley's actions were so quick the eyes could scarcely follow them. One arm grabbed Amos up against him, and at the same instant a long, thin blade appeared in his hand. He held it inches from the boy's throat. He backed away from the table, dragging him with him.

"Move out of the way," he snarled.

At first Amos was so frightened he couldn't move. Then he let out an agonized wail, "Ma... ma!"

Callie screamed. "Amos!" She tried to stand. Her cry scared Abe and he let out a piercing scream.

"You bastard!" Jason yelled. "You were going to kill all of us! Why? For God's sake! Why?"

"Stay back!" Hartley's face had taken on the expression of a cornered wolf.

Annie Lash's thoughts flew wildly, crazily. How could she have ever thought he was handsome?

"Put the boy down!" Jeff crouched to spring, a knife in his hand.

"Move out of the way or I'll cut his throat!" Hartley had backed to the wall beside the door.

"No, you won't. You don't stand a chance without him."

"Jeff...er...son, please!" Callie was almost hysterical. Her agonized scream was heard over Abe's loud, frightened cries.

"Get out there, you black, bungling bastard, and saddle my horse," Hartley shouted. Antone was so frightened his shoulders were hunched and his head hung between them as if he were trying to hide. His eyes went from Hartley to Jeff. Jeff nodded and he sidled out the door.

Amos was almost out of his mind with fright. His eyes were large and wild. Tears flowed down his freckled cheeks. Hartley held him in a grip so tight he could hardly breathe, but with every gasp of breath he called for his mama.

Anger blazed in Annie Lash. She had never before felt the desire to kill. On the trail she had acted automatically when she shot the robber, but now she wanted desperately to kill Hartley Van Buren for what he was doing to Amos. Callie's screams filled her ears. She reached over and jerked the crying baby from her arms.

"Don't hurt him! Please...don't hurt him," Callie pleaded. "He's just a...little boy!"

"Stay back or I'll kill him," Hartley snarled.

"Take me...take me," Callie pleaded and moved toward him. "Take me and let him go!"

"Shut up and stay back!" There was desperation in his eyes as they shifted wildly about.

"You hurt that boy and you'll wish you were dead a hundred times over," Jeff warned.

Hartley backed out the door with Amos held like a trapped animal against his chest. The child's terror-filled eyes were fixed on his mother.

The horrifying scene danced before Annie Lash's eyes like a terrible nightmare. Oh, dear God, she prayed, let me wake up and find this is a dream.

Jeff was at the doorway almost as soon as Hartley cleared it. He held his arm across to prevent Callie from running out into the yard.

"No, Callie! Don't crowd him," he said sharply. He moved quickly and was out the door.

Annie Lash followed after Jason, who seemed to be in a shocked stupor. Abe had ceased to cry and lay against her, hiccupping and sucking his thumb.

Hartley stood at the corner of the house, his eyes roaming the landscape. Antone was in the barnlot, trying to catch the skittish mare.

"I'm the one you want, Van Buren," Jeff called. "You came to get me. I'll throw my knife down. I'm not armed." He moved into the yard with his hands in the air.

Hartley ignored Jeff and yelled to Antone. "Get a horse, any horse, and put a bridle on it!" He started across the yard with Amos screaming and crying.

Callie made an inarticulate sound in her throat and started forward. Jason grabbed her arm and held her. Sobbing with terror, tears streaming down her face, she swung her fist and hit him square in the face.

"Gawddamm you!" she screamed. He loosed his hold and she jerked free.

"Ma...ma! Ma...ma!" Amos screamed with every breath.

Hartley didn't see the wolf-dog when he first came out of the shadows beside the shed, but Annie Lash did. The dog stood on stiffened legs, his head low, his eyes on Hartley, his teeth exposed in a silent, vicious snarl. The hair stood up on his back from his neck to his extended, bushy tail. Annie Lash stood mesmerized, knowing something was going to happen.

"Ma...ma!" The boy's agonized wail rent the air.

Hartley turned and saw the dog the instant he sprang. His natural instinct moved his arm up to shield his face, taking the knife from the child's throat. The force of the dog's weight knocked him to the ground and he lost his hold on Amos. The child fell hard and rolled free of the tangled bodies of the man and the dog.

The sounds now were a mingling of vicious growls from the dog and short, desperate cries from Hartley. Jeff rushed in and scooped Amos up in his arms and thrust him at Callie. By the time he turned back it was too late to help Hartley. He lay sprawled on the ground, his throat open, his windpipe torn from it. The wolf-dog stood over him, hunched, ready to attack again, his muzzle wet with blood.

"Oh, my God!" Jason croaked.

Annie Lash turned her back and buried her face against the babe in her arms. She fought to control her heaving stomach. When she looked again, the wolf-dog was moving away toward the shed, dragging his hind leg, his head low. Jeff was kneeling beside Hartley. The torn arteries in the man's neck poured blood onto the ground. She put her free arm around Callie and urged her away. Amos had both arms wrapped about his mother's neck and his legs locked about her waist, clutching her as if he'd never let her go.

The two women stood holding onto each other, the two children between them. The last few minutes had taken a toll of their strength. Callie crooned to her son, and pressed kisses on his wet little face.

"It's all right, my sweet baby. You're all right, now. Oh, my little boy—"

When the shot came the sound was so abrupt and so unexpected that Callie screeched and Annie Lash jumped with fright. Her first thought was of Jeff. Oh, God! Where was he? She looked wildly around and saw Jason reloading his gun as Jeff ran toward him.

"No, you fool! No!"

"I'm going to kill the black sonofabitch who was going to poison us! Stay out of my way, Jefferson!"

"You, fool! If not for him we'd all be dead!"

"I'm going to kill him, I tell you. I'm going to

kill him!" Jason's voice was shrill and the words coming out of his mouth were almost incoherent. He was bordering on hysteria and his hands shook so he could hardly hold the gun.

Jeff reached out, yanked the gun out of his hand, and slapped him on the side of his face.

"Get yourself together!" he commanded sharply. "Your assassin friend is dead! Go get something to cover him with. Hurry up!"

Jason stumbled away, keeping his eyes away from the gruesome sight on the ground.

A few minutes later, Annie Lash heard the sound of a running horse. She looked up to see Will riding recklessly into the yard. He pulled the animal up so sharply it sat back on it's haunches. He jumped from the saddle and ran to where Jeff was covering Hartley's body with a canvas.

"What the hell happened? I heard a shot."

"Jason was shooting at Antone."

"Who is it?" he asked anxiously and lifted the canvas.

"Hartley. He had grabbed Amos and the wolf-dog killed him. Jason thought Antone was in on the plot to kill us."

"Then ya was right?"

"I was right. Godamighty, Will! It was close. The sonofabitch was going to kill all of them in order to get to me," Jeff said as if he couldn't believe it.

"The sonofabitch fuckin' bastard!" Will cursed. "God, Jeff, if ya hadn't a got 'em..." His words trailed off.

"I didn't, the wolf-dog did."

Annie Lash and Callie, unable to bring themselves to go inside the kitchen, sat on the benches under the porch roof. Each held a child in her arms. Callie crooned to Amos, trying to assure him that he was safe. Jason walked restlessly up and down.

Will came around the end of the house. He ignored Jason and went straight to Callie.

"Ya a'right?"

She nodded. "Oh, Will! It was terrible. I was never so scared in all my life. Poor Amos ... poor baby ..."

Jeff, with his hand firmly attached to Antone's arm, spoke from the end of the porch. "Let's go in and have a cup of tea. I think we deserve one."

Will took Amos from Callie's arms and carried him into the house. The thundercloud look on his face dared Jason to comment. He sat down on the bunk with the boy on his lap. Jeff came in pushing Antone ahead of him. The black man hovered near the door as if he were about to flee. His eyes were large and fearful and kept wandering toward Jason.

Annie Lash set out mugs and poured tea, avoiding the pot of fish chowder as if it were the plague.

Jeff stood beside Antone. "We have this man to thank for our lives," he said. "He made sure that I saw him pour the contents of a bottle Van Buren gave him in the soup." He waited a moment for them to absorb what he was telling them. "I was sure Van Buren was here to kill me after Annie Lash found the snake in my boot. I was watching for him to make a move, but, my God, I never dreamed he would attempt to kill all of you in order to get me!"

Annie Lash's face went white. "Oh, Jefferson—why?"

"It's a long story, sweetheart—one I'll have to tell you now. First, we've got to get rid of this batch of poisoned soup and make sure none of the animals get to it."

"Suh," Antone spoke in a shaky voice. "I put rivva water in de chowdah." He reached inside his shirt and brought out two small bottles. One was empty and one full of a clear liquid. "Mastah say dis make de flavah, but I seed 'em put hit on meat fo ol' dawg down to Saint Louis. Ol' dawg fall daid." He shook his head. "Me doan kill li'l chil', me doan kill missy." His eyes rolled toward Annie Lash and he held out the bottle to Jeff.

Jeff took the bottle and looked at it. "He would have killed you when he realized what you'd done."

"Yas'sah."

"How long have you been with him?"

"Hartley won him in a poker game last winter," Jason answered, impatience making itself known in the tone of his voice. Then, as if compelled to say what was on his mind, he blurted, "I don't understand any of this. Why was he going to kill me, too?"

"Stupid, as usual, Pickett." Will spoke from the corner of the room where he sat cradling Amos in his arms. "He was working for Aaron Burr. His job was ta keep me'n Jeff from gettin' to Virginny to testify at the trial. If he'd a killed ever'body here, he was goin' to try to ambush me, 'n there'd be no witnesses. Ever'body he hired to do his dirty work bungled the job. He had to try 'n do it hisself. Jeff had it figured out after the snake crawled out of his boot."

"But why was the sonofabitch going to kill *me?* We were going into the keelboat business together!" Jason said with disbelief. He took a square of cloth from his pocket and wiped the sweat from his face.

"Ya bastard!" Will snarled. "Can't ya think of nothin' but yore...blasted self? What about Callie and the boys? What about Annie Lash?" In his anger, Will stood up. The only thing that kept him from hitting Jason was the child that clung to his neck. "How come ya let that murderin' shithead get his hands on this here youngun?" he demanded.

Jason started to reply, then changed his mind. Self-preservation was uppermost in his mind. Nothing that had happened here today was going to change his plans, and so he'd be better off if he didn't antagonize Will Murdock. If the man was willing to fork out the money so he could have Callie and the kids, Jason would damn sure take it and let him have them. Besides, he hadn't been able to get the girl, Maggie, off his mind. He was going to have her. He'd have money now to take her to New Orleans. His heart began to hammer at the thought.

"Do you know if Van Buren carried Antone's papers with him?"

Jeff was talking to him, and he pushed thoughts of Maggie to the back of his mind. "I don't know for sure, but I think so."

"Well, he's going to lose him in another poker game."

"What do you mean, lose him in a poker game? You can't do that. Hartley's dead and that nigger'll go to pay off some of his debts. He owed me, too." Jason looked sulkily at Antone. "I figure I've got as much right to that nigger as you have."

"You figured wrong, Jason. This *man* is going to be free."

"But...that nigger's worth a fortune!" Jason sputtered.

"Don't cross me, Jason!" Jeff shouted, his voice trembling with anger. "This is a man! He's not a horse or a mule. He's a man with a brain! He used that brain today and saved our lives at the risk of losing his own. You'll not make any mention of him when you leave here. Is that understood?"

Jason's lips curled in a sneer. "Papa was right about you, Jefferson. You're a fool! You're a sanctimonious fool and you'll never have any more than this chicken coop here in the back of nowhere."

"I feel sorry for you, Jason." Jeff looked at his brother so steadily that he turned his eyes away.

"What are you going to do about that beast that killed Hartley?"

"Nothing. Absolutely nothing!" The look on Jeff's face dared his brother to argue the matter.

Annie Lash watched and listened to what was going on as if she were suspended somewhere in a void, somewhere outside herself. The information Will let drop so casually about him and Jeff stunned her. A fluttering that began in her heart settled in the pit of her stomach and refused to go away, even as she pressed her hands tightly to it.

Jeff hadn't bothered to tell her he was going to Virginia or when he was going. Virginia seemed half a world away from Missouri. What was she suppose to do while he was gone for a year, or possibly more? Of course, she would stay here and occupy the homestead! He wanted a wife. A wife to give him a son so the Merrick name wouldn't die when he did.

Annie Lash felt drained, remembering. Jeff had said on the raft that he wanted to leave something behind to show that he had passed through life. He was going to use her as if she were a brood mare to be assured his lineage was continued! Perhaps his seed was already growing in her belly. He had known he was a hunted man and that there was a good chance he'd be killed.

She looked at him with new eyes. He had been very clever in winning her over. Her stomach did a slow turnover and tears of disillusionment filled her eyes.

CHAPTER
EIGHTEEN

An hour after he died, Hartley Van Buren was buried without ceremony of any kind. Henry and Jute dug the grave; Jeff and Will placed the canvas-wrapped body in it. They filled it, marked the spot with a flat board, and went back to the homestead.

Antone sat on a stump in the yard. He was still dazed by the midday events. He had never been thanked for anything before. He'd never had a white man shake his hand. There was no one to say, "Do this, do that." No one objected if he sat on the stump or went to the creek for a drink of water. He had even eaten his fill of the fish chowder that no one else seemed to want. It was all very confusing.

"Dat boy gwine need he'p to straight his head out," Henry said sorrowfully. "If'n y'all doan mind, me'n Jute'll take 'im 'n tell 'im how it gwine to be."

"That's a good idea, Henry. It's going to take him awhile to get used to being free. If anyone can help it's you and Jute. Tell him that if he wants to stay here and work, he can have wages, not as much as you and Jute to start, but later, when he learns. And he can have a mule and a piece of land to build on."

"I tell 'im, Masta Jeff. Him do 'pear like a city nigger. But we he'p 'em if'n he wants de he'p."

"That's all you can do, Henry. Offer your help and see what happens. The man's earned the right to make a few decisions for himself."

Jeff was surprised to learn from Callie that while they were burying Hartley, Jason had saddled his horse and ridden off in the direction of the Cornicks.

"Did he say if he was coming back?"

"He didn't take his things. Jefferson... will he leave tomorrow?" Callie sat in the rocking chair holding Amos. The child was still suffering from his experience with Hartley and refused to leave Callie's arms, except to go to Will.

"Don't worry. He'll be leaving."

Jeff left Will and Callie together and went across to Annie Lash's room. She was bending over her trunk. She finished folding a dress, laid it in the trunk, and closed the lid.

"I'd like to look at Zan's things if you have time to get them," she said quietly.

"I'll get them for you later this afternoon. Right now I just want to be with you, hold you." He came toward her.

Annie Lash stepped away from him and stood

behind a straight-backed chair, her hands gripping the top for support.

She broached the subject without hesitation. "I've been waiting to discuss some matters with you. This has been a difficult day for all of us, and especially for you. But what I have to say is important to me."

"Can it wait while I kiss you?"

"No, it can't wait." She lifted her head a little higher, straightened her back, and forced herself to look directly at him, keeping her face calm and her feelings well bottled up inside.

Jeff waited. He couldn't imagine the reason for the resentment she was showing despite all she could do to cover it. His dark eyes searched her face. The moment stretched.

Finally he asked, "What is it you want to say?"

She took a deep breath. "First, I want to hear what you have to say. Are you and Will going to Virginia to testify at the trial of Aaron Burr?"

"Yes, we are. I was going to tell you when—"

She held up her hand. "Stop right there. You were going to tell me, but you didn't. I think now I was too hasty when I committed myself to marry you, Jefferson. I've known you for such a short time. I realize I know nothing about you at all." He started to speak and she held up her hand again. "Let me finish. You were honest with me when you stated your case the night on the raft. You wanted a wife to produce a son, so a part of you would remain after you were gone. I said no to your...ah...proposition. Now I believe you changed your tactics. How conniving of you to bring me here, woo me with sweet words, and leave me while you go chasing off to Virginia—that is, if you live so long!" Her rising anger showed in her eyes and in the tone of her voice.

"And you think that what happened to us that night down by the river was a farce? An act on my part?"

"I've no wish to recall that night," she said and hid her hurt with anger. Too many whispered words and stirring kisses had been exchanged in the dark of the night for her to feel comfortable airing the memory. She turned her face away from his probing eyes.

A strange, haunting expression came over Jeff's face. "I would have told you in time."

"When? In time for me to wave good-bye to you?"

"I don't understand why you're so angry."

"Of course you don't understand. You're not the one who was deceived."

"I never deceived you. I was trying to keep you from worrying, dammit!"

"That's good of you, but I'm a grown woman. I intend to share everything with my husband. I think I told you that before." She breathed deeply, trying to stay calm. "I want to leave here. I'll stay until Jason goes, because I don't want to cause more heartache for Callie."

"And my heartache?"

"You cared nothing for mine. It appears to me that you and Jason have more in common than I at first believed."

A look of angry frustration ran rampantly across Jeff's face. "I made my commitment to go to Virginia long before I set eyes on you," he said angrily. "You've no right—"

The spitting anger fairly sizzled in her clear, blue eyes. "But had you intended to share your life with me to the fullest, you would have told me that!" She shook her head and blinked back the tears.

"Let's forget this senseless quarrel, sweetheart," he said wearily.

"Senseless?" Her argument burst forth in a torrent of words. "What kind of marriage did you expect ours to be, Jefferson? Was this bond between us so fragile that I was not to even know you were targeted to be killed, that one day soon we would say good-bye and not see each other again for more than a year, if then? I warned you, Jefferson, that I wanted more out of marriage than that."

His face was stiff with anger. "You have no right to ask me to choose between my duty to my country and you."

"No, I don't. I'm not asking you to do that. I'm *telling* you that I have made a choice. You're not the man I want to be with for the rest of my life. Go to Virginia. I'm not asking you for anything except to help me leave here as soon as Jason goes."

"Why don't you leave with him? The two of you would make a good pair!"

Annie Lash almost shrank from the fury that radiated from him. The raking tone of his voice as he ground out the words, the burning darkness of his eyes as he glared at her, told her she had stirred up a raging demon in him, but she met his trembling rage with well-feigned assurance.

"I'm sure he would escort me as far as Saint
Louis."

"Goddammit! Don't push me!"

Annie Lash had not stirred from behind the
chair, but when Jeff came toward her, snarling in
the red glory of his rage, she moved quickly and
was by him in a flash, running out the door, through
the dogtrot, and into the yard.

"Annie Lash! Come back here!"

She hurried past the shed, darted through the
barnlot, scattering clucking hens, and turned
toward the creek. Only then did she stop and look
back. Thank God, he hadn't followed her!

Anguish overshadowed reason. She had to be
alone to sort out her thoughts. So much had happened it was hard to comprehend it all. She walked
quickly along the path she and Jeff had taken the
night they walked to the river. A poignant wave
of homesickness for her father and Zan over-
whelmed her as she walked among the trees they
loved. Tears filled her eyes, and she longed with
all her heart to be back with them in the cabin on
the Bank.

It was cooler in the woods, where only an occasional bright ribbon of sunshine hung between
the big trees. She picked her way unhesitatingly
and surely, detouring around brush growth and
logs, avoiding the soggy depressions, keeping to
solid ground. She had never been this far from
the house alone, but her mind was so full of the
events of the last few hours there was no room
for fear.

The river lay ahead, hidden by the trees. She

reached the bank where Jeff had lifted her down. This time she turned to crawl down the steep bank backward and came out onto the bluff overlooking the river. The long ribbon of water shone like burnished pewter. A narrow sandbar, white as alabaster, stretched from the opposite bank and was lost in the distance.

Annie Lash sat down on a felled log and gazed downstream. It came to her that the river was a gateway to all the land beyond. As she watched the river race on, a multitude of buzzards landed on the sandbar, stretched their wings, and turned their backs to the sun, low in the west. Two deer ambled out of the woods to drink in a pool formed by the back water, and a whippoorwill swooped overhead, trailing his melodious, repeated cry. Behind her, the woods came alive with pleasant cheeps and chirps and rustlings. The late afternoon was serene and beautiful. With her hands clasped tightly together in her lap, she sat stone still and blocked all thought from her mind.

There was no movement and no sound that she could recall. Abruptly, she was swept backward over the log. A hand from behind her clamped over her mouth and nose and an arm tightened about her throat. She had only a moment of panic before she lost consciousness.

When Jason saw the opportunity to leave the house without having to answer questions, he took it. He was totally fed up with his brother's high-handedness. How was he to know that Hartley was Burr's agent? Damn Hartley! He'd used him to get to Jefferson. There wasn't going to be a

keelboat business. He could see that now. By God!
He'd been dragged back into this godforsaken
wilderness for *nothing!* He recalled the last
thought because it wasn't true. The trip, facing
Jefferson, the beating by Will had all be worthwhile. He would get money from Will to divorce
Callie, and he had found a *jewel* that, when polished, would make him a fortune.

Maggie had been constantly in his thoughts.
Even while stunned by the news that Hartley
meant to kill him, he was angered by the thought
he would have died without having had her. His
heart beat wildly at the prospect of seeing her
again. He put his heels to the horse and rode down
the rutted path toward the Cornicks. When he
came onto their land he skirted around so he
wouldn't be seen passing, and rode on toward the
Gentrys'. He didn't have a plan. He hadn't decided if he was going to make a formal call or
hang around in the hope of seeing her. It was
decided for him.

Several miles past the Cornicks, almost in the
same place where Jefferson had waited for him
and she had appeared out of the woods, he saw
her. He pulled up the reins so suddenly that the
horse reared. Forced to gentle the animal, he had
to take his eyes off her, and when he looked again
she was gone. He cursed under his breath and
had to restrain himself from punishing the stupid
horse. She wouldn't have gone far, he reasoned.
She was more likely watching him from behind
a bush or a tree. He smiled slyly to himself and
dismounted. He walked around his frightened
horse, patted him and talked softly to him, all the

while scanning the dark woods for a sight of her.

Suddenly she was there, standing beside a tree as she had been the day they met by the river. She blended so perfectly with the background it was almost as if she were a part of it. The skirt she wore was nut brown, the shirt only slightly lighter in color, the sleeves rolled up past her elbows, revealing arms as pale as her face. Wrapped around her tiny waist was a wide piece of buckskin that brought her small pointed breasts into prominence. She stood as still as a doe, one hand resting on the rough bark of the tree.

With great effort, Jason let his eyes pass over her while his heart pounded like a hammer on an anvil. He turned his head slowly away from her and then slowly back again, and saw that she had moved closer, like a small, shy animal. He gave much thought to what he would say before he spoke.

"Hello, Maggie. I think you frightened my horse."

He glanced at her and then away, but the picture of her stayed in his mind. She stood with one thin shoulder against the tree trunk, as though she had been there for quite awhile studying him. Silence surrounded them. Jason was quite sure he had never waited in such breathless anticipation before. Every nerve was atuned to her.

"Ya hurt him." Her voice came from the side and he turned slowly to see her coming toward him.

He stood stone still as she approached. Her movements were so fluid that she seemed to skim the ground. Jason couldn't take his eyes off her.

She had eyes only for the horse. She passed beneath the animal's head without the top of hers touching it, reached up, and put her hands on either side of its face and pulled its head down so she could whisper in its ear. The sounds she made were soft coos and low murmurs. The animal stood quietly, its ears twitching as if listening, and Jason stood watching her as if mesmerized.

Close up, her beauty had an even more devastating effect on him than it did from a distance. He caught his breath and at that instant she looked up at him, fixing her eyes on him in a faintly sulky expression. They were long eyes, genuinely hazel in color, like a flashing gem between her beautiful, thick, dark lashes. They attracted and held his attention irresistibly, as did the pale, warm gold of her skin and her soft, red mouth that looked so innocent.

"Why do ya look at me like that?"

He had thought he'd spent no more than a few seconds in his scrutiny, but it must have been longer because she looked suspicious and resentful, like some tiny, shy bird that would take wing and fly if he made a sudden move. He was careful not to do so.

"You're very beautiful and I like to look at you."

"Yes," she said, and shrugged.

"How old are you?" He smiled his most charming smile.

"I'm not a child," she said quickly. The sulky expression dropped from her eyes and was replaced with one of haughtiness. "I've had my woman's time for this many years." She held up four fingers.

"Oh, I never for a moment thought you were a child," he said gravely. "I knew you were a woman full grown."

She moved around to the side of the horse, then behind it.

"Don't go behind the horse!" Alarm caused him to say it rather sharply.

She laughed and Jason knew why she had haunted his thoughts, drifted in and out of them like a strange, sweet mist. He'd seen that smile before! It was on a painting in one of the great mansions in New Orleans. An artist had painted a portrait of the face of a girl he had seen in a dream. It was a great work of art, and many people would have paid a high price for it; but he refused to sell. He had carried his picture all over the world searching for the girl. When he failed to find her, he had killed himself. This was the girl! This beautiful, elusive creature was the girl in the painting, and if he could get her to New Orleans—

"He won't hurt me. See?" Maggie swung gently on the horse's tail, patted his rump and the hind legs that could lash out with such devastating force. The animal stood perfectly still.

My God! he thought. She's not like anything I've ever seen before! If she beckoned, a man would cross half the world to get to her. She whirled around. The full skirt of her dress flared out to reveal tiny feet encased in low, beaded moccasins. Jason had never seen anything so perfect, had never known anything like the tide of feeling that swamped him when she looked at him and smiled. He knew that whatever he had to give, whatever he had to do, he had to have her.

"Do you dance, Maggie?" he asked casually when she whirled again.

"A'times."

"Will you dance for me?"

"No."

"I'll give you something pretty."

"I'm no beggar," she said haughtily.

"I didn't mean that," he said quickly and cursed himself for a fool when he saw that he had offended her. "I just meant that you are so very beautiful you should have beautiful things."

"I am beautiful, but I don't want anythin'." She said it completely without vanity.

"Where did you live before you came to Missouri?" Jason was desperate to keep her talking.

"Kaintucky."

"Have you been to a town bigger than Saint Louis?"

"I don't like towns. People're hateful." Her mouth looked unhappy and sullen.

Jason laughed. "Not to you. I don't see how anyone could be hateful to you."

"They are. Women hate me. They called me a witch and were goin' to burn me. Pa had to move."

Jason laughed again. "Are you a witch?"

"I don't know." She lifted her shoulders in a shrug. Not a trace of a smile touched her mouth. "I only had to look at their men and raise my hand. They'd leave their women and come to me." She tilted her head defiantly. "I did it sometimes 'cause they were mean and hateful to me and to Ma and Pa."

Jason felt a tightness in his chest and a throbbing ache in the pit of his belly that made him painfully aware of his desire for her. He had never practiced abstinence and he had been awhile without a woman. Indulgence of his sexual appetite was one of his greatest pleasures. He'd had many women. He'd pleasured himself in every possible way with women of every color and creed. None of them had ever set his blood afire like this little backwoods nymph.

"How would you like to see New Orleans and wear fine silk, have men bow at your feet and bring you jewels?" Jason showed her a ring he had taken from Hartley's pack just before he'd left the house. "This is a fine gem. See how it sparkles? Would you like to have it?"

"I don't like it."

"It's worth a lot of money."

"I don't need money."

"But it's beautiful. The color matches your eyes. It would make you even more beautiful if we put it on a ribbon and tied it about your neck."

"I don't want to be more beautiful."

Jason's patience snapped and his hand lashed out and grasped her arm. "Then what do you want, dammit?"

Instantly, she began to struggle and hit at him with her free hand, but her strength was nothing compared to his. He held her easily and drew her to him.

"I didn't want to do this, but I will if it's the only way." He was breathing hard, not from the exertion of holding her, but from the lust within him that tore at his loins like cruel, sharp spurs.

It was like holding a small, spitting cat. She hissed and clawed. She tried to bite him and when she couldn't, she butted him with her head. Her struggles only made him the more determined to have her. She pursed her lips and let out a long shrill whistle before his mouth clamped down on hers. Holding her wrists behind her with one hand, he fastened the other beneath her chin and pried her jaws apart with his thumb and forefinger. His tongue lapped the sweetness of her mouth and white, hot flames licked at his groin.

As soon as his mouth left hers, she whistled again. Jason scarcely noticed that, or the fact that their struggles had frightened the horse and he had shied away. He threw her to the ground and fell on top of her. Her struggles were beginning to irritate him and he slapped her. Almost instantly he was sorry, but it was too late to recall the blow. She would never be his now, except by force, and by God, if that was the only way he could have her, that's the way it would be!

He yanked her skirt up and saw that she wore nothing beneath it. Dark curls nestled between her legs and he buried his hand there while she writhed under him. She whistled again. He withdrew his hand and slapped her again, hard.

"Stop that!" he snarled, and jerked at the fastenings on his pants. His fingers fumbled in their frenzied haste to release that part of him that was swollen and rigid and ached so desperately.

Small mewing and gasping sounds came from her as she fought to free herself from his pressing weight.

"God, but you're beautiful! Even fighting mad, you're beautiful. Will I be going where no other man has ever been?" His happy, jubilant laugh rang out.

He shifted his body to lie full-length on hers, pressing his sex against her writhing body. She whistled again, but the sound was lost as he clamped his mouth to hers and ground his lips against her clenched teeth. He lifted his head just enough so he could see her face.

"You beautiful little...slut. I want to ram this up into your belly!" He flexed his hips and pushed the hard length of his arousal against her. "I can't wait to feel *that* inside you!" He continued to talk to her while he pried her legs apart with his knees and lowered himself onto her, breathless with anticipation, his insides churning to a painful depth. He grasped his elongated sex in his hand, desperately seeking admittance into her small, writhing body.

Jason felt a dull thud as something hit his back. It was seconds before he felt pain. The strength suddenly left his arms and he toppled over onto his side, unaware when the girl slipped out from beneath him. A gushing of something, warm and wet, come up and out of his mouth. His fingers turned into claws, reaching out...seeking...A foot against his body pushed him over. He felt an icy chill start in his legs and then cover his body. He was cold...cold.

"Help...me..." The blood bubbled up when he spoke. Oh, God! He was dying! He looked up into a fierce, dark face; the eyes were wild, the lips drawn back in a vicious snarl. The devil! The devil had come for him! This was his last thought before the knife slashed a path across his throat.

Light looked down on the mutilated body of the man he had just killed. His trousers were open and his male parts exposed to the sun that shone through the branches of the trees. Such fury was on him that he could barely restrain himself from slicing them from his body. Instead, he spit on them.

"Dog!" He spit again, this time on the still, lifeless face. He wiped his knife and returned it to his belt, rolled the body over with his foot, and held it there while he pulled the thin steel from between the shoulder blades. He rolled him back over and left his face and privates exposed to the sun as if to add more insult.

When he turned from the man he had just killed he opened his arms. Maggie flew into them. Not a whimper had escaped her lips, nor was there a tear in her eye. Her arms encircled his neck and he lifted her off her feet, burying his face in the soft curve of her neck. She could feel the trembling in his body and sensed his desperation by the way he strained her to him.

"I'm a'right, my love," she crooned in his ear. "I knew you'd come. I only had to wait fer you."

"*Mon Dieu*, my little one! I'll not leave you again!" He set her on her feet and brushed the tangled hair back from her face. His fingers gently touched her bruised, swollen flesh, and he cursed. "Did he violate you, my pretty one?" His dark eyes examined her anxiously, her large emerald ones questioned him. "Did he go inside you?" he asked gently.

She shook her head vigorously, and he clasped her to him again and held her for a long, quiet moment.

"I'm yore woman, Light."

"You're my woman—my angel of a woman. I'll let nothing hurt you." His voice vibrated with tender emotion. She stood quietly while his hands moved over her, brushing the dirt and leaves from her dress and hair. He put his hands on her shoulders and held her away from him so he could examine her swollen lips and bruised face. Anger reflected in the bright gleam of his dark eyes.

"I would kill him again and again!"

She lifted a hand and her fingers traced the frown that drew his brows together. "It be a'right, now."

"How did you know I was coming this way?"

She smiled, but only one side of her swollen mouth moved, and lifted her shoulders in a shrug. "I jist knew you were comin'. I was awaitin' for you."

Tenderly, he kissed the side of her soft, red mouth that was distorted. "You were waiting for me to pass this way," he repeated softly. "It is enough to know for now. *Mon Dieu*, my sweet pet! I must guard you well, my jewel, my love, for you have become precious to me!" He kissed her face again and again, finding the broken flesh and licking it with his tongue.

"Does it make you happy to be with me, Light?"

"Very happy, my pretty one."

She laughed, a soft trilling sound that came musically to his ears. Her small arms tightened around him, hugging him. It seemed to Light that at that moment a great swell of joy washed the torment from his soul.

When he held her away from him so he could look down into her face again, it was with gentle firmness. "Do not be so foolish again, my little one," he scolded gently. "When you are alone you will not get so near a man that he can pounce on you."

"He hurt the horse, Light. But I do as you say." She reached up and laid her palm against his face, he turned his lips into it, and she smiled, holding his eyes with hers until his dark features relaxed. He smiled and cherished a joy he had never expected would be his.

"Come, my wood sprite," he said softly. "We must go. I have the painful duty of having to tell *mon ami* that I killed his brother. Come, let's get the unpleasantness over."

CHAPTER
NINETEEN

"Where was Annie Lash off to? She cut out like
a Injun after a spotted pony." Will came out to
where Jeff stood beside the house.

"She's just now found out about Burr trying to
kill us and that we're going to Virginia for the
trial. She's madder than a wet hen because I didn't
tell her. I'm giving her some time to cool off. Goddammit, Will. It seems like everything piles up
on a body all at once."

Will glanced at the worried look on Jeff's face
and then away. It would be another blow to his
friend, he thought, when he told him he wasn't
going to Virginia. He was staying with his sweet
woman, wed or not. But he'd keep that bit of bad
news for another day. Jeff had enough to deal with
right now.

"Annie Lash ain't no scatterhead, she'll come

'round," Will said as he picked up a twig, whittled a point on the end of it, and stuck it in his mouth.

"When did you meet up with Jason?" Jeff asked quietly.

"Ya noticed, did ya?"

"I didn't think he'd run into a tree," Jeff said dryly, his face turned away, his eyes scanning the woods along the creek for a sight of Annie Lash.

"He come to the shed 'n I jist happen to be there, so I whacked 'im. I never tol' ya I wouldn't whack 'im, Jeff. I tol' ya I wouldn't kill 'im."

In spite of himself, a fleeting grin crossed Jeff's face. "Where do you suppose he's off to? He certainly wouldn't go visit the Cornicks or the Gentrys unless they had something he wanted. He may be going to ask the Cornick boys to ride with him as far as Saint Charles."

"He'll be back afore he goes, ya can bet on that!" Will felt the weight of the bag of coins inside his shirt. He knew Jason wouldn't leave without the money he'd promised him.

"Isn't that Light coming in on Jason's horse?" Jeff asked, and moved away from the house.

Will narrowed his eyes and watched the riders approach. Light was riding Jason's horse and Maggie, riding astride, was on the spotted mare Light favored. He looked at Jeff's set face and felt a premonition of more trouble.

Light rode up to within a few feet of them. He tossed the reins to Will, slid down, and reached up to lift Maggie from his horse. He turned and looked Jeff in the eye.

"I killed your brother."

Both men stared at him with astonishment.

Light stood with his feet spread, his body rigid. His piercing black eyes held Jeff's. Maggie stood close to him, both hands clasped about his upper arm, looking up into his face.

Jeff looked steadily at the expressionless, dark face of the man who had been more like a brother to him than his own kin. It took awhile for the full import of his words to hit him. Jason was dead! Light had killed him!

"I know you, Light," he said slowly. "You wouldn't have killed him without a reason."

"I killed him while he lay on top of my woman. I did not know who he was when I threw the knife. Had I known, I would still have thrown it." A mask of fury came over the scout's face. "But I knew who he was when I cut his throat," he said dispassionately, despite the anger that was on him.

"He...a...was forcing himself on Maggie?" Jeff looked at Maggie. She had turned to face him. Her face was swollen and bruised, her lip cut and bleeding. He knew what Light said was true without seeing the evidence. Light didn't lie.

"I was on my way here when I heard her whistle. He was forcing his way into her." Rage was in the scout; he let it boil out; his voice vibrated with it.

Maggie took Light's hand and rubbed his arm soothingly. He looked down at her, his face softening; he placed his hand behind her head and drew her to him.

"I'm sorry," Jeff said slowly. "I didn't know that side of Jason."

"He lies yonder, beyond the Cornicks. I would not soil my hands to bring him to you."

"I understand." They stood silently for a moment, then Jeff heaved a big sigh. "I'll have to go tell Callie. We'll have to ... go get him, Will. Are Jute and Henry still here?"

Will nodded. "I'll hitch up the wagon." He walked away, leading the horses.

"I will tell the *madame*," Light said.

"No, my friend, I'll do it. Stay with Maggie." Jeff laid his hand on Light's shoulder and squeezed it when he passed him.

Callie was sitting in the rocker holding Abe. Amos was asleep on the bunk. Jeff stood in the doorway for a moment and looked at them. Here was a family any man would have been proud of. Any man, except his own brother.

Callie took the news calmly, as he knew she would. Jeff told her everything, even about Light's offer to tell her himself.

"I'm sorry for you, Jefferson," Callie shook her head sadly. "And I'm sorry it had to be Light to do it."

"I think no less of Light, Callie. I want you to know that."

"I know. There's nothing I can say that will ease your pain, Jefferson. Jason was your brother. Your mother loved him. His life was not for nothing. He left two sons. Let's pray to God they don't turn out like him."

"Will's gone to get Henry and Jute. They'll take the wagon and go get him. It'll be late when they get back. We'll have the burying tomorrow."

"A'right, Jefferson. The Cornicks'll come and Silas'll say the words if you want him to."

"How's Amos?"

"The poor little thing's worn out. He's cried till there's no tears left. Will rocked him to sleep."

"He thinks a heap of Will."

Callie suddenly realized that Jeff looked tired and older. She wondered why Annie Lash wasn't here to comfort him. She had heard him calling for her to come back when she went running out of the house hours ago.

"Where is Annie Lash, Jefferson? Is something ...wrong between you?"

"Nothing that can't be straightened out." He got up to leave. "This has been quite a day," he said wearily.

Henry and Jute brought up the wagon and Light gave them directions. Will walked down to open the gate so the wagon could pass through.

"Stop by the Cornicks, Henry. Tell them the burying will be tomorrow before noon."

"Yas'sa, Mista Jeff." Henry slapped the reins over the backs of the mules; they strained at the harness and the wagon moved away.

Maggie stayed close to Light, either holding his hand or grasping his shirt sleeve.

"Callie's in the house, Maggie. If you'll go in, she'll give you a cup of tea and bathe your face." Jeff looked at her swollen face and wondered how his brother could have done such a thing. She was scarcely more than a child, in mind, despite her great beauty.

Maggie shook her head vigorously. "Where is your woman?"

"She went down to the creek. She may have gone toward the river. I was just going to look for her."

"Jeff," Light said sharply. "You say your woman is not here?"

"No..." He looked at Light and a cold ring of fear begin to form around his heart.

"*Mon ami,* I must tell you the news I bring. I learned in Saint Charles two men ask about you and Will, then go upriver on the other side. They are called Branson and Collier. I know of these men. I hear much bad things about them. They hunt men for money. One is old, one is young. The old one is from the Trace. He may know you."

"I've heard of Branson. He's cold and he's mean. He wintered a few times with Jackson, the man who was going to blow up the MacCartney place a few years back."

"It may be they come down the other side of the river, cross over and wait."

"My God! That's what they'll do! I've got to find Annie Lash and bring her back to the house. If they're who I think they are they may be watching for a chance to grab a hostage to force us to come to them." The words exploded from Jeff's mouth.

Will came up the path. "What's wrong? Gawdamn! Don't tell me somethin' else happened!"

"Remember Branson from the Trace? Light said he and a partner were asking about us in Saint Charles. They left there and came upriver on the other side. Now what the hell would they be doing here if not looking for us?"

"Shitfire! Branson's knowed up 'n down the big muddy fer a thievin', killin' varmit what would split his ma's throat fer a dollar!" Will took off his hat and wiped the sweat off his brow with the sleeve of his shirt. "Gawdamighty!" he said suddenly as a thought came to him. "The riverman who wanted my lip said he'd *overheard* the agent hirin' a man to do the job. Van Buren must'a seen what come downriver, thought it was Branson and he'd bungled it. He come on with Jason to do it himself. Hell! Branson'd not got here yet!"

"It holds together," Jeff admitted. "I'm worried about Annie Lash. If they get a hold of her—" He broke off his words and turned anxious eyes toward the creek. "She's been gone an hour. Something's not right. I'm going to look for her."

"I'll get the rifles 'n come." Will started toward the house.

"I go with Jeff," Light said. "Stay with the women, Will. Maggie is not afraid of you."

"Yo're a better tracker," Will admitted. "Jeff'll be obliged fer yore help." Will took off on the run toward the house.

Light looked toward the sun, then down at the shadow made by a fence post. "The days are long. We have three hours."

Light's words chilled Jeff to the bone. They didn't hold out much hope that they would find Annie Lash strolling down by the creek or sitting on a log somewhere pondering what she considered a serious problem between them. They implied she was in real danger, but he was already aware of that. Oh, sweetheart, he groaned silently. She'd not done one foolish thing up to now, why did it have to be this day of all days?

Will returned and shoved a rifle in Jeff's hand. "Need another blade?"

Jeff shook his head. "I'm afraid, Will. I hope to

God we meet her coming along the path, but I'm afraid."

Will had never heard his friend voice a fear before, and he knew his fear struck deep. There was nothing he could do or say to ease his worry.

"Don't worry 'bout here. Come night, 'n ya ain't back, I'll close up the shutters."

"Go with Will, little one. Stay close, and do as he says. I will be back for you." Light put Maggie firmly away from him.

"I want to be with you, Light," Maggie said and put her arms around his neck. "But I obey my man. I stay with Will and wait for you."

Light kissed her on the forehead, pulled her arms down from around him, and loped after Jeff.

Annie Lash came awake the instant the water hit her face. Her eyes flew open to see a bearded face inches from her own. A rough hand clamped across her mouth as soon as the man saw that she was conscious, and his arm pinned her to the ground.

"Don't make a sound or I'll split yore gullet." The words were breathed into her face on a putrid breath.

Terror boiled up in her as soon as she comprehended his words, and she tried to squirm away but she was powerless to move. The strong arm held her to the ground. Her feet refused to move. They felt as if they weighed a ton.

"Mmmmmm!" She was too frightened to heed the warning and frantic sounds came from her throat through the hand over her mouth. In full panic, she pushed at the man holding her, hit him with her fists, and tried to kick him.

"Be still!" He slapped her so hard her head rolled to the side. "I done tol' ya ta hush."

The hand over her mouth slipped beneath her chin. The thumb and forefinger squeezed viciously into her cheeks, forcing her mouth to open. A cloth was shoved inside and another wrapped over it to keep her from spitting it out. She was hauled to her feet and now, with her arms gripped on each side, she could see her captors.

Her terror-filled eyes traveled from one to the other. They were two of the most unsavory looking creatures she'd ever seen. They looked more like animals than men. Straggly beards sprouted on their faces like stiff, dead weeds. Their hands, and the skin on their faces, were cracked with dirt and soot. Their buckskins were dirty and ragged, and their moccasins were tied on their feet with strips of rawhide. One was tall, lean, and old; the other was shorter, fleshier, and younger. Had she not been so frightened, the smell of them would have made her sick.

The younger man held her while the other one bound her hands behind her back. He leaned toward her, putting his face close to hers. She could smell his sour breath and see his rotting teeth. She turned her face away, then looked back in horror as she felt his rough hand on her breast. She jerked her body backward and lashed out at him with her foot.

He laughed without a sound. "I likes 'em ta fight. We'uns 'll take ta fight outta ya. Hit be a long spell since I humped me a white gal."

Annie Lash renewed her struggles. The man behind her gave her arms a savage wrench upward. Excruciating pain shot through her arms and shoulders when he tightened his hold brutally. She thought she would faint from the pain that knifed through her.

"Listen good, gal. You's a little lever we didn't know we was agoin' ta get, but we still don't need ya. If'n ya make more trouble than ya's worth to me, I'll slit yore throat 'n throw ya in ta river. Hit makes me no never mind." His hand cracked sharply against her cheek and ear.

The blow was sudden and unexpected. Her head was flung to the side. Stunned, Annie Lash tried to focus her eyes on the man in front of her. Her jaw felt like it was broken and her ears rang. She was whirled around and a twisted, bearded face floated into view.

"Ya understan'?"

She nodded. Her pleading eyes went past him to the young man who stood behind him. The lascivious look in his eyes and the spittle leaking from his loose mouth almost caused her to drift back into total unconsciousness. Instead, she fought to keep the bile from rising in her throat and choking her.

"Her'll make dandy bait."

The older man, still gripping her arm, pushed her ahead of him through the brush that lined the river. When the brush was around them and they were well concealed, he jerked her to a stop, tied a long leather thong to her bound wrists, passed it under her arm, and took off at a faster pace, leading her like a leashed animal. The younger man followed behind.

Annie Lash staggered in her haste to keep up. Branches slapped at her, tearing at her face and hair. Once she stumbled and the jerk on the rawhide thong almost brought her to her knees and pain knifed through her. The man behind her tormented her by nudging her buttocks with the end of his rifle. She knew he laughed when she twisted and turned to avoid the prodding, but no sound came from him.

When the way was clear, the man in front moved at such a brisk pace that Annie Lash was forced to trot to keep up. The gag in her mouth prevented her from taking gulps of air into her lungs and they felt as if they were on fire. She had no time to think of anything. All thought was blanked from her mind, and she concentrated completely on staying on her feet and trying to keep up to prevent the jerk on the thong that brought such vicious pain.

She lost all sense of time and direction. They pushed on through the woods. At times the ground sloped upward and the trees became thinner. The evening sunlight was brighter as it made its way through the leafy branches. Annie Lash stumbled along, swerving to avoid the tree trunks and thorny branches.

They entered a darker, thicker part of the woods. The man ahead of her stopped so suddenly she ran into him, her mind so numb with fatigue that it failed to register his action. He turned angrily, placed his palm over her face and pushed hard. She fell heavily against a tree trunk and sat there, dazed, trying to gather her wits about her. Her head seemed about to explode and she was floating. She whirled and floated through space filled with shooting stars, soared and dived again. Finally, she went spinning off into a black void. For the first time in her life she had fainted.

When Annie Lash opened her eyes the two men were hunkered down beside a pack, gnawing on what looked like a piece of dried meat. There was not a shaft of sunlight in the clearing. The sun had gone down, she thought disparagingly. It will be dark soon. Jeff will never find me! Her next thought was that she wished she hadn't awakened, and her next was fear of what might have happened to her while she was unconscious. The end of the thong lay on the ground and the men were not facing her. She moved and raised her body to a sitting position and leaned against the tree, but she didn't have the strength to get up, much less to run.

She shook the hair from her eyes and took stock of her surroundings. They were in a heavily wooded gulley filled with tall trees and dense undergrowth. Vines the size of a man's arm rose from the ground and twined around the huge trunks of the trees and disappeared in their lofty branches. The ground she sat on was damp and she could hear water gurgling over rocks. Weak tears filled her eyes and sobs tore at her dry throat. She tried not to think about the dirty cloth in her mouth. Using all the self-control she possessed, she forced back the tears and commanded her heaving stomach to behave, knowing that if the contents came up, they could choke her.

The younger of the two men looked around and caught her looking at them. He stood, wiped his hands on his pants, and came to stand over her. She tried to scoot around the tree to get away from him, but he stepped on her skirt and held her.

"Ya ain't agoin' nowhere." He dropped to his knees and brought his face close to hers. "Her's a purty 'un, Branson." He rubbed his fingers across the part of her face not covered with the rag that held the gag in her mouth. She tried to jerk her head away. He chuckled low in his throat and edged closer. It was more like an animal growl that came from him than a laugh and it came louder when he rubbed his maleness against her upper arm and she cringed. She heard the snort of laughter that came from the older man. It was a short guffaw.

"Yo're horny as a jackrabbit, Coll. Did ya ever see 'un a them studs take down a she? Whooeee! He's on 'er like mud on a fence, apokin' at 'er, 'n her asquealin'. Ya'll have yore bit a tail soon's we done what we come to. So jist take it a mite easy." His tone of voice changed abruptly from friendly to one with authority when he spoke again. "Ya ain't goin' ta be on 'er first, nohow. Ya kilt that thar Injin gal back thar afore I got me a turn on 'er. I'm takin' this'n first. Ya cin have my leavin's."

Coll jumped to his feet. "Hold on thar! Now ya jist hold on," he snarled. "Ya didn't even see this'n. I seed 'er. Ya didn't know 'er was thar. Yo're missin' yore know-how, ol' man! I ain't lettin' ya on 'er first."

Annie Lash was so terrified she could scarcely comprehend the man's words. It was all she could

do to focus her eyes. She was floating in a sea of
terror and misery. The rawhide that bound her
wrists was cutting off the circulation and her hands
were getting numb. She flexed her fingers and
tried to shift her position in order to ease the pain
between her shoulders. She closed her eyes for a
moment, thinking that if this was a nightmare she
would wake up. Her eyes flew open when she
heard what Coll was saying.

"I'm ahavin' 'er now!"

"Ya try hit, 'n I'll gut ya, here 'n now." There
was a deadly promise in Branson's tone and Coll
recognized it.

"Hit ain't right, but . . . soon's we get done with
that thar white-headed bastid—"

"Hit's goin' ta take some gittin' to git 'im. Ya
don't know that thar bastid. I do. He's foxy, got
the eye of a eagle, the guts of a mule, cin tract a
duck across a pond. Once he gets his teeth in, he
don't let go."

They were talking about Jeff! The knowledge
hit Annie Lash like a blow between the eyes. This
pair of animals had been hired to kill Jeff and
Will. Oh, dear God. First Hartley Van Buren and
now this! They were using her to lure them to
their deaths. That's what he meant when he said
she would make dandy bait!

"Whose woman air ya?" Branson asked. Annie
Lash shook her head. "Air ya Merrick's woman?"
She shook her head again. "Then she's ta other'ns.
Murdock's. He ain't alettin' nothin' of his go. He'll
come fer her. He's soft fer women. I seed him
shoot a feller o'er a dirty ol' squaw. Feller was a

goin' ta let a pup suck her tit. Murdock shot 'im. He ain't got no sense a'tall."

"Ya left a trail a yard wide," Coll said with disgust. "They ain't goin' ta have no trouble trackin' 'er, if'n they do it afore night."

"That's why I done it. I ain't wantin' ta piss along. I want ta get it done."

Coll squatted down beside Annie Lash again. "Soon's it's done I'm goin' ta have me a time with this gal." He touched her neck with rough fingers and she tensed. He put his nose to her skin and sniffed. "Ya got a funny smell ta ya, but it makes no matter. I ain't had me nothing fer so long I 'bout ta bust my buckskins."

Branson snorted with disgust. "'Bout ta bust, is ya? I ain't blind. I seed ya ajerkin' on that thing."

Coll grinned sheepishly. "Won't be no need fer it t'night." He quickly plunged his hand down the neck of her dress. Annie Lash went wild with fear and butted his nose with her head. He let out a yelp and grabbed her by the hair. Excruciating pain shot from her scalp to her neck.

"We got us a fighter, uh?" he gritted. His fingers plunged into her dress again and found her nipple. "How'd ya like fer me ta pinch these pretty li'l thin's off ya? Huh?" He gripped her tender flesh brutally and she couldn't hold back the grunts of pain that came from her dry throat.

"Stop diddlin' on the woman." Annie Lash heard the command through the sharp, black edge of pain. "Ya gotta keep an eye peeled, hear?"

"I jist agivin' 'er a taste a what she's goin' ta git."

Annie Lash fought with all her limited strength
when the rough hand moved up under her skirt,
trying to force its way between the thighs she kept
tightly together. Her mind refused to record the
obscenities being inflicted on her and she momentarily blacked out. When her mind began to
function again, she realized that she was praying
fervently to die, and the fingers had left her.

"Tie 'er ta the tree so she cain't crawl off," Branson ordered. "We got ta git us set fer what we're
agoin' ta do."

Coll wrapped the leather thong around the tree
trunk and tied it. He moved over beside Branson
and they talked in low tones. By straining her ears,
Annie Lash could hear most of what they were
saying.

"Air we goin' ta do same as we done ta other
time we took bait?" Coll asked.

"He ain't goin' ta come awalkin' in here like
other's is done. He ain't doin' nothin' till he sees
if'n his woman is a'right. I figure we ort ta scatter.
He'll circle round ta see what we's up ta. While
he's a doin it, we pick 'im off." Branson looked
around and pointed. "Scutter up that thar tree.
Pick ya a spot so ya can see the woman. If'n ya
git one a 'um in yore sight, shoot 'im. I'll git the
other'n. If'n jist one comes, we'll sashay up ta the
place 'n get the other'n."

It was almost completely dark, but light enough
for Annie Lash to look at the older man while he
talked. He was cold and as dangerous as a coiled
snake. He's like Zan would have been, she
thought, if Zan had taken the same trail. Despair
swamped her. They had got her tied here like a

Judas goat. Her mind tumbled with thoughts. Her last words to Jeff were so hateful, so senseless, like he said. Her own stupidity had caused this to happen. Running off like a silly schoolgirl!

Every minute that passed seemed like an hour to Annie Lash. Her head throbbed viciously. The thong was biting into her wrist and she desperately needed to swallow. Half of her wanted Jeff to find her, the other half fervently hoped he wouldn't. Branson expected Will; but if anyone came it would be Jeff, and they were waiting to kill him.

Darkness came quickly, making it impossible for her to see but a foot or two in front of her. An owl hooted and frogs croaked. From the far distance came the cry of a night bird. A slight breeze rustled the leaves in the tree above her. There were no other sounds at all, except the night sounds.

For the first time since she had been abducted, Annie Lash allowed the tears to come and made no attempt to stop them. The pain in her head and the ache in her hands and arms was nothing compared to the pain in her heart. Her selfish, impulsive action would cost Jeff his life. Oh, God, she prayed, let me wake up and find that this is a terrible dream. She wanted a chance to tell him she loved him and that she was sorry.

CHAPTER
TWENTY

Annie Lash began to concentrate all her attention on the sounds around her. She heard a night bird call again and again, and wondered if it was a bird or if there were Indians in the woods. An owl hooted from a nearby tree and then took off on lazy wings, dodging between the branches. The peeper frogs in the backwaters of the river sang their nightly chorus. She strained her eyes, but not a shadow moved.

Once she heard her father telling Zan that the minutes preceding inevitable danger were the slowest minutes of a lifetime. She had not understood what he meant at the time. Now she did. The minutes seemed like hours as she waited. Life was suddenly very precious. For at this moment in time she could hear and feel as she had at no other time in her life. Waiting to be killed she realized that this must be the way a soldier felt before a battle. Her senses were honed and alert. The smells and the sounds she had formerly ignored or forgotten were now remembered and appreciated.

Annie Lash heard the lonely, dismal call of the whippoorwill, then the monotonous hoot of an owl. On the other side of the clearing, near where the thick forest loomed, she thought she saw movement, but the night was so black she couldn't be sure, and her eyes became glued to the spot. There was movement! A dark form glided toward her, moving slowly and smoothly. Inch by inch it advanced, the seconds passing as minutes.

Swifter than thought a second shadow leaped upon the first, swinging a hatchet. The first shadow parried the blow with the thrust of a knife. Then began a duel in which strength and fury were matched against savage cruelty and cunning. The one dodged the vicious swings of the hatchet, any-one of which would have crushed his skull. The other, nimble as a cat, avoided every rush while he waited to kill. Annie Lash caught a glimpse of a white head and her blood raced to her ears and pounded there. The fight ended abruptly when a knife thrusted deeply into a human chest and an agonized cry rent the darkness. One shadow crumbled, fell, and slowly straightened out on the damp ground.

At that moment, from the depths of the trees above came a swelling cry that ended in a wail like that of a lost soul. Following the sound was a dull thud, a grunt, and the sound of something falling through the branches above her head. Then a limp and heavy body hit the ground to the right of where she cringed against the tree. She closed her eyes tightly, not wanting to see. When she opened them a man loomed over her.

"Are you all right?"

Jefferson! Oh, thank the blessed Lord! Fingers worked at the rag tied across her mouth. She spit out the rag and gagged.

"Two," she croaked. "There are...two."

"We got them both." He cut the thong that bound her hands and she cried out in pain when they fell apart.

"Jefferson..." She could scarcely get a sound from her dry throat.

"Can you stand?" He lifted her to her feet.

"I think so," she whispered hoarsely, her throat and mouth so dry they felt as if she'd swallowed sand. She wanted him to hold onto her, but he moved away.

"*Mademoiselle?*" Light was beside her and took her arm when she staggered on numbed legs.

"Oh, Light! I'm all right." She rubbed her hands together and moved her shoulders to relieve the ache between them. "I was so scared. Jefferson..." He bent over the man on the ground and his back was to her. "I'm sorry. I'm so sorry. My foolish action almost cost you your life."

"And yours," he said curtly. "Did you get their weapons, Light?"

"*Oui.* I will bring them and the pack."

Jeff reached out and took one of the long guns from him. "I'll carry this. Are you ready to go?" he asked Annie Lash.

She nodded, then thinking he didn't see her,

murmured, "Yes. Thank you. Thank you both. I don't know—"

"Let's go then," Jeff said, cutting her off abruptly.

Jeff led off through the trees. Annie Lash stumbled after him on wobbling legs. He was angry! He was very angry and she was afraid she was going to give way to a storm of weeping. She continued to put one foot before the other while she fought a losing battle with her rebellious stomach. Her head whirled and her stomach churned. When she could control it no longer she staggered a few steps to a small tree, grabbed hold of it so she wouldn't topple over, and the contents of her stomach came spilling out. She moaned with pain when she opened her jaw. When it was over she wiped her face and mouth on the hem of her dress, grateful for the darkness that had prevented them from seeing her.

Jeff took her arm in a firm grip and they walked at a slower pace. She had broken out in a cold sweat when her stomach convulsed, and now she was trembling violently. She hated the show of weakness. But somehow pride surfaced to give her strength and she plodded on, determined to be no more bother to him than necessary. Her heart rejoiced that he was safe. He had escaped the assassins once again.

"How did you find me? It was so dark."

"It wasn't hard. It was still light when we got there." His words were clipped, impersonal.

"It was light? Then you saw—"

"If we'd gone in then, he'd have used you as a shield, killed you. We waited until we could get them one at a time."

"That's what they were going to do to you. They thought Will would come alone."

Jeff didn't reply and they walked on in silence.

At the bank Jeff sprang up, reached down and pulled her up beside him. There were no hugs and tender kisses like the ones they exchanged the last time he had helped her up the bank. He was as remote as a stranger and if not for the warm clasp of his hand beneath her elbow, she might as well be alone in the darkness.

Her head throbbed painfully and she was deaf to the sounds of the night that only a short while ago she heard so clearly and in the past had so often pleasured her. The worst part of her pain was buried in the back of her mind and it floated on the periphery of her thoughts, tormenting her, reminding her that by her foolish, selfish actions she had spoiled something that had been so very beautiful.

The house was in total darkness when they came up the path from the creek. Jeff's hand left her elbow and formed a cup around his mouth. He gave out the low, mournful cry of a mourning dove. Instantly, a shadow separated itself from the house and came to meet them.

"Did ya get 'er?" She recognized Will's voice.

"Yeah."

"She a'right?"

"Yeah."

"And them?"

"Dead."

Through the dark haze of pain Annie Lash registered in her mind this short exchange of words. They were talking about her life and Jeff's. How can they discuss what happened in so few words? she thought, with the distant part of her mind. She felt lightheaded, like she was floating. The torturous walk was making every step known to her aching body.

When they reached the house she didn't bother to raise her head until Callie's arms enfolded her. Then the dam broke and the agony of the day and especially the last few hours bubbled up and out of her in an eruption of tears. She was led blindly to her room. Jeff let her go without a word. Safely behind the closed door, Callie lit a candle and turned to look at her ravaged, swollen face. her hair stringing wild and loose from her braid, and her dirty, torn dress.

"Oh, you poor thing! I was so worried. Are you sure you're all right?"

"I'm just tired and my head feels like a thousand hammers are pounding on it." She looked at Callie through eyes streaming with tears. "I'm so glad to be back here with you, Callie. Those terrible men that took me had come here to kill Jefferson and Will. They caught me down by the river. They said I was bait. I knew they'd do terrible things to me before I died. I was scared for Will and Jefferson, too."

"Light came to tell us—" she hesitated. "He told us the men had come upriver. Oh, Annie Lash, why did you wander so far from the house?"

"Maggie wanders all over." That was the only defense she could think of.

"Maggie's not like us. She's different. There's something not quite real about that girl." Callie poured water in the washbasin. "Get out of that dress. Let me help you wash up so you can get in the bed. This has been a day none of us will ever forget."

"How's Amos?" She lifted the filthy dress over her head and pulled off her shoes and stockings.

"He's sleeping. He'll be fine in a day or two."

"I'm sorry I ran off and left you, Callie, after I promised to stay near."

"That part was all right. I'm just so thankful you're back and the men didn't do what they came to do." She smiled. "We're all still together. That's what's important."

Washed and in a clean nightdress, Annie Lash sank down in the bed, her aching head loving the feel of the soft pillow beneath it. She stretched out her sore limbs. It was pure heaven to be in the soft bed.

"Tell Jefferson I'm sorry for all the trouble I caused him," she said behind a yawn.

"Here he is. Tell him yourself," Callie said and slipped out the door.

Her eyes flew open and there he was, staring down at her. She wanted to cry again. She lay in stunned silence, wanting to tell him how she felt, but even her numbed mind knew he was in no mood to listen. His face was streaked with dirt and sweat, and his eyes, dark and as cold as the bottom of a well, raked her face.

"Jefferson—" She tried to firm her quivering voice.

The tension in him was so strong that she was shaking from it. She couldn't reconcile this Jefferson with the one who had lain in this bed with her and made such tender love to her only last night.

"Get a good rest. I have plenty to say to you, but it'll wait till later." With that he turned away from her, blew out the candle, and went out the door, closing it behind him.

She lay in the dark, filled with misery and bewilderment, her mind going in a thousand directions until her tired body overcame her tired mind and she dropped into a dreamless sleep.

Annie Lash woke from a nightmare in which she was wandering on a vast open plain looking for Amos. She pushed herself up onto a bent elbow, blinked, and swept the hair back from her eyes. The ghost of a headache was still there, but she felt vastly improved. Shaking off the fogginess, she flipped back the covers and sat up on the side of the bed.

Did she hear Biedy's voice? She tilted her head to listen. Yes, it *was* Biedy's voice; scolding, commanding, cajoling. What was she doing here so early in the morning? But was it early? The light coming in through the window told her it was not early morning. She went to the washbasin and splashed water on her face and dried it with the towel.

Callie opened the door and came in. "Mornin'. Feelin' better this mornin'?"

"Much better. Is that Biedy's voice I hear?"

"Yes, Biedy is here, as is Silas and three of their boys. Mr. and Mrs. Gentry, Maggie's folks, are here, too."

Annie Lash's eyes closed. "What's happened?"
she asked tightly, opening her eyes to look at
Callie.

"That's what I wanted to tell you before you
came out. You were too tired last night. Jason is
dead. The neighbors, out of respect for Jefferson
and the boys, have come for the burying."

"Oh, Callie!" Annie Lash sank down on the bed
and pulled Callie down beside her. "How did it
happen?"

Callie repeated what Jeff had told her before
he and Light went to look for her as well as the
lesser details Will had provided during the long
wait.

"It's wicked, I know," Callie said softly. "But I
can't be sorry, except for Jefferson's sake. Jason
had a demon in him at times. He would never
have been happy and content at anything. He
didn't know how," she added sadly.

"Ah...poor Jefferson! Do you realize all that
happened to that man yesterday? Hartley tried to
kill all of us, and then took Amos. His brother
coming to such a tragic end! Then, if that wasn't
enough, he had to come for me, knowing men had
come to kill him!" Annie Lash felt chill bumps
pop out on her neck and arms when she thought
of the accusations she had flung at him before she
ran off into the woods.

"It seems it's always been this way for Jefferson. He's had to get Jason out of first one thing
and then the other. He even had to provide a home
for his brother's wife and children. But he has you
now to stand by him and help him. If ever a man
deserved to be happy, he does." When Annie Lash

didn't answer, Callie got up from the bed. "Get dressed and come on out, or Biedy will be in here to see about you."

The group that gathered around the box that held Jason's body were there out of respect for Jeff. Silas and Biedy sang "Rock of Ages," his deep tones and her melodious ones united in beautiful harmony. Silas read a scripture from the Bible. Annie Lash couldn't help thinking how Jason would have sneered at the simple service.

Jeff stood on one side of the grave with his hat in his hand. Callie, holding Abe in one arm, her other hand holding tightly to that of her older son, stood on the other side. After the service was over, they all stood silently while the Cornick boys filled the grave. After it was filled, Biedy handed a bouquet of wild flowers to Amos.

"Lay them on your pa's grave, Amos," Callie said gently.

The child took the flowers and placed them carefully on the heap of black dirt. He was dry-eyed and solemn. Then, instead of returning to his mother, he went to the end of the grave and took Will's hand. Will swung him up in his arms and carried him back to the house.

There was a flurry of activity in the kitchen as the women laid out the noon meal. Biedy and Mrs. Gentry had brought food and it was placed alongside the hastily prepared meal Callie and Annie Lash had put together. There were enough men to fill the table. Amos took his seat beside Will. The women waited their turn to eat, talking in low tones out of respect for the occasion, fetching extra bread and refilling mugs with strong, hot tea.

While the women ate, Annie Lash told of being taken by the woodsmen. They wanted to know every gory detail. But she couldn't repeat some of the things that had happened to her. They were brought to mind often enough each time her sore nipple touched her dress, and now, when she was unable to eat the baked chicken Biedy had brought or the nut pie which Mrs. Gentry was so proud of. The large, purple bruise on the side of her face caused the women to click their tongues in an expression of sympathy, and shake their heads.

It saddened Annie Lash when she realized no mention had been made of Jason during or after the meal. Usually at a time like this the talk was about the one who had passed to the "great beyond," but the people that gathered here talked of crops, river trade, and the chance that the Missouri Territory would become a separate state. Neither Light nor Maggie were present, but she didn't think of that until later.

Annie Lash was glad when it came time for the company to leave. Her head was pounding anew with nervous tension. Jeff had not looked at her, not even one time, that she was aware of. The strain was beginning to tell, and she was having a hard time concentrating on what was being said to her. When the food baskets were repacked, she and Callie walked out with Biedy and Mrs. Gentry. Silas brought the wagon around to the gate.

"Thank you for coming, Mr. Gentry," Callie said. "If you need help with anything a'tall, send us word. Biedy, you know we're obliged."

"Ain't no call fer ya to be feelin' obliged," Biedy said and tied the strings of her sunbonnet firmly under her chin. "What's neighbors fer, anyways? I was saying that to Martha, here, on the way over. What's neighbors fer, I said, if'n they don't come in time a need? Ya know Marthy's man is brother to the other Gentry. I jist couldn't be keepin' them straight, so it's Marthy 'n Gladys. Marthy's Maggie's ma. That Maggie scared the wind 'n water outta me at first. My, that child comes 'n goes like a butterfly! My land, she likes my pie. Sometimes I jist leave her a piece out on the porch 'n put a bucket over it. Come mornin', it's gone. It worried me somethin' awful at first. Now I don't pay no never mind. Silas, air ya ready? Ya was rarin' to go afore I got my bonnet on. What ya standin' there palaverin' fer?"

Finally, the wagon was loaded and the boys were mounted on their horses. Silas slapped the reins against the backs of the mules and the wheels begin to roll.

"Bye," Biedy called. "Bye. Y'all come, now. Don't bother to give no notice, just pull out and c'mon. Silas 'n the boys'll get us a big old tom turkey. Silas says he seen some what'd weigh..." Her words faded away on the warm June breeze.

"Do you suppose we'll ever know what those turkey's will weigh?" Callie asked as they walked back to the house.

Annie Lash smiled. "Biedy is a happy woman. One of the happiest I've ever known."

Callie caught sight of Amos running across the yard toward her. His small face had a smile that split it in half.

"Look what Will caught. He said tie a string on its leg and I can hold it. He said it won't hurt it none."

"What in the world?" Callie bent to see what was in his small, cupped hand. When they opened, a giant junebug flexed its large, green wings and flew away.

"Shitfire!" Amos said and stomped his bare foot.

"Amos Pickett!"

Callie made a dive to grab him, but he eluded her and raced to Will, who was coming up from the creek with a bucket of water. He set the bucket down and caught the child in his arms. Callie watched, a small, tender smile on her face, then turned back toward the house.

CHAPTER
TWENTY-ONE

The sun had gone down; evening shadows softened the outline of the huge cedar trees whose
tops reached for the sky. It was the time of day
poets wrote about; the gloaming, they called it.
To Annie Lash it was the lonesome time of day.
She wondered if her life had been different, if she
had someone to share it with, would she feel the
same about this golden time of the evening?

The strain in her relationship with Jeff had
placed her in the position of a guest in his home.
She felt now as she did when she had first come
here, an outsider. She had waited all day for the
opportunity to talk to him. He had come to the
kitchen to eat his supper and gone out. He had
been distantly polite, quiet, as if there was much
on his mind. What to do now was a burning question in her mind.

Feeling tired and alone, she looked out over

the land she thought she'd call home and tears misted her eyes. She had wanted to be completely honest with Jeff. She loved him and she had thought he loved her enough to be completely honest with her. She was ashamed that she had not waited for a more appropriate time to tell him of her disappointment in him for not telling her he would be away for a year or more. It was one of the few rash things she had done in her life. That, and running off toward the river. Mercy! she thought desperately, he'd never forgive her for that.

She left the bench on the porch and went to her room, struck a spark, and lit a candle. On an impulse she took down the oil lamp she had brought from the cabin on the Bank. It had been washed and filled with oil. She seldom used it as a candle was usually sufficient.

The light reached into every corner of the room and she immediately saw that Zan's pack had been placed inside the door near the washstand. The sight of the familiar, soft leather bundle brought a lump of homesickness to her throat. She rubbed her hands over it lovingly before she lifted it and placed it on the bed. It was heavier than she had thought it would be, or else she was weaker than she thought she was. She untied the straps and laid out the contents.

There were several small leather bags of coins. She opened one of them and peered inside. Gold coins. She didn't bother to count them. She pulled the drawstring at the top of the pouch and placed it beside the others. The extra socks she'd knit for him were there and a change of buckskins, as well as two sets of clean underdrawers. Zan had always been clean, she remembered. He had wrapped several well-oiled knives in a soft doeskin. In another packet was a silver spoon and a gold pocket watch with the picture of a sailing ship engraved on the back. The only other thing in the pack was a flat package, wrapped in oilcloth and tied with a thong.

Annie Lash laid all the other things aside and opened the package. Inside was a well-worn picture of a girl. The edges of the portrait were jagged and crumbly. She looked at it closely and her heartbeat picked up speed. It was a picture of her mother, Lettie; a miniature painted by the artist who had spent the winter with her mother's family The same artist had produced the pictures she had in her trunk. The likeness was of her mother when she was very young. The eyes that looked back at her were large and light blue. Her hair was parted in the middle and pulled back with puffs over her ears. How in the world had Zan come to have it? Why hadn't he shown it to her? Did her pa know about it?

She laid the picture aside, and with trembling fingers unfolded a paper and held it to the light so she could read the faint words written there.

Dear Lash,
   I take pen in hand to inform you that I will be wed to Charles Jester on the morrow. I love him, Lash. He is a staying man, a good man, and he loves me. You, my dear Lash, will always follow the next river, go over the next mountain or wherever your wandering feet will take you.

You and your kind will open the West. Charles and his kind will stay and hold what you have gleaned from the wilderness after you have moved on to new frontiers. You will always have a special place in my heart. I will remember you always. May God go with you and keep you.

Lettie

Annie Lash read the short letter through several times. Dear Lash, it had said. So that was where she got her unusual name. Her mother had said she was conceived in love. Was it possible that she loved both her father and Zan? It was certain that Zan loved her. She folded the picture and the letter in the leather and wrapped them in the oilskin, then tied it with the thong just as Zan had. So much was explained; Zan's devotion to her, his concern and help when her father was struck down, his mention of her mother as he lay dying.

She placed Zan's possessions in his pack and put it in the bottom of her trunk. As long as she had that, she had a part of Zan and a part of her mother, too. She blinked rapidly to hold back a flood of tears, then finally she was no longer able to control them and let them stream down her cheeks.

Later, after she had washed and put on her nightdress, she sat on the edge of the bed and brushed her hair, raking the soft bristles from the top of her head down the full length of her hair that hung to her hips.

The door opened and Jefferson stood there. Annie Lash glanced at him and then away, shocked, confused, embarrassed. He had such an odd expression on his face that she was frightened, too. He looked at her for a moment, then came in and closed the door.

"Did you find Zan's pack?"

"Yes, I put it in my trunk."

"Why are you crying?"

"I'm not."

He came to her and put his hand beneath her chin and raised it. She looked at his grim face, then lowered her eyes. He turned her face so he could see the bruises and breathed a curse. He dropped his hand and moved away from her.

With downcast eyes, she continued to brush her hair. Her arms moved automatically, although they felt like each held a leaded weight.

She fully expected to hear the door open and close behind him. When there was only silence, she glanced at him, then gaped with astonishment. He had removed his shirt. The lamplight shone on his muscled shoulders and blond hair. As stunned as she was, it registered in her mind that he had been in the creek. His hair was wet and his shirt was damp from being pulled onto his wet body. He ignored her surprised stare, sat down on the bed beside her, and pulled off his boots.

"I talked to Silas today. He'll be here a week from Sunday to marry us." He got up and set his boots beside the wall.

"You what?"

"You heard me. Light is taking word to the MacCartneys and the Witchers up on the big river. They'll be here. We'll make as big a to-do about it as we can on short notice." He worked at the fastenings on his pants.

"You should have consulted me before you made such big plans." She stood and began to braid her hair.

"Leave it down. I like it that way."

"I like it braided. And you can—"

"You heard me, Annie Lash. Don't give me any of your sass tonight! Trouble's been heaped on me the last few days like flies on fresh cow shit. I'll not have my wife adding to it!"

"I'm not your wife!"

"You're the same as!" He glared at her and jerked his britches down and stepped out of them. She quickly turned her eyes from his naked body. "I'm going to tell you this one time! I'll not tolerate disobedience when it comes to keeping you safe. You were told not to go toward the river alone. You did and almost got yourself killed. You're willful and headstrong, Annie Lash Merrick. But remember this: I am the head of this family. I expect to be obeyed!" He shouted the last words.

"You...expect? Ha!" Annie Lash's independent heart pounded with indignation.

"Get into the bed, over next to the wall."

"I will not!"

"You will, or I'll spank your butt!" The look on his face said he would do it.

Her pride fought with her desire to do as he said. She hesitated, then slid beneath the sheet and moved over to the far side. What in the world was she doing? This was not the kind of marriage she'd dreamed about. True, she loved him desperately; but she couldn't face the years married to him yet living alone. Her mind was filled with these thoughts and she had to tell him.

"I'm not going to marry you. I'll not stay here as your wife while you go traipsing off to Virginia."

"I'm not going to Virginia."

"Well!" She flopped over to look at him. "Why didn't you say so, for goodness sake?"

"You didn't give me a chance." He blew out the lamp and got into bed. He reached for her with strength that defied her to resist and pulled her into his arms. He lay on his back, his arm pressing her to his side, and heaved a big sigh.

"Oh, Jefferson, you make me so...angry!" she whispered and snuggled against him, her heart singing, so happy she wanted to weep.

"And I will again, love. You can count on it. Now, be quiet. I've got a lot to tell you, and I think I'd better do it before I make love to you, or I'll forget half of what I want to say." He planted a tender kiss on her forehead.

With Annie Lash clasped tightly to his side, he told her about his life in Virginia. He told her about his mother and father, and how, after his father died, his mother married a rich planter. Pickett spoiled his own son, Jason, by giving him everything and demanding nothing from him, but his stepfather had come to hate Jeff. He suspected him to be the bastard of Tom Jefferson, his enemy, because he had been named after him, and because of Tom Jefferson's devotion to his mother.

"There was no truth to it. I had a legitimate father, whom my mother loved very much. His name was Wilson Merrick, and he was a good friend to Tom. While we're on this subject, I'll tell you, because I want no secrets between us. Will is more than likely the bastard son of the president. Tom settled a large amount of money on him a long time ago, but as far as I know Will has never touched it. He feels resentful, and who's to blame him?"

"Does Callie know this?"

"Not unless Will told her. He was willing to give up that fortune to buy a divorce for Callie. Jason had agreed to it. There wasn't much he wouldn't do for money."

After that he explained everything from his and Will's part in gathering evidence against the traitor, Aaron Burr, to the reason why Light killed Jason.

"I understand why Light acted as he did. He would have done it even if he hadn't fallen in love with Maggie. To him it was justice. He's lived in his own private hell for so long; I hope he'll find happiness with Maggie. They're going away together. Light's taking Maggie and going up the Missouri; going west where few men have ever been. They'll see things never seen before by a white man."

"Do you envy him?" she asked shyly.

"No. I've had my taste of opening new frontiers."

"Maggie will be happier," Annie Lash murmured. "People don't understand her. Her beauty is more of a curse than a blessing." They lay quietly, his hand caressing her arm as it lay across his chest. "I hope they find their Garden of Eden."

"They'll find it, darling. Just like we've found

ours." He searched for her lips and found them, kissing her deeply.

"Light was on his way here to bring me news of the men coming upriver, but also to bring me a letter, when he found Jason with Maggie." He felt compelled to hurry and finish what he wanted to say so he could get on with the loving. "It took the letter a month and a half to get here. Burr's trial date was set ahead. Not even his agent, Hartley Van Buren, knew the trial had already started. Will and I would never make it back in time to testify."

She lay quietly for a long while. "Is that why you're not going?"

"Yes. In all honesty, I must tell you that if I thought there were a chance of getting to Virginia before the trial was over, I'd go." Jeff could feel her soft body next to his begin to withdraw, and he tightened his arms, holding her close. "It would be my duty, sweetheart. I took on that job before I met you. I'd have to finish it."

"But why didn't you tell me you'd be going and that I'd be left here to live alone? Didn't I have the right to know that the man I love might not live to see the child we were making? Did you ever stop to think how I would feel, waiting here for you, wondering if you would ever return?"

"Yes, I thought of that. I almost didn't tell you my feelings for you because of it. But—" He wrapped her in his arms and crushed her to him. "I'm a selfish sonofabitch! I wanted you so much that I ached for you. I thought it would be easier to die knowing my child lived on in the body of the one I love above all others, where I'd planted him during the happiest moments of my life."

"You still should have told me," she said stubbornly, but breathlessly, too.

"I didn't want to see the light go out of your eyes, sweetheart. I didn't think I could stand to see you sink down into the pit of despair you were in when Zan died. You've been so glowing, so soft and warm, so loving—"

"I'm a woman, Jefferson," she said against the warm skin of his neck. "I'm a woman who wants to share everything with her man."

"You will from now on, darling."

"Then this business with Aaron Burr is over?"

"As far as Will and I are concerned it is. All we've got to worry about now is this business of getting married." His voice teased for the first time. His hands were pulling at the gown wrapped about her thighs. "I don't like this thing. Why did you put it on?"

"Will and Callie are getting married, too!" Her laugh was one of pure happiness. "I put this on because I thought I'd be sleeping alone until you sent me back to Saint Louis." She raised her hips so he could tug the gown higher.

"Whatever gave you that idea? I told you that you would never sleep alone again." The gown came over her head. He sighed with contentment and rolled over onto his back again, taking her with him.

"Jefferson!" His name came shiveringly sweet from her lips.

He settled her on top of him and spread his thighs to make room for hers to lie between. His hand found her smooth rounded bottom and he smacked it sharply.

"That was for scaring the life out of me." His whisper rasped in her ear.

She could feel his body's arousal, responding to the softness of hers.

"You were so angry," she whispered into his furry chest.

"You're damn right I was. I was boiling mad. I died a thousand times while we waited for darkness."

"I'm sorry, darling. I'll behave. I promise." Her hips made a slow circling movement, grinding against his arousal.

His hands clutched her buttocks and pulled her up so his lips could reach hers. She closed her eyes, panting and breathless, pliable beneath his caresses. His hands roamed her back, his hard belly caressed the softness of hers. The fur on his chest excited her nipples to hardness. His mouth trailed across her cheek to her ear, and teased it with a soft, warm breath and darting tongue.

"I love you. I can't image life without you, now. I hope Zan knows that you'll be with me forever."

"He knows, my woolly-headed darling," she crooned and sank her fingers in the tight curls at the nape of his neck.

His hand caressed downward along her spine to press her hips close to his. He rolled, tucking her beneath him, and they came together with a heat that melted them into one, oblivious to where one body left off and the other began.

"Ahhh…" The sound came from deep in his

throat. "There's nothing more wonderful than the feel of you surrounding me. We fit together so perfectly." He was huge and deep inside her. "Oh, Annielove...I was walking and thinking...I was so scared! What if I failed to find you? What would I do if they had already—Oh, my sweet love, I would have died if that had happened."

"I'm sorry, darling. Please forgive me." She locked her arms about him and pressed her lips to his mouth.

A heavenly feeling began to build as Jeff's motions grew more and more frantic.

"Forgive *me*," he whispered, and with a long breath he thrust at her full force. Her body responded to him, and as they emerged from a long, long, unbelievable release, she felt the tremors rippling through his body and heard him whisper reverently, "Oh, God, I love this woman..."

27 million Americans can't read a bedtime story to a child.

It's because 27 million adults in this country simply can't read.

Functional illiteracy has reached one out of five Americans. It robs them of even the simplest of human pleasures, like reading a fairy tale to a child.

You can change all this by joining the fight against illiteracy.

Call the Coalition for Literacy at toll-free **1-800-228-8813** and volunteer.

Volunteer Against Illiteracy. The only degree you need is a degree of caring.

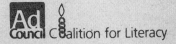

Ad Council Coalition for Literacy